THE VILLA, ONCE BELOVED

Also by Victor Manibo

The Sleepless
Escape Velocity
Dead Note

The Villa, Once Beloved

Victor Manibo

an imprint of Kensington Publishing Corp.
erewhonbooks.com

Content notice: *The Villa, Once Beloved* contains depictions of/references to: alcohol use, authoritarianism, blood, bugs, classism, consensual sex, death, dementia, drug use, emotional abuse, ghosts, gore, gun use, incest, miscarriage, monsters, murder, natural disasters, physical violence, queerphobia, racism, sexism, sexual assault of women and girls, sleep disorders, state violence, transphobia.

EREWHON BOOKS are published by:

Kensington Publishing Corp.
900 Third Avenue
New York, NY 10022

erewhonbooks.com

ISBN 978-1-64566-138-2 (hardcover)

First Erewhon hardcover printing: December 2025

10 9 8 7 6 5 4 3 2 1

Printed in the United States of America

Library of Congress Control Number: 2025940691

Electronic edition: ISBN 978-1-64566-140-5

Edited by Diana Pho
Interior design by Kelsy Thompson
Images courtesy of Adobe Stock/Irfan Mulyana and 404 Not Focused

The authorized representative in the EU for product safety and compliance
is eucomply OU, Parnu mnt 139b-14, Apt 123
Tallinn, Berlin 11317, hello@eucompliancepartner.com

To Sean, my beloved, once and forever

THEY PRACTICE THE FOLLOWING CEREMONIES *when one of their chiefs dies. First, all the chief women of the place go to the house of the deceased. The deceased is placed in the middle of the house in a box. Ropes are placed about the box in the manner of a palisade, to which many branches of trees are attached. In the middle of each branch hangs a cotton cloth like a curtained canopy. The most principal women sit under those hangings, and are all covered with white cotton cloth, each one by a girl who fans her with a palm-leaf fan. The other women sit about the room sadly.*

There are many porcelain jars containing fire about the room, and myrrh, storax, and benzoin, which make a strong odor through the house, are put on the fire. They keep the body in the house for five or six days during those ceremonies.

Every night about midnight in that city, a jet black bird as large as a crow was wont to come, and no sooner had it thus reached the houses than it began to screech, so that all the dogs began to howl; and that screeching and howling would last for four or five hours, but those people would never tell us the reason of it.

—from the accounts of Antonio Pigafetta, chronicler of Ferdinand Magellan's circumnavigation, a month after landing in the Visayan islands including Leyte and Samar, April 1521

APRIL 7

MONDAY

THE WALLS OF THE STONE MANOR GLEAMED DULL under the moonlight. The masonry, weathered by what now had been a century and a half, finally seemed to show its age. What once was the pride of the Sepulveda clan—no, the pride of the entire province, the jewel of Leyte—looked as though it was built with chalk, under threat of collapse from the faintest breeze.

This was how Don Raul Sepulveda saw his ancestral home as he beheld it from the driveway, barefoot in his nightclothes. The stiff wind and the cloud-laden sky told him typhoon season had arrived much earlier than expected. He worried about the coconut plantation, tallying in his mind the acreage he might lose, but more than that, he worried about Villa Sepulveda, fixed in the firm yet absurd belief that the manor would dissolve in the rainfall.

The old man fastened his robe, which did little to prevent the chill from seeping. Arms wrapped around himself, he made his way through the garage and into the silong and its maze-like walls. He felt his way through the dark, guided by the mahogany posts of the manor's foundations, until he found the room where the groundskeeper stored the tools that, for weeks, had been waiting to be used. He took the shovel and the pickaxe down from their hooks. He felt their heft in his hands before placing them into a wheelbarrow. He took an electric lantern too, the only one that had some charge left. Bags of cement languished next to stacks of marble tile. He felt his blood pressure rise.

Raul had unfinished business, and he didn't have a lot of time.

He carted his implements toward the back of the manor. Past the veranda, he traversed the large expanse of lawn, stopping as he reached a depression close to the stone fence that bounded the villa from the plantation's groves. Under his instructions, the groundskeeper had erected bamboo stakes to demarcate the plot for the don's project. Raul squinted to find them and thanked his stars that Tiago had tied a tattered shred of red cloth at the end of each stake. This should not take too long. He set the lantern down by the wheelbarrow. Shovel in hand, the old man began to clear the soil.

His eyesight had not left him in his dotage, and he found little difficulty in spotting the rocks that needed to be sifted. The difficulty came in getting them off the ground and hauling them back onto the cart. He didn't mind the roughness under his bare feet, or the chill wind that turned his skin into gooseflesh, but the strain on his back and the tightness on his forearms worsened with each load.

At length, Raul began to slow down, both to give himself a respite and to make as little noise as possible as he placed the rocks into the cart. The crickets' chorus wasn't loud enough to drown the clang of rock on metal, and he didn't want to stir his wife from sleep. Catching him at work in the dead of night wouldn't surprise her; she knew of his plans, and she knew of his bullheadedness. Still, he wasn't inclined to get into another argument, to be mocked for his folly. Oh, how he longed for those days when she never gave him back talk.

Once the wheelbarrow's load was heavy enough to support him, the old man sat on its lip for a rest. He gazed upon the manor once again. His papa, and his before him, had boasted that Villa Sepulveda had been built from stone dug from the very land they owned. They boasted too that the men of the family built the place with their own hands, with calluses to show for it. Raul easily dismissed that claim. His forebears had laborers, retinues of able-bodied peasants. He saw them himself, and when his time came, he too had his own army of workers. They would have been doing the backbreaking work instead of him, if he hadn't fired the architect and the contractors, if he hadn't berated every single mason, one after another, until they all quit, until no one in the entire town was left to take the job. No matter. He had exacting standards, and if no one could meet them, then he would do what his father and his grandfather had only claimed to do. He would build something with his own two hands. He would erect the mausoleum himself.

All the Sepulveda patriarchs were laid to rest in a graveyard on the west of the property, on a hill far enough away from the groves and where the trees had long been cut down. The family had a special dispensation from the bishop that let them eschew the Catholic cemetery by San Isidro Church. And when Raul broke ground to build his mausoleum, he did so without obtaining a special permit from the municipio. "This is our land," he'd said, "and we've been here even before the diocese was established."

Raul resumed his work with more vigor, out of spite for the lesser men who'd left him to toil on his own. He imagined the laborers laughing at him as they did when they walked away from the job, shaking their heads at the crazy old man. He imagined his late papa too, and his lolo, both looking down at him, their arms crossed in smug expectation. "I'll show you," Raul spat between heaving breaths. With each load, he imagined his great-grandfather who'd built the stone house, his grandfather who'd replaced the quarry and planted the coconut groves, his father who'd bought the neighboring parcels and expanded the plantation to cover an entire face of the mountain. Raul wouldn't just restore Villa Sepulveda to its former glory—though he knew such revival was only needed because of his own neglect—he would preserve the family's legacy, more than any other Sepulveda before him did. The mausoleum, strong and grand, would stand on this spot for centuries, protecting them all.

His vision for the project was influenced by mausoleums of antiquity and great monuments he'd seen in his travels. It had to be sizable, as he planned not only to house himself and his wife in it; he wanted to move all the other bodies from the family graveyard. He planned on exhuming the noble Bartolome, the enterprising Oscar, and Raul's own father Claudio, the fierce general, plus their wives who'd been laid right next to them. The family had only ever considered the patrilineal heirs to be entitled to a plot. The long series of first-born males and their wives. Not even the second-born sons, nor the daughters, were on the hill. They were in the town cemetery, side by side with other members of the extended Sepulveda clan, both the ones who were legally acknowledged and those who were not. And, boy, were there a lot of those.

A gust whistled through the palms of the coconut trees. Raul heard a rustle in the overgrown grass beyond the bamboo stakes. He stilled to listen. His lands didn't have wild animals, Tiago and the farmhands made sure of that, but just the same he lowered the rock he was holding.

The rustling grew louder, this time from another corner of the plot. The scrap of tattered cloth danced in the breeze. Raul squinted at the gaps beyond the tall grass. It was probably

Tiago's cur, Askal. "Haaaaa—" the old man half yelled, hoping it would scurry away. The rustling stopped.

In measured steps he made his way back to the silong to get a bolo, just in case. He found one with a worn leather scabbard and slung it around his waist. He returned, setting the lantern closer before swiftly resuming his work. If he were an honest man, he'd admit that his haste was out of fear, but he told himself that it was out of annoyance with all these interruptions. He had a plan, and it needed to be done now, before the torrents came.

Before death came for him.

He had seen its omens and heard the cries of its herald. His time was coming. The mausoleum needed to be built soon—for himself, for every Sepulveda buried on the hill beyond the stone fence, and for the sake of the few Sepulvedas still living. He wasn't crazy; he just happened to be the only one who could see all the signs.

The mausoleum hadn't always been the plan. At first, Raul only wanted to spruce up the graveyard, update the markers, and most critical of all, build some sort of enclosure. Tiago had told him that wasn't necessary—the site had been unmolested for decades—but he'd be happy to maintain it more often, especially after the don and doña's return from the States. Yet Raul insisted. He contracted a builder to erect a stone fence around the plots. In the last few weeks, however, Raul grew to believe that a fence was not going to be enough. His ancestors had to be locked up in marble. When the contractor said the section of the hill was neither large nor stable enough for the structure, the old man was only too happy to have it built much closer to the manor. They would be better protected that way, he said. At first, he never spoke of what these long-dead bodies needed protection from, but in those moments when he lost control of his tongue, he would say it. The balbal was lurking, eager to come dig up the corpses and devour them.

It didn't matter if they were bones and dust at this point. The monster wanted them, and Raul wouldn't let it have them.

The electric lantern dimmed. He gave its case a couple of hard taps, which only caused it to flicker and then die.

The tall grass shook violently. The rustle was all he could hear now; the crickets had grown silent. The old man placed a hand on the bolo's hilt. In the corner of his eye, he saw the dog's hindquarters dive into the brush. He called out to it. "Hoy! Kadna ngadi!"

Askal turned toward the call but then disappeared into the shadow of the trees that lined the stone fence. Raul followed the dog, shambling on the uneven ground. It was easy to miss the rotting head of coconut in his path. The pain came first, then the fall, flat on his face, having failed to brace himself in time.

Groaning, the old man lifted his head. Inches away, a smooth, white stone stuck out of the soil. It gleamed even in the dark. He lifted it with his fingers, brushing the dirt off.

It was a bone, the joint of some small limb.

Raul flung it away and hurried to get himself upright. As he did, more bones caught his eye. Underneath the dislodged soil were the ends of long, narrow tapers: five human fingers, still held by a knot of wristbones.

He knelt up, legs quaking in pain and dread. Then, a shadow came before him, darkening the unearthed bones. Raul raised his head at the hem of a flowing gray skirt.

The figure floated above the ground, its soiled feet and blackened toenails peeking from underneath tattered cloth. A low murmur issued from above him, repetitive and pressing. The words sat on the edge of comprehensibility. He stumbled onto his rear and found himself beholding a pale, faceless woman.

Raul froze, every part of him paralyzed. His joints locked in place, and no sound came out of his open mouth. Even his eyelids couldn't blink to shield him from seeing. The specter raised an emaciated finger, her veins pulsing blue beneath the paper-thin skin. She hovered closer, pointing at him.

He began to hear the woman's words as though they were whispered right into his ear. Tears streamed down his face. He recognized her now.

Then, the icy tip of her finger touched his forehead.

With impossible force, the old man fell back as though pushed into an abyss so dark and vast it seemed to consume all of him, and the villa and the land it stood on, the coconut trees, the bones, all those bones, the whole island, the oceans, the planets, all light and all life and the very universe itself. An eternity seemed passed as his consciousness screamed, trapped in a leaden, unmoving body, calling for his wife, for God, calling for mercy, begging, begging, begging until his fall was finally arrested.

Yet instead of landing on the dirt among the weeds and the carabao grass, his body found a soft landing. Everything remained dark, but in due course, his sight was again aided by the moonlight streaming through embroidered lace curtains. Above him he saw the drapery that hung over his four-post bed.

A nightmare, he told himself. That was all it was. He'd had another one.

Raul wiped the sweat off his brow. His robe had been soaked with sweat, and worse, his pant legs were drenched with piss. "Putang ina!" he cursed as he sat up. The incident brought him back to the worst nights of his Alzheimer's, before the treatment worked. He may have regained his faculties and his memories, but he'd also gotten night terrors alongside them. Part of him still felt the price was not worth it. He swung his legs over the side of the bed. He had half a mind to call for help, but he wouldn't stand for the shame of having soiled himself.

Then, a great figure overcame him, pinning him back onto

the mattress. It fell on him with the force of the Almighty's fist. The wooden bed frame cried from the impact, its creaks joining the old man's bones as they cracked. He screamed in pain.

A massive hand, or hands, he could never quite tell, held down his head. His vision adjusted to the dark and he saw a naked gargantuan straddling him, crushing his torso and pinning his limbs. A giant, he thought, but no—it had too many parts. What he thought were thick folds of fat turned out to be several bodies. Arms and thighs, heads and backs, bellies and breasts and buttocks, all writhing against each other, piled on top of him, on top of each other, growing and expanding into a living monument, a pyramid of flesh. Starving mouths, agape with yellowed teeth, moaned with the old man's muffled groans, and their frantic breaths matched his own as the monstrosity grew to reach the canopy, tearing the sheet that hung above the bed. Raul felt his rib cage collapse, his insides pierced by his own brittle bones. He coughed up blood and his mouth became a fountain of red spray that rained on the sheets and the undulating bodies that kept growing and crushing and forcing him to take his last gasp, choking in his own blood.

In the morning, after Doña Olympia arose from her own four-post bed, and after she made her way across the hall into her husband's bedchamber, the first thing she noticed was the window. Odd that Raul would leave it open. Did he want to be feasted on by mosquitoes? As she went to shut it, she noticed her husband's face. He was drained of all color, and his hands clutched his chest. His mouth was agape and so were his eyes, which stared fixedly, almost maniacally, at the canopy above his bed.

The doña screamed, throwing herself onto her husband's

cold body. The caretaker, Remedios, tried to shield her away from the master's corpse, but Olympia refused. She tearfully held onto his arm, her body half collapsed onto the floor by his bedside. She reached for his hands and enclosed them in hers. She wailed. Fifty years. Who was she without him? Had there been life before Raul? She didn't remember anymore. She wailed and wailed, her eyes an unstoppered dam. Half a century's worth of sorrow was only interrupted by a feeling of roughness on her skin. Olympia unclasped her hands around the rigor mortis of Raul's fists.

With effort, she opened his petrified fingers. Then she found, to her utter confusion, enough to stem the flow of tears, that her husband's palms were completely covered in dirt.

April 9

Wednesday

Her eyes peeled open, but all Sophie Anderson saw was darkness. Sleep clearly hadn't helped with the exhaustion, and with the thin air and disorientation, she'd forgotten to take off her eye mask.

In the dim light, her cabin looked like her dorm room, only better appointed, slicker. It sure wasn't smaller by much. The display panel on the wall came alive as she sat upright. She fumbled with the controls on her bedside and after a few clumsy attempts, she pulled up the flight map. The tiny airplane icon blinked on a downward slope over the Pacific.

Five more hours.

She was certain they'd be closer by now. As it turned out, she hadn't slept as long as she thought. Well, at least she got a nap in. She reached for her phone.

No new messages. The same emails stared back at her no matter how much she refreshed. Updated links to the shared drives, follow-ups from her course advisor, reminders from her research partner. That last one closed with "Have a safe and fruitful trip." An unwritten postscript: *Two weeks is a long time to be gone during your junior year, so you better find a way to get stuff done.* Unread newsletters and journal articles, an ad for Instacart that she didn't send to Trash; the $10 off promo code would still be valid when she got back.

On her video console, the carousel of movie selections remained unchanged too. She shot another text to her friend Coralie. *i didn't know there was a new gladiator sequel*, upside-down smiley face emoji. It went through, but as with the others before it—*thank fucking god they have wifi*, and then *this is wild af*, followed by a snap of the cheese plate and champagne flute that greeted her in her luxe cabin, and then *adrian says hi btw*—she knew it, too, would go unanswered for a few more hours until shift change at the clinic. All the futile scrolling and texting was a bid for distraction. Sophie could at least admit that to herself.

She pulled up the flight map again and noticed the date had already changed. While she slept, she'd crossed the date line and jumped into the future. She stared at the airplane icon, willing it to fly faster. It followed a dotted arc that straddled the ocean over Hawaii, over nothing but water, sloping back down to SFO. A surge of exhilaration rippled in her veins. The trip marked a lot of firsts: her first time on a plane, for one, and in such style too. It was also her first time outside the country. Before this, the farthest she'd gone was leaving Ruskin to go to Stanford. Her father had protested, argued there were plenty of fine community colleges in Nebraska, as though they were comparable. No, Sophie would go to the finest school that would give her scholarship money. She would leave the farm. She would find herself, whatever that meant to a sixteen-year-old, but she'd known it required getting as far away from her parents as possible. On the map before her she imagined her own path from three years ago: The fifteen hundred-mile drive down the I-80 on the beat-up cobalt blue Dodge she bought with money from her late shifts at the Dollar General in Hebron and a small fundraiser by the church choir. Over the deserts of Nevada, the forests of Utah, the mountains of Colorado, Sophie drove for twenty-four hours, only stopping twice, so eager was she to start her life out west.

Now here she was, going farther than she'd ever gone before.

Yet the decision to go on this trip had been fraught, and she felt uneasy traveling on a chartered jet, all expenses paid. Until today (yesterday?) she didn't even know that planes could be built like hotels, with suites, showers, a stocked bar. To allay her misgivings, Adrian had been quick to point out that his family didn't usually travel this way when they visited the Philippines. His comfort and familiarity in these surroundings cast this claim in doubt.

More than that, she worried about spending that much time in the Sepulvedas' ancestral home. There simply were too many opportunities for a misstep. Sophie was liable to struggle whenever the conversation inevitably veered into Filipino. She'd misunderstand a word, or she'd make a rude gesture, or be overly polite. She'd be unable to stop from wincing whenever the family referred to their coconut groves as the "plantation." She'd somehow offend the elders, or the help, the way she felt she sometimes did whenever they spent time in the homes of Adrian's trust fund buddies, despite his assurances that she was doing great, she was perfect, in fact. She was fitting in nicely. She never quite cared about fitting in then, but now . . .

And then there was, of course, the fact of the funeral.

A low rapping came from the other side of her cabin door. It slid open as soon as she said "come in."

Adrian entered and sat by her bedside. "Hey there . . . did you get some sleep?"

"Not as much as I'd like."

He gave her hand a kiss. "I'm sorry."

"It's not your fault."

"Yes, well. You're here because of me." Adrian pulled a baggie out of his jeans pocket, and though the lights were turned low, she could tell it wasn't your standard bag of multicolored gummies. "You sure you don't want some? I got six hours on just half a gummy."

Sophie swatted his hand away playfully, turning toward the open door. Across the aisle, his parents' cabin door was shut.

"Look, I'm telling you, they don't care," Adrian said. It was somewhat attractive, the way he was so cavalier about sneaking contraband into another country, but it was also another stinging reminder of how he moved through life so differently from her.

"I don't want to give them the wrong impression, that's all."

Sophie asked him about his film, and it was Adrian's turn to see if anyone heard. He smiled askew, recognizing her attempt at evasion. He stowed the baggie away and slid the door shut. "Been at it for a while," he answered. "Sorting through pics, old home videos. No time like the present, right?"

"In more ways than one. Is it . . . helping?"

"I like seeing what he was like when he was younger. Before the Alzheimer's. He was a lot funnier than I remember."

"You know," Sophie started, gently, "you could just reminisce about your lolo. It's okay. You don't have to get your work done while you're at it."

Adrian smiled wryly, a glint in his eye. "Lolo would disagree—that would be . . . inefficient. And maudlin. Two things he hated."

Sophie thought Don Raul Sepulveda would also disagree about the subject of his grandson's secret project, but this was not the time for snark. A personal documentary about the Sepulveda clan and its thorny history in the style of *Stories We Tell* and *Sherman's March* would be too vérité for his family's taste. It was bad enough that Adrian majored in film, but his course mentor loved the pitch, and if he does it right, it was likely to get him into the honors program.

"Besides, I'm already missing school so soon into the quarter," he continued. "I might as well come back with some progress."

Sophie couldn't blame him. There was guilt over the secret, over the subject matter, guilt over the very fact that his grandparents were cozy with—were closely related to!—a dictator. Guilt over his circumstances, his privileges, the very clothes he wore and the very Gulfstream they were on. Adrian had plenty he'd want to avoid, and if he could use schoolwork as a means to distance himself from them, how could she fault him?

"Is there anything I can do to help?" she asked.

Adrian leaned in and caressed her ear lobe. He knew how much this calmed her. "I just want you to get some rest while we can. We still have a way to go."

"Yeah, I know."

"You know you have nothing to worry about, right?"

"Yeah."

"Everything will be fine."

"I know that too."

She sounded abrupt without meaning to, and she hugged him to make up for her tone. His grandfather had just died. His family was beset with grief, as was he, and that grief was compounded by travel fatigue, jet lag, and soon, the sensory strain of having to acclimate to the tropics. She was supposed to be here to support him, yet there he was, taking care of her again. She knew the questions still swimming in his mind, the same ones he'd asked several times in the last few days. Was she comfortable? Scared? Stressed about meeting the rest of the Sepulvedas? And what about going this far from home? To the Philippines, of all places? She raised her head and saw them all in Adrian's downcast, slightly bloodshot eyes. She'd been giving him hollow assurances; she didn't really have any answers. At the very least, she could do things for his sake, like she promised herself she would.

"All right," Sophie said, holding out an open palm.

Adrian drew the bag from his pocket and held it up in front of her. He grinned. "Pick a color."

By the time they arrived on the island province of Leyte, the high had worn off, but the haze did not lift. It became a new haze, caused by the noontime heat that prickled her skin and the humidity that sapped her of strength. Sophie felt rested at least, knocked out on half a dose.

The sign greeted her as she descended the boarding stairs. *Daniel Z. Romualdez Airport*. From Adrian's stories, a not-so-distant cousin of his late grandfather's.

Bodyguards with dark sunglasses waited on the tarmac. The cars would be slightly delayed, they informed Adrian's father Eric as he descended the plane. He took the news without a hint of annoyance; if anything, he seemed overly gracious toward the men, as though he'd inconvenienced them. His wife Margot only smiled meekly.

Sophie had only met them once, two years ago, during her first Stanford Family Weekend. As she'd expected, no one came to visit her, but less expected was Adrian's offer that she spend the weekend with his folks. For one, their relationship was so new. For another, she assumed quite reasonably that his parents would want alone time with their only child, even if Adrian didn't sound too psyched about it. Didn't he at least want to give them a tour of the university grounds, show off his hastily tidied off-campus bachelor pad for their inspection? He brushed the idea off. What he'd been most excited to show off was her. Sophie thought it was the most romantic thing.

She didn't realize how serious he was. From the very

first moment of introduction, Adrian sang her praises, casually dropping how tough and selective the computer science program was, and how she was top of her class, with a full course load and research assisting, not to mention extracurriculars. Adrian segued to discuss their activities with PASU, the Pilipino American Student Union, but he soon found his way back to talking about Sophie. Eric seemed genuinely impressed, and Margot even teased that she hoped Sophie would be a good influence on her son.

Sophie took everything in stride, ignoring the undercurrent of cringe. She instinctively knew that Adrian admired her achievements, but she'd never been raised in an environment that lavished her with praise. Roy and Frances Anderson were humble Midwestern folks who rarely showed pride or gave encouragement. They never wanted to spoil their daughter. Said daughter might have also believed that their restraint was tinged with resentment at how exceptional she'd become, despite everything. It was a new and foreign feeling, being lauded by someone who loved her. That was the reason for her unease, nothing more. Affirmation felt good, and in time, she could get used to this. She could come to enjoy it, even. Seeing the glimmer in Adrian's eyes as he spoke, she felt well on her way.

The afternoon was a greater success because Adrian's parents, deftly deploying that upper-class conversational sidestep of anything unpleasant, avoided asking about her own parents' absence. Sophie was relieved she didn't have to use any of the excuses she'd prepared on behalf of Roy and Frances, who would have balked at the idea of having to explain themselves, let alone have their daughter apologize to complete strangers on their behalf. She was also relieved that the big question was raised only once—*yes, I am Filipino*—and then the topic was swiftly dropped after some noises of approval. For a moment she worried that Eric might test her by conversing with her in Tagalog, but there had been none of that, not even a vernacular aside between father and son. No questions about her background, no "Do you know so-and-so?" or "Where in the Philippines, exactly?" This unspoken dance lasted throughout that brisk February afternoon. Now, Sophie doubted she would be quite so lucky again.

Margot sidled up next to her under the shade of the Gulfstream's wing. She'd changed into a black satin top, lightweight for the climate but still appropriate for the occasion. Meanwhile, Sophie's flannel was getting soaked in sweat. "*Someone* should have warned you," she clucked at her son outside of his earshot. "But don't worry, the cars have good AC. The villa too."

"Oh, I'll be all right."

"You know, I was you, once. It was a while ago, but I still remember," Margot said. "It's okay—no need to hide it. This all takes some adjustment." She shielded her eyes and pointed at the low clouds in the distance, over the ocean. "It'll cool down soon anyway."

Sophie caught her breath when she realized she was now standing halfway across the world from where she'd started. A strange sense of awe surged in her. She was finally *here*.

"I'm sure I'll acclimate," she replied absently.

"And I don't just mean the country," Margot said with a conspiratorial grin. "The Sepulvedas can be quite a handful. You and I gotta stick together, kid."

"Thanks, I'm gonna need all the help I can get." Sophie said with a straight face. There was something absurd about the idea of having Margot as her guide and ally. Her sherpa with the Sepulvedas, this tall, blonde New England WASP dressed in head-to-toe Dior, standing right next to a private jet. But yes, Margot did know what Sophie was getting herself into, and they were both outsiders, of a sort.

In time, their entire party was whisked away into gleaming white Bentleys. It would be another two hours from the airport before they would arrive at the Sepulvedas' ancestral home in a secluded mountain town named Maalin, and by then, Sophie would have been traveling nonstop for twenty-two hours.

Her window views had changed from late-afternoon San Francisco to the murk of the Pacific, the first glimmers of dawn over the Philippine islands, the lush green provinces that she should know by name. Now, through tinted windows, she witnessed the Tacloban cityscape—the tangle of traffic, the sidewalk stalls selling everything from fruit to hardware supplies to flimsy plastic toys from China, the streets lined with billboards and banners mostly in English: *Grand Opening! Live More Today. Re-elect Romualdez for Mayor. 50% Off Sale! Tough Times Call for Beautiful Measures*—morph into suburbs. Along the narrow highway stood squat houses, most painted in pastels, their wooden fences each enclosing a small backyard with trees of plumeria or papaya. Eventually, these all gave way to dense shrubbery and the thick woods where no houses stood, signaling their convoy's entry into the countryside.

At first, Sophie thought it was just the tall mahoganies casting shade, but soon enough her view was obscured by raindrops. Seen through darkened windows, the storm clouds seemed to loom lower, closer. A thunderclap followed a streak of lightning.

"It's coming," the driver said, in an oddly cheerful, almost apologetic manner.

"Didn't know it was supposed to rain," Adrian replied.

"Yes, sir. It's a typhoon. They've named it Lorena."

Adrian leaned forward to peer out the front windows. "It doesn't look too bad."

His remark seemed to summon the storm. A torrential downpour came upon them, obscuring their view with a thick curtain of water. In mere seconds, noon seemed to turn to dusk. The car sounded like it was being pelted by hailstones as it winded through the asphalt highway.

"Storm signal number four, they say. The first one this year. Good thing your plane came on time."

The driver's phone rang from its dashboard mount and a gravelly voice came through on speakerphone. "Paghinay-hinay, utoy. Peligroso hit kalye." The driver responded, first sounding annoyed, then resigned, all in the same language that Sophie didn't understand. She couldn't pick out any English either. She turned to Adrian, who looked as puzzled as she was.

"You speak Waray?" the driver asked after he hung up.

"No. Just Tagalog," Sophie answered. It was a stretch, and Adrian smirked. She'd gotten a lot better since she joined the PASU, but languages always tripped her up, spoken languages at least. French had been her talon d'Achille in high school. Give her a math problem or lines of code any day.

"No? Tsk, tsk. Just like Sir Adrian. Always Tagalog," he replied jovially. "That was my father, from the other car."

On the mention of a father, Sophie noticed that this driver was younger than she first thought. He might have been her age, though she couldn't fully see his face enough to be sure.

"Is everything ok, Kuya Dante?" Adrian asked.

"He said he will slow down, and we should also. So we don't get into an accident. Sir Eric is worried. But this is just a little water. We will get out of it soon." The driver slowed and turned the radio down. From the rearview mirror hung a rosary with beads made of sky blue plastic. He rubbed its suspended crucifix between his fingers, then made the sign of the cross.

The convoy proceeded in a crawl for another hour. Adrian alternated between wakefulness and slumber, but Sophie wanted to stave off sleep until nighttime to better cope with the jet lag. Already it was becoming difficult, her eyelids drooping. The sound of the torrent kept her alert at least.

They drove past a gray stone arch. The streets grew denser, and so did the houses, the low commercial buildings selling agricultural equipment and fertilizers, the telephone poles.

Welcome! Mabuhay! Municipality of Maalin, Province of Leyte

"We're almost there," Dante announced. Adrian peered out the window and his face betrayed a sullenness Sophie recognized too well. She reached out and held his hand. He patted hers gently and gave her a smile.

Not long after they passed the threshold, the sky brightened somewhat. Sophie could again see the other car ahead of them.

"That wasn't so bad," she said to herself.

"Yeah, maybe not a signal number four then, huh?" Adrian answered.

"Yes, sir, it is," the driver replied. "We're just in the eye."

Maalin was a pass-through kind of town. One main throughfare, a town plaza with a small church, a few stalls that passed for a market. It seemed deader, too, on account of the weather. The stretch of civilization did not last long, and the car soon turned toward the mountain road. Shortly, they were once again surrounded by trees and vegetation: endless rows of coconut trees flanked the way, as far as the eye could see. Their fronds, lush and slick with rainwater, looked like verdant sheafs of giant needles, erupting from slender trunks that gathered both palms and fruit. Each tree teemed with young coconuts of a pale green shade. It was the same shade, Sophie thought, of the innermost husks of late-season corn.

When Adrian first told Sophie about his family's plantation, their relationship gained a dimension more vital than the romantic fervor that bloomed from their shared interests and heritage. Yes, he was rich, but he was always humble about it; often it seemed that his privileges pained him. Learning about the family business told her that there might be a humility in the Sepulvedas too. They were farmers. They took care of the land, and it took care of them. So well that their business managed to thrive on both sides of the ocean. Sophie's own family hadn't been so lucky; the struggle to keep their modest farm afloat seemed like the Anderson birthright. It gave her another reason to flee Nebraska. Yet despite their families' divergent fortunes, Sophie, raised the way she was, knew one thing to be true: Stewardship of the land required a purity of spirit that few possessed. Adrian might not be a simple farm boy himself, but she was gratified to know he was at least part of that legacy.

Sophie turned to Adrian. "By the way, you never did tell me how your lolo died." He gave her a look as though he'd been jolted by a charge, a flash of forgetfulness. Dante watched her through the rearview mirror. The hush weighed on Sophie. *Did I say something wrong?*

"He . . . his heart gave out in his sleep."

"Sure," the driver muttered.

"At least that's what they've told me. What, is there something else?"

"Ah, well, you know . . . your Lola Divina has very strong opinions about . . . things."

"That she does." He gave Sophie a knowing look.

"What kind of opinions?" she asked.

"It's not right for me to talk about it," Dante replied sheepishly. "Best for you to hear it from them. We are close anyway. Another ten minutes, maybe."

"Aw, c'mon, Kuya," Adrian said. "We promise we won't tell."

"I don't want to scare Ma'am Sophie," he chuckled.

"Oh, Adrian's told me the stories," she answered. Every great house found itself the subject of provincial lore, and the older the house the more baroque the lore. Adrian had shared it all with her—the ancient records, the second- and third- and fourth-hand accounts, the oral histories he'd unearthed in the course of researching for his film. He'd also warned her about his great-aunt, the reclusive widow and Don Raul Sepulveda's younger sister. Divina executed the don's wishes from across the ocean and made sure the business ran smoothly despite the distance, doing the same for Adrian's father once Raul handed over the reins. Yet for the people of Maalin and beyond, Divina always had a reputation that was by turns pitied and feared; some called her mad, cursed, just like the once-stately manor she inhabited.

"Yeah, Sophie knows," Adrian told the driver. "How Villa Sepulveda's a nexus of bad luck, which you have to admit is ridiculous given how good the harvests have always been. How Lola Divina's a witch, that there are monsters lurking in the hills, ghosts and such. None of which I've seen in all the times I've come back, by the way—and I've been looking."

"So, what, does she think there's something more to her brother's death?" Sophie asked Dante. "Something—supernatural?"

Dante grunted. "They're not all true, the stories. People here like to exaggerate."

"Well, which ones are, then?" Sophie asked. Adrian shot her a look that said, *He's fucking with us.* "True, I mean."

"Isn't that the question." The car slowed to a crawl. "We're here."

The gate of wrought iron rose up from the land like a lady's comb, its teeth fine and even, their pointed tips like the blades of the palms glistening in the rain. This frontage had been a later addition to replace the low stone fence that still bordered the rest of the villa, Adrian told her, put up by his great-grandfather, a conscript in the US Army back when America still laid claim to the islands. Don Claudio had seen sprawling farms and plantations in his travels to the South, and he thought, rather accurately, that his ancestral home looked like the ones in New Orleans or Mississippi. Villa Sepulveda, too, was nestled among acres of farmland like a jewel hidden in a sea of green, and, as with any precious object, it needed protecting.

There were stories—for, indeed, this was a storied house—that the Sepulveda who dug the first hole into which the casa's foundation would be laid built the place to be a summer retreat for his reclusive wife. They were Spanish aristocrats who'd fallen on hard times and so chose to move to the colony, which had become a booming port after the Crown opened the Port of Manila to the world. This at least was the story carved onto the plaque by the double doors, put up by the National Historical Institute. It designated the manor as a Heritage House, one of about sixty great homes spread across the country, all built in the same period and architectural style, all owned by once-noble families.

Of course, Adrian mused, the NHI couldn't have put the real deal on the plaque: that the plantation house, nestled in the mountains with its fresh air and bountiful food, with its seclusion, was not a mere summer home for when his great-great-great-grandfather Ilustrísimo Señor Bartolome Sepúlveda, a marqués from Valladolid, tired of Manila and the business he conducted from the capital. The house had in fact been meant to hold his wife Dorotea, who had gone mad from homesickness and had to be hidden away from society. It had been 191 years since, and who knew what the truth was anymore, but the tale's shadowy nature ensured the legend would persist, and Adrian personally found that story more interesting anyway.

Past the gate, more coconut trees lined a gravel driveway of such length that one traversing would have no sight of the plantation house until they'd nearly reached the end. Yet with the afternoon turning into night, Sophie only got a darkened view of the ancestral home.

The manor was long and wide and had only two levels: The lower one was built with coral stone and adobe blocks laid in a brick pattern, like a European castle. Into its walls were carved arched windows that looked like the embrasures of a fort. The top floor was built with coconut lumber, stained and polished a deep brown that looked black in the nighttime. Its windows, all closed, had the typical checked pattern of capiz, polished and pearly white, beneath which were balustrades of carved wood, their intricate scrollwork matching the columns and pilasters. Its scalloped terra-cotta roof hung far over the entire structure, shielding a large swath of its perimeter from the rain.

The Bentleys entered the zaguan, a garage carved into the side of the manor that looked less a carriage port than a tunnel. Its arched beams and sloping ceiling seemed to be caving in on them. Sophie held Adrian's hand to ease her claustrophobia.

When she emerged from the van, she was met by a dour-faced woman with a tight bun of gray hair partially obscured by a threadbare veil. She wordlessly snatched the suitcase from Sophie's hand. Sophie smiled and thanked her, suddenly hyper-aware of her status as an outsider. When Adrian got out the van, the woman's demeanor changed like a switch. Her face lit up from within, and she wrapped Adrian in a tight embrace.

"This is Manang Remy," he introduced. "She's the caretaker of this place. And this, Manang, is my Sophie. The one I've told you about."

Sophie extended a hand, and it floated in the air for far too long before the caretaker made to reach for it.

The old woman looked at Sophie warily. "Remedios. Welcome."

The folds of her face deepened as she took Sophie in. She then called out to Dante, asking him to take the bags and lead the guests to the upper floor. The driver responded in Tagalog or Waray, Sophie couldn't tell, though she deduced that Dante was the caretaker's son given his playful, irreverent tone. That, and how he called her Nanay. That word, she recognized at least.

Remedios looked past the vehicles, out of the zaguan and

up at the dark skies. She made to cross herself and muttered what sounded like a prayer. Sophie only caught the end.

Gaba.

That one, she didn't recognize.

Once Remedios had shut the carport doors, Adrian gamely took the caretaker's arm and let her lead them past the carriage tunnel. Behind them, Adrian's parents trailed, escorted by the two drivers. They all walked past a large, empty expanse before reaching the main hall of the silong and its storage rooms.

The party reached the main entryway and its double-high mahogany doors braced with a thick piece of lumber that looked too heavy for two arms to lift. Dotted with ironwork studs, the doors' surface bore intricate carvings of foliage and what Sophie first thought were birds, until she leaned in and saw they were cherubs.

Sophie made her way up a grand staircase, its balustrades as ornate as the door that led toward it. More foliage, more cherubs. The spindles were as close together as the steps were, and the steep incline made the journey feel longer and more arduous than it first appeared. Sophie reached for the waxy smooth railing and startled at how warm the wood felt under her touch.

A tall statue of the Virgin Mary greeted them on the foyer, standing on a large round table, resplendent in the warm light that emanated from the grand sala beyond it. This iteration was painted lighter, and somehow younger, than those Sophie had seen before, and this one did not carry the child Jesus. If it weren't for the powder blue gown and the white headscarf, she might have mistaken it for a lesser saint. She looked around her, at the caretaker and the driver, at her boyfriend's parents. The bereaved who had yet to set aside the pleasantries attendant to arriving from a journey, who were soon to be confronted with their destination. Sophie peered into the Virgin's eyes, downcast yet vital, and she felt filled with compassion.

Adrian's father led them all into the sala mayor, a well-appointed room with dark hardwood floors, high-backed chairs, and fulsome bouquets—lilies, hyacinths, gladioli, and roses, all white—in tall cut-crystal vases atop console tables and pedestals. In the center hung a wrought-iron chandelier, but the illumination came from gilded candelabras that stood on each corner of the chamber, their arms dripping with gold leaves and candle wax. The capiz-shell windows, holding their own against the whipping winds outside, glowed in the warm light, as did the stamped tin ceiling of burnished bronze, patterned with tendrils of choking vines.

On one wall hung a massive oil painting, the Sepulveda family portrait: don and doña in the center, their three children right beside them. They all wore traditional garb. The men wore barong tagalog made of gossamer white organza; Olympia wore a Filipiniana gown with puffy sleeves and a high bodice. Her youngest child Kai did too. This made Sophie wince; the piece may have been commissioned years back, but Adrian's auncle likely disapproved of the portrayal, what with the overly feminine dress, the cheeks blushed, lips rouged, hair twisted in a chignon.

Soon enough, Sophie saw it: the gleaming gold casket that bore Don Raul Sepulveda, former provincial governor, father of three, grandfather of one. She'd never been to a wake before. That was another first. She'd seen it in movies and thought the open casket would be better than the alternative, but it wasn't. She imagined the lid slamming shut, unable to withstand its own weight, and felt a knot in her stomach.

Two women flanked the deceased, dressed in head-to-toe black. The famed Divina was just as Sophie had pictured her: She wore an embroidered black mourning dress and wrapped herself with a black manton de Manila, its fringes cascading over her shoulders. A string of rosary beads coiled around her left hand, and she held a damp, white handkerchief in her right. She dressed not solely for the present occasion; she'd worn the exact same attire every single day since her husband died thirty-nine years ago. Today, however, she wept for her brother underneath her lace veil, the bags under her eyes smeared with mascara.

Beside her, Doña Olympia Sepulveda received her eldest. Once Eric, Margot, and Adrian had kissed and hugged and given their mano, Sophie at last approached her. The first thing she noticed was the beauty mark on the apex of the doña's left cheekbone. A flaw that elevated one to perfection. Sophie had heard it before, but she'd never truly understood what people meant by "a terrifying beauty." Maybe it was because of the fact that she was a stranger intruding upon a family's most vulnerable moment. Maybe it was because of the surroundings, the dizzying ogees and filigrees that adorned each surface, the heady aromas of disparate cut flowers mingling with each other. Maybe it was the finery, the pearls that hung on the doña's lobes, the diamonds that weighed down her fingers as she extended her hand for a mano. Whichever it was, Sophie was in awe of the woman, and she trembled as she took that hand, then bent down like a beggar, touching her forehead with the back of Olympia's palm.

Olympia gave her an absent look. Sophie's heart sank. Had she not been expected? Divina leaned in to remind her sister-in-law. The doña bore a look of one who'd forgotten and had been quickly, soberly reminded. Sophie stated her condolences and gave a slight bow, unable to help herself. Olympia lifted Sophie's chin with her hand and when the light caught her face, the old woman began to weep.

"Welcome, hija. So good to finally meet you. I'm sorry it had to be under these circumstances."

Olympia raised an arm and reached out for her elder son. "Enrique . . . " She nestled her head in his arms and let the emotions overcome her.

Sophie watched as son held mother, Eric straight-backed and straight-faced. His wife stroked his back in commiseration, but it did not at all appear that he needed it. Sophie hadn't seen Eric cry, or even tear up, in the whirlwind of the days prior to the unplanned trip, not in the past day and a half they'd been on the road, not even as he came face-to-face with his dead father. He kept a composed, dignified grief, and to Sophie it seemed to be for his benefit as much as his family's.

Adrian hadn't been so restrained, having cried the second he hung up the phone when his father first called with the news. They were in Sophie's dorm and the two of them had just had sex, their postcoital high amplified by weed. Adrian wept like a child in her arms, his tears mingling with their sweat. Now, he seemed to follow his father's suit, keeping his emotions behind a slowly softening facade.

"It hits different, being here," Adrian sniffled into Sophie's shoulder. She led him toward a divan and ran her hand through the waves of his hair.

"Would you like to see him?" she asked. She noticed how he'd steered clear of the casket since they arrived. "I'll be right next to you."

Adrian nodded and peeled himself from their seat. He took Sophie by the arm, marching like a man about to be executed. His tension reminded Sophie of her own. The sense of claustrophobia returned as they approached the casket. Adrian carefully placed his palm over his lolo's cold hands, as though touching a flame. Finally, he broke down, sobbing uncontrollably.

Sophie held firm by his side, but soon began to weep herself. She took in Raul's pallid features, the strong brow, the regal nose, the cleft chin. He was as Adrian had described him, an older version of Eric, but Sophie saw some of him in Adrian too. The family resemblance allowed Sophie to silence that part of her that felt like an interloper. The deceased was a stranger, yes, but he was loved by the man she loved. And the man she loved was hurting. So were the others all around them, whom Adrian also loved. She turned to the dolorous faces that surrounded her. She'd never experienced death firsthand, but she knew that no kind of death ever came easy. This one, though, must surely be worse. The sudden and unexpected nature of it, the way Raul was so looming and central a figure in these people's lives. Sophie cried for them and with them, and she hoped that in doing so, she could bring them some comfort.

In Villa Sepulveda, everything that mattered was on the upper level. Sophie understood this as she walked its wide hallways, the dusty caverns of the silong beneath her feet, the first floor essentially a raised cellar. On the top level, the wood panels were made of luscious mahogany, lovingly polished to a gleam. Large double doors led into anterooms that led into larger rooms filled with art and antique furniture and artifacts from the family's travels. Some doors had been left open, and through what seemed like a den and a conservatory on her left, then a dining hall on her right, she could see from one side of the manor to the other.

The main corridor that led from the grand staircase split off into two hallways. Remedios led Sophie down the longer one, and soon the caretaker parked Sophie's suitcase by an open door. As wordlessly as she came, Remedios left before Sophie could thank her. Once more, as though the passage through halls and arches had transported her to a place so far away from the sala where she sat with a family grieving its patriarch, Sophie became keenly aware that she might be unwanted. She resented herself; at some point, she had turned into the kind of person who cared about being wanted.

Her assigned room was larger than she expected. Too large for just one person, but Adrian did warn her that his family would pull out all the stops for a guest. The bed was a four-poster, with a sheer linen canopy beneath a long-armed ceiling fan that squeaked as it rotated. The breeze invigorated her, and she was grateful that the storm at least brought a needed chill.

Sophie sat on the edge of the bed and rolled her neck. Travel fatigue slowly sloughed off her. She ran her hand across the cool dampness of the sheets and felt grateful, too, that the Sepulvedas were conservative. She loved being with Adrian, but she could do with a massive bed all to herself. She laid back, legs hanging off the edge of the bed. Soon, sleep threatened to visit her. She sighed wearily and lifted herself off the bed. Olympia hadn't given the new arrivals a lot of time before everyone had to gather for evening prayers.

Next to the bed loomed a massive armoire that reached up to the ceiling. Sophie stood before its mirrored doors and straightened the plain black shift dress she'd changed into. She never liked black, nor worn anything so severe and austere. She liked vibrance, a bit of color. Until very recently nothing in her wardrobe would have fit the occasion, and she'd needed to buy a week's worth of the most funereal clothes she could afford.

She tried to tame her tousled hair with her fingers, too tired to dig through her luggage for a hairbrush. As she did, a streak of white light flashed right next to her image in the mirror, then suddenly disappeared. Sophie shook her head. She was more tired than she thought. She rubbed her bloodshot eyes, which only made them sting.

"And who are you supposed to be?" said a voice from behind her.

The figure leaned on the doorway, arms folded. Sophie thought she was seeing things again, for the man looked just like the one laid out in the casket down the hallway. This one, though, was much younger, with a fuller head of jet-black hair, and sans the old-man moustache.

"You must be Javier. I'm Sophie, Adrian's girlfriend."

She tried to go in for a handshake. She didn't know why she did that; she was never quite so formal. The man kept his pose and took her in. Sophie's hand floated unreceived, and so she eventually felt forced to withdraw it. She'd heard about Adrian's uncle, the black sheep whose temper was rivaled only by Don Raul himself. The coldness bordering on discourtesy was unsurprising.

"You've been crying," he said evenly.

"Oh, it's the flight. The thin air. Plus, I haven't gotten much sleep."

"Yes, all that. And the crying."

"And that." She sighed, relenting. "I'm so sorry for your loss."

"Funny, I didn't think you would be quite so . . . "

"Emotional?"

"Filipino. When I heard Adrian was dragging his corn-fed Nebraskan girlfriend all the way out here, I imagined he'd be bringing some blonde, white girl like his mom."

"Nope, just me. I'm Filipino, but I am corn-fed and Nebraskan too. Hope that's not too dissonant for you."

His face darkened. "Someone knows big words."

Sophie had shorter, choice words to deploy but thought better of it. The man had just been orphaned of a father. He was allowed to lash out, and she'd bear it, for now.

As though he had tired of her, Javier's attention wandered into the room—he looked up at the stamped ceiling, the slowly spinning fan, the lightbulbs that started to flicker in their receptacles shaped like bluebells. For a second Sophie feared he would breach the threshold, but Javier remained fixed in his place.

"I hope this'll do for you," he said. "It's not quite the Belvedere manse."

"I wouldn't know . . . I've never been. I hear it's gorgeous, though."

"Cliffside, with a view of the Golden Gate. Don't tell me Adrian hasn't brought you?"

Javier's sly look piqued an already sore spot. There'd been brunches and birthdays with Adrian's parents, but always in the city. He'd never even mentioned bringing her over to his childhood home, which was just slightly over an hour from campus, and just across the bridge, not even for Thanksgiving or Christmas. Sophie believed him when he explained his lolo's Alzheimer's outbursts, but a small part of her always wondered if he'd kept her away for a different reason altogether.

"That's weird, don't you think?" Javier continued, seizing on her stunned silence. He rubbed his chin affectedly. "I mean, his other girlfriends have definitely stayed over, as far as I know. Well, maybe one day. I heard they just renovated the guesthouse. You should give it a go when you get the chance."

"Thanks." The monotone response was not taken as a signal to depart like Sophie had intended.

"On second thought, it's probably for the best that Adrian never brought you around to Belvedere," Javier answered, his face turning grave. "If he had any sense, he would've spared you from all this, too. You know, they say bad luck follows anyone who steps foot in this house. Businesses go under, hearts get broken. People go missing, die by freak accident. That sort of thing. That's why people never visit. Townies speed past the gates. Maids never stay on too long either, no matter how well Auntie pays."

"Adrian's told me all about the cursed villa. Is that why you've never come back home?" she asked, like a dare. Javier arched an eyebrow. "Yeah, he's told me about you, too."

"I was born here, little girl. Had my childhood here."

"That's good for you. Can't scare a nonbeliever, unfortunately."

"Oh, I don't believe all that either. I know the real deal. And that's what I'm trying to tell you." Javier whistled faintly, and it seemed to harmonize with the whistling winds outside. "It's not the villa that's cursed. It's the family."

A low rumble answered for her before she could say a word. Then, a sharp thunderclap, swiftly followed by another. Sophie startled, not so much at the sound as at the total darkness that enveloped her when the lights cut out.

It struck Javier how different it looked. How the house that loomed so large in his mind was in reality an altogether inferior place. He'd seen every sort of manor one can think of; manors were all he'd ever seen. His family's holdings all over the world were stately; so were his friends' homes, his private school lodgings, the Midtown Manhattan penthouse he lived in through college, and the various estates that comprised his firm's portfolio. Villa Sepulveda bested them all. Calling it his childhood home gave him an exotic cachet, and he liked to tell stories about the manor (a historical landmark, officially) whenever the subject came up with his clients. *How do you have such good taste?* they'd ask. *Why did you choose this career?* He took every chance to boast of the villa. *Well, see, this house I grew up in . . .* And they would eat it up, lost in the romance of worlds past and distant, of a faraway yet familiar place, of patricians in their tropical paradise. Javier would omit how he hadn't been back to the villa since the Sepulvedas moved to the Bay when he was eight, but when could he have returned, really? Not when he was young and the family's exile, though ostensibly voluntary, was strictly enforced by his father. Not when he'd been cast out, as poor as he'd ever been, struggling to find his footing for years. Not even after he built his real estate business, a self-made man, and traveled all over the world, for by that point it had been far too long. By then, the manor ceased to be a real place and became a cocktail party story, sometimes a prelude to a sales pitch, a point of conversation to be used for some sort of gain. As Javier stood in it now, three decades older, he realized that the Villa Sepulveda of his stories was merely one of his imagination. Here, rather, the chambers were cramped, the halls narrow. The antique furniture, though tasteful and authentic, was ill-preserved. The dusty artifacts looked like they could be found at any Sunday-afternoon flea market in the city. Tarnished, like his memory. In the silong where he located the stockpile of wine, the ceiling hung lower and seemed to cave in. Maybe he should have come back sooner, if only to blunt his disappointment. Stripped of the mystique with which he had, over decades, imbued it, Javier saw how the once great villa was pitifully, heartbreakingly small.

He turned the tumbler of tuba in his hand, swirling the amber liquid. The sharpness of fermented coconut mingled with the sting of kerosene from the gas lamp. He slowly rocked on the rattan chair, and it creaked almost in rhythm with the call and response in the oratory. The caretaker's son barged into the den, mop in hand, but made to retreat upon seeing Javier.

"No prayers for you? The old ladies won't be pleased," Javier warned. He waved in Dante, who then proceeded to sop the rain by the shuttered windows.

"Still have to clean. God won't mind if I skip this one."

"Do you pray at all?"

Dante stopped what he was doing and mulled the question over. "I think work is my prayer."

"You know what that means? That makes Papa your god."

"He does scare the shit out of me," Dante laughed heartily.

"He's very Old Testament–style. A jealous and vengeful god." Javier took a sip of his drink and winced. "Though even that might be too generous."

Javier surprised himself with his candor. Railing at Sepulvedas was one of his life's great pleasures, but Dante was not part of this. At most he was an innocent bystander, and at worst, he'd endured three months of Olympia's exacting demands and Raul's scattered wrath. Or perhaps that was what gave Javier license to be quite so open. Discussing Raul's temper was an apology of sorts, the most he could muster on his father's behalf. He was old and sick for a long time. Not well in the head. He began to tell Dante about the forgetfulness, the dementia. The hallucinations. Then there was the drug trial.

"It worked and brought his sanity back. And then he decided to return here."

"He looked normal when he first came," the younger man said, pensive. "Strong and quick for his age. But the last few weeks . . ."

"That's because he wasn't done with the treatment. No wonder he became a blubbering idiot again."

Dante cleared his throat.

"I made sure Papa got the best damn doctors. I traded in a ton of favors to get him into an experimental program, paid for everything too, even though everyone disagreed. And then he threw it all away. I'm pretty sure he did it just to spite me."

Javier reached for the bottle. He extended the refilled glass to Dante. He refused, but leaned his mop against a wall and took a chair. "Why would he do that?"

"Why do fathers hate their sons, why do sons hate their fathers?" Javier asked. He took in the younger man, who looked little more than half his age, twenty-five at most. Dante's rapt attention was palpable in the dim, fluttering lamplight.

The mention of paternal dynamics made Javier feel ancient.

Dante wasn't bad-looking at all. He reminded him of some of the boys from his single years. The wispy, meek, down-to-earth types that he once had a yen for. That he himself once was, before he'd felt the need to transform himself into someone more like his husband Connor, all mass and firmness, cut like a marble god. The muscly, athletic type who only ever fucked someone who looked like him.

"It wasn't all bad," Javier continued. He leaned in, stopped rocking his seat. "I had great memories in this house. Papa didn't hate me until much later."

He told Dante about how he was even the favored son at one point. Relatives and friends had always remarked on how Javier resembled his papa. They shared the same brow, the same nose, the same intense look in their eyes. Enrique was Raul's heir, they said, but Javier was his clone. His "carbon copy." He had memories of himself and his father wearing identical tailored suits, posing for photos at parties in the governor's mansion in Tacloban. Don Raul had bought Javier a horse the same color as his own, and for his fifth birthday party, Javier was Tonto to his father's Lone Ranger.

They had the same brash temperament too. Eric was always more sedate and introspective, and though he was the firstborn, it was Javier that some people called Raul, Jr., or just Junior, which was close enough to his name. Javier loved it, and his kuya resented him for it. Their father knew this, too, and relished it. Worse, he toyed with his sons' emotions and pitted the brothers against each other. *I do have a favorite son*, he used to tell them. *But I won't say who*. The competition drove Eric and Javier to strive in school, to follow orders better and more consistently, to be the better son. Their father only had enough affection for one child.

"But we were boys. Naturally, we teamed up and raised hell," Javier said, laughing. "We loved playing pranks on our parents."

He recounted one stunt they pulled, that one summer when he and his brother had only learned how to swim. One of the farmhands had taught them in the family pool. It was large, ten feet deep on the far end. Javier still recalled its crystal-blue water, remembered how proud he felt when he first finished a crosswise lap. He remembered the dwarf coconut trees and their palms that shaded him when he swam, remembered the pool parties his mother threw. The luaus, the tiki torches. The guests who would come over for the weekend and take up room in the manor. It all seemed so suburban American. A pool, here, in the middle of nowhere? What use did it have here, where a short drive would take you to the sea, to a pristine, glimmering beach?

"Papa liked to make me and Kuya race each other. Up the north lawn to the boundary wall and back, every morning. For exercise, Papa said, but it was also for his own amusement, I think. The winner got a crisp fifty-peso bill," Javier said. "Neither of us cared for the money, though. It was all about the bragging rights. Nine times out of ten, Eric won. It's not fair, I'd complain. Eric was taller, his limbs were longer. You know what Papa said? 'If you swam as hard as you whined, then maybe you'd win.'

"Kuya started to feel bad for me, and so one time he threw the race. I only kinda guessed, but Papa was sure that he did. He dragged Kuya out of the pool and shook him senseless. 'It's bad enough that your brother's weak, I won't have you be like him too.' Oh, he was livid. He twisted Kuya's arm, and when he tried to squirm away, he almost pushed Papa into the pool. Can you imagine? Thank God Papa caught his footing. When he did, he smacked Kuya across the face. I felt so bad for him. He was only trying to do something nice for me. And so I thought we could punish Papa. I came up with the idea of pretending to drown. I thought, that'll teach him. Maybe he'll be nicer to us if he realizes we could die. Kuya said it didn't make sense for both of us to die. Papa would see right through it. So he said he'd be the one to drown; after all, he's the one who got hit."

"That's so messed up," Dante replied.

"I was supposed to run into the house crying and screaming. Kuya was supposed to hold his breath and play dead. We thought it would be so fucking funny, seeing him panic, jumping in the water all dressed in his barong and his leather shoes."

"And did he?"

"Well, so I came in yelling for help like a maniac, right? I really sold it too. The maids panicked; your mom was there too, I remember. I kept shouting, 'Papa! Papa!' and bawling my eyes out, but our nanny found me first. She rushed to the lawn and jumped in to 'save' Kuya. Papa came too, but he didn't get in the water. He was dry as a bone. Meanwhile, there was our nanny, sopping wet and frazzled and crying. She was sure Kuya had drowned."

"Poor woman! You boys were horrible."

"Yeah, she wasn't part of the plan. We felt really bad for her," Javier answered, taking a long sip of his drink. "God, I can still see her face. The worst of it was that Papa blamed *her*. See, we weren't allowed to be anywhere near the pool without an adult around. So he fired her."

Dante's face soured and Javier felt a pang of regret. "Yeah, I guess it wasn't too funny. But me and Kuya got our punishment too. It was the first time Papa ever hit me. I was seven. A smack to the side of the head. I don't know what it was, maybe I got so used to roughhousing with Kuya, but I didn't even flinch. Instead, I hit him back. Gave his thigh a couple punches."

"God. Then what did he do?"

"He pushed me off my feet and kicked me like a dog. He got a taste for it that day, hitting me."

"I'm sorry," Dante stammered. Javier waved it off.

"We left for the States soon after that, but all my days in this house were blissful. All except that morning by the pool. I still get traumatized every time I watch *Sunset Boulevard*," he scoffed, but Dante didn't seem to get the reference.

"But there's no pool here," Dante replied after a while. "Are you sure that wasn't at the governor's mansion?"

"There used to be. That was part of our punishment. The pool was expensive to maintain, and our farmers also worried about chemicals seeping into the soil, though I don't know if that was a real risk. Plus with the typhoons and the landslides, it was too much work to keep clean. The prank was the last straw. Papa had the pool filled in right after that."

Javier stood and slid a window open, just enough to gesture toward a spot northwest of property where a grove of dwarf coconut tress stood among the tall cogon grass. A gust of wind carried raindrops into the den, spraying them with a cool mist.

Dante stared at him, a forlorn look in his eye. Javier cocked his head and smiled. "What?"

"Do you forgive him?"

The question took Javier's breath away. He downed the last of his tuba. The drink burned its way down his throat. "Can't forgive someone who hasn't asked for it."

"What if he did?"

"He had plenty of chances," Javier answered. "But he never asked, and he never changed either. You know, he never came to my wedding? And he always opposed our plans to have kids. He said we'd just ruin them. He said this to my husband's face. The height of his Alzheimer's, when he lost his mind, was probably the kindest Papa ever was to me."

"I see . . . " Dante started hesitantly. "You haven't been back here since you were a kid, right?"

"Not to this house, or this country."

"I know he's passed on, but . . . isn't it easier not to come back?"

Javier swept his gaze across the contents of the room. He resisted the impulse to say the cliché—that it was his duty to be a good son, despite it all—or the snarky—that he needed to make sure his papa was dead—or the sentimental—that he sought closure for himself—even though they all had the benefit of being true. Instead, he responded with something more practical and equally true.

"The will. I want to see what he left me."

Javier stood by that window for a while, long after Dante excused himself. The rain did not deter him; neither did the lack of drink.

He looked out into the distance, at the tops of the coconut trees, the cogon of the unmanicured lawn and its plumes whipping in the breeze. He saw something in the high grass and, for a second, thought it was just another dwarf coconut, denuded in the typhoon. No, someone was out there, solid and unmoved by the storm. Not the caretaker or the groundskeeper either, no one from the family; all were still in the oratorio murmuring their prayers.

He didn't know how, but he was sure that a specter stared directly at him.

Before he could turn away, it lifted its arm and reached out to him. Dread gripped his chest. Javier lowered his head and looked away, the way he'd been taught to do when encountering a vicious dog, then slowly slid the shutters closed.

Dinner was a candlelit affair. The smoke from the tapers intermingled with the steam from the rice, the trays of red snapper served escabeche style, and the terrines bearing a pork stew with pineapple chunks. There was a tragic splendor to the feast, Sophie thought, especially given the empty seat at the head of the table. At the other end, Olympia stared at the spread with near-catatonic stillness. Indeed, no one made a move to commence the meal until Eric finally entered the dining hall. He stood there for a while, caught off guard as everyone looked at him, expectant. He gripped the back of the chair, a lump forming in his throat as he finally assumed his father's place.

Divina led grace. She thanked God for the bounty before them, for the opportunity to gather, even under the worst of circumstances. Her voice cracked as she pleaded for the eternal repose of her beloved brother. No sooner had she said "Amen" than Adrian reached for the rice and a bowl of beef stew. He served Sophie, explaining every offering. "This one's the caldereta, which you've had before, and the pork is called humba—it's salty and vinegary but also sweet." He scooped a mound of rice onto her plate and doused it with the humba's brown sauce before doing the same for himself. Sophie picked off the chunks of pineapple with her fork; she'd never liked the fruit's mouthfeel. Adrian's eyes narrowed. "All right, let's not do that. You're missing out. It's better with the pineapple, trust me. The sweet and the sour . . . " He smacked his lips. She lifted a piece to her mouth, and as she chewed deliberately, she caught Javier watching her with a grim sort of amusement.

There was talk of the weather and its continued assault on the island. Divina complained of the timing—the storms seemed to come sooner each year, but April was still early for typhoon season. And to have the first one be a signal number four, too.

"I'm only glad you made it," Olympia said, turning to her sons.

"Let's just hope Kai does too," Eric answered. "They're still grounded in Manila."

Javier snorted. "Don't tell me you're buying that story."

Sophie turned to the vacant seat next to her, the table setting untouched. Adrian had told her stories of his auncle. They were a real modern nomad, not the digital kind that proliferated after work-from-wherever became standard. They'd been living the drifter life since they were old enough to leave the Belvedere mansion sixteen years ago, and they hadn't returned since. The family got the occasional check-in at least, choppy video calls from the jungles of Guatemala, or the mountains of Bhutan, or some village outside Zanzibar, always somewhere Kai would describe as "spiritual" or "transcendental," but they never, ever came back home. They'd never been to Villa Sepulveda either. Scheduled arrivals did not fit their vibe, and were impossible besides, when one is coming from some semi-off-grid silent retreat in Ushuaia.

"I don't care where they are or where they're coming from," their mother stated. "As long as they're here by the Friday vigil."

"Tiago says the soil might be a problem," Eric replied. "Let's hope things clear up before then so the dig is easier on the men." Margot suggested that talk of graves might not be the best dinner conversation. He patted her arm reassuringly and continued. "What do you think, Auntie?"

Divina chewed intently on a piece of fish as if chewing on the question itself. "The masons will be here, and if not them, then we could always task a couple of farmhands. They'll work no matter the weather or the condition of the soil. We won't need to worry about them. The guests, on the other hand . . . "

Sophie had been wondering about all the chairs and tables laid out in the sala mayor, and in the smaller chambers too. The Sepulvedas expected a lot of mourners.

Adrian piped up. "We don't have to rush, do we? I mean, can't we wait the storm out?"

Divina took a sharp breath, hand on her breast. "My child, don't you know? Holy Week starts on Sunday. It's bad enough that we have to bury your lolo, but on the week of the Lord's passion too?" She signed herself with the cross.

"It's not ideal, but we could push it out until Tuesday, Wednesday at the most," Olympia added. "Beyond that, the bishop will not perform a funeral rite. No one can, not until Easter."

"Well, I don't plan on sticking around for that long," Javier muttered, stabbing his fish with a fork.

"Javi, please." Olympia's voice was thin, tired. "Easter could be an option. It's the day of the resurrection, at least. It will be symbolic."

"That's insane. Papa will be dead almost two weeks by then."

"If it means having to wait, then we wait. At least we can be sure the plot is ready and the guests have enough time to travel. You know how important your papa is in these parts. The people will want to pay their respects."

"Not counting his ill-fated return, he hasn't lived here since the eighties. None of us have, except for you"—he brandished his fork at his aunt before turning back to his mother—"and I doubt anyone in this province cares about any of us."

Olympia pouted. "That's not true. If you must know, no less than *the president* cares. And his mother too. They're arriving Friday afternoon and staying with us for the weekend."

"You've gotta be fucking kidding."

"Calm down, Javi," Eric hissed.

"Are they actually coming, or did they have their staff send regrets? I don't remember seeing his name in the mass cards or on the flower arrangements either." Javier lifted his whiskey glass and winced.

"Well, Imelda is your Papa's cousin and they're still family," Olympia insisted. "Naturalmente they would want to pay their respects. So, yes, they are coming."

"But, Ma, that's not the best idea, is it? If they come, Papa's funeral is going to be a bigger circus than it has to be," Eric replied, wiping his brow. "I wish you'd told us beforehand."

"I can't believe this is even a discussion," Javier added. "You haven't even spoken to these people in decades!"

The brothers continued arguing with their mama. Sophie

and Adrian exchanged worried looks. Already Adrian's documentary gnawed at him; she could only imagine how this news disturbed him. She knew how he felt about the Marcoses, and she herself felt a sympathetic kind of anxiety.

Before Adrian, she knew little about them. The dictatorship happened so long ago and she never learned about it in school; Roy and Frances never had occasion to mention it either. Sophie had only seen depictions of Imelda Marcos, the first lady who owned thousands of designer shoes, and all she knew of Ferdinand Marcos was that he was a dead, deposed dictator. She knew just as little about his only son Ferdinand, Jr., only that he got elected president in a landslide vote a couple years back. Right around the time she met Adrian. He taught her about the Marcos family's bloody grip over the entire nation. He got her to read books, watch documentaries, learn about martial law and the dismantling of the very form of government to centralize power, the republic's transformation into an autocracy. The presidential plunder amounting to billions of dollars. The abductions, the rapes, the tortures, the extrajudicial murders of anyone who dared stand up to a tyrant.

And now, said tyrant's wife and son were coming here, staying under the same roof.

As Javier's voice began to rise above everyone else's, Divina slammed her palm on the dinner table.

"Tama na 'yan. Pagod ang mama ninyo. Ipagpabukas na lang natin ang usapang 'to."

A hush settled over the room. Sophie looked to Adrian, who shot his great-aunt an imploring look. Divina turned to Sophie, regretful. "Oh, I'm so sorry, hija. English only from now on."

"Thank you, but it's fine, really. Pretend I'm not here."

She meant it too. All attention was now on her, and she wanted to disappear.

For a long time, only the scraping of utensils on china

could be heard. Sophie was at least relieved that the arguments ground to a halt. The plates were cleared faster, the teas and desserts served sooner. Remedios came out with coupe glasses brimming with buko pandan, and Sophie perked up. The dessert was a new favorite, one that Adrian had introduced her to. She savored the clean, fragrant cubes of pandan jelly, the supple strips of young coconut flesh. The power had been out for some hours, but its cream still had a slight chill.

"Good, right? Much better than the ones we got before?" Adrian asked her.

"That's because it's all-natural," Eric cut in. "Manang Remy made the pandan jelly herself, none of the jarred stuff, isn't that right?" Eric turned to the caretaker, who nodded with pride. "And the buko, well, that goes without saying. Best in all the world, right outside our doors. Hopefully, we don't lose much after this storm. The past year's harvest has been particularly sweet, and we got good volume too . . . "

Adrian sighed with boredom, but Sophie had to agree. Her senses may have been dulled by the fatigue from her journey, but she could taste the difference in the coconut.

Olympia tapped her teaspoon against her cup as though to halt the small talk. Eric and Javier visibly tensed. She broke her silence and turned to Sophie. "So, hija, tell me. What is it you study?"

"She's a genius," Adrian answered, emphasizing the last word. He lifted her hand and pecked the back of her palm. "I could never wrap my head around what she does."

Olympia waited expectantly, and Sophie didn't know where to begin. Genius was such a loaded term. Almost no one lived up to the label, herself included. If using her was Adrian's way of impressing his family, then it was destined to fail. She understood that it stemmed from his own insecurity about being an artist, but something about that moment in particular made

Sophie doubly resent him, even though she knew he wasn't doing it on purpose.

"I don't know about that . . . but I'm a computer science major. I do a lot of coding, programming, that sort of thing. It's intellectually challenging but incredibly dry, I'm afraid."

"Aw, don't be so modest. Tell her what you're working on," Adrian said. "It's very cool and not boring at all."

Sophie had no desire to put the entire table to sleep, but they were all turned to her. "I'm assisting on a research project about neural networks for natural language processing." Her nerves got the better of her and she started prattling about learning algorithms, recursive systems, hierarchical tree-based structures, child and parent nodes. She'd never quite gotten her layman's spiel down, and she floundered to explain every term as soon as she'd said it.

Adrian's lola had a bewildered look on her face, the one older people always had when she talked about her work. Sophie's own grandma was much the same way, rest her soul, but quite unlike her, however, Olympia's manner seemed to have a veiled wariness. Something about how she didn't seem to be listening to the words, but rather watching Sophie's lips move, catching every gesture and eye flutter.

"Basically, we're working on ways to improve predictive text-to-speech machine translation models," she finished. "The end goal is a better way of building programs to help people communicate with each other. Programs that are better than Google Translate."

Javier swirled his tumbler and took a swig of whiskey. "That explains your vocabulary," he replied. Adrian raised an eyebrow.

"Your parents must be very proud," Olympia said, her tone devoid of the sentiment. "If you don't mind me asking, which part of the Philippines are they from? It's just that Adrian hasn't really shared much about you . . . yet."

"Ah, Mama. You know how teenage boys can get. Adrian's very private about his relationships," Eric said, seeing his son's unease.

Sophie knew this moment would come at some point, and the first night's dinner was as good a time as any. Get it out of the way early and she wouldn't spend the rest of the time worrying.

"My folks are from the Midwest, actually. Nebraska. Ethnically, my dad's side is white, mostly Scandinavian, I think, but far back. My mom's family is German and Irish two generations back. The Filipino comes from my birth parents, whom I never knew."

Sophie hoped her tone struck the right balance: breezy, so she wouldn't get the pitying looks she received much too often; matter-of-fact, to impress the idea that adoption is no big deal; firm, so as to discourage any follow-up questions. She failed.

"Oh, my. And it's your first time here?" Divina asked.

"Yes. Again, thank you so much for having me." She turned to Adrian. "It's a difficult time, and you've all been so kind and generous."

"And you never met them at all?" Divina continued. "Do you know anything about them?"

Sophie shook her head. "I did one of those ancestry tests, but that didn't tell me anything except that I'm 99.2% Filipino."

Adrian's great-aunt pressed on. "So what was it like growing up in Nebraska? I don't expect a lot of Filipinos live there."

"Not in Ruskin, where I'm from. It's a very small town. Probably not that much different from here in terms of population."

"That must be so . . . difficult," Divina said. There it was, the pity. Not from the fact of adoption, but close enough. The older woman's tone reminded Sophie of Barbara Walters, warm and almost familial, but with an undercurrent of authority. Sophie recognized this as an attempt to disguise officiousness. She was used to it, but more than that, she felt that she owed it to this family to indulge their prying. So she kept talking.

"It wasn't all that bad. I felt different from everyone, but even that can be comforting sometimes. My parents helped a lot." This spiel, Sophie had perfected since Stanford and the need to repeat the story with every new friendship—or, more often, with every tactless busybody. She talked about her humble upbringing, her mom and dad, the broad strokes of the adoptee experience, following a script she'd developed over the years. She'd aimed to come across as completely secure. Confident and fully formed, her history notwithstanding. The Sepulvedas, she assumed, would expect nothing less of the girl who dated Adrian.

"Being here now, do you feel a connection?" Divina asked. "Does it feel like, I don't know, a . . . homecoming of sorts?"

Sophie mulled the question. Her true answer wouldn't sound so kind. She'd just gotten here. Given time, perhaps this place could feel like home. Perhaps she'd feel the things she'd seen in films and read in memoirs about people removed from their country of origin. That swell of belonging. *This is where I am from, where I have every right to be*. Filipinos had a term for it: lukso ng dugo. Feeling your blood leaping out of yourself when encountering long-lost relations. An innate knowledge of one's lineage and kin. Sophie hadn't felt anything of the sort since she'd arrived. Not yet, but oh, how she yearned for it. She never did, before Adrian. She'd been blissfully oblivious of that bond with her heritage, but the more she fell for him, the more that bliss fell away, replaced by a desire she hadn't known she'd had. If not for Adrian, she wouldn't have started to care about where she came from. She still wondered sometimes how much her life would be different if she hadn't joined Stanford's PASU and hadn't met him. He was the one who introduced her to Filipino food—Ruskin didn't even have a single Chinese restaurant. After him, she listened to OPM, Original Pilipino

Music, and watched too many Star Cinema rom-coms. She still watched them dubbed, but Adrian patiently taught her Tagalog. He encouraged her to read books and memoirs, turned her onto Rappler and This Filipino-American Life.

At times it felt very *My Fair Lady*. Sophie was clay ready to be molded, a Filipina Eliza Doolittle who somehow needed to be more Filipina, and Adrian was happy to be Henry Higgins. It wasn't all surface, though. Not for Adrian. It was never just about the food, or clothing, or art, though those things did matter. It was an education for her soul. He wanted Sophie to cherish her heritage the way he did, and that meant showing her the bad and the good: the colonial history, the growing pains of a fledgling republic, the ancient and modern tragedies of its people, their vices and vicissitudes. "You gotta know all of it to fall in love with it, flaws and all," he'd told her once. "And I'll show you how."

She didn't know how to love it yet, but she wanted to, flaws and all. She wanted this place to feel like home.

"Yes, a homecoming. That's exactly what it is," she answered Divina. "I feel so . . . welcomed here, thanks to you all." Her gaze roved the room and landed on Olympia, whose lips were drawn in a thin smile. "You have a lovely home, and a lovely family."

Adrian gave Sophie the quick and dirty tour after dinner. Each bearing a candlestick, they walked the halls past darkened rooms, not so much to show where was which as to give Sophie her bearings, in case she needed something in the middle of the night. Adrian's room, unsurprisingly, was past a turn on the opposite end of the hallway, as far away from Sophie's as possible. He didn't find this nearly as amusing as Sophie did, and was in fact quite miffed at being treated like they were a couple of horny teenagers. Between their two rooms were his parents', Divina's, and the lady's bedchamber. For obvious reasons, the master bedroom, the one where Don Raul had died, stayed unoccupied.

"So whose room am I in?" Sophie asked. "Please tell me they didn't kick Kai out to make space for me."

"Trust me, there's plenty of space. You're in one of the guest rooms. Besides, no one's even sure if Kai is coming," Adrian replied.

"Not even for their dad's funeral?"

"Let's just say it wouldn't be the biggest surprise if they didn't show. They've had a lifetime's worth of dinners just like the one we just endured."

Adrian helped Sophie unpack, made sure she had everything she needed. What she really needed was a shower, but the power was down and so was the water heater. The shock of cold water would keep her awake when she should be cutting down on her sleep debt. She also needed wi-fi, and her phone could use a charge.

"You're a sweetheart, but I have this covered, babe. You should go to bed," Sophie said. "Look at you—you can barely keep yourself upright."

"I'm fine for a while. I don't think I can sleep, honestly."

"Do you want to talk about it?"

She swept the hair off Adrian's face. He had an air of melancholic absence to him, like he was lost and overwhelmed in his being lost. He drew a gummy from his pocket absently and held the baggie out to her. Why the hell not. Sophie took one as well, doing a mock toast before swallowing.

"Seeing him is too much," he started. "I loved Lolo Raul. Sure, he's not perfect. And he scared the shit out of me. Still does, even dead. But underneath all that, he loved me too. He didn't have to say it."

"He never did?"

"Not to anyone. Not the entire time I've known him." Adrian choked up. "And he thought film school was a joke, always made snide remarks about my 'hobby.' I mean, I got into fucking Stanford and all he said was that it was a waste of time and money. *His* money. Like it wasn't Dad and the farm that paid for everything. He blamed Dad too. I should be in business school, Lolo'd say, and it was Dad's fault for spoiling me."

Sophie had heard of Raul's renowned severity, but by the time she'd come into Adrian's life, his lolo seemed less like a vicious lion and more like a meek lamb. Adrian had told her about the old man's addled brain, the way he'd put salt in his tea, the times he'd roam the halls late at night, naked, calling out for Ayam, a dog that he had when he was a child. Raul sometimes snuck out of the mansion, fleeing the night nurse and running through the gardens, all the way to the cliffs that overlooked Belvedere cove. These stories painted a different man from the one Sophie heard about now.

"I can't tell you how happy I was to move out," Adrian continued. "I mean, I was excited for college and all, but being away from Lolo was a definite upside. He was either a monster or a burden and I was just . . . so sick of it." He hung his head, chuckling. "Fuck, that's cold. I'm sorry. I don't know why I said that."

"Just let it out," Sophie replied. She understood why Adrian might have previously needed to gloss over the ugly parts of the dead man's life. She also understood his need to unload them now. "Families are complicated. But I'm sure there were good parts, right? Think about that instead."

Adrian nodded, then fell into Sophie's arms and wept. She soothed him, rocking him like a child. She thought this part would be difficult. She'd had tragedies in her life, and she was touched by death as soon as she came into this world, but she herself had never had the chance to grieve. Nor had she needed to console another in their grief. Yet doing that now for Adrian seemed like second nature.

In time, Adrian hushed. He stared at the candle flames. Sophie dried his cheek.

"I'm so glad I decided to bring you here with me," he said with a quaver in his voice. "But I hope none of this changes your feelings about me. This . . . is a lot to handle. As far as first times go . . . and my family . . . "

"Like I said, families are complicated. And you're all hurting."

"It's not just that. It's also that other thing . . . the Marcos thing. My heart literally stopped when Lola mentioned them," Adrian said. "I don't know what I'll do if I come face-to-face with any of them."

"Look, we'll deal with it if it happens," she told him. "It sounds like they might not even come to the funeral. It'll make good material for the doc, at least."

Adrian frowned. She knew making light was not the right call, but Sophie didn't want him saddled with more guilt than he already was. He'd only just confirmed what she'd always suspected: that his film project was at least in part an act of rebellion against his family, who disapproved of his choice of career, who viewed him as a disappointment. "The personal is political" was how he had initially pitched it to his program mentor, who didn't grasp how personal this was to Adrian. *Blood Relations* would document both the Marcoses and the Sepulvedas, starting from his great-grandfather and Imelda's mother, who had been siblings. "Not quite *The Act of Killing*, more like *The Look of Silence*."

By Raul's generation the blood tie was already at a remove, but the families' bond—social, economic, and political—was just as strong during the dictatorship; at least, that was what Adrian's research has unearthed. Leyte was a small province, after all, and it all belonged to the same extended clan, even to this day. How did the two families flourish before the president took power? How did they fare during the decades of martial law? And then when Marcos fell? How did it all make Adrian

Sepulveda feel, coming from that place, that lineage, with that proximity to power and perfidy? How did it feel learning that another Marcos was now president? *It was such a rich period,* his mentor had said, *that era in your country's history. And the topic's in vogue too! There's so much to mine here, especially from the Filipino American perspective. Do it right and this film might get you to Sundance.*

"You know how much I admire your passion," Sophie continued, taking him into an embrace. "But remember what I keep telling you: Whatever the Marcoses did, that has nothing to do with you, no matter how related you are. You disapprove of them and what they did and you've put your beliefs into action. That's all that matters to me."

Adrian sighed. "I love you, Sophie. I don't know how I'd survive this without you."

"And you almost didn't want me to come," she said, giving him a playful jab.

"Yeah, what the hell was I thinking."

Adrian leaned in to give her a chaste kiss, but the two of them broke off when a knock came through the door. Eric's muffled voice asked, "Anak, are you in there? It's time for bed." The doorknob jiggled.

"Coming, jeez!" Adrian called out with no effort at hiding his contempt. "He'll be treating me like a damn kid all week," he complained to Sophie.

She shrugged. "Their house, their rules."

"Yeah, well." He gave her another kiss, one not so chaste this time, before they both opened the door.

Eric peeked into the room and smiled awkwardly at Sophie. "So sorry for the interruption. Just came to get this guy. I hope you're settling in all right?"

"Yeah, Dad, she's fine," Adrian answered, annoyed. He waved his arm at the room. "See? Now can we get out of here?"

Eric bade Sophie good night and escorted his son toward the far end of the hall. She watched their candle lights grow fainter and then closed the door.

Sophie blew out her candle. She lay on the bed, listening to the hard rain hitting the tile roof in an unceasing fusillade. The winds were still whipping the trees, and the windows creaked against the blows. Then, a clicking and buzzing sound cut through the noise. The white linen canopy above her bed began to crest and fall like a wave. A breeze passed above her, grazing her skin.

The ceiling fan had gone on. She turned to the writing desk and saw that the indicator on her laptop charger had lit up.

The power's back.

Sophie thought about reaching for her phone, but the breeze was so calming, and she was so tired, so she let the sounds of the storm lull her to sleep.

That night, Sophie dreamed about her mother. Not Frances Anderson, but her biological mother, or at least who Sophie imagined her to be. What she looked like, what she smelled like, what it felt like to be carried in her arms. She imagined her mother having long, jet-black hair just like her, and her skin was the same warm tan. Her mother had kind, roundish eyes, and a button nose with a low bridge. She had an oval face. Adrian once showed her this movie, *On the Job.* "It's a modern classic. Neo-noir but distinctly Filipino, not a Hollywood knockoff. It got a standing ovation at Cannes." She indulged Adrian's snobbery, a minor hazard of dating a filmmaker, but she didn't care much for the movie. Still, it left a lasting impression: It was the first time she'd seen Angel Aquino, and she was struck by how the actress mirrored Sophie's vision of her own nanay. From then on, she'd always imagined her like the actress.

In truth, her mother might look nothing like that at all. Sophie had never seen her nanay, not even a photo. That was for the best. She didn't want to see the images from the news, or from federal records.

Sophie was nine when Roy and Frances told her how she came to be their daughter. She was strong and mature enough, they'd told her, and they didn't want to hide things from her. Besides, her inquisitiveness could no longer be kept at bay, and their attempts at ignoring Sophie bred a palpable resentment.

"She was smuggled into America," they'd told Sophie, "seeking a better life for you." This last part, Sophie knew, was one of the Andersons' benevolent additions to the case history they received from the foster agency that took care of her while her placement was determined.

The cold facts from the ICE report and the local news story were these: Her nanay was one of eight men and women who flew from Manila to Mexico City, and were then loaded into vans for the trip up the coast. None of them had identity documents. Shortly before the border, they were moved into a long-haul truck with a container that had a false back. The cramped and dark conditions were uncomfortable, but that part of the voyage, from Hermosillo into Tucson, was supposed to last no more than five hours. It wouldn't have imperiled anyone, not even the pregnant woman. The compartment had jugs of water and a box of saltine crackers. Coyotes didn't want their cargo to die.

As Roy and Frances recounted the little that they knew, Sophie felt—not imagined, felt—what her nanay must have gone through. The heaving and panting in the back of that truck, her entire body slick with sweat, her mind reeling in fear. Her baby pressing on her bladder, every small bump in the road threatening to unleash its contents. She must have prayed to the Virgin Mary, using her fingers as rosary beads, stopping only when the truck slowed into the border inspection.

The shootout occurred after they crossed into Arizona. Gang wars, the border agents speculated. The driver and his shotgun rider's bullet-ridden bodies were splayed in the front cab. In the back, two men supposedly protecting innocuous shipments of toasters and flat irons were likewise gunned down. At nighttime, smugglers tended to steer clear of the roads to avoid encounters such as these, and so the authorities didn't spot the truck until three days later, deep in the desert. Even if there hadn't been a dust storm, they wouldn't have found it easily, and certainly not in time. When they opened the compartment, all but one of its occupants had either suffocated or died of thirst.

"You were born in the back of that truck. It was a miracle you survived." It was the only time she ever saw Roy cry.

In her mind's eye, Sophie saw her nanay, splayed out on the metal floor of the pitch-black compartment. She felt her sweating, crying, her stringy hair, the blood running down her legs, the iron smell mixing with that of afterbirth and shit. Did the baby's cry give her hope for survival, or did it plunge her into despair? Or did the despair only come when her companions' wails turned into whispers, before their breaths turned into silence? When came the smell of death? The ripe corpses steamed in the darkness. Her nanay mouthed her goodbye. Sophie saw herself, bloody, naked, the mother's cord tangled around her neck like a noose.

"You are a miracle."

That night, her first night in Villa Sepulveda following her own long and arduous journey, Sophie found herself in that truck once more. The deeper she slept, the more vividly her nanay's face became, as clear as she'd ever seen it, as though it was a memory. As though she'd met her mother, as though her mother stood before her now.

The desert fell away. The truck, the dead coyotes, the container vessel and its cargo vanished. All that remained was her nanay, her nameless mother, standing tall with an open hand reaching out for her. Sophie felt alert, alive. She held out her hand, not quite asleep, not quite awake either, struggling in that in-between place, waiting for a touch that never came.

DSC_20250302.docx

Source: A003C005_20250302_DivZoom.mov
[AUDIO CUTS OUT FOR A FEW SECONDS AROUND
00:08:04
00:11:47
00:13:13]

Divina Sepulveda-Cuesta: We'll have much to discuss of the men, and so I would like to begin with the woman without whom our house would never have existed. Dorotea, the marquesa, was a great beauty. This much is known. She was refined and well educated too. The royals envied her, or so we've been told, and they all sighed in relief when her husband Bartolome decided to move to the colony. This was in 1834, right around the time when Spain opened the Port of Manila to world trade. However, the couple didn't settle in the capital. Bartolome wanted to build a country house in one of the Visayan islands. No one knows why he eventually picked Leyte, but, here we are.

Adrian Sepulveda: You sound like you don't like it there.

DSC: Oh, I do. How can I not? This is the land of my heart. It's just . . . interesting how these things happen. The marqués could have easily picked another island, another colony, even. Our family might have ended up in Mexico instead—imagine that!

AS1: Tell me more about Dorotea.

DSC: Now, her—***she*** didn't like it here at all. She sorely missed society. She missed the courts, the exhibitions and salons . . . a quite relatable sentiment, to be honest. Living here must have made her feel like a cloistered nun. The mountains offered cool air and good food, but Leyte had none of the culture she craved. Things haven't changed much, and even back then, the plaza was spare: a couple of food stalls, a wet market, and a capilla that doubled as a school. You see, at the time, this was true of most of the country. Leyte didn't even have a city, let alone one that could compare to European capitals. The nearest large town, Ormoc, was a two-hour carriage ride through rough roads. Manila was two-day journey by boat. Even if the capital was closer, it was hardly a cosmopolitan city either. It would have been only a slight improvement if her husband decided to settle there and made Villa Sepulveda merely their country house.

AS1: What happened to her?

DSC: She made the best of it. Having a lot of money helped, and her children did too. Four of them, and each inherited her renowned good looks. She died young, though . . . only a decade after she moved here. They say she died of loneliness.

AS1: I've heard some stories . . .

DSC: I'm sure you have. But you did say you want a factual account, no? The real deal, as you called it.

AS1: As real as you can give me.

DSC: Real and unadulterated. On with the family tree, then. Bartolome and Dorotea had four kids: Oscar, Mario, Jacinta, and Luz. Jacinta died of the flu when she was little; Mario was a spendthrift who met his fate at the end of a thief's dagger, so after the marqués passed away, it was only the eldest and the youngest left to fend for themselves.

AS1: Sounds tragic.

DSC: Very. But unlike his father's, Oscar's life was marked not by tragedy or scandal, but by prosperity. You see, my lolo was tenacious. Ambitious. By the time he came of age, Bartolome's holdings on the peninsula had suffered years of drought and poor harvests. The trade in luxuries between Manila and Mexico had severely dwindled too. As the heir, it fell to Oscar to save the Sepulveda fortune. He found salvation here, in this island's acres of coconut trees. He founded Sepulveda Farms and turned the wilderness into a moneymaker. He also enlarged the family and thus ensured that the family name continued to live on. He married Mercedes, the daughter of a rich doctor from Cebu. She was an indio, much to Bartolome's dismay, but she was a dutiful wife and mother who sired Oscar seven sons.

AS1: No daughters?

DSC: One. Soledad, fittingly named. Oscar shrewdly married her off to one of Leyte's great families, the Romualdezes. They were indios too, but that began to matter less around the turn of the century. As for—

AS1: I'm sorry, Romualdez as in Romualdez-Marcos?

DSC: The very same one. Surely you know this already.

AS1: Seems like I don't know nearly as much as I thought.

DSC: We'll get to them later. And so—Oscar and Mercedes had my father, Claudio; then there was Paciano, Gabriel, Soledad, Manuel, Fidencio, and the twins Lorenzo and Leonardo.

AS1: Huh. Another firstborn.

DSC: Why, yes, hijo. You come from a long line of firstborn sons.

AS1: Now, I've heard stories about Great-Grandlolo, but for this project, let's pretend I don't know anything . . . please, tell me about Claudio Sepulveda.

DSC: [Sighs] How does one talk about their father? Bueno—General Claudio Sepulveda was born in 1929. The Philippines had been sold to America by then, but Spain's influence still gripped these islands. Castilian blood flowed in Papa's veins, but he was also a US national, a subject of Uncle Sam, so you could say he was the son of two nations. He even fought for the American army and helped kick the Japanese out of this country. When General MacArthur returned to this very island like he promised, Papa was right by his side. He was only a lieutenant then, but MacArthur saw great promise in him.

Papa was a war hero, a soldier through and through, but he also kept up his responsibilities to the Sepulveda name. After the war, he devoted his energies to building on the successes of his ancestors. He didn't do it through farming and landholding, but through managing the family the way he managed his military affairs. At that point he had risen in the ranks of the Philippine Army and, not unlike a strategic military decision, he chose to marry my mother, Elisea, heiress to the landed Jimenez clan. I hope you don't find me harsh in saying so, but that is the truth of it.

AS1: No, of course not. Please, go on.

DSC: Mama played no small part in the Sepulvedas' continued success. She contributed more than her name and her family's land: She was the power behind the throne. She prevented his siblings from ousting him from the company, which would have been an easy feat as Papa got promoted to general and spent more time away from Leyte. Mama also had the idea to expand the farm's business. The international coconut trade was booming in the sixties and she took advantage of it. Sepulveda Farms began exporting more goods: coconut lumber, coconut oil, and tuba, the coconut wine that graced the tables of Leyteños more often than any other alcoholic beverage. Before then, the company only sold these goods for the local market, but Mama, who basically ran the business at that point, took the risk.

The tuba export trade didn't take off, but the oil and lumber did. Coconut oil was especially huge with our US partners. Still is. Go to the beauty aisle of any Walmart—all those major brands are our customers. Soaps, shampoos, lotions, makeup . . . detergent too, for laundry, dishwashing. The fruits of our fruits are practically in every household in America. [laughs]

AS1: I didn't realize we owe so much to Great-Grandlola.

DSC: Our futures are secure because of her smarts and her courage. I'd like to think I take after her.

AS1: And finally, we come to Lolo.

DSC: The next in line. I'm happy to answer questions about Kuya, but it might be best to hear directly from the source. You do know I hate to speak out of turn.

AS1: That's not a problem at all. I've arranged to interview him at some point. For now, we can talk about something else. Maybe let's circle back to the Romualdez branch of the family . . .

April 10

Thursday

The walls of Villa Sepulveda were adorned with fine art by European masters. Lesser works like a portrait study by Matisse, a couple of Goya's court paintings. One was of a duke from Badajoz who had no relation to the family, bought from the artist himself by the Marqués Bartolome Sepulveda. It surprised Javier how easily this piece of trivia came back to him after all these years, after a single bleary-eyed glance. Neither his fitful sleep nor his hangover made him forget, and the longer he stayed in the manor, the more he would discover, for better or worse, how deeply the family's lore had been ingrained in him. His father's repeated bombast about his ancestors, even after the migration, had made them as indelible as the fairy tale heroes lovingly read to him by countless nannies, as the lives of saints recounted by his mother and taught to him at Sunday school.

The ducal Goya was reputedly part of Bartolome's efforts to appease his wife, a compromise that to Javier never seemed adequate. In his mind, the fact that Dorotea suffered from boredom, which grew into ennui, then grew into a more sinister kind of darkness, leading her to drown herself in the bathtub, was tragic but hardly surprising. This place could drive one to despondence and suicide. There'd been legends that the manor was originally built as a sanatorium for a mad noblewoman, but that was untrue: Dorotea only went insane after she'd lived here for a decade.

The marqués and marquesa's own portrait hung in the study, though that one was by a nameless artist from Alicante. There hung, too, on the hallway that Javier now traversed on his way toward the dining hall, a daguerreotype of Bartolome and Dorotea, together with their four children. Another family portrait, from shortly before the nobles' deaths, showed only three of these children all grown, together with their spouses and their own children. The portrait was virtually a mural: seventeen subjects in all, captured in a canvas that took up an entire wall in the sala mayor, before the later generations replaced it with their own portraits. Now it hung in the hallway between the master's bedroom and the lady's bedchamber. Though expertly painted, Javier knew it wouldn't fetch a price remotely close to the Goyas.

Javier's own grandfather, General Claudio Sepulveda, had the most images in the house, mostly photographs from a time when they were rare and expensive. The general saw the turn of the century, the sale of the country from the Spaniards to the Americans, and he lived through several wars, including the one against the Japanese, ending foreign rule for the first time in four centuries. Every stage of Claudio's life had been documented, from his studies in Austria and Switzerland to his conscription in the US Army, his military career under two flags, and his rise in the ranks of the nascent Philippine Army. He had a strong jaw and an aquiline nose, a legacy that he passed on to Raul, and then to Javier. He now stared at one of these photos; the gloss on the pane was like a mirror.

His survey would make it harder, he knew, when it came

time to partition the villa and its contents. There would be little gained from the more recent items, but the others had value beyond the historical or cultural. The masterworks would be easy to unload, and he had plenty of contacts who'd take interest in Spanish-era Filipiniana. Javier still intended to take what he could get—*looting* was how his husband Connor crudely put it—but he recognized now that each sale would come with a bit of a sting.

Sophie woke up sweating. Her vision adjusted to the faint light that filtered through the capiz. The fan had stopped blowing. She slid the windows open. The sun was low and there was no warmth over the land. In the far distance, fog rolled down the hills and settled on the tops of the coconut palms. She scanned the vista and noticed large depressions in the tree lines—gaps where trees had fallen. Closer by, trunks and fronds and heads of coconut piled atop each other by the stone wall that set the manor's boundaries. At least the sky was clear.

She lumbered to the writing desk and checked her phone. *April 12, 2025. Saturday. 5:52 a.m.* A handful of emails had come in overnight: university announcements, ads. Another ping from her research partner, disguised as an update: He'd sorted the segment of broken code that they'd been trying to find for weeks, thank God, and it would be ready for her fresh eyes when she got back or whenever she got the chance, no rush, really, they had more than enough time before finals. A text from Coralie: *so how filthy rich are we talking about?* Sophie began to type but saw that she had no wi-fi. The phone had barely charged overnight, too. She tried the fan and lights, and nothing. The lone signal bar flickered on and off, then flatlined.

Sophie caught a glimpse of herself in the mirror and

decided to change. She couldn't step out of the room wearing the clothes she'd slept in: A ratty Ethel Cain shirt with a bacon-y neckline and short shorts. Modesty required something longer and appropriate for a wake, something that Olympia would approve of. She chose a black blouse that covered her shoulders and a pair of white linen pants that was roomy enough to look like a long skirt at first glance.

Her door creaked even as she opened it gingerly. Sophie tried to listen for signs of life, but it seemed the rest of the household was still asleep. Phone in hand, she went down the hall, turning where she remembered the kitchen was supposed to be. She needed a strong cup of coffee, stat.

She was struck by how Villa Sepulveda looked so different from last night. The curtains were drawn and the windows still shut, but light managed to creep in and made the place look warm, serene. The moldings seemed alive and inviting to the touch. Sophie turned down a corridor toward what she thought was the west side of the manor, where the dining room had been. The kitchen should be near enough to it. What she found instead were more rooms, some with their doors open. There were small chambers, for recreation or for a specific purpose, Sophie couldn't tell. One looked like a sitting room, one seemed to be a small office, all of them furnished with what were surely antiques.

In due course, Sophie reached the grand hallway that led into the sala mayor. Her relief was short-lived, startled by the open casket and the man that lay in it, exposed and solitary. Had they really left him like this overnight? Was that the custom? She approached and peered down at Don Raul. No longer cast in shadow, he looked younger than the seventy-four years he'd lived, this despite the stern look on his face, which seemed less in repose than in a state of suspended agitation, like a bowstring pulled taut without any hope of release.

He reminded Sophie of her own father, Roy. He, too, lived

in a perpetual state of tension. If he didn't stress about the harvest, he stressed about his wife, who suffered from undiagnosed depression, or his daughter, who was still technically a teenager, albeit in her final year, and who in any event was her own person now, and had been for a while. Sophie tried to never give him cause to worry, but good grades and keeping out of trouble could only do so much. The only solace Roy found was in prayer, and he felt most at peace every time he came home from church. She missed him, sometimes. Since she started at Stanford, she hadn't gone back home, not even for Thanksgiving. Each year she told her parents she had to do extra credit to maintain her scholarship, or that she had to work in the lab for extra money. They believed her; money was always tight, though they all knew it was ever only partly the reason. The truth was she never wanted to return.

In her final years of high school, Roy had become more militant about his faith and what he thought that faith required. What he'd been told it required—by church leaders, community elders, people who had the knack for melding the tenets of their religion with the prevailing political winds. Roy too easily swallowed the talking points and began to infantilize the teenage Sophie. She was a pure, innocent thing to be protected and saved. He forbade Sophie from wearing makeup and dresses that didn't reach below the knee. He demanded that she grow out her undercut because it made her look like a lesbian. He scared off every boy who dared to come close to her. He disallowed her from going to prom, even after Sophie swore she was going with her girlfriends. He almost would have stopped her from leaving the state to go to college, unattended, dorming with strangers, living with hormonally charged frat boys. Her mother, Frances, was barely better. She sang at the Keystone Methodist Church, had done so since she was a teenager, and though she hadn't hardened the way Roy did, she never opposed him either, save that time she'd sided with Sophie and persuaded her husband to let their daughter leave for Stanford. Sophie often thought about the day she set out west, pulling the Dodge out of their driveway at the crack of dawn, both her and her parents forgoing goodbyes.

Sophie felt a sudden desire to touch Don Raul's hands. She wanted to impart some warmth to them. He looked so hard, so cold. Despite him being a stranger both in life and in death, Sophie felt some kinship to Don Raul. That Adrian resembled him helped too.

She wondered about her own biological father, what he might have looked like, whether she'd taken after him somehow. Whether he was still alive, or dead. If he was, Sophie hoped that at his wake, someone, too, had seen the loneliness and coldness of his death, and that that someone felt a desire to ease it.

The sala suddenly brightened. Remedios had arrived and began drawing the curtains. Sophie greeted the caretaker with a hint of apology, as though she'd been caught being where she shouldn't be.

"Is it customary to leave him alone overnight?" Sophie asked.

"He was *never* alone. I kept vigil. I only left for a moment to go wake Tiago and Dante."

"Oh? Do you live nearby?"

Remedios didn't answer, only moved to the window closest to the casket and slid it wide open. Petrichor suffused the room. She raised her arm and pointed into the distance. Near the edge of the stone wall stood a thatched-roof cottage with a bamboo fence and a narrow patio. Dwarf coconut trees surrounded it, as well as a couple of bananas and a trellis of ripening gourds. Beyond its enclosure stood a rusty pickup truck, its cab covered with a black tarp. Dante was clearing the dead leaves and branches that had collected on top of it.

Remedios watched her on intently, arms crossed like a drill sergeant.

When he was done, Dante started to drive off. His mother yelled out to him in Waray. Sophie only caught the word "ingat," which she knew meant "be careful." She and Adrian had recently started to bid each goodbye with the phrase, though in a tone sweeter than the caretaker's.

"Your home looks nice," Sophie said.

The caretaker shrugged. "It's close."

"Has your family always lived there?"

"Since I was born. My parents also. The Sepulvedas have been very kind to us."

Remedios turned to the open casket, then crossed herself. She blew the candles out and fluffed the bouquets in the vases, setting straight the stems that had drooped overnight. She did this with a tenderness that Sophie hadn't yet seen from the caretaker, and the young woman couldn't help but admire her devotion.

"Is there something I can help you with?" Remedios asked, noticing Sophie's attention.

"Yes, I . . . is the power out again? I can't seem to get onto the wi-fi." She waved her phone forlornly.

"My husband got the generator running last night but we turned it off at sunup. Fuel's not infinite, and we don't need lights during the day. If you need hot water for a bath, I'll put on a kettle." The offer, aside from being logistically unusual, seemed inauthentic.

"No, but thank you," Sophie answered. She checked her bars. "And there's no cell reception either, I guess."

"It's hard to get a signal here. Especially indoors." Remedios pointed toward the grand staircase that led to the front door, the gesture more dismissive than solicitous.

From outside and in the daylight, Sophie finally got a good

look at the place. The terra-cotta roof seemed ablaze under the warmth of the morning sun. The capiz of a few yet-unopened windows seemed to glitter. The manor was more exquisite than it first appeared, and larger too. She understood now how easy it was for her to get lost in it.

She aimed her phone at an angle, and took a wide perspective shot. A curious fascination grew within her the longer she gazed up at Villa Sepulveda. Was it possible to fall in love with a country house?

She paced around its stone walls, not straying too far from the structure, and got a peek into the embrasure windows on the lower level. The silong. Adrian had explained how houses had always been elevated that way ever since the people of these islands learned how to build houses. First on stilts, then on sturdier foundations, but always with the hearth itself away from the ground. This was in case of floods, especially common in Leyte, or in case of wild animals roaming about. Typically, the gap underneath was no more than a crawlspace for olden huts, where precolonial families kept their tools or chickens. For the nobles, it was where they kept their slaves. That feature didn't disappear with the arrival of the Europeans and their architectural style; the silong just got bigger. In the case of ancestral homes like Villa Sepulveda, it was big enough to hold carriages (or, more recently, luxury sedans) and equipment and rooms upon rooms of household help. But that was in the past, back when the manor still bustled, before the family went to America. Now, most of the silong's rooms were unoccupied. Sophie peeked into a half-shuttered window. A thin stream of light revealed a large room with spare fiberboard walls. Scattered across the expanse, like eerie stalagmites, were statues and furniture covered in dust-covered drop cloths.

Waving her phone around, she ventured further toward the back of the house but still had no luck getting reception. She looked toward the groves beyond the fence line, searching for higher ground.

As she neared the southwest corner of the manor, she found her path impeded by a large satellite dish. Its base had ripped from wherever it had been affixed, though the bolts were intact. The dome was cracked, the antenna bent. Sophie looked at her phone again. The display was woefully stuck at *SOS*. Frustrated, she decided to go back the way she came, following the sound of voices, silverware, the Sepulveda house coming to life.

"Does anyone have any goddamn reception?" Javier asked as he sat at the bustling banquet table, his reddened eyes fixed on his phone. Everyone shook their heads. Remedios explained that the generator had been turned off, and in any case, the broadband satellite had been downed by the typhoon. Javier groaned and flung his phone aside.

The breakfast spread had exactly three components: a tray of garlic fried rice, a large platter of fried eggs ranging from soft and yolky sunny-side up to well-done, and a platter of breakfast meats. There was longganisa, short and stubby pork sausages bursting out of their casing; tocino, strips of pork belly cured in so much annatto that made them a vibrant shade of red; and tapa, dark slices of sirloin cured in vinegar.

The table chatter mostly revolved around everyone's recovery from the long journey. Margot acclimated quickly, though Eric complained of the jet lag. "It hit me like a semi. Tossed and turned all night." He looked like it too; he lazily chewed on his tocino like a goat.

Adrian, meanwhile, ate with gusto. "I couldn't sleep either. Good thing the wi-fi was on for a while. Got to doomscroll myself to sleep." He turned to Sophie, who daintily sipped on her coffee, her every movement slow like syrup. Yet she didn't seem tired, more blissed out. She barely touched her food. When Adrian noticed this, he took her fork and stabbed a piece of tapa for her.

"It tastes better with this," he said, dipping it in the chili-onion-vinegar sauce. She opened her mouth and chewed with a smile.

"It's like jerky," she said.

Adrian laughed. "Yeah, I guess. Better though, right?"

The banal conversation made Javier reach for his phone again.

"Trying to reach Connor?" Eric asked. Javier nodded hesitantly.

Eric and Margot shared a meaningful glance. The family had expected Connor, and all were surprised when Javier arrived at the villa solo. "I hope everything's all right with him. We were so looking forward to seeing him again. I'm sure Mama was, too. It's been a while."

Javier sensed the veiled rebuke—Eric definitely viewed it as Connor's duty to be present for the funeral, the same way his wife was here, pried away from the demands of her job—but he let it slide. It was too early for arguing, and he had a simmering hangover. "There was a last-minute emergency session at the assembly," Javier answered. "The capitol needed Connor's vote. He'd be here if he could." His curtness ensured that no further discussion would be welcomed.

He couldn't stand to tell them that Connor had moved out and wanted a divorce. Javier never could endure pity or shame, let alone the judgment. They would all think it was his fault somehow. That he did something to deserve it. He'd always been a difficult son, brother, nephew, uncle; no surprise he'd be an unbearable husband too. To top it all, they were gay; they were never built for marriage. It was doomed from the start. All that might be true, but Javier wouldn't take any of it regardless. He spent his entire life making sure than no one, especially his father, saw him as a failure, and he would maintain the charade, even in his death.

The meal proceeded in an awkward silence. Javier spoke again only as Remedios began clearing the plates. "So, while the old ladies aren't here . . . does anyone want to tell me how he really died?"

Eric sighed, setting down his coffee. "He died in his sleep, like Mama said."

"He's seventy-six and had no heart problems. No health problems of any kind, not even high blood pressure at his age. All he had was the Alzheimer's. Are you telling me a man like that just dies in his sleep? C'mon, Kuya."

"Well, what do you want me to say?"

"I don't know. Shouldn't we order an autopsy or something?" Javier said.

"And what would that tell us, aside from the fact that he's dead?" Eric answered, his patience thinning. "Besides, Doctor Almario saw to the body, the police chief too, and they both agree. It was simply his time."

"Look, I spent too much time and money getting his head screwed on straight," Javier stated. "It's bad enough that Papa just decided to abandon his treatment, then uprooted Mama and moved her back here, away from us, but then he went ahead and died too. So forgive me for wanting some answers."

"Oh, so now we see what this is really about," Eric said. "It's all about money with you, isn't it?" Margot hushed her husband and suggested that the kids to move to another room, but she failed on both counts. Eric kept going. "No one forced you to pay for that experimental treatment, Javi."

"And no one complained when it worked. I didn't hear you say anything after the old him came back and made your life easier. Not even a 'thank you' for not having to deal with a lunatic anymore, running wild around the house and flinging shit at the maids."

"Fuck, Javi. Have some fucking respect!" Eric's voice boomed. "You never paid for those treatments for Papa's benefit, and especially not for mine. That was all for you—to ease your guilt at having me take care of him. Because that's what you do. You throw money at your problems. God forbid you take some responsibility."

The argument had been a recurring one, a broken record that's been on repeat since Raul's mind started to slip three years ago. Eric had always said he was happy to take care of their father, no matter how difficult it got. Senile dementia was common, and dead brain cells were impossible to resurrect. Besides, he didn't want to subject the old man to drug trials, probes, and surgeries, no matter how physically fit he was for his age. Yet Javier was as headstrong as his father, and he refused to accept that there were no other options than to nurse Raul for the remainder of his life.

"It's too early in the day for this," the older brother answered calmly, catching himself. "You don't want answers. You want a fight, like you always do. But I'm not gonna give it to you. Not here, not now."

Javier himself didn't know what he wanted. He had questions, he had rage, he had guilt. His kuya was right. He was spoiling for a fight. He'd been so used to clashing with Raul that he didn't know how to stop.

After a while, the caretaker spoke. "It was bangungot," she said with an almost fanatical confidence. "That's how he died."

The hush that fell over the room was total and immediate.

"Don Raul wasn't crazy or sick. Every morning, he woke up and did his calisthenics before breakfast with Doña Olympia. Afterward, they would sit in the sala and he would play the piano for her. In the afternoons, he liked to walk around the property, sometimes all the way to the lumber mill or to the warehouse. Some days he was even strong enough to help Tiago with yardwork.

"He only had problems at night. He never slept soundly in the entire three months since he and your mama returned. At first, we all thought it was jet lag or the change in weather. Or maybe he wasn't used to the bed here, or he missed the sound of the sea lulling him asleep. He only ever got five hours of sleep a night, and it was rare if he didn't wake up in the middle of it.

"The last few weeks, he started having nightmares. Really horrible ones. One time, he was being chased by a flaming angel; another time, it was ants. Doña Divina and I found him screaming down the hall, rolling on the floor, and begging for us to get them off him. The worst one was demons. Almost nightly he screamed, 'They're coming after me,' swearing they're invading the villa. He said he heard scratches from behind the walls, keening from outside the windows, but of course no one else heard anything."

Remedios paused, considering her next words. "Don Raul gave everyone a fright, but more than that, the nightmares became . . . violent. He sleepwalked, and when he did, he often flailed his arms, yelling, as though he was fighting with someone, or fighting them off. And your mama . . . well, you know about her high blood. Being woken like that every night was bound to give Doña Olympia a heart attack."

"And so she moved out of the bedroom," Javier said. It didn't escape his notice that his mother had been sleeping in her own room, a detail she'd omitted in one of their several calls of late. She had also downplayed how bad it had gotten, no doubt in shame.

"She still used the master bedroom during the day; all her clothes are there," the caretaker answered. "But at night, she slept in the other room. That was also when she asked me to start sleeping in the manor, one room over from Don Raul, to keep an eye out. It was my job to guide him back to bed if he had another one of his fits, which was almost every night. Until . . . "

"Until what?" Javier asked.

A knot rose in the caretaker's throat. The entire room waited, hanging on her unfinished story, but she couldn't say more. Or rather, she didn't want to. Javier saw an almost rabid denial in the old woman's face, like the face of the condemned being dragged into a dungeon.

"Until the one nightmare that killed him," Eric said somberly. He turned to his brother. "Did you know about any of this?"

"No. Obviously, Papa had a hard time adjusting. Another reason why coming back here was a fucking terrible idea."

"He had night terrors," Margot said with pity. She gave Remedios a slight nod. "That couldn't have been easy."

"But what's . . . bangungot?" Adrian asked.

"It's like dying of fright," Javier answered. "A nightmare so bad it kills you."

"For real? What actually happens though? Like you have a heart attack or stroke or something?"

"Kind of. Your body seizes up and ceases functioning, basically. There's some medical explanation for it that I'm not familiar with, but it's like sleep paralysis--"

"Only much worse," Remedios cut in, a harsh, disapproving look on her face. "Many have died of bangungot. Healthy people. Happy people. People who weren't troubled by nightmares. Bangungot is not something to be explained by medicine. It's a malevolent being. The bangungot is a nightmare made flesh in the form of a demon."

"Oh, come fucking on," Javier said, laughing. "That's not what killed Papa."

"I'm sorry, Sir Javier, but that is what happened."

"So Lolo had a sleep paralysis demon," Adrian interrupted, shaking his head. "That's . . . well, I don't know that they're fatal. Or real, for that matter."

Just then, Divina entered the room, dressed in her signature head-to-toe mourning clothes. The scapular that hung down her neck bore an emblem of heart behind a cross and a lick of flame above it. Though a dark veil obscured her face, her dismay was evident for all to see.

"Look, it's not some demon, all right? It's not bangungot," she said with annoyed urgency. "It's the curse that killed Raul. Now, if you're all done eating, your mother and I are waiting. It's time for the novena."

The family filed into a long room bounded on one side by a row of pews, and on the other, an antique altar, its shelves crowded with icons and candles and crucifixes. Javier was filled with nostalgia as the oppressive smell of candle wax and sampaguita garlands tickled his nose. He'd almost forgotten about the villa's oratorio, which his mother always boasted could rival the town church. Here, too, they had grand icons, like the Sacred Heart, Jesus with his chest splayed open, San Miguel Arcangel with his wings and his sword, and San Francisco in his monk's habit. Beside him was San Isidro, the farmer and local patron, holding his bundle of grain and his sickle.

Olympia was situated dead center and handed out prayer booklets, directing everyone to kneel in their place. Javier, last to arrive, stood by the door. As his mother did the sign of the cross, she gave him a stern look. *Maybe tomorrow*, he told himself. There were nine days of these repetitive orisons and he'd already missed the first two; she should be happy he even showed up.

The matriarch led the Sepulvedas in responsorial prayer,

and they answered her according to their booklets. "Lord, hear us. Christ, hear us. Lord, have mercy. Christ, have mercy," they all said in a timely yet lifeless cadence. Javier made a token effort, mumbling along. Boredom made him quit trying when the novena reached the part that invoked the saints, the seemingly interminable roll call of intercessors: "San Juan Bautista, pray for us. San Mateo, pray for us. San Lucas, pray for us. San Agustin, pray for us . . . "

His aunt Divina, as usual, spoke loudest. She looked filled with the spirit as she prayed, and the sunlight through the window cast upon her a sort of halo. Which saint was the sorrowful widow again, the one in perpetual mourning clothes? Javier wondered which his aunt believed in more: religious tradition or provincial superstition. She sounded definite when she dropped mention of the curse, as though she were stating that the sky was blue, that the sun rose in the east. He himself hadn't thought of the infamous Sepulveda curse in years, let alone believed it, but if anyone was bound to, it was Divina. The curse took her husband, she had always maintained. Did she need the legend to ease her grief? Did it somehow preserve her faith in a god that would never be so cruel as to take her new husband so soon? Maybe. People cling on to whatever they can to feel good, even if it meant believing one or two or ten things all irreconcilable with each other.

Once the litanies were done, Olympia rose from her pew and approached the altar. She placed an open palm against a framed picture of Raul, which Javier hadn't noticed before. It stood among the saints. She withdrew her hand and kissed it. Javier caught his mother's tear-filled eyes. His Mater Dolorosa. She gestured at the empty space next to her. He'd never been able to resist her, not for long, anyway, and so Javier squeezed himself into a pew and kneeled as she did.

People always said Javier was a mama's boy, but it was not quite as simple as that. She was his consolation prize for

Raul's apathy and later antipathy; in some respects, he was hers too. Olympia's husband ignored her, and so did her firstborn. Whatever attention she would have showered Eric she gave to Javier instead. She took her little boy everywhere: to church, to museums, to tea with her amigas. Even when the teenage Javier began to assert his independence, the two of them went on their mother-son jaunts into the city, roaming the hilly streets of San Francisco, shopping in the Mission, brunching at the marina. Once, she'd even taken her around the Castro to visit a local artist's studio. When he finally came out as gay, that first Christmas break he was back home from NYU, Javier wasn't surprised that Raul blamed his wife and her "feminine influence."

The misdirected anger made it easier for Javier to forgive her for what she'd done in response: After Raul had cast Javier out of the family, she, too, cut ties with him. He supposed his papa didn't leave her much of a choice. He knew how Raul Sepulveda was. Yet two decades later, Javier still needed to suppress the nagging thought that even if she'd been given the choice, Olympia never would have picked the consolation prize.

"Eternal rest grant unto Raul, O Lord. And let perpetual light shine upon him."

Javier's jaw clenched. His father was onto his eternal rest, but everything felt unfinished. It wasn't the curse, the bangungot, or whatever bullshit the elders clung to; there must be a logical reason behind his death, and though Javier hadn't yet found what that was, he was haunted by the feeling that he was somehow responsible. Wasn't it he who wanted his papa to have a clear mind? Didn't he need the old man to remember all the horrible things he'd done, to live with their weight in his waning days, for wasn't it unfair that he'd been blessed with forgetting while Javier still suffered? What if the experimental drugs, or their abrupt cessation, gave Papa his night terrors? Javier stewed in these thoughts as the rest of his family mindlessly mouthed their prayers. By the time they made the sign of the cross, Javier had rendered himself guilty. The judgment let him ignore the more insidious emotion that lurked beneath: that as much as he bore the blame for it, Javier was much more relieved that his father was dead.

The caretaker's favorite part of Villa Sepulveda was the veranda. She enjoyed sweeping the azulejos every morning, and though her back had been giving her trouble for years now, Remedios Ilagan savored the weekly task of polishing the ornate blue tiles with the dried half shell of an old coconut husk. At the end of a long day's work, she liked to sit on one of the deck chairs, feel the breeze rolling down the leeward side of the mountain, and watch the late-afternoon sun set the slope aglow in amber light.

That view and the cool twilight air now eased her fingers as she did the work of braiding palm leaves. Unlike most of the town, which bought theirs from the vendors in the plaza right outside San Isidro for the Palm Sunday mass, the residents of Villa Sepulveda had always made their own palaspas. It was an annual tradition stretching back as far as she could remember, and one that she had always looked forward to: The palm-making sessions brought necessary mirth before Holy Week, the most dismal time of the year. The maids and the women of the house gathered over ginger tea and rice cakes, gossiping and commiserating as they worked. Splintered fingers were a small price to pay for the camaraderie, one that Remedios willingly paid. It was the rare time that made the household feel as one, and made her feel part of the family. But that was a long time ago now, no more than a distant childhood memory. The staff had long since left, scared off or lured away to better jobs, and the Sepulveda family had been whittled down by death and departure to America. For the last four decades, Remedios was the sole holdout of the tradition, sitting at the very same table, no tea or cakes, with a basket of palms on the seat beside her. Her husband Tiago had always said she should just buy from the kids in the plaza. Dante hadn't joined her since he was a boy, mother and son bonding over a chore that she never really viewed as a chore, and Remedios knew that he only joined her now to indulge her.

Remedios weaved four blades languorously. Raul's death weighed on her, and the storm had made all her labors heavier. If not for Typhoon Lorena, she would be managing two other maids and a cook. The temporary staffers Doña Olympia had hired for the funeral all lived in town, and none of them wanted to take up the maid's quarters in the manor's silong, one convenient staircase away from their jobs. How foolish, passing up free lodging like that and choosing to pay for a tricycle for a round trip, too. And for what? For fear of a curse that had never and would never harm them? And now the weather made the already treacherous trip impossible. Now, she had to run the whole manor by herself. It was already a strain when Sir Eric's family came home for their annual summer trips, but now everyone was here, even the siblings who never came home, and a stranger too.

Remedios scowled as said stranger emerged from the house. The young woman brandished her phone and swept it across the air like divining rod. All day, all she'd cared about was the damn signal. She couldn't wait to leave, could she? The caretaker set down her palaspas, halfway done, watching Miss Sophie. She was beautiful, sure, but Sir Adrian could do so much better. If he wanted someone so . . . American, he could have just picked someone like his mother. As it was, Sophie was another Ma'am Margot—someone that she'd have to address in English, but worse, because Sophie was supposed to be Filipino.

"See, what did I tell you?" Adrian said as he came out to the veranda. He carried a video camera, sweeping it from one end of the property to the other. "Isn't this view amazing?"

The caretaker resumed her work, pretending not to listen to Sophie's half-hearted and inauthentic reply in a tone she'd had since she arrived. Like nothing was ever satisfactory, as though nothing here made sense.

More than the couple's carefree banter, it was the presence of the camera that ruined the occasion's solemnity. The boy was always so kind, Remedios thought, and so she tried to forgive the impropriety. As it was, he seemed only interested in capturing the manor and its surroundings. But she never understood why people would take pictures during wakes and funerals, let alone video, like it was some birthday party or wedding. She had overheard him say it was for a film project, but what kind of project was this? It seemed more like the two were taking vacation videos.

Dante, who had his own stack of palms next to him, called the couple over to the table and asked if they wanted to help make palaspas.

"Don't pawn your chores off to the guests," Remedios hissed.

"We might as well be useful," Adrian replied eagerly.

Dante distributed the palms and showed them how the blades could be braided to make one thick stalk that opened up into a fan. Remedios observed Sophie like a hawk. The girl nodded along, but Remedios saw her stiff demeanor and sensed her standoffishness. *She must think she's too good for this,* the caretaker thought.

She wasn't even Catholic, Remedios almost said out loud, as Sophie shared how her parents attended a Methodist church (whatever what was) and took home the palms from the Palm

Sunday service to hang it on their front door. "But they weren't made from coconut leaves. They were much smaller fronds, I'm not sure what kind. And they're simpler, too. No braiding or pretty ribbons like these," Sophie explained as she took a length of red satin and tied off the handle of her first palaspas.

"Times like this, I really get to appreciate the coconut tree," Dante said, tying off another palaspas. "From root to crown, no part of it is wasted. Truly the tree of life."

"But these palms kind of stand for the opposite, don't they?" Sophie remarked mindlessly. She continued, noticing how she'd caught everyone's surprise. "I'm sorry, I didn't mean to . . . I just meant, the people of Jerusalem waved the palms when Jesus returned to the city . . . and then a few days later he was sentenced to die, by the same people, in a trial by acclamation."

Remedios felt the blood rush to her face. Adrian caught the old woman's glare and quickly added, "Wow, you really know your Sunday school, Soph. I mean, I had twelve years of Catholic school and barely remember the stories."

"Don't call them *stories*," Remedios said. "They're the Gospel."

The group worked in silence for a time. The string lights came on and illuminated the veranda just as the sky darkened. Tiago had started up the generator again. Adrian and Sophie immediately reached for their phones, breaths held in expectation, and then made noises of disappointment.

"So, Manang Remy, I wanted to ask you something," the boy said when the repetitiveness of the task had settled. "And I hope you don't get offended, okay? You know I love you," he added, chuckling. "But you're, like, a really religious person. Do you really think Lolo died of bangungot?"

"He did. Why does everyone keep doubting this?" Remedios said firmly. "I saw what he looked like, and so did Doña Olympia. It can't be anything else."

Dante laughed. "Yeah, but Nanay, you only saw him the

next day. Maybe it was just a heart attack. Maybe he died peacefully in his sleep." He suddenly turned glum. "Isn't it better to remember him that way, instead of . . . dying in pain?"

In her heart, Remedios agreed with her son, but saying so would have been another lie. There was no hiding or denying the look on Raul's face when he died. It was not a serene passing. He was in agony; it was as clear as the stab in her chest she now felt as she recalled him.

"And a sleep paralysis demon?" Adrian asked. "You don't find it, I dunno, inconsistent with your beliefs?"

"Not everything can be explained by religion. I have an uncle, he was a priest. Almost became a bishop, too. He said that priesthood is a lifelong journey of questioning your faith. The church doesn't know everything, and even they acknowledge the existence of demons."

Dante agreed, recounting a story about an exorcism in Davao. Out of nowhere, a six-year-old girl had started speaking in low, incoherent growls, acting like a feral dog. After doctors confirmed it wasn't rabies, her family turned to the parish. Three priests had her tied up to a bed while she thrashed and roared, her limbs twisted in agonized resistance. The priests prayed over her for ten hours, trying to cast out the demon that possessed the child. "It was all over the news. And it looked just like in the movie—except her head didn't spin," Dante chuckled. "They almost drowned her in holy water too. I don't know that it worked, though. She fell into a coma and died after a week."

"Not having an explanation is one thing," Sophie answered, more toward Dante than his mother, whom she couldn't look directly in the eye. "But how do we even know it's bangungot and not something else?"

Remedios put down her finished palaspas. "I know what I've seen in this house. And I know it was an evil force that took Don Raul's life." She took another bundle of palms and began weaving them. "Looking back now, I think his nightmares about demons were omens. The bangungot is a nightmare made real, in the form of a large, grotesque demoness. She sits on her victim's chest, crushing and suffocating them until they die. No one knows why or when she comes, only that when she does, there is no escape."

"Except death," Adrian added in an affectedly baritone voice. He grabbed Sophie's side and she yelped, startled. His laughter carried in the stillness of the night. Their giggles only ceased when they caught the caretaker's glare.

Adrian raised his chin at Dante. "So maybe that curse is real after all, huh?"

Remedios crossed herself. "Gaba."

"Is that what that translates to?" Sophie asked. "I'd heard it but I wasn't sure."

"Oh? I thought curse was 'sumpa,'" Adrian added.

Dante shook his head. "'Sumpa' is Tagalog, and it is not the same thing. 'Sumpa' means curse, but it also means a promise."

"As in, I promise to curse you." Adrian snickered.

"But gaba is Waray. And it can only mean one thing," Remedios warned. "A great misfortune."

Sophie's face turned grim and the caretaker felt a flutter of vindication. She tied off a bundle of braided blades and asked the girl, "So, has Sir Adrian told you about the curse of Villa Sepulveda?"

"Only that it's a local legend, nothing more," Sophie replied. "You have a big house in the middle of a jungle, and people are bound to make up stories. I mean, this manor has a long and documented history. It makes sense that some of it would get distorted over the centuries."

"Like the legend about Bartolome's wife Dorotea," Adrian added. "The mad marquesa whose ghost supposedly roams the halls."

"Psh! This house has no ghosts," Dante replied.

Sophie asked, "So, what, did Dorotea curse the place . . . ?"

"No, nothing like that. More like this house was unlucky from the very moment it was built, for the reason it was built—to be an asylum for Dorotea," Adrian replied. "Isn't that right, Manang Remy? So, when bad things happen, it's all because the manor's cursed. It doesn't help that Lola Divina has been living here like a recluse. Talk about bad PR."

Remedios sneered. "All everybody sees are her mourning clothes, but the townsfolk forget how she manages the farm. The employees all answer to Sir Eric, but Doña Divina is the one who's here to get things done."

As for the curse itself, Remedios chose not to correct the boy. Easier for him to dismiss it as a silly story exchanged by backwards people. He wasn't born here, wasn't raised here, and he only ever experienced the bounty of the plantation. He wouldn't understand, let alone bear the truth.

"And the chismosas also forget all the good the governor's ever done for Leyte. Everyone is happy to gossip about the family's misfortunes, but we wouldn't even have ports and paved highways if not for Don Raul. And the jobs! Why, everyone came to work for the farm, even people from far away. It wasn't just the Sepulveda family who prospered, this entire region did. But now, all they talk about is the 'haunted house' and all the disasters."

"What disasters?" Sophie asked.

Remedios put down her palaspas, taken aback at the question. Adrian seemed equally interested. *They really have no idea, do they?* She didn't know where to begin—the typhoons, the landslides, the malaria, all the deaths that followed. Surely Adrian would at least know about Doña Divina's husband, or his great-grandfather, who died around the same time?

"You shouldn't listen to any of it," Dante answered instead. "It's all idle talk. That is just how people are. They remember the bad and forget the good. And they still believe in myths and legends. Everything bad is caused by gaba."

"And Lolo's death is gonna be part of that now, isn't it? They'll say the gaba continues."

"They just don't know," Sophie answered. It was unclear to Remedios whether the girl's sympathy lay with Adrian or the simple-minded barrio folk. "I mean, seriously, no one who looks at your family and knows the real deal could say that the Sepulvedas are cursed. If anything, you all are the exact opposite."

"I still don't know what to think," Dante said. He gave his mother a mischievous look. "Gaba or heart attack, who knows. All I know is the dirt."

Remedios clucked, keeping her head down and her focus on her task. "Ignore him. He doesn't know what he's talking about." Any stronger of a response would only egg him on, and she didn't want her son spouting hurtful nonsense.

"Makes more sense than bangungot or the damn curse," her son continued. "Pasintabi, Sir Adrian . . . but when Nanay and your lola found your lolo, his hands and nails were dirty, like he had been digging in the ground."

"Digging? I don't understand."

"I think he was working on his mausoleum when his heart gave out, but no one listens to me. I mean, I saw his tools. The wheelbarrow was out, and the lantern was still on the next morning," Dante insisted. He pointed into the distance, where the bamboo stakes still stood. "You know how he can be stubborn sometimes. I don't know why he was working at night or how he ended up--"

"Ano ba, anak! The doctor already said no," Remedios said sharply. "He died in his sleep, in his bed, where we all found him. And that's the end of that."

For dinner the second night, they served pastel de lengua. "Ox tongue," Adrian explained, "but it's just like any cut of beef, only more tender." That did little to comfort Sophie, who took painfully slow bites of her eggplant salad to delay getting to her main course. She usually wasn't this sensitive. She'd eaten an alligator burger once, cookies made of cricket flour, deep fried frog legs, but this medallion of tongue was still too close to its original form, especially as it had been doused with creamy mushroom sauce that only reminded her of phlegmy spit. Its sinews did look like a filet's, but she could still make out the taste buds on its bumpy surface. She looked around the table. Everyone savored their lengua without hesitation, even Margot, who caught her staring. Sophie cut into her tongue, swallowed the bite, and chased it down with a drink of water. Despite its appearance, the gravy helped convince her she was eating a regular sirloin. With effort and, she hoped, calling little attention to herself, Sophie eventually finished her plate.

Unlike the previous night, the dinner conversation left her out this time. Sophie was relieved to blend into the background, as inconsequential as the empty chair reserved for the yet-to-arrive Sepulveda sibling. It started out promisingly. The table reminisced about the manor's halcyon days: Past Christmases with Raul, the never-ending series of themed birthday parties, company soirees, charity balls, and campaign fundraisers, all organized by Olympia, who told her stories with self-satisfaction.

"All this only makes me think about the future of this house," Javier stated, slicing into his lengua. Olympia protested, casting a conspicuous glance toward Sophie, but Javier never seemed the type to care for protocol. "Are we keeping it?"

"Por Dios, por santo! How could you even ask that?" Divina cried.

"Well, Kuya has always thought about selling, haven't you?" Javier answered, to his brother's obvious chagrin.

Eric cleared his throat. "We keep the plantation and its subsidiaries, naturally. As for the manor itself, well, it costs a lot to maintain, especially with the requirements of the landmark commission." Every year, the house had to be done up for inspection, which always seemed to uncover a necessary repair or update. A reinforcement here, replacement there, all still in keeping with the original craftsmanship of the place. "We're basically paying for bragging rights, and it's not cheap."

Divina held a palm over her forehead as though she was going to collapse. "Hijo, you cannot say that. Please, tell me you're not even considering it." She turned to her sister-in-law, stern-faced.

Olympia nodded in agreement. "We are not destitute, far from it. We'll manage the upkeep, the same way we have for years. But it's not just about the money. We must keep Villa Sepulveda for as long as we can. It's our duty. This house has been in the family for centuries. I won't see it pass to some stranger just because you children see no value in it."

"That's not what I said," Eric countered. "I love this place, but it also hasn't been home for forty years. I'm just trying to keep an open mind."

"I say sell it," Javier answered. "I have no fond memories of this place. I'd rather have the spending money."

Divina stifled a cry. Javier reached for her hand. "Selling doesn't have to mean you'll lose your home, Auntie. We can work out a tenancy deal with whoever ends up buying. Maybe the provincial government, or the National Historical Institute. That's what they've done to the other ancestral homes. They could convert the first floor into a museum, make some money, that kind of thing."

"Oh, and have the masses walking in and out of here while I have my morning tea?" Divina exclaimed. "I would much rather not!"

"And what would your papa think if he were here? A

museum, tour groups? The masses invading?" Olympia added, her voice rising. "Think of the invasion of privacy, the pilfering. And think of the disgrace! Pimping the manor out like a common prostitute. Why, our ancestors would turn in their graves! Your papa never would have said yes."

Javier leaned in with a snarl. "Well, he doesn't get a vote, now does he?"

"There's no need for that. The body isn't even cold yet," Eric snapped. "Besides, the question of who gets a vote isn't up to you. It's up to Papa's will."

The room fell silent. The mention of Raul's will promised to turn an ugly conversation even nastier. No one spoke for an uncomfortably long time, until Olympia settled the matter. "It makes me sick how we've devolved into quarreling over spoils, and so soon too." She shot Javier an icy glare. "All will be settled fairly in due time, but one thing is certain: This place will never leave the family's hands, not for as long as I live."

Every unhappy family is unhappy in its own way, Sophie thought to herself. Adrian mouthed "I'm sorry," his eyes filled with shame.

Divina broke the ensuing lull, her voice petulant. "Besides, it's not like anyone will buy this place anyway. It's gained a *reputation*."

The brothers groaned in unison. "The villa has seen its share of bad luck, but it's not cursed," Eric said, repeating the last word with incredulity.

"How many times have we said this? Gaba is more than just bad luck. It is a curse in every sense of the word," his aunt replied. Her voice was even, remarkably different from the usual highs and lows of her manner. "It's easy to dismiss it because you kids never saw the worst of it. Never *lived* the worst of it. But your parents did. So did I."

Olympia cast her head down, almost in reverence. At the

other end of the table, Eric crossed his arms. "Mama, Auntie, I'm sorry, it's just not part of my belief system."

"Belief has nothing to do with it," Divina replied. "Whatever happened, happened. And you can't judge the reasons we ascribe to them when you don't know the full story."

Divina likened it to the Ten Plagues of Egypt. Everyone who knew about the Sepulveda curse agreed that it started with Typhoon Saling. "It was one of the strongest typhoons the country ever saw, and certainly the worst that Leyte had ever seen. There were landslides, too, caused by the storm surges. Millions in damage, entire towns disappearing from the map. Hundreds dead and missing. And that was only the opening salvo." The storm coming down outside the manor, battering the roof as they dined, only served to underscore Divina's ominous tone.

Light poles were still down, roads still uncleared, when the next tragedy struck: A plague of malaria ravaged Leyte, with the town of Maalin seeing the highest casualties. Villa Sepulveda itself had not been spared; three of their maids died, not to mention a handful of farmers. Many believed that the toll wouldn't have been as high had doctors and medicine been able to make their way to the province.

That belief wavered when hordes of crocodiles began to attack the countryside. They were found in the streets of the Maalin, in the coconut plantations, in the grain silos, truck stops, churchyards. Places too far away from the coast and the estuaries where the beasts resided. Everyone still talked about the story of the schoolteacher who lost both legs after a buwaya surprised her in her classroom early one morning.

"And then there were the beetles," Divina said. Before she could continue, Olympia broke her silence, to the table's surprise. Her face was as bleak as her tone.

"They covered the face of the land so that no one can see the land; and they ate what is left to you after the storm, and they ate every tree which grows in the field, and they filled our houses, and the houses of all the servants and of all the Egyptians; as neither your fathers nor your grandfathers have seen."

"Is that Exodus?" Margot half whispered to no one in particular.

Olympia ignored her and continued to describe the large black scarabs that laid waste to groves all over Leyte and beyond. It was a common enough pest in those parts, but never before had they descended with such ferocity. Swarms covered the trees like a slick and scaly armor, felling the ones that hadn't already been downed by the typhoon.

"They had long, pointed horns. Pesteng yawa, quite literally. The devil's beetles."

"They ruined everything on this island, but Sepulveda Farms was hardest hit," Divina interjected. "Your papa had to sell some acreage after that."

"Is that why you left?" Adrian asked his lola.

"It was . . . one of the reasons."

"Because it didn't end there," Divina said. "There was also the warehouse."

Divina had been weepy since they all arrived, but this moment seemed to be her first show of genuine sorrow. She spoke of her husband, Melchior, the peasant who won the heiress's heart. Even after marrying into the family and moving into the villa, he still wanted to work the land and stayed on as a farmhand. He died one exceptionally hot November morning, only a few months after the wedding: The roof fell in on one of the plantation's warehouses, crushing everything and everyone inside. Along with eight others, Melchior was buried under tons of husked coconuts.

"I went from bride to widow in the span of a season," Divina said dourly. "And then shortly after, I took on a new title. Orphan."

Her and Raul's mother died young, of colon cancer, but

Don Claudio lived to a ripe old age of eighty-four. His aneurysm was not entirely unusual, considering. The shock mostly came from how it had manifested: The general was in the back lawn target-shooting coconut heads as he always did on Saturday mornings. The maids were summoned by the sudden cessation of the gunshots, and when they found the master of the house, he was collapsed on the grass, blood leaking out of every hole in his head.

"That was right before Christmas 1985, the only year this house didn't see a Noche Buena," Divina said with regret, over her father's death or the lack of a feast, Sophie couldn't tell. "So now you see how dark that period was. One heartbreak after another after another."

"I knew about Lolo Claudio and the warehouse, but not in full detail. Just the broad strokes," Eric answered, and Javier nodded in agreement. A first. "And I sure didn't know about the Biblical plagues bit."

There'd been no sense recounting it, Olympia explained, especially not after moving to the States. The challenges of rebuilding their lives in a new country left little time to dwell on the past. Besides, California was supposed to be a fresh start for them, and so the villa, once beloved, was forsaken with all its tragedies.

"But you did know about the curse, at least?" Adrian asked his father.

"I did, but I was nine when it all happened, and I thought the grownups were just trying to scare me," Eric answered. After a pause, he laughed. "Javi, do you remember that one nanny we had? The one who liked to scare us into going to sleep? She said the witch would come after us the way she came for our family."

Javier nodded half-heartedly. "Yes . . . this was already in Belvedere, right? Mila was her name, I think."

"That's right. Oh, she was such an odd duck." Eric then

proceeded to reminisce about the pranks they pulled on the nanny. Sophie saw how hard the man tried to change the subject and the mood. Adrian did too, and he helped by riffing with his father and uncle about their boyhoods. Margot started to look bored and soon interjected.

"So, there was a witch who 'cursed' the family?" she asked, gesturing with air quotes.

"I actually don't know," Eric answered. "I don't think I'm quite clear on that part of the family lore."

"Witch or not, there must've been someone. Right, Mama?" Javier said, like a challenge. "After all, you did say gaba is retribution. So, who did Papa piss off?"

Olympia dropped her utensils. "That's just uneducated barrio talk. I won't deny the coincidences, and the catastrophes were all real. Like your auntie said, we saw it and we lived through it. But your father didn't piss anyone off, and there is no witch."

"That doesn't really answer the question," Javier countered. "Where does this curse come from? What do the taga-barrio say?"

The two old women stared at one another, each waiting for the other's cue. When the wait had gone on too long, Olympia finally spoke. "Gaba is retribution, yes, but it is more like karma. You do something bad, something bad happens to you in return. It's not sorcery or some witch's spell. It's part of our culture, and it's how people here like to make sense of random misfortunes. 'Oh, the general must have done so-and-so, the governor might have acted this way or that, no wonder all the harvest is poor, makes sense that their livestock fell ill,' things like that." She looked at Divina again, who hid behind her veil.

"Well, there was one thing," Divina said.

Olympia pursed her lips. "Back then, most of Leyte worked for us. Farmhands, lumberjacks, truck drivers, line workers at the mill and refinery and distillery. We treated them well and paid them well, more than any other farms would. The workers flocked here from all over the country and stayed with us for years. But they were unhappy with Marcos. He imposed this . . . 'coco levy' which taxed farmers, but it was a tax on us farm owners too. And it had a noble purpose: All the money went into a fund intended to improve the coconut industry and help the farmers directly. The tax was supposed to be a temporary pain for long-term gain."

"So this is about . . . tax policy?" Adrian asked.

"Not even our own tax policy, mind you," Olympia continued. "The workers had a union—we never stood in their way of forming one—and the union was very anti-Marcos."

"And I'm guessing the fund didn't end up helping the farmers, did it?" Adrian asked sharply. Sophie could tell where this was going, and she only hoped that Adrian would talk to his still-grieving grandmother with more gentleness.

"We all know what they did," Javier answered.

Olympia continued. "There'd been protests, even before the corruption got revealed. Things really started to heat up around then, late 1985 to '86. Sepulveda Farms drew some of the ire that the farmers wanted to direct at Marcos. They knew how close our family was to the president, and we were the largest coconut producer in the country at the time, so we were an easy target. There were strikes, and our workers quit en masse. All our businesses suffered. And then Typhoon Saling struck. The townsfolk blamed the tax on us and blamed all the disasters too—the typhoon, the malaria, the pestilence. With Melchior's death, and then Papa's shortly after, everyone on the island started saying it was gaba. The universe was taxing us for the way we taxed them."

"They even blamed monsters on us, can you believe it?" Divina said, tut-tutting.

"Oh, yes, I remember. This is where you'll see how the rumors and myths got distorted." Olympia took a sip of her wine. "The barrio folk just kept tacking on detail after detail, saying they heard this or saw that, on and on until the real story got muddied. They said that they'd seen a balbal lurking around in the groves by the foot of the mountain, right around the time after my papa died."

"Wait—what's a balbal?" Adrian asked, taking the words out of Sophie's mouth.

"It's a local legend, like the kapre or tikbalang," Divina replied, then turned to Sophie. "You've heard of these?"

"I've heard of the aswang, which is kind of like a vampire, right?" she said. She'd read a collection of Filipino horror stories and had always been fascinated by how similar folkloric creatures were across time and cultures.

"You mean the CIA's vampire?" Javier added sarcastically. The entire table looked at him in confusion.

Javier began to explain how in the fifties, the CIA staged deaths to look like aswang attacks. They planted corpses in the jungles of Quezon and punctured their necks to make it look like the bloodsucking cryptid had been attacking the countryside, in order to scare communist rebels that had been hiding in the mountains. "There's no aswang, or balbal, or tikbalang. It's all horseshit, and worse, it's weaponized horseshit. Psyops, just like this gaba. It's superstition used to rob people of their agency and control them."

"Well, that's a cynical view of our culture," Divina stated. "There's no harm in teaching the children about the country's folklore, especially when they're taking such an interest. The balbal happens to be one of our more fascinating monsters." She turned to Adrian and Sophie and she took on the manner of a fireside storyteller trying to both scare and entertain. "It's a very tall, very thin demon covered in fur, with long claws and sharp teeth. It does look like the aswang, without the long, bloodsucking tongue. It also differs in one important respect: The balbal only feeds on corpses. A carrion feeder."

"So it can't hurt us, right?" Adrian's tone was almost mocking. Divina carried on, oblivious.

"Unless provoked, I suppose. But yes, it only eats corpses. The more rotten, the better. Human corpses best of all. It stalks cemeteries after burials, digs up the coffins, and then brings the bodies into its lair to feast on them. But before it leaves and goes up the mountain, it does one last thing." Here, the old woman lowered her voice. "It rips out a small tree from its roots, takes the trunk, and puts it inside the open coffin to replace the dead body. Legend says it's to trick people, to create the illusion that the body was still there. No one ever claimed that the balbal was smart. Personally, I think it's something else. Some sort of ritual, or remuneration. Its idea of paying back after having taken."

"Sounds to me like a cover story concocted by graverobbers," Javier replied.

"I suspect some enterprising thieves have used the legend as a smokescreen, especially back during martial law," Olympia said. "There was a lot of death going around, and there followed reports of coffins being exhumed and emptied of their contents. I don't know if the stories were true or exaggerated, but it's easy to see how the townsfolk would have their imaginations running wild."

"Great." Javier rolled his eyes. "So we have: a malaria outbreak and a beetle infestation and crocodile attacks and falling roofs and stolen taxes and corpse-eating monsters," he said, counting each with his fingers. He turned to Sophie with a sardonic grin. "Bet your family doesn't have that kind of fucked up lore, huh."

"You're forgetting the storm that started it all," Adrian added. "Typhoon Saling."

"And Saling!"

"And the witch too," Eric said.

"I thought there was no witch?" Margot asked, giggling.

Adrian shook his head. "There was never a witch, though that's part of the lore now too. Damn, Villa Sepulveda really does have everything."

Javier smirked. "With the right kind of marketing, we'll have buyers beating down our gate."

Sophie couldn't resist laughing along, despite the elders' dismay at the rest of the family's jests. After all, when grief becomes unbearable, one must laugh to help from going mad. And at least for Sophie, the laughter was essential: It quieted the coil of unease in the pit of her stomach, brought on by the knowledge she'd had to digest with her meal.

Everyone turned in early that night. There were no postprandial conversations in the conservatory, and the old ladies' evening prayer seemed cut short. Jet lag caught up with Adrian, whom Sophie expected would hang out in her room until his dad once again called him to bed. There was still no reception or wi-fi, and she tried to entertain herself with a slim Agatha Christie volume, but even a murder in the Mideast proved an inadequate distraction. She decided to unleash her restless energy and slipped out of her room.

She wandered aimlessly, familiarizing herself with the place. The lamps were still lit, which made her task easier. Alone, and after the day she'd had, Sophie saw the manor in a different light. There was a lot of misery behind all the finery. The artwork and photographs told one story, and the people—the family—told another, a fuller, richer account. She found all of it fascinating. This place was messy, and beautiful in its messiness. And the Sepulvedas, whether meaning to or not, had shared all that with her. Even as stories of demons and curses unnerved her, Sophie drew from them a strange sense of pride.

She reached the foyer and stopped dead in her tracks. A hooded figure stood by the statue of the Virgin Mary. Water dripped from its arms; puddles collected by its feet. It saw Sophie and lurched forward, startled as much as she was.

"Who are you?" the figure asked, revealing the face under the hood. Sophie recognized Adrian's auncle, Kai. They were just as Adrian had described: shaved head, pierced eyebrow, thrifted threads from head to toe. Slight, almost waifish, youthful for someone in their thirties.

"You must be Kai. I'm Sophie, Adrian's girlfriend." She extended a hand, which Kai pulled into a hug.

"Glad to meet ya," they answered, blithely unaware of how damp they made her. Kai paced around, eyes roving and wide, almost hypnotized. "Do you feel that? It's unusually cold in here, no?"

"Well, you are soaked."

"Oh, yeah, trouble with the gate. The driver was a trooper, though." They peered into one room and down the hall before heading into the sala mayor. The sight of the coffin didn't seem to register with them. "This place . . . it's so different from what I imagined . . . but yes, no, the cold. I don't mean because of the storm. It's a cold place. It has a cold aura. It's so strong. Do you feel it?"

"I'm sure I don't know what you mean." Sophie smiled politely. She'd expected as much from meeting Kai. They were a child of the earth, a Burner with the whole world as their playa. Needless to say, they were into all sorts of mysticism and the occult. Their backpack, festooned with pins and patches of indecipherable sigils, doubtless contained a tarot deck or some divination crystals. "But I can see you're shivering. Maybe you should go get changed before you catch a cold?"

Kai narrowed their eyes and made to respond, but then Tiago came up the stairs carrying their luggage.

Soon, the rest of the family had been roused from their

rooms to meet the final arrival. Greetings and hugs were exchanged. No one minded or even remarked on Kai's damp state.

"I bet myself you wouldn't make it in time for the funeral," Javier said.

"Ah, well, either way, you win, huh?" The siblings half hugged awkwardly.

Olympia teared up at the sight, and her youngest child swept her into their arms.

"I'm sorry it took me a while," Kai said.

"It's quite all right. What matters is you made it." Olympia stroked Kai's back, like lulling a baby to sleep. She settled on one of the longer couches and gathered her children around her. She wiped her cheek with her laced sleeve, though tears continued to flow freely. "You know, this is the first time we're under this roof. All five of us." Her voice cracked as she spoke, and Kai began to weep.

Eric, too, was overcome with tears. "I know Papa is pleased to see us all together."

When the crying died down, Kai told them about their travel—the various ordeals surmounted to arrive in the Philippines from a remote Argentinean hillside, the flight delays and cancellations, and the eventual need for a private charter "because that was the only way anyone could be bribed to ignore all the typhoon alerts."

In turn, the family gave Kai an overview of the weekend's arrangements: the next day's vigil, the services for Saturday's funeral.

"There's an evacuation warning, didn't you hear?" Kai said. "No one's gonna come. No one can. I'm honestly amazed I made it here in one piece."

"It's like the universe conspiring, huh?" Javier said mockingly, waving his fingers around like a magician.

"This storm will pass tonight," Olympia stated. "We have nothing to worry about."

In due course, everyone retired for the night. Adrian and Sophie led Kai to their room, which was down the same hall as theirs. She hung back a bit, allowing auncle and nephew to chat. She knew how excited Adrian was to see Kai again, whom he'd viewed more like a cool older sibling.

"I know we're supposed to be miserable wrecks right now, but I'm really psyched you're here," he told them. "It's been, what, four years?"

"Yeahhh . . . got tangled up in some things, you know how it is."

"All right then, tell me all about it. What have I missed? Where'd you go, what did you do . . . ?"

"Hmm. Where to start," Kai answered with a distracted sigh. Their attention seemed to catch on every detail in the manor, and they strode with deliberation. Or was it trepidation? "There it is again," they said, apropos of nothing. "Do you feel that? The cold. Tell me you do."

"Uhm, no? But I'm also not dripping wet," Adrian said.

Kai turned to Sophie, holding her by the wrist. "You're not from this place. You've never been here before. Same as me. You must feel something different. *See* something different."

"I'm sorry, I really don't."

They looked at her with disappointment. Sophie couldn't tell if it was because they believed her, or because they saw through her lie.

For she did feel a shiver come up her arm, felt a gust of cold air brush against her face in the stillness of the half-lit hallway. Sophie admitted as much to herself when she was finally alone in her room. She chalked it up to jet lag. Her energy level varied throughout the day, not to mention her mental acuity. Intrusive thoughts and odd sensations were to be expected.

She tried to ignore these as she went through her bedtime routine. She did her meditation exercises, her yoga stretches on the hardwood floor. She lotioned, brushed her hair, massaged her scalp, feeling the muscles in her head loosen. Yet she couldn't stop thinking of the Sepulveda family curse. There must be a straightforward, earthbound explanation for everything that happened. She didn't know how crocodiles would travel so far inland, or why the coconut warehouse collapsed, but the malaria and the devil's beetles were probably caused by the typhoon. Adrian must have thought so too. Just like him, she was an atheist, a fact that should never be spoken in this household. She was willing to make the sign of the cross and read the prayers, but she was a nonbeliever. She didn't believe in superstition or the supernatural either. Her interest was purely cultural; the stories were an amusing facet of this country that she didn't fully understand quite yet.

In time, Sophie fell asleep.

She tossed and turned and stirred awake, her sleep coming and going in bursts. She dreamed of a spectral figure, dark and shrouded, standing in the corn fields of her family's farm. Then, the farm melted away but the specter remained. It now stood in the tall grass of the villa's plantation, among the coconut groves. Then she saw it on Stanford's main quad, then the veranda of Villa Sepulveda as she lazily tap-tap-tapped her feet on the azulejos. The places and sensations bled into each other, but always the specter was in the distance. She couldn't tell if it was a man or a woman; its face hid behind a hood that reached all the way to the ground. Yet she knew it watched her. Waited for her.

Sophie shot up from bed in a cold sweat.

The sun had already risen. She lay there, panting, staring at the undulations of the linen canopy with bloodshot eyes. She was both tired and wired. Damn the jet lag that she should be over by now. Damn her midafternoon coffees. And damn all that talk of monsters and bangungot. Propelled by agitation, she rose and changed out of her dampened shirt.

She stood before the giant armoire's mirror, looking as

worn as she felt. She tidied her hair and then saw it again. A small blot of light, right by the reflection of her face.

She spun around, puzzled but determined. It took some pacing around the room, tracing the source of the light, but soon enough, she found it. A gouge in the wall, no larger than a quarter. The grain and shade of the wood made it easy to miss.

She leaned into the wall, slightly on tiptoe, and peeked into the hole with trepidation. She saw straight out into the hallway with a clear view of the room opposite hers, and of the end of another hallway that led down to the sala. Sophie pulled back, slamming her hand on the wall. She had no doubt about it. It wasn't just any hole. It was a peephole.

April 11

FRIDAY

"That's a peephole, all right," Adrian said, stunned. He turned and tilted his head, trying to ascertain the limits of his view. "Fuck, that's creepy."

It's more than just creepy, it's a goddamn breach of privacy, Sophie wanted to say, but she caught herself. Already she thought it was a bit much that she'd camped outside his bedroom for over an hour until he was up. She hadn't wanted to wake him and seem too hysterical.

He traced the rim of the peephole. "It's smooth. It's been here a while."

"And it's too big a hole to be an accident."

"This used to Great-Grandlolo's room. Why would this be here?"

"Babe, I really don't care about that right now. I just want it . . . I don't know—gone!"

Adrian looked at her with amused concern. He paced across the room and lifted a coatrack that hung next to the armoire. He placed it right in front of the hole. "Ta-da," he said, flourishing his arms.

"This isn't funny. I barely had any sleep," she complained.

"What, because of this?"

"No," she said nasally. The last thing she needed right now was Adrian poking fun at her nightmares too. "It's the jet lag still."

"Yeah, it always takes me a couple days to recover." He hugged her in sympathy. The gesture soothed Sophie; her body wanted to fall asleep in his arms, but her mind was persistent.

"Look, I'm grateful to be here, really, but you can't just put guests in rooms with peepholes."

"Whoa, okay, I didn't even know about it till you showed me," he answered. "And we don't know that it's a peephole, necessarily."

"You just said it was!"

"I mean, yes, it does look like it, but there could be another explanation—I don't know!"

The two froze mid-argument when Remedios spoke. "It is for spying," she said, hands clasped as she stood on the open threshold. "Not into the room, but out."

"Out?" Adrian asked. "Manang Remy, that doesn't make sense."

"It does, to the amo of the house. These holes are as old as Villa Sepulveda itself. They're there to look out on the staff. To make sure they did their duties," she explained. "For their own privacy, the amos blocked the holes with a frame or a painting. Some used a stopper too, to prevent eavesdropping. Not that there was much risk of that. Maids feared punishment more than they loved gossip."

Both dread and outrage crept up Sophie's spine each time the caretaker used the plural. How many holes were there, exactly? "That's so . . . " She grasped for words, her frustration cresting. "Wrong. Just plain wrong."

"Please tell me Lolo and Lola never used these," Adrian said warily. "Or Great-Grandlolo."

Remedios pursed her lips. "This room has been vacant for a long time. And all the other villas have these, not just ours. It's nothing unusual."

"*All* the others?" Sophie asked with alarm. How many holes looked into the sanctity of how many rooms across this country? "What kind of—this—this was how they all lived?"

"It is the amo's right."

Adrian would later translate the word to Sophie. Amo meant master or superior. Not gendered. Sophie wondered if it derived from the Spanish. Amo: love, as a verb.

"This is so fucked up," Adrian said as the caretaker left them. "Amo's right, my ass."

"We should plug it up," Sophie told him. "And search the room for other holes. Search all the rooms, while we're at it."

The suggestion took Adrian aback. "I don't think it'll go over well if we start going into rooms and feeling up walls, Soph."

"You heard Manang Remy. This is a feature of this house, and there are several of them. My room can't be the only one that has it," she answered firmly. "And I doubt that these peepholes were made to only look out into the hallways and not into adjoining rooms."

Adrian's face was inscrutable, on the edge of indecision. "I know it's just your family here," she continued, "but you know I'm right. You don't think it's weird to have men walking by a peephole to my room?"

Adrian replied by snapping into action. He moved furniture around, stood on the bed and the desks, feeling each wall from floor to ceiling. When both were convinced that there was only the one, they plugged it up with one of Sophie's balled-up scrunchies.

Once done with breakfast, the young couple skulked around the manor to hunt for more peepholes. They started with the room opposite Sophie's, but found it was locked. It was a guest room, Adrian said. Where Manang Remy used to sleep when he tended to Don Raul's nightmares. They decided to search the exterior walls instead, and found no hole. They went down the row, next searching outside the lady's bedchamber. It took time to find one, but thankfully Kai and Olympia had had a late start to their day and were still in the dining room. The peephole had been hidden behind a bird-of-paradise watercolor. Adrian lifted the frame and said, "Gotcha!"

Just then, Margot walked down the corridor with a confused look on her face. Adrian tried to dissemble and said he was just admiring the art. It was likely an attempt to shield his mother from worry, but Sophie could see Margot wasn't buying the lie.

"I found this . . . peephole. In my room," Sophie said, head bowed. She and Adrian weren't doing anything wrong; they were uncovering wrongdoing themselves. Yet she still felt guilty, as though she shouldn't have been leading Adrian on this quest, or shouldn't have been questioning how this house was built. At the very least, she shouldn't be stalking about other people's rooms. She showed Margot the smooth, dusty hole under the painting. Margot bent over to peek in, but changed her mind at the last minute.

"Kind of a backwards way of treating the help, no?" Margot said with a shiver. "Who does this?"

"Our ancestors, apparently." Adrian hung the frame back on the wall. "It really freaks me out, and Sophie too. I mean, we're all family here, but it doesn't feel right to have her sleep in a room with a peephole."

"Or anyone, for that matter," Sophie added.

Margot began to agree but then said, "Oh, I see where you're going with this. You know it can't happen, kid. Separate rooms—those are the rules."

Adrian whined, asserting that *that* wasn't the reason at all.

He just wanted Sophie to feel more secure and comfortable. Sophie tried to chime in but the mother and son had gotten into their own debate about discretion and responsible adulthood. Margot apologized to Sophie. "You're good kids, and I trust you both," she said, then turned to Adrian. "But your dad and I already said no. Besides, the lolas wouldn't like it. Maybe Kai would be willing to share the room?"

"No, I wouldn't want to be a bother," Sophie answered. She didn't want to involve the rest of the family. Her concern started to sound so infantile now. It was just a hole in the wall. She shouldn't need company at night. Besides, they'd covered it up already. "I think I'll be fine now that the initial shock's worn off."

"Good," Margot said, heading into their room. "As for me, I'm gonna see if there are peepholes in here."

"Sorry, babe, I tried," Adrian said once his mother closed the door.

"I know. It'd make me sleep better, having you there, but I think I'll be fine. Really."

"I'm so not used to this. Mom and Dad have always been sex positive. Now they've become super conservative, being all 'appropriate' and shit. Death in the family, Holy Week, I know all that, but it's not like we're going to fuck while they're praying over Lolo or something."

His grumblings aside, Sophie knew Adrian would always do the right thing. He'd always been the good son. It was one of the many things she admired about him. He was obedient and thoughtful, and he made time for his family. Even when he disagreed with them, he was never disrespectful or hostile. She recognized, too, that there was a hint of envy in her admiration of him. Filial piety never was a feature in her upbringing. Her folks were civil with their parents, and the extended family celebrated Thanksgiving and Christmas together, but they were mostly uninvolved and uninterested in each other's lives.

It was not very Asian, she'd learned, and not very Filipino at all.

Adrian asked if she'd like to hunt for more holes to plug up, but Sophie said no. She saw how concerned he'd grown and she tried to act breezy for both their sakes. Instead she told him she felt tired and wanted to get some rest.

Despite the size of her room, the breadth of the villa's chambers and corridors and vistas, the murmurings of her claustrophobia had returned. Yet after some thought, she had to admit that she didn't really feel spied on. Not through the peephole, anyway. That wasn't the cause of her unease. If anyone or anything had watched her as she slept, Sophie was convinced it was in the room with her last night.

Javier expected the day to be chaotic. After all, it was the day before the funeral, when the final vigil would be held, when all the supposed mourners would be packed in the sala mayor, trading their condolences with cups of coffee and pastries. The women would be bustling to stage the manor (flower arrangements fluffed, chairs filed in straight rows, refreshments laid out tastefully) for visiting dignitaries, not the least of whom would be the president and his family. Javier never actually thought they would come; he was as firm in his disbelief as his mother was in her belief, but he nonetheless indulged her. He would also indulge her yelling that roused him from bed.

Olympia's voice boomed down the halls, and everyone gathered in the sala to see what the fuss was about. Before her stood the groundskeeper and the driver, both with hangdog looks on their faces. When at last her eldest son had arrived, she asked the driver to repeat the news he had just delivered.

Dante had gone to Maalin at daybreak to collect supplies from the market. The meats, produce, alcohol, and other sundries would have been delivered days before, if not for the storm, which appeared to have passed overnight. As it was, he was surprised the warehouses were staffed, even though most of the town had hunkered down in their homes or evacuated. On his drive back to the estate, the road rumbled. He saw it through his rearview: A section of the mountain had collapsed, sending soil and boulders crashing down the slope. It was as though a giant had scooped up the mountainside and formed a hill that blocked the road all the way to the bluff. Dante had clutched the rosary hanging from his mirror and sped back toward the manor.

"I must have missed it by half a kilometer," he said.

He and his father Tiago had just returned, having set out again to assess the damage. The landslide was massive, cascading down the slope to the bluff, and cutting a wide swath that reached all the way to the downhill route. Villa Sepulveda, intended as a retreat, was built on a secluded incline; the road that led to it formed a loop. The landslide blocked both paths that converged into the main road toward the town.

"So we're fucking stuck here," Javier said.

"Bueno, call the municipio and have trucks sent over to start clearing the road," Olympia said. "Call the capitolio, if you have to. We have guests coming."

"And the funeraria. The church, too!" Divina added, crossing herself. She turned to the groundskeeper. "How bad could it be, really? We can't bury my brother without a service."

Tiago cleared his throat. "Señora, you might need to see it to understand. We've never seen anything like it. If you'll remember, the Typhoon Yolanda landslides took a week to clear, and this one is much worse."

"What will we do, anak?" Olympia asked Eric. "Your papa needs to be taken to church. What about the mass? And the reception—how will people get here? Dios mio, the guests . . . the president . . . "

"We'll have to postpone," Javier answered. Given the weather, it was foolish to even think that his mother's plans could come to fruition. Already it was too good to be true when the storm abated after their first night; Javier knew it could turn at any minute. At least now this landslide should inject a dose of reality. "We have no choice."

"Well, we can't postpone. Not next week," Olympia argued. She turned to Tiago again. "What about a tunnel?"

The question was met with incredulous cries. Kai leaned over to Javier. "Um, I don't get it. Why can't we bury him next week?"

"Holy Week starts Sunday, and no religious services are allowed."

"Oh, right. But I'm sure the church makes exceptions for emergencies, right?"

"It's not just burying the dead," Remedios interjected from behind them, the look on her face as stern as her voice. "You're not allowed to do *anything*. No TV, no music, no gatherings, not even a mournful one. Not even mass. No one should leave the house. Patay ang Diyos. God is dead on those days, and that's when all the demons come out."

Javier rolled his eyes. More demon talk. He had a faint recollection of Holy Weeks from his childhood in the villa. The eerie silence, the marathon prayers, the endless stories about Christ's torture and death. He recalled the superstitions too—how people seemed more prone to accidents during the week, how wounds incurred never healed, how the forces of evil exploited God's absence to wreak havoc. He got these stories from his elders and nannies alike, who all seemed to enjoy instilling fear more than inspiring reverence. What use was all that for, especially now? They were in the middle of not one, but two natural calamities. No one has so far asked how the town fared during the typhoon, or whether settlements had

been crushed under a mountainside, but these people were concerned about timing a funeral around religious bunk.

"We should dig the grave anyway," Olympia commanded. "The rain already stopped, and the road work must be ongoing as we speak. So we will have the funeral as planned. If the president can't come, I am sure he'll at least lend us one of his choppers. It's the least he could do. We can have the bishop airlifted."

Everyone fell as silent as the man laid out in the casket. No one wanted to say it, not even Divina, who had a preternatural inability to hold her tongue. There couldn't possibly be a funeral, they all knew that, and not even Olympia's iron will could make it so.

"And what if it rains again?" Javier asked. "Or, God forbid, what if no priest or bishop allows you to drag them out here?"

"Then we do the funeral after Easter," Eric said. "A week should be enough to clear the road, and then we can have everything according to plan. Bring Papa to San Isidro, then the procession home."

Kai raised a reluctant hand. "After Easter? Uhm, what about . . . " They cocked their head toward the casket.

"The embalming will last for at least two weeks. Papa will be fine. The cool weather helps too."

Javier lazily draped himself onto a wingback chair. "C'mon. We have everything we need right here. The grave will be in our literal backyard. The mourners are all in this room. The guest of honor"—he lifted an arm in salute—"has been ready for days. We don't need a church mass. We can still bury him tomorrow, priest or no priest."

Divina clasped her hand over her mouth, muffling a horrified scream.

"A mass isn't strictly required for Catholic funerals," he continued. Javier would know; he'd known enough queers disowned by their families and their religious communities, even in death. "The service doesn't have to be done on site, and it can be done any time: before, during, or after the burial. And we have, what, five able-bodied men here? We can dig the grave, set him down, say our prayers and all that. Then, in a week or two, do a memorial service in church, with all the guests and grandeur as planned."

"Pero, hijo, that is simply not how things are done!" Divina screeched, crossing herself. "No priest! How can you even suggest it? Especially given how . . . "

"How he passed." Olympia finished the thought somberly. "He needs to be blessed, hijo."

"Oh, come on. Not this bangungot bullshit again! Maybe—maybe—I'll buy that he died of fright, but crushed by a demon? We're not seriously putting everything on hold so we can, what, do an exorcism? This is ridiculous. We have to face the facts here—"

Olympia wrung the prayer book she'd been holding and screamed. She flung it at Javier's head, almost hitting him. She marched toward her son, each heavy footfall punctuating her words.

"We—will—wait—for—a—priest—and then bury your papa!"

Javier held his mother's glare. For the first time in his life, he saw in her what he'd always seen in his father: an adversary. He readied a number of choice comebacks, the way he would have if Raul were the one screaming in his face. *No amount of blessing will save his soul*, he thought of saying. *There isn't enough holy water in the world to wash him clean.* Was it a priest that she needed, or the adulation of her precious guests? Javier had been so used to fighting, and so self-satisfied in his acts of rebellion, that he didn't know how to stop himself.

Even his very presence in Villa Sepulveda was one such act. Paternal love certainly wasn't the driving force that brought him home; it was the need to confirm the old man's death. And now that he was sure, Javier had no one left to fight against, except maybe this widow in front of him, fraying at the edges, falling apart before her entire family.

Javier rose from his seat. He turned to Dante, standing behind his father.

"Let's go dig a grave."

DSC_20250308.docx

Source: A003C017_20250308_DivZoom.mov

Divina Sepulveda-Cuesta: And so, this rumor about the madhouse. Let's set aside whatever you've heard, whatever is the "official" account in the National Historical Institute's records, all that. Here's the truth: Villa Sepulveda wasn't intended as a mere country house, but neither was it a sanatorium for Bartolome's wife, whatever the people in this region say. [clicks tongue] It indeed was a hideaway of sorts, though not because the marquesa was insane, but because she was beautiful. Bartolome couldn't stand the masculine competition, and so he whisked her away from all the men who hounded her in Spain. That was it, nothing more.

Adrian Sepulveda: So not a madhouse. But like you said earlier, Dorotea must have felt like a nun locked up in a cloister.

DSC: A wedding ring never proved an effective deterrent for the nobles and upstart merchants who had ill intentions with his wife. Bartolome probably felt the distance necessary. The capital wouldn't do either, as it also swarmed with other men. Younger, richer men, sometimes. And so yes, Dorotea was hidden away. She was his and his alone. Trouble was, the expectation of fidelity didn't go both ways. In his travels between Alicante and Manila and Mexico and Leyte—the handful of times he could be bothered to visit his wife and kids—Bartolome had numerous affairs and fathered many bastards.

AS1: Do we know anything about his other kids?

DSC: No. I'm sure there was a lot of gossip and claims made, but they've been lost to time. They kept these details secret, as you might understand. Between Dorotea's reputation and his younger son's profligacy, not to mention the reversals in his business ventures, Bartolome couldn't afford more scandal. Thankfully, my lolo Oscar did not inherit his father's cheating ways, and his many children were all born within his union with my Lola Mercedes.

AS1: And what about the general?

DSC: I suppose things come in cycles, because Papa was much like his grandfather Bartolome. Don Claudio was a renowned ladies' man. It didn't help that he was this five-star general, with his spiffy brown uniform, bars on his shoulder, and, as with all the men in the family, he was very handsome.

AS1: He got a lot of attention.

DSC: And he enjoyed it. There was a long-standing and mostly private affair with an haciendera from Samar, another with a movie star in Manila. This was after he'd been stationed at the army HQ. I saw how these affairs broke Mama's heart. [long pause] There are days . . . days when I think her dying at fifty was a bit of a blessing.

AS1: We can take a break if you'd like.

DSC: [shakes head] I still remember, there was always an "incident" whenever Mama threw a party here in the villa. Men getting handsy—Papa mostly, if not his compañeros and underlings—their wives getting jealous . . . there were always whispers and giggles in some room or alcove, in every dark corner away from the festivities in the sala. Oh, yes, I know it all too well.

AS1: Oh, yeah? How so?

DSC: Hah, bueno, I was a very inquisitive girl. Mama knew how to throw a ball, and naturally, I stayed up for these parties, with or without her permission. [sighs] And then, when I became old enough to attend, I saw these antics with my very own eyes.

AS1: You probably have stories about every high-ranking soldier and politician from that time. The secret trysts of the rich and powerful . . .

DSC: I do, though I admit, it's the kind of knowledge I wish I didn't have. Especially when it came to Papa's own predilections. You don't understand how heartbreaking it was. I've often had to contend with questions about some stranger's paternity. 'So-and-so is your brother,' some ill-meaning gossip would tell me. 'See how you share the same nose, the same chin.' It got worse when he died in 1985. All these bastard sons and daughters crawled out of the woodwork asking for their slice of the pie . . .
[long pause]

Let's not use this last part, hijo. I don't think it's relevant anyhow . . .

AS1: This is all background. Preliminary, for my notes. I'll need to reshoot at some point and so this won't end up in the final cut. But don't think about any of that, Lola Divina. It'll be better if we just treat this as a conversation . . .

there's no recording equipment, you're not in an interview, and I'm not a filmmaker. It's just you and me, talking. [pause] I really do value these calls, Lola.

DSC: As do I, hijo. I get few reasons to get excited anymore, fewer reasons still to revisit the past. So, thank you. And, very well, where was I? Ah, yes, Papa's alleged bastards. I don't know that there's much else to say about that, anyway. None of the claims ever got proven, thank God.

AS1: That doesn't mean they weren't true.

DSC: Fair enough, but certain things still carry weight. One doesn't become a Sepulveda just because the men of the family happened to stray. Paternity matters. Acknowledgment matters, too. Papa was many things, but he was never a deadbeat. He never shirked his responsibilities, even ones he detested. He was a soldier. Duty and obligation were paramount to him. If he indeed had a child with another woman, he would have supported both child and mother. And so we would have known, me and Kuya.

AS1: It's a good thing Lolo Raul didn't follow in his father's footsteps, at least from what I can tell.

DSC: True. He's a one-woman man through and through. Have you spoken to him yet? I'm sure he can fill in the details I missed.

AS1: It's been hard trying to pin him down, plus with the time difference, we've had to cancel twice already. Lola Olympia says he's getting better but I'm starting to get worried. How is he, really?

DSC: He has his bad days, but otherwise he is as sharp as ever and still strong as a bull. There's no reason for you to trouble yourself. We're taking good care of him. You'll get his story soon enough.

Filipinos gambled at wakes. This seemed blasphemous, but Sophie didn't want to say anything. Wasn't there a story about Christ losing his shit at the temple, driving out the merchants, flipping over the gamblers' tables? Playing tong-its in the salon while a man lay dead across the hall seemed just as sacrilegious, but there was very little they could do aside from wait. There was no news from the outside world, the reception being completely down. A card game seemed a fine way to pass the afternoon, but did they really need to bet money on it?

Sophie tried in vain to disguise what she was doing. Her attention turned more to the game than the paperback she was supposedly reading, and why wouldn't it? Lunch—roasted pork belly and salmon sinigang—had induced a food coma that lulled Adrian to a siesta, and so she was left alone with a rare chance to be a fly on the wall, observing the Sepulvedas in their natural state without everyone doting on their heir and his girlfriend. Indeed, Margot seemed more at ease than Sophie had ever seen her, and even the taut sinews of Divina's face appeared to have slackened. At first, Sophie thought the card game served merely as a distraction from the morning's tension, but the two women seemed to genuinely relish playing. The caretaker Remedios rounded up the third, but stood from the table before long. She had to ready the meats for supper, and Margot teased that it was the worst timing, as she was just about to clean Remedios out. Margot stacked her one-peso coins and chuckled.

Divina called Sophie over to the table to take the empty spot. Despite her unease, Sophie thought it might be rude to decline; besides, she couldn't pass up the opportunity.

Tong-its was similar to rummy, a game she'd played countless times with her parents. It, too, involved building runs or sets of three or more cards, what they called "bahay," which literally translated to "house." Within an hour, Sophie picked up the variation well enough to outperform Divina and even caused Margot's fortunes to turn. The thought of throwing a hand or two crossed Sophie's mind, but that wouldn't go over well. Tong-its required reading your opponent, and Margot would be canny enough to catch it. Besides, Adrian's mother seemed like the kind of woman who would respect someone who bested her.

It struck Sophie how easily Margot fit into the family. She was blonde, blue-eyed, a Boston Brahmin from an ancient whaling family–and to top it off, a high-powered intellectual property attorney, a partner in the largest law firm in the world. Yet there she was, in her sweats (black cashmere, but still), hustling her eccentric aunt-in-law and the help, comfortably trading jests and idle chatter. She stood out only in how much she didn't—Margot didn't call attention to herself, didn't fuss about any of the food, didn't seek any translations or explanations. She wasn't out of place. Two decades of marriage and yearly vacations at the villa might have done that, true, but Sophie still studied her as though she might reveal some other, useful secret.

"Again?" Divina exclaimed when Sophie put her cards down to win another round. The old lady flung her coins in front of her. "Are you sure you haven't played this before?"

Losers dealt, and Margot handed out the cards with confident ease. "You know, I'm glad we get to spend some time without Adrian. Get to know each other."

A wicked look cut across Divina's face.

"You don't have to worry about me," Margot added. "I'm cool."

Sophie smiled. Every mom thought of themselves as a "cool mom," and no one ever was. Margot was a badass, but she was not a cool mom. Type A lawyers could never be cool moms.

"Ask away."

"Adrian's given me a rundown of sorts. Just the usual

things. Details you might find in a resume or your college application. Your major, internships, accomplishments, all that. The boy can't stop talking about how smart and well-rounded you are, and I hope I don't need to tell you that Eric and I are impressed." Sophie felt herself blush. Margot, trying to defuse the awkwardness, took on a lighter tone. "But that's all so blah, don't you think? I wanna know the side of you that's not about school, not on paper, you know what I mean?"

"Yeah, I think I do. So, uhm, nothing about Stanford then. Got it. Well, I could always talk more about Nebraska."

"Yeah, tell us what that was like," Margot answered. "Do you miss it?"

"All the time." Sophie figured any other answer would invite concern, and not the good kind. "School's been great, but there's no place like home, you know?"

"There was something I wanted to ask, from the other night," Divina said. She leaned in, drawing her words out. "So, you never knew your birth parents?"

"No, unfortunately not. It was a closed adoption," Sophie answered. The truth was plenty complicated, and as painful to recount as to hear. She didn't want to be a downer.

"And your adoptive parents are both white, yes?"

"Very white."

Margot shifted in her seat at the word. She drew a card and put down a straight set of diamond face cards.

As each player took their turn, she shared stories about Roy and Frances, third-generation corn farmers. Salt-of-the-earth types. She made sure to paint them as simple, but not simpleminded. She spoke of how she missed them; that part wasn't a complete lie. She also told them about Ruskin, Nebraska, population 160, and how she missed the quiet of the corn fields, the comfort of wide-open spaces and the boundless sky. She hadn't felt it anywhere else, except maybe there and now, amidst the coconut plantation. She was one of three

Asians in her entire village, and the only Filipino for miles and miles. To their credit, her parents never shied away from her Filipinoness. They took pains to make sure Sophie never felt uneasy about being brown in a white town, in a white country, different from everyone around her. More than being transparent about her adoption, they encouraged her to connect with her culture, if she so desired. That she never did so was not the Andersons' fault; it was hers.

Sophie looked out the window at the hillsides that hadn't collapsed, at the trees that weren't leveled overnight. The storm yet lingered, but as their game progressed, it calmed to bursts of drizzling.

"The kids at school called me coconut," Sophie said with a bittersweet smile. "Brown on the outside, white on the inside."

"How cruel," Divina said, placing a ten of diamonds on Margot's set.

"The thing is, they didn't really use it as an insult. At least they didn't think they were insulting me. It was like, *Sophie's not so different from us.*" She omitted saying how she herself never viewed it as an insult. To the contrary, it felt affirming to be told that how she looked didn't matter. Who she was inside, *that* was what mattered.

"Still, calling anyone names, especially racially charged ones . . . that's so demeaning," Margot said, going out with another set and winning the round. "Good thing you got out of Ruskin." That last word dripped with condescension, and Sophie winced. That was still her hometown, but she decided to brush it off.

They covered less fraught things, too—her interests, which included video games and mystery novels and, of late, karaoke. Sophie enjoyed this part of the conversation; Margot had begun to speak to her like a friend and Divina seemed more like the chatty old lady at the grocery store than the shut-in everyone in the neighborhood gossiped about. The game also helped distract Sophie and encouraged her to be frank. At one point they circuited to her relationship history, with a passing mention of the ex-boyfriend whom she'd broken up with only the day before she ran off to California. Sophie thought it a misstep, but the two women didn't seem to care, even going as far as to cheer the decision.

The topic had the benefit, too, of coaxing them to tell her about Adrian's ex-girlfriends, something he'd mostly kept to himself. He'd told her about Lexie, the one right before her, the high school sweetheart who dumped him just as he started Stanford. When he and Sophie first met, he was very open about the fact that he still stung from the breakup, though not quite so open as to tell her the sordid details, only that Lexie had cheated on him.

All this time, Sophie thought that Lexie was Filipino too. Looking back, she had no reason to assume so. She hoped the surprise didn't show on her face when Divina snarkily mentioned "the perky blonde thing" and how unfortunate it was that "the cheater" would forever be in the family Christmas photos. Margot winced at the description, though freely took a jab at the girlfriend prior, Vanessa, who'd also cheated and broken her baby boy's heart. A two-timing airhead, Margot called her, before adding, sotto voce, "Just like her mother." Unavoidable in the exchange was the discussion of the girls' families—they'd all gone to the same tony private schools and the rarefied circles the Sepulvedas ran in were small. Soon, the two women seemed to have forgotten about Sophie, going on about this girl and that, and Adrian's unfortunate string of bad luck.

"But you, my dear, are different," Divina finally told her, as though this should flatter her. Sophie felt the exact opposite. They'd all been rich, white, from good families; that was Adrian's type, until her. He brought them all to Belvedere, spent holidays with them, involved them in his life to such an extent that the Sepulvedas, even the one who didn't live in America, knew them intimately. Her mood soured, but she kept up a congenial façade. As more cards were lain on the table and more gossip exchanged, all she could hear were her own insecurities.

Here I am, girlfriend of, what, three years almost, only now meeting Adrian's family for the first time. I barely know anything about them, and whatever little I know, they knew much less about me. Yes, she was different from his exes in a lot of ways, but one overshadowed the rest: *I'm the only one Adrian kept hidden away in shame.*

Once she'd repaid all the coins that Margot had lent her to play with, Sophie excused herself from the game. On her way back to her room, she got lost in the halls again. She turned down the wrong way, toward the kitchen, the conservatory, the dining hall. She saw the corridor that led to the oratory and recognized that she'd gone too far, and to the wrong side of the manor too. She doubled back, following a route that seemed familiar. She had used an oil painting as a guidepost, the Spaniard in a doublet and a ruffled collar, but that didn't help either.

She passed a room with its door slightly ajar. She hadn't seen it before, nor been down this small hallway. A sliver of light showed a glimpse of an office illuminated only by a desk lamp. All the curtains had been drawn. Inside, someone was sobbing, moaning in pain. Sophie slowly opened the door and saw Adrian hunched over a desk. His shoulders were shaking. It was only as she came closer that she saw that the man was in fact Adrian's father.

Eric startled, but unlike last night, he didn't bother with any pretense of composure. The man was crying, and he seemed close to collapsing as he gripped the back of the large leather chair. He barely acknowledged Sophie, casting only a teary sidelong glance.

The sight was jarring. In the short time she'd known the man, Sophie had begun to view him through Adrian's eyes. He always kept his emotions close to his chest, the son said of the father. He hid them from everyone, for his own benefit and for those around him that looked to him for calm and stability. He was also stingy with praise, with expressions of pride or joy, more so with negative emotions like disappointment. "So goddamn repressed," Adrian had said. Sophie surmised that the complaint also applied to paternal grief, and she'd seen as much in Eric's behavior since they met at the airport. Witnessing him now so raw and unguarded made Sophie feel she'd done something wrong.

"I'm so sorry," she said. "Is there something I can do—"

"I'm—I'm sorry. Please forgive me."

The plea wasn't directed at her. Tears and snot mingled on Eric's face. She had never seen a grown man cry so much in her life. Still, she replied softly, "It's all right. It'll be all right."

"Papa used to sit me on his lap behind this very desk. I still recall the scent of his tobacco, his coffee with cream. He'd be reading his morning paper while I doodled on his bills and letters, pretending to be the governor. He let me stay on his lap even as visitors came by with official business. He'd tell them he was training me. That I was his little gobernadorcillo."

Sophie couldn't stand to look directly at the man as he cried and reminisced. Her gaze roamed the room as she stood there, uneasy. Shelves of books and bound journals collected dust alongside trophies and plaques honoring the province, the governor, the family. It took a while for her attention to land on the desk, where crumpled sheets of paper were scattered about. A page stood out to her: *Last Will and Testament.* It was marked up in thick red ink, parts struck out here and there, frantic large X's over entire paragraphs. Chicken-scrawl handwriting peppered the margins with incoherent ravings. *No! No! No! More than you deserve! Damn you all to hell!*

Sophie flushed with embarrassment. She wasn't supposed to see this either. Yet she couldn't help herself, and Eric didn't seem to care. He rested his head on the desk, his weeping muffled by the wood.

Sophie came closer. The papers were more legible to her now. A listing of assets, addresses of several buildings, valuations in the tens of millions of dollars. A catalog of their entire portfolio, in the hundreds of millions: Sepulveda Farms; Sepulveda Securities, Inc.; Sepulveda Land Development Corp.; Sepulveda Family Trust. And all these were just from the first few pages. Whatever Sophie had learned about the family through Adrian's downplayed stories (and through her Google searches), it nowhere near captured the extent of the family's wealth.

Don Raul's grievances were also clearer: The annotations struck out the names of his children where they appeared, his wife's too. Each mark and each expletive was so vigorously scrawled, the papers' furrows formed rough tears.

Sophie averted her eyes only when Eric raised his head, but not quickly enough. He made an effort to put away the papers, but the sheets were now as damp as his face. He fumbled with them for a while before giving up.

"Papa always said it is a father's sacred duty to give his children a better life than he ever had. That's what he did, and what his father did before him, and his father before him. Every generation better off than before. He really must have lost it in the end." He gestured at the document bleeding in red ink. "This is not a will. This is more of a suicide note. But it doesn't change things, not legally. It's not even signed. Still, it's a peek into where his mind was. And it hurts to see how tortured it was."

"I'm so sorry," Sophie answered as she retreated from the desk. "I shouldn't have . . . "

Eric reached for her. "No, it's quite all right. You've already seen it anyway." He wiped his face dry and gathered himself. He looked her in the eye, and Sophie saw a shift in him. "And please don't tell Adrian about this. I don't want him worrying. I especially don't want him thinking that his lolo felt that much hatred against the family. It'll only hurt him to know, and we don't want that."

"No, of course not."

"Papa was a great man who did great things for this country. He helped so many people, not just in this province, but everywhere, even when we were already in America. But he was also a difficult man, Sophie. A very difficult man. I'm sure Adrian has told you stories."

"He didn't tell me a lot," she admitted. "But I know he loved his lolo very much."

"And he loved Adrian. More than anything in the world. More than anyone."

Sophie couldn't miss the rancor in that last sentiment. Eric continued, making no attempt at hiding it. "Papa gave him a hard time, but that's only because he wanted Adrian to be better. He is the future of this family. And, as Papa never failed to remind me, he's my greatest achievement."

"You've raised a good son," she replied, measuring her words carefully. There was no way to wade into this without causing offense or heartache. "I'm so lucky to be with him."

Eric shook his head. "I'm sorry, I don't know why I'm telling you all this . . . I just . . . I'm overwhelmed, is all."

Tears began to flow anew, and he turned away from Sophie. He buried his face in his hands as he wept. This went on for a while, Eric having seemed to have gotten his second wind, and Sophie felt stuck. She had the notion to stay, but a greater part of her wanted to flee. She'd been a sounding board, an emotional outlet, but she didn't bring the man comfort. It only then occurred to her that it wasn't her place to do so, nor should she have to, regardless of how she found herself in that position. She shouldn't be here. And so she decided to step away and quietly leave.

As she did, Eric took hold of her and fell into her arms. She didn't know how to react. His total lack of inhibition felt surreal, as did the whole encounter. Sophie felt trapped. The man's tears dampened her shoulder as he spoke. She could barely make out the words. Some were in Tagalog, some in Waray. He was addressing his father again, begging for forgiveness. Pity overcame her discomfort, and Sophie felt her arms rise and wrap themselves around Eric.

"I'm sorry, too," Sophie heard herself say. "But I should go."

Eric extricated himself from her. He had an imploring look on his face. "Look at me. What would Papa say if he saw me?" He reached for her again, but when he caught what he'd done, he released her hand. "Thank you, Sophie."

"It's okay. Really."

"And as I said, I think it would be better if we kept all this to ourselves, just for now. Out of respect for Papa's memory." He tapped the surface of the desk with his fingers. "They can't know, not Adrian or anyone else."

Sophie was never one to keep secrets; she found them insidious, even those intended to spare one's feelings. Secrets had a way of engendering more secrets, and worse, they tended to spawn lies. She thought of Adrian, of the rest of the Sepulvedas, who had been nothing but kind to her, whose acceptance she'd been yearning for. She wouldn't have told them anyway, would she, even if Eric hadn't asked? And so she told him yes, and she told herself she'd keep the secret just this once.

The bamboo stakes that marked the mausoleum plot were still there. Javier passed them as he walked toward the hill west of the property, carrying a couple of shovels. Behind him, Dante drove a wheelbarrow laden with folded-up tarps, pickaxes, a bamboo ladder, and jugs of water. Javier stopped by one of the stakes and imagined the structure that his father had intended. He touched the ragged piece of red cloth that hung on the end of the bamboo. This was where it happened, he thought bitterly.

At the top of the hill was a smaller plot similarly marked with stakes. Javier scanned the two rows of graves—the stone crosses, the marble angels, the headstones with their carvings smoothed out by time—and looked at the space awaiting his father. Dante lay down the tarps next to it, over the untouched plot of grass where Javier assumed his mother would eventually go.

Javier could tell from the uphill trek that the soil was very damp, and that he'd spend the next few hours digging mud. Dante was more optimistic. Javier didn't know if he was only trying to make the task sound easier than it was, or if he actually shared Olympia's view that the day's downpour was "only a drizzle."

Javier had never dug a grave in his life. Neither had Dante, though you couldn't tell by the way he prepared the space and instructed Javier. He showed him how to use the shovel effectively. "If all goes well, it should only take us three or four hours. Even if it is all mud, which it won't be." The estimate seemed too promising, but Javier was ready. Anything to get himself away from that house, and the longer the better. Between the two of them, they likely wouldn't finish till sundown.

This part of the hill was quite flat, which made for an easy start. Javier quickly found his rhythm. He dug his shovel into the wet ground, pushed it in with his foot, lifted, then swung. The unearthed soil made a satisfying thwap as it hit the tarp.

He took a good look at Dante and how he handled his

tools. He was more than a driver; he was an all-around at the plantation, and he had the body to show for it. Unlike Javier, who spent half his free time at the gym only to build vanity muscles, Dante's physique was hard-won through arduous labor, which made it as impressive as it was attractive.

"You're a quick learner," Dante remarked after a while.

"Maybe I was a gravedigger in a past life."

"You could be one now, the way you're going. The job doesn't pay well, though."

Javier asked him about his job, what exactly it entailed. Dante said he did whatever needed doing. Technically, he was in the farm's payroll as a field hand, but his shifts were flexible since he also helped his parents maintain the villa. He did pickups for the household or the warehouses, and he drove Divina around, mostly to and from the church to attend mass or visit her husband's grave. It explained why the old widow seemed so taken by him and treated him almost like family.

"So you've been here your whole life," Javier said. "Don't you ever feel like leaving?"

"Not my whole life. After high school, I went to Tacloban for college. Leyte Normal. I wanted to become a schoolteacher," Dante answered. He took a break, leaning on his shovel. "But I dropped out after a year. It didn't feel right, college. I missed the farm. I think this is where I'm meant to be."

A faraway look crossed Dante's face, taking in the mountain, which seemed even greener after the rain. Javier almost felt like he understood what Dante meant, even though the last thing he ever wanted was to be bound to this place. The afternoon wore on and the two men continued to dig, taking only short rests to wipe the sweat off their brows. They traded more stories about life in Maalin, the business of coconut farming. The more Dante spoke, the more Javier understood why he wouldn't want to leave. He was as much part of the land as it was part of him.

A couple of feet into the pit, Javier's shovel clanked against rock. Dante handed him the pick. With that and a shovel, he pried the rock loose from the soil. They dug around it together, and when it was freed, the two men lifted it and flung it over to the side.

"I thought it was treasure," Dante said, snickering. He told Javier about the Yamashita legend, about the Japanese general who kept his loot in the Philippines during the occupation. Bars of gold and bags of jewels were buried in the mountains or stashed in caves all over the country, and all told, it was allegedly the largest World War II–era hoard yet to be recovered. Javier laughed, not deigning to hide his skepticism, even as the younger man seemed to defend the legend.

"It's how the Marcoses got rich, they say. They found one of the secret caves."

"You don't actually believe that, do you? That is very much not how they got rich."

"Yes, yes, I know they stole from the people—" Dante said without regard to the Sepulvedas' relation to the Marcoses. "But they were already rich before martial law. Before he became president. At least the Romualdez family was. And the treasure was how they got to own most of Leyte."

"Man, we're more likely to hit skeletons than gold up here."

"Sabi mo eh. If I find gold, I'm not sharing it with you," Dante said with a wink.

Javier laughed, covering up a pang of envy. Dante knew about the villa, the history of this land and its people. In a deep and intimate way, he knew all the rumors, legends, and lore. Javier couldn't say the same about himself, even though he was nominally the owner of these parts. His last name was on the deed, emblazoned on the sides of the farm's equipment, printed on the stickers placed on every head of harvested coconut, but that was all he had. Despite his strong sense of ownership, he felt undeserving of this place and everything it could give him. Of everything it had given him.

"Did he take care of this land, my father?" he asked Dante. "I know you didn't get to know him long, but what do people say?"

"He was a good governor. Everyone agreed on that. He built highways and bridges and schools. He was a good boss to the farmers too. Hired good managers and paid fairly."

"Even with the coco levy?" Javier asked. "Did you know about that?"

Dante nodded. "People don't talk much about that. It's still a sore subject. There's a big division between the pro- and anti-Marcoses. The fighting died down for a long time but started up again during the election. And then Marcos won, so . . . " He gave a half-shrug. "But anyway, when people talk about your papa, it's mostly the good things, I think."

"Leaving is a good way to make people forget your flaws."

Raul was a politician, a very charismatic one. He won the governorship at the young age of thirty-one, and not just on account of his matinee-idol looks. He would have been senator if he hadn't decided to leave. Something tells Javier that his father could've easily made the people of Leyte forget his flaws even if he'd stayed.

Yet it was equally true that the family's migration to California benefited Raul in terms of forgetting. Time cooled the farmers' ire, quelled the rumors of malfeasance and complicity with the dictatorship. If the curse was to be believed, their move also prevented further catastrophe from befalling the family. The more he thought about it, the more Javier became convinced of his father's cowardice. It was never about greener pastures or a fresh start; Raul Sepulveda feared consequences and fled. That was what really happened.

"Well, I'd leave for America too if I had the chance," Dante said, starry-eyed.

"Living there isn't as easy as you think, especially starting out. In fact, it gets very lonely."

"Really?"

"The place we moved to, Belvedere, was a very rich, very white town. My English was good but not perfect, and I had an accent I couldn't hide. The kids in school made fun of me constantly. Eric was no help. He was two grades ahead of me, and he was too cool to be hanging out with his baby brother. At some point, the bullying wasn't just about me being Filipino anymore. They started picking on me because I was *soft*. I'd made a few friends, all of them girls, because they were kind to me. That didn't help." Javier laughed, hiding his hesitation. "The boys stole my stuff, pushed me around. I got into a lot of fights. You know how it is. They called me faggot. I was eight. I didn't tell anyone about the trouble I was having in school, but I didn't have to. Papa noticed the scrapes and bruises I hid under my jacket."

"So what did he do?" Dante asked.

"Nothing, at first. He'd also begun to notice how I moved. How I swished rather than swaggered. How I crossed my legs with my ankles touching, like a woman, not with one shin atop one thigh, legs spread out, like a man. How I ran listlessly. 'Like a girl,' he'd said. I think he realized I was gay well before I did."

Javier observed how Dante had been reacting to his monologue, and he sensed how the younger man tensed when Javier said the word "gay." It was confirmation enough for him.

"Papa kept it to himself, but I sensed a growing rift between us," he continued. "He'd decided that I could never be his clone, his carbon copy. I could never be his 'Junior.' Not the way I am. I think that was around the time he stopped loving me."

When the hole they'd dug was about chest deep, Javier's arms started to ache. Dante seemed to tire as well, though he looked less fazed than how Javier felt. He watched Dante intently, the way his damp shirt clung to his body, the way his biceps flexed and relax with each motion. Javier tried to keep pace, unsure whether he was trying to prove something to Dante or to himself. Either way, Javier wouldn't let up. He powered through, going as fast as the pain would allow.

That was the permanent tension with Javier and the men he felt drawn to: He always wanted to *be* them and he also wanted to *best* them, and the more he bested them, the more he wanted them. It was the same even with his husband Connor, whom he'd first met at a circuit party seven years ago. Thousands of sweaty, shirtless men dancing to techno in a large warehouse in the middle of Berlin. He and Connor had vied for the attention of the same muscle-bound man, and the pursuit commingled with the competition commingled with the cocaine to produce a ravenous and irresistible desire.

When Dante slowed down and rested on his shovel, finally declaring that he was done, that they'd dug deep enough anyway, that familiar thrill of conquest raced through Javier.

A thin, brown dog came running up the hill and stopped at the edge of the pit. Dante's face lit up. He petted the dog as it licked his sweaty cheek. "This is Askal. Short for 'asong kalye'. Street dog. Tatay found him roaming the highway when he was still a puppy."

"If you don't mind me saying," Javier said as he stroked the dog's head, "you're a good-looking guy. Haven't you ever thought of moving to the city, even for a while? It must be hard meeting men here."

Dante froze, stunned. Javier continued, "I'm not misreading you, am I?"

"No, you're not. And it's okay. I'm actually relieved to talk about it. There's not many people who I can feel comfortable opening up to." Dante said this last part matter-of-factly, which didn't stop Javier from feeling aflutter.

"Your parents know though?"

"They don't like to talk about it. Doña Divina knows too, I think. It's been a long time since she's teased me about finding a nice girl to settle down with. In some ways, I'm blessed. I've never had problems with anyone because of . . . what I am. Still, life here can sometimes feel isolated."

"How do you deal with it?"

"I drive to Tacloban sometimes. Other towns too. There are men everywhere; they're not that hard to find."

"Oh, I'm sure it's not a problem," Javier answered snarkily. "Not for you at least, huh?"

"No, no, I don't mean it that way." Dante blushed. "I mean, I don't feel much of a lack, being here. And I'm young. There's time for me to find someone. If I don't . . . well, I'm not scared of being alone. I don't think I'll be too lonely about it either."

Javier took the bamboo ladder and climbed his way out of the pit. The dog's tail wagged furiously, expectantly. He held Dante's forearm, assisting him as he did the same. The two men stood against each other, their bodies a hair's breadth away. Javier inched closer.

"Well, we don't want you feeling lonely, now do we?"

He leaned over, touched his lips to Dante's. A chaste kiss, but then Dante responded passionately. The boy's eagerness dispelled the twinge of shame lodged in Javier's chest; indeed, it heightened the thrill of the indiscretion. Javier wrapped his arms around Dante and his hands roamed underneath his sweat-soaked shirt, feeling his body undulate with each heavy breath. Javier moaned in pleasure as Dante's mouth explored his neck. The two kept at it, more torridly the more they came undone, ignoring the dog that circled their feet as it whined for attention.

Later, well after the palms had been burned and the bodies lain, after she'd stared into the abyss, Sophie would recall her third night in Villa Sepulveda and tell herself, *I should have seen it then*. To be sure, no one has the gift of such foresight, and at that time, she was yet new to this land and its beliefs. She still thought dreams were no more than the mind's way of assembling and reassembling the day's experiences, a mysterious yet natural process bound by the principles of science.

She'd told herself as much when her eyes shot open in the dead of night, seemingly awoken by nothing but her own subconscious. She was in the same room, but it was bright, as though lit by a spotlight. She could hear nothing, not even the sound of her breathing.

"I must be dreaming," she whispered.

The light, blinding white, came from near the door. By the wall where she'd placed the coatrack. Through the peephole. She was sure she'd stoppered it, and just as sure that the hole wasn't big enough to let that much light through. She flung away the sheets and floated off the bed. She felt no fear or affront, only a strange curiousity. She stood before the light, casting her shadow on the room. She bent down slightly and peered in.

The light was cool, almost calming, very much unlike staring into the sun. She blinked and turned, trying to see what shone this light, what else was out there. "Hello?" she heard herself call out. Her voice was faint and it echoed. A shadow swiftly passed over the hole and she averted her gaze.

The room fell dark. Unable to help herself, for this was merely a dream, after all, she peered into the hole again.

She saw a slick surface, dark and viscous. Red like blood. It blinked.

She pried herself off the wall and rushed back to the bed. The room was bathed in a sultry red glow. *Wake up*, she told herself. *Wake up wake up wake up!*

She opened her eyes. Sounds returned. The coatrack stood where it had been. There was no hole, no light, no bloody eye staring back at her. She breathed a sigh of relief. A trickle of sweat ran down the side of her temple, and she tried to wipe her brow dry, but found that she couldn't. Her arms twitched ever so slightly, but otherwise did not move. Her legs too. She was awake, she was absolutely sure of it. She could see around the room, and her thought process was lucid and logical. She remembered her dream and recognized it for what it was, but this was different.

This was reality. And the reality was that she was paralyzed.

She tried to lift her head and failed. At the edge of her vision, right by the foot of her bed, Sophie sensed a presence. The specter was back. It loomed, watching her.

Its hood had fallen away and she could now see that the figure was a woman, tall and thin, shrouded by a thick head of jet-black hair. She couldn't make out her features, but she knew it wasn't anyone in the family. Not Olympia or Divina, definitely not Margot. Not even Remedios. She tried to speak, but her lips only trembled, unable to make a sound. Why couldn't she move? Her heartbeat grew as loud as her panicked thoughts.

The woman came closer and lifted her ropy arm. Her flesh looked as gray as the dusty blouse she wore. She pointed toward the peephole.

Sophie blinked, shut her eyes hard, then opened them again. The vision remained, immovable like a statue, unmoving like her. Sophie struggled, willing herself free of the invisible hold that gripped her body. She wished to rise up, run out of the room, scream, turn the lights on, cower under the sheets and pray, do anything, anything at all besides lie there helpless, with only two equally useless options: keep her eyes open or closed. In the end, she chose the latter, unable to bear her plight. If Sophie couldn't will her body awake, she would will her mind back to sleep, and that way escape the woman that tormented her.

April 12

Saturday

"What do you know about sleep paralysis?" Sophie asked Kai the next morning. She thought it better to give them a watered-down version of what had happened; she didn't want to seem erratic or odd, even to the person who'd be the most receptive to such behavior. After all, they only just met, and this was hardly a normal kitchen-counter topic. Sophie stuck to the physical aspects of the experience: her frozen joints and muscles, her unresponsive bones, and her eyelids, the only part of her that responded to her will.

"I've never experienced it before, but I think I just had a bangungot."

The word was cumbersome. Sophie had never been able to perfect the nasal "ng" sounds; her accent was as misplaced as her syllabication. Adrian had patiently tried teaching her how, lengthening each part as he spoke it—"baa-ngoo-ngot"—but her attempts just ended in guffaws. Kai, however, wasn't the least bit bothered or amused by her pronunciation, which Sophie thought was kind.

"I've had those, yeah. They're not the most pleasant thing,"

Kai answered. They took a pouch from their hoodie pocket and placed an assortment of dried leaves, twigs, and buds into a tea ball. They poured the kettle's contents into their mug and handed Sophie hers, one filled with instant coffee. "Did you freak out?"

"A little. It was surreal more than anything. I was mostly conscious but I couldn't tell the dream from reality. It was like they overlapped. Only thing I knew for sure was that I couldn't move."

"That's classic. They say it's a potassium deficiency." Kai took a banana from the fruit bowl and handed it over. When Sophie refused, they chuckled. "Yeah, I think that's bullshit too. Well, if you believe the legends from these parts, it's an obese spirit sitting on top of you."

"Yeah, I've heard the story from Manang Remy."

"I would never discount otherworldly beings. On the drive up, I sensed a lot of chaotic energy all over this island. From the mountains, the groves, everywhere. And this house . . . Good thing I packed this." Kai drew a necklace out from under their shirt. Its dark teardrop pendant shone at the end of a fine silver chain. "Black tourmaline. Wards off bad juju. I just wish I had sage too."

"For burning?"

"I don't suppose that grows around here, huh?" Their brow furrowed, as though they were formulating a plan.

All this talk of mysticism reminded Sophie of the alleged wiccans she'd met at Stanford: dabblers who dug the aesthetic and trappings but didn't truly understand what they claimed to practice. She was positive this country had sage or something like it; trouble was, Kai didn't even seem to consider that this place, too, had its own brand of witchcraft.

"Anyway, a demon's not what caused your 'bangungot' or whatever they call it," Kai said. They were as Americanized as Sophie, but they didn't mangle the word.

"What do you think it is, then?"

They gave Sophie a curious, prodding look. "Wellll . . . have you heard of astral projection?"

Kai proceeded to talk about the veil between the spiritual and the mortal planes, and how dreams were gateways between the two, a one-person portal to another dimension. The feeling of paralysis happened when one's consciousness awakened as they traveled between these worlds, risking the severance of the mind-body connection.

Sophie wished she could repay Kai's kindness with credence, but she didn't understand any of it. She couldn't, especially not before she'd had her coffee. Yet she politely nodded along to the impromptu lecture on the paranormal, making half-hearted noises of courtesy. Kai was undeterred. "And when people think they see sleep paralysis demons, what they're seeing are not flesh-and-blood monsters. They're inhabitants of another plane of existence. Spirits."

"You mean ghosts," Sophie answered, immediately regretting the word and her tone.

"Look, you can believe me or not, I'm so used to it," Kai said dispassionately. "No one ever takes me seriously until they have to. Until it's too late. I'm a Cassandra, and like a true archer, my words never miss the mark."

A tad dramatic, Sophie thought, resisting the urge to laugh. "I'm sorry, I sounded really judgy just then. Please, don't let me stop you."

Kai explained the concepts at great length, how a ghost was worlds apart from a spirit. Sophie couldn't see the difference. She didn't believe in ghosts to begin with, not even after seeing an almost lifelike vision standing by her bed last night. She remained convinced that what she saw was a figment that her brain—the same high-alert, sleep-deprived, occasionally medicated brain that had been soaking up stories about demons and witches and curses—overlaid on the little of her room she could see during her first bout of sleep paralysis. What she experienced must have been some severed link between her consciousness and her body. Synaptic misfires, a grim hallucination, nothing more.

"And you just tried to sleep through it?" Kai asked when they noticed how Sophie had drifted off.

Right then, she felt a stab in her gut, a nagging sensation that deafened her to Kai's question.

The woman from last night. Sophie had seen that face before.

With haste, she took Kai's hand and led them down the hall in search of a picture. They went past each bedroom, Sophie scanning photographs from various eras: old relatives, family vacations, landscapes of Leyte. They turned around and went down another corridor, one that mostly had paintings. Finally, Sophie found what she'd been looking for, in a spot by the door to the oratorio, right before the turn toward the conservatory.

It was a faded photograph of the Sepulvedas. The patio furniture looked newer, shinier, and the moldings were better maintained, but the columns and blue tiles of the veranda were unmistakable. In the center between two posts stood Adrian's great-grandparents, the general Claudio Sepulveda and his wife. Beside them were Divina and a strapping figure, whom Sophie assumed was her dead husband Melchior; on the other side were Raul and Olympia, and in front of them were the two boys, Eric and Javier, when they were maybe six or seven.

Behind them and off to the side, almost out of frame, was a woman. She stood by one of the posts, her hands clasped. Sophie leaned in closer. She was young and frail and had long black hair, fine and straight, that fell on the sides of her face. She had an oval face and piercing round eyes that looked directly into the camera.

It was her, the woman from her bangungot.

Sophie gasped. For one horrified moment, she thought

she saw her mother. The mother she'd never seen and never known but had always imagined in her mind. She was there in her dream, and there in her room, and now she was there in this old photograph. She checked for a date. The bottom-right corner read June 16, 1984. Sophie did some quick mental math—the woman looked like she was in her early twenties at most; she'd have been born in the sixties, which would make her over forty in 2007, when Sophie was born.

"It can't be her," she whispered to herself. For a moment she assumed that last night was a repeat of her dreaming about her nanay, but no, this woman was a different person altogether.

"What are you talking about?" Kai asked.

Sophie pointed at the woman. "Do you know who that is?"

"No . . . I've never been here, remember?"

Footsteps came from around the corner, and Kai caught a glimpse of Eric. They called out to him and asked.

"Oh, that was our yaya. Our nanny. I forget her name—Alana, I think. She was very kind . . . " Eric called out for Javier, who'd just then plodded out of the dining room with a mug of coffee. "Hey, remember our yaya? What was her name again?"

Javier squinted at the photo. "Alondra. How could you forget, Kuya, after we put her through hell?" He laughed, playfully smacking Eric's chest with the back of his palm. The display of fraternal bonhomie jarred Sophie.

"No, we didn't," Eric answered before turning to Sophie. "I was a good boy, I swear."

Kai gave their brothers the side-eye. "Regular angels, I'm sure."

"This pic was about two years before that," Javier said, ignoring the sarcasm. "Which means I must've been five here."

"Yeah, I think I remember now," Eric continued. "She was with us till we moved to the States. She took real good care of us."

Sophie stared at the woman in the photo. Something about her must have imprinted itself in Sophie's mind. But which came first, her seeing visions of Alondra, or her seeing this photo? Or maybe she was asking the wrong question. Sophie asked, to no one in particular, "Where is she now?"

"She's dead."

Remedios strode down the hall, her bearing as stiff as her words. "She died in childbirth a month after you all left. It was a complicated pregnancy, and an awful tragedy. Mother and son both didn't make it."

The doña seethed with displeasure. Remedios could tell the thoughts that ran through Olympia's mind while leading the morning Angelus. Whatever hope she had for the funeral had been washed away with the rain. The attendants from the funeral parlor were supposed to be here by now, loading Raul onto the hearse that would take him to the Church of San Isidro. The bishop was already supposed to be here as well, leading the fifth day of the novena in the family's oratorio. Now, Olympia had to do it herself. Her voice had the clipped cadence of concealed rage. And when prayers concluded and the young ones tried to do the mano, she presented her hand stiffly, pushing them away, her jeweled rings digging into their foreheads.

After all were done with breakfast—a tense and mostly silent affair—Olympia declared her decision. The funeral would be postponed to the following Sunday. She announced this evenly, and it was met with nothing but resigned agreement. Easter seemed apropos, she said, and would allow enough time for the roads to be cleared and the guests to arrive.

"I don't think we can expect guests, Mama. The countryside will still be a mess. They might not risk traveling," Eric replied carefully. "And besides, families will have plans for Easter. Not to mention the parish and the diocese."

"They will certainly move things around for Raul. Don't be so negative, hijo. The church will be available for us, and there will be guests. Including the president and Imelda."

Javier groaned. "And what are we supposed to do for the next seven days? Just wait?"

"And I've already booked my flight for Thursday," Kai added.

"You three wanted me to move the funeral, so I did. What else do you want from me?" their mother snapped. "We need to inform everyone immediately."

Olympia called out to Remedios, who confirmed what the rest of the household already knew: There was still no reception, and so no news. They might be able to find a connection uphill or closer to town, toward the road blockage, but that would take a short drive.

Adrian was quick to volunteer. Finals were coming up, and he and Sophie needed to send emails to professors if they were going to miss more days of class. Eric demurred, but in the end, it was agreed that they should maximize their chances: Remedios was to accompany the kids on the way downhill, while Tiago and Dante would try finding a signal up the mountain.

It continued to drizzle, but the shower was light. Kai joined Adrian and Sophie last-minute, complaining that they couldn't take the boredom. They all trudged down the gravel driveway in their raincoats, then past the gates, which took effort to swing open. The narrow asphalt road stretched straight in both directions.

Endless coconut groves bordered their way. Adrian walked ahead of everyone. He had brought his camera and didn't seem to mind the rain spattering on his lens. He swept the camera across the verdant landscape. "This is all part of the farm,"

Adrian said dejectedly, pointing out trees that were felled by the typhoon. "Dad told me it takes about seven years to grow one from sapling to maturity, and you can kind of judge from the tree heights when and where typhoons have hit."

"You know, we've never experienced a typhoon in April," Remedios answered. "Bagyo season is not until July."

"Climate change," he answered. "And it's only going to get worse."

He rambled on about extreme weather patterns, but that hadn't been the caretaker's point. It was touching to hear how much the boy knew about the trees, and how deeply he empathized with the farm's plight. But neither he nor his auncle or girlfriend knew these islands. They didn't know when the ocean and the skies unleashed their fury, or when such fury was unleashed by other forces. Remedios had seen the increase in the storms' number and severity; she knew of climate change. What they were in the middle of was not that.

After about a mile, the group passed the farm's warehouse. It was an abrupt change from the rows of identical trees, and a needed distraction too. Kai was near ready to give up, the trek turning out to be longer than they anticipated. But if they couldn't get a signal, they at least could do some exploring.

The building itself was no different from any other warehouse or barn. It cut a wide rectangular swath through the land, and its red roof stood in sharp contrast to the greenery surrounding it. The sign, in bold letters the same light green color as a young coconut, read

Sepulveda Farms: A Family Business Since 1872

Adrian captured the length of the sign, moving this way and that to film it from different angles.

"This wasn't the one that . . . ?" Sophie asked the caretaker. The building was two stories high and twice as long, its walls made of concrete; its visible foundations were of solid steel, and so were the ventilation shafts that supported the roof.

"They built this after the collapse. The old one was much smaller."

"Oh, yeah, I think I saw this back at the manor. There was a big, blown-up photo of the ribbon-cutting," Adrian said. "You should see what Auntie Divina looks like with a hard hat instead of her veil. So cringe."

Remedios bristled. No one ever gave the poor woman enough credit. At the time, Doña Divina had just lost her husband, her father too, and the rest of the Sepulvedas had left her to be an unofficial liaison and figurehead while they absconded to the States. Obviously, she didn't want to show her face and gladhand with the farmers and the priest who'd come to bless the site. She didn't want to pose for photos, especially not at the very site where her Melchior had been pulverized by tons of coconut heads only months before. Back then, all the young widow truly wanted was to die. "Merciful saints, let me join my husband!" she would cry over and over while huddled in her bedroom. Remedios's heart ached for her, and she remembered thinking then, as she still did now, that it must be part of Divina's curse that her death be withheld for as long as possible.

"I saw that picture too," Sophie answered. "And you're right, babe. This used to be a lot smaller. And made of wood. The roof wasn't red, it was brown. A thatched roof. That must've been why it collapsed."

Kai crossed her arms. "Huh, I think we're in the presence of a mythbuster."

"Your lolas were saying how the warehouse collapse was completely unexpected, but maybe it was just really old and damaged," Sophie continued. "I mean, even if it had been a few months after, maybe Typhoon Saling didn't take the building down, but it could have weakened the foundation. No offense or anything, but none of us are buying into this curse, right?"

Kai tsked. "I believe in curses; I just don't believe in this one. Gaba, or whatever. It smells like horse manure to me."

Remedios held her tongue. All week she'd been careful, sensitive to the signs. She'd been trying to make the family aware. But if these kids can't be reached, then they can remain ignorant at their own peril.

Adrian laughed, pointing the camera at his auncle's face. "You brought two sets of tarot cards and your wrists are covered in crystals. Are you saying you don't believe in the supernatural? In karma?"

"Karma's different. That's about action and consequence and the universe maintaining a balance. It's not something that can be weaponized out of some personal vendetta, like this gaba," they answered haughtily. "Plus, karma is part of a religion and philosophy. It's not some small-town myth."

"I don't know, it sounds pretty similar to me," Sophie said in a teasing tone.

"It's not, because you can't run away from karma. Didn't Mama say the disasters stopped once our family went to the States? Karma doesn't work that way," Kai replied, suddenly taciturn. "It follows wherever you go."

Remedios had withheld any judgment of Kai, but she felt she'd learned enough in the one day she'd known them. They could avoid believing gaba, forsake their family in search of freedom, but this youngest sibling, the one who fled and always flees, must know that their feet could only take them so far. Their family's legacy was everywhere and now stood in front of their very eyes. Was the old warehouse ill-maintained? Probably. It was built with the trees that had been felled to lay its foundation, and coconut lumber was not immune to termites. If the Sepulvedas hadn't been so overwhelmed with a string of disasters, they might have discovered that the damage the fanged critters had caused. The family might have clung onto that detail to explain the unfortunate tragedy that befell their laborers.

Remedios knew the truth, however. Everyone who lived

through that time knew: The storm and hollowed-out lumber did not kill those farmhands.

"There's no escaping this one either," Remedios finally said. "Now that you're all back here."

As she expected, the kids just made light, rolled their eyes, and moved on.

They walked up to the front of the warehouse. Adrian had the thought that the tuba stores might be in there too, and the bar stock back at the manor was running low.

"It's not stealing," he argued when Sophie tried to deter him. "It's ours to begin with." Finding the personnel entrance locked, he tried to pry open the loading gate. When that, too, didn't budge, they went around back, but the door was locked as well.

"Hey, guys . . . take a look at this." Sophie pointed to the spot by the cornerstone on the building's rear wall. Remedios didn't have to turn to know what it was. The makeshift marker etched into the concrete. Eight names etched into the caretaker's memory. Doña Divina's husband was last on the list. Melchior Cuesta. Right below was the date: November 3, 1986. Carved with a spade as the cement dried, the letters weren't as neat and elegant as the sign up front, or the plaque of the National Historical Institute that hung by the manor's front door, but to Remedios, the memorial was just as important.

"Those who survived the tragedy helped build the new warehouse," she explained, "and they made this . . . headstone."

The young ones read the names in silence. To the caretaker's surprise, Adrian didn't choose to record this part. "Did you know any of them?" he asked her.

"Every single one."

Sophie, the stranger, crouched down and ran her hand through the grooves. She lingered there for a while, long enough that Adrian and Kai became restless and decided to find another way into the warehouse. "Maybe through a window or something," Adrian suggested. Remedios cautioned against this, but her attention was divided.

"Do you mind telling me how it happened?" Sophie asked.

Remedios recounted the event much the same way Divina did two nights ago, and with nearly as much emotion as the widow had. "When word reached the villa, we still held hope that the farmers could be rescued. Every available hand came to dig through tons of brown coconuts, ready to risk their lives if the entire building collapsed after the roof. But when we got here, it was clear to see. No one could've survived." She paused, her hand trembling. "Melchior's body was first to get dug out. It was completely crushed. His head was caved in like it was run over by a truck. That was how we found the others too." As though it might allay the girl's evident sorrow, she added, "Their deaths came quick. They probably didn't realize what was happening until it did."

Sophie's interest was only half as surprising as her response. Tears fell as she read the list of names, as though she knew who they were and what they had gone through. Despite her predisposition, Remedios couldn't find it in herself to doubt the girl's sincerity, and she herself felt a renewed grief for these men whom she hadn't thought of in a while. She placed a gentle hand on Sophie's shoulder. "Come, hija. We should go find the other two before they get themselves hurt."

The sky cleared, but much to Sophie's dismay, that didn't solve her communication woes. The downhill excursion was a bust. Signal bars popped in for a few seconds, but not long enough for a call or even a single text to get through. The groundskeeper and his son also returned unsuccessful. The men said they'd try again in a few hours, closer to dusk.

At the villa, everyone pretended to while the afternoon away, playing cards or doing chores, but they all simmered in frustration, Sophie included. She needed a connection badly. Her professors needed to be notified that she'd be absent a bit longer, and the research fellows might need something from her. Less important—she'd been wanting to look up all the new words she'd heard but was too embarrassed to ask about, to fact-check all the historical trivia and cultural tidbits she'd learned.

Brandishing her phone, Sophie set out of the manor without telling anyone. The soil was wet, and with each step, a thin layer of mud clung to the bottom of her flip-flops. She awkwardly paced past the crescent of the porte cochere, past the algae-flecked fountain of a broad-winged angel, down the driveway lined with neat rows of dwarf coconuts. These smaller trees had survived the brunt of Typhoon Lorena, losing only some of their foliage, but in the groves beyond, treetops were almost naked, with only a sad handful of palms hanging on for dear life.

As she neared the villa's gate, she noticed a small enclosure on the southwest lawn. A garden. Unlike the main gate, its low iron fence was polished and rust-free. Indeed, this small plot seemed to be in better shape than the manor itself. Its cast stone statues (more angels) were unblemished, and its hedges of camellia and hibiscus and jasmine were well-tended. The groundskeeper took pride in his work, Sophie could tell. Despite the deluge, or perhaps because of it, every leaf and petal looked shiny and fulsome. She ambled between the hedges, grazing the leaves with her hand. The lush jasmine scent was intoxicating, almost hypnotic. She plucked one of the tiny white blossoms and inhaled it longingly. She dropped it, startled by a mosquito biting her arm.

Just then, her phone beeped. Sophie squealed. A lone text made it through the one-bar signal that pulsed on her screen. An identical text came in right after.

Verizon Wireless: Welcome to the Philippines! You have

Travel Pass, which gives you unlimited data and calling for the next 24 hours . . .

She spun around, arms outstretched, fishing for reception. The tiny, little bar seemed to flicker less as she paced away from the gate, off of the driveway. Sophie let the invisible thread lead her. Fixated on her phone, she proceeded around the garden in halting steps, mindless of where she was going, until at last she was stopped by the villa's boundary wall.

The bar stayed steady. Sophie furiously refreshed her email and browser to make sure she was online, but she was met with just old messages and blank white screens. "Damn it!" She reached her arm over the stone fence. She thought about jumping over. The walls were made of coarse, uneven blocks stacked atop each other, all slick from the rain. She decided to find a gap instead. She looked up and down the perimeter and found a section where some of the stone had collapsed. She clambered over the pile, soiling her clothes in the process.

As she skipped over the gap, she found a large dog waiting for her on the other side. It sat on its hindquarters, alert and expectant. It looked like a greyhound, if the breed came in brown. On its neck hung a silver tag.

"Hi, buddy," she said, slowly coming closer. She wasn't afraid of dogs, even strange ones. They always warmed up to her easily, and she was good at predicting their temperaments. This one was a trained dog, and it stood at attention, not in aggression. "Why are you out here? Did you get lost?" A refugee from the typhoon, probably. Sophie held out an open palm to let it sniff her. It responded by licking her fingertips, but before she could pet its head, the dog ran off.

Sophie chased after it. After bounding a few yards, the dog stopped and turned, seeming to wait for her. Once she got closer, it sped off again. Sophie began to understand. The dog was trying to show her something. She looked back at the fence, and at the manor beyond it. She wasn't too far away, but what was she doing? She checked her phone. Two bars.

"Good dog!" she exclaimed, refreshing her email again. A text came in from her roommate.

Tell me EVERYTHING

Quickly followed by another, then two more.

Also you wont believe who I saw at oconnors . . .

Well? Hows it going?

Maam?? Hello?? Are you alive???

Sophie started to type her reply but was interrupted by the dog's whining. A few yards away, it seemed to be circling something in the grass. She almost ignored it, but it whimpered like it was hurt. When she reached it, the dog launched into a full run, yelping and moaning.

Sophie called after it but it didn't heed her. And so she ran after it, worried it had gotten hurt or that it might get lost deeper in the groves. That dog belonged to someone, and it might not find its way home. Sophie kept chasing the dog, which kept running and yelping as it went. Her flip-flops snagged on grass and twigs and branches, and then, she lost her footing. She tripped on a coconut, falling flat on her face.

She raised her head and found herself staring down a gleaming black beetle. It was as big as a child's fist and its long, curved horn resembled a fishing hook. It seemed to stare Sophie straight in the eye.

She lifted herself off the wet ground and the beetle halted its advance. Then, it flapped its wings, whizzing toward her. "Jesus, fuck!" she shrieked, shielding herself. She felt the creature's heft as she swatted it away. She scrambled back, flinging her limbs, checking herself and her clothes to make sure it wasn't on her anymore. She couldn't find the bug, but she still heard its buzzing. Then, the sound grew louder and louder until it drowned all else. And that was when she saw it.

A coconut tree, high as a house, covered in the scales of thousands of black scarabs.

The scarabs hissed and buzzed as they crawled on top of each other, dug into and around others in their swarm. From the base all the way up to the crown, the creatures left no gap. The fruits hung heavy with their bodies, the palms too, the blades drooping under the weight of their pestilential passengers. The tall, dark pillar looked like a gigantic snake, its scales moving in waves, ready to strike.

The sound was deafening, the sight debilitating. Sophie froze in awe and abject terror. And there were more. Other trees had been engulfed too. All around her dark spires seemed to explode into fountains of shiny carapaces.

It began to rain. The creatures on the tips of the palms struggled to hang on and fell from above like black, jagged hailstones.

When at last she managed to rise from the mud, Sophie ran as fast as she could, never looking back. Her mind raced as fast as her feet. *How—why—what the hell is going on?* The buzzing seemed to follow her, and all over her body she could feel the rough scratches of legs, horns snagging on her clothes and digging into her skin. She didn't look down. She just kept running. The rain obscured her vision, but past the tall cogon, she caught sight of the manor's terra-cotta roof. She sped toward it and mounted the border wall with effort. Once over, she strode toward the house, limping through the ache caused by her stumble.

"Sophie!" Adrian stood in the porte cochere by the front door. Seeing her state, he rushed out. "What happened? You're hurt."

"I—there was—I saw—"

Adrian took her into the foyer and sat her on a bench by the staircase. He knelt before her and inspected her left ankle.

It didn't look swollen, at least. When she'd caught her breath, Sophie realized that she'd lost her phone.

"Fuck. Lemme go look for it before it gets drenched," Adrian offered. "You stay here."

"No! Don't go back there!" She gripped Adrian's wrist, and he was too startled by her reaction to argue.

"Babe, what happened? You're starting to scare me."

Sophie told him about the garden and then the dog, how she tried to lead it to safety and how instead it led her deep into the plantation. "And then I saw them . . . the horned beetles."

She didn't know how to explain it. What she'd witnessed seemed literally incredible. She remembered the curse and her own disbelief at the yarn spun by the elder Sepulvedas. She remembered, too, how Adrian poked fun at them. She didn't want to be the prissy American girl who was disgusted by bugs, but more than that, she didn't want to be the kind of person that believed in silly superstitions.

"One flew right at me and I freaked out and . . ."

"And you took a tumble. Aw, my poor baby." Adrian pulled himself closer and gave her a peck on her forehead. "But I think I can handle a few beetles. We need to get your phone."

Just then, the groundskeeper came into the foyer through the door that led from the zaguan. He was sopping wet.

"You all right?" Tiago asked, though he seemed more preoccupied with drying himself off.

"Uhm, well, Sophie . . . fell," Adrian tried to explain, almost apologetic, as though she'd done something wrong. "And she lost her phone out in the groves."

"And there were beetles," Sophie added. "A shit ton of them."

Tiago crossed his arms as though warming himself and asked, "Where exactly?"

The old man wasn't as old as she'd first thought. His head had turned all but gray, and his mustache had too, but past all of that, he looked more than a decade younger than the don and doña. His skin was tanned leather from working under the sun, most likely, and it had barely any furrows, save for a long scar that ran down his right temple.

"The south lawn, beyond the wall close to the garden. There was a clump of trees a bit farther out," she answered cautiously. "And they all had black beetles on them. It should be near those."

"About this big?" Tiago gestured with his fingers. "With a horn in the middle?" Sophie nodded vigorously. "Pesteng yawa," the groundskeeper cursed. He'd have to tell the plantation's foremen, who'd need to smoke the trees quickly, but how, in this weather? "How bad was it?"

"It's the biggest swarm I'd ever seen."

Tiago muttered more curses. "I didn't think they would come back, but here they are. Just like my wife keeps warning me about."

"Oh, no, not you too, Manong Tiago," Adrian said. "This isn't gaba. I mean, it's gotta be because of the typhoon, right? Pests come out after the rain, don't they?"

"Some do, some don't."

"Maybe these beetles are like those cicadas, the ones that only come out every seventeen years, I think?" Adrian turned to the two others, who gave no hint of recognition. "Some insects have long life cycles. I saw a documentary about that once."

"But forty years?" Sophie asked, skeptical.

"I don't know much about insects, except what I've seen," the groundskeeper answered. "And what I've seen is that these beetles never get flushed out after a storm. That only ever happened once, with Typhoon Saling. Back when all this talk of a curse started up. I am not saying I know what brought on the storms or the pests or whatever else, but I know one thing: There is no such thing as gaba or karma or anything like that."

"Huh. Somehow I thought you'd side with the old ladies on this," Adrian replied smugly.

Tiago wrung the hem of his shirt, dripping onto the welcome mat. He formed a circle with his fingers and whistled. Shortly, a large brown dog bounded in from the zaguan. Sophie's heart leapt. The groundskeeper patted the dog as it frisked itself dry. "Suffering is a part of living. It comes when it comes, and it doesn't need a reason. And the only thing we can do is endure."

Sophie's third dinner at the Sepulvedas featured none of the friction of the prior evenings. The tension lingered in the way the family moved stiffly and avoided each other's lines of sight, but everyone seemed too dejected or too tired to argue. Polite compliments were exchanged over the food—the steaming pots of shrimp sinigang and chicken curry, the trays of grilled pork belly—but not much besides. Sophie was happy to eat in relative silence. She was ravenous, having had little rest overnight, her fatigue compounded by the day's events. She ate to stuff herself, hoping to induce a nightlong food coma that would silence thoughts of beetle swarms, crushed farmhands, dead governesses, and her sense of utter isolation. She resolved to look for her phone tomorrow morning. The storm seemed to have passed. The skies were clear, almost cloudless. The moon was full. Best case scenario, her phone hadn't been bricked by the rainwater and the cell towers would be working again.

Margot fell ill after dinner. The family was gathered in the drawing room, and while the tense silence continued, it grew more companionable as rounds of tong-its progressed. She began to break out in cold sweats as she played her hands and drank her digestif, but soon it became harder to ignore.

Divina was first to remark her concern. "Hija, you don't look too well. Are you quite all right?"

"I think the shrimp is not agreeing with me," Margot answered. "But I'll be fine."

Sophie saw through the act but understood; she, too, wouldn't want to be the sensitive American guest whose constitution couldn't handle food outside her comfort zone.

"Are you sure? Maybe you should lie down for a while?" Divina offered. Margot shook her head. She began to reply but her voice broke, as though she was choking.

"Here, drink some water. We can't have you getting sick," the older woman said, now panicking. Even the blissed-out Kai got off their seat to assist, spurred by Divina's agitation. "Remedios . . . "

Margot did as told, but when she put the glass to her lips, she started gasping for air, unable to swallow. She got up to leave and almost collapsed, her hands shaking as she steadied herself on her chair back. Eric came over and wrapped an arm around his wife. Margot gestured toward the hall and he reflexively led her to the bathroom, from which the sounds of heaving and retching soon came.

"This never happens," Adrian explained later, in Sophie's room. He seemed more confused than concerned. "She's always had an iron stomach. And she's been here enough times, she never needs to acclimate." Sophie did notice how jet lag hadn't seemed to affect Adrian's parents as much as it did her, despite them being older and Margot being, well, not from here.

"How about you, by the way? You've been okay with the food, right?" Adrian asked.

"My only complaint is that my body won't let me eat more. Everything was so yummy."

"I know! A definite downside to coming home is having to hit the gym extra hard when I get back." Adrian pouted theatrically but turned serious once he sensed a shift in Sophie's mood. "Yeah, I know. We'll have to go back eventually. This isn't exactly a vacation, but at least we get a longer break."

"I just wish I had my phone at least," Sophie replied. "And wi-fi. I'm missing so much already and I'm sure the lab's . . . "

"Don't worry, babe. We'll go look for your phone first thing tomorrow," Adrian said, hushing her. "As soon as it's light out, we'll retrace your steps. We'll cover every inch. Then, after we find it—which we will—we can head down the road again and try to catch some bars."

"To think, if it wasn't for the typhoon, this'd all be done by now," she said. "But you're right. I'm sure we'll find it. I'm sorry I'm making this about myself, with everything else going on."

"Aw, c'mon. It's me who should apologize. You're the guest getting stuck here for longer than you bargained for." He plunged onto Sophie's bed back-first.

Even though she knew Adrian hadn't intended it, being called a guest came with a sting.

"I'm sorry things are a mess with the funeral and all," she said, stroking his hair, giving his scalp a light massage. His temples always grew so stiff when he was stressed.

"I'm just glad Lola finally agreed to postpone," he answered. "I mean, there was no way we could have done it. It's weird too—she's not usually this rigid. That was Lolo's style."

"She's grieving. I can see why she'd want everything to go the way she envisioned."

"But it's not just that. You see, my lola can be a bit . . . vain. I'm not questioning her grief, but part of this is also for show. All the traditions, all the rituals and fanfare that we can't have now. Lolo encouraged that side of her, of course. Gave her everything she wanted, made sure she always got her way."

"He was like your dad," Sophie said. "Devoted. A wife guy."

"Yeah, I guess my dad is a wife guy," Adrian answered. "I wouldn't say he's like Lolo though. Growing up with all of them in the same house, I saw how different their relationships were. Dad's just as devoted as Lolo, but Lolo was *very* traditional. He gave Lola whatever she asked for, but he also expected her to comply with everything he said. I don't think I've seen her disagree with him ever. You know she never learned how to drive? Never went anywhere without him. Never could. It was kind of fucked up. And Lola was happy to go along. All those Bible verses about the wife submitting to the husband and shit, she embodied them."

"Was she happy?"

"Seemed like it. But can anyone really be happy in a marriage like that?"

Sophie contemplated Olympia's life and how trapped she must have felt. How helpless. Yet Olympia was comfortable too, Sophie knew that much, and comfort can forgive a lot of things.

"With Mom and Dad, though, well . . . it's not like that at all," Adrian continued, speaking with admiration. Dad ran a multimillion multinational business, and Mom ran a prestigious law firm, the top companies' go-to for high-stakes patent and copyright litigation. "They're a power couple, and I don't think they could be unequal, like Lolo and Lola were. Like, if Dad ever acted up, Mom would definitely give him hell," Adrian said, chuckling. "She's not a trophy housewife, plus, she's too badass to submit to anyone, even her husband."

A marriage of equals had always been a dubious concept to Sophie, and her skepticism seemed inversely proportional to Adrian's faith in it. He believed in it so much—and wanted it for himself, it seemed like—that he didn't even notice how much more impressed he sounded talking about his mom, and how, at least in Sophie's mind, Margot was in fact more impressive.

It seemed, too, that Margot called the shots in the marriage. True, she agreed to live in the manor with the Sepulvedas, and yes, she came to the Philippines every year because Eric needed to, but the rest of Adrian's stories were about Margot's choices taking primacy. She decided where they bought their vacation homes (in Savannah and in the Apennines); she decided where Adrian went for private school; she hired the staff in the Belvedere manor and they responded to her. She even acted as an advisor to Sepulveda Farms, with Eric officially or informally consulting her before making major business decisions. She decided to only have one child, despite Eric's and his parents' desire for plenty more. Sophie thought back to the couple's interactions since they arrived, and Sophie did notice a lot of deference on Eric's part. Sophie was convinced that their marriage, strong as it seemed, was as unequal as Raul and Olympia's. Only, it cut in favor of the wife.

"I mean, the reasons are obvious, right?" Adrian asked. "Dad couldn't pull all that traditional Filipino values shit on someone so independent and successful, let alone a super WASP-y Boston Brahmin."

"And if he'd married a Filipina?"

He paused, chewing on the question. "Dad grew up in the States. He was ten when he moved. So I think he could have married anyone and he'd still act the same. He wouldn't be conservative like Lolo at all. I think him growing up seeing his parents' marriage would've turned him off of that kind of relationship. I mean, I myself grew up seeing it and I for sure know I don't want *that*."

"So, you want a badass wife who'd give you hell if you ever acted up, huh? You sure you don't want a trophy?" Sophie teased. "You don't want some pretty little thing who'll follow you around and be at your every beck and call?"

"I want you." Adrian blushed, a diffident look on his face. "Okay, so I don't want you to think I'm mentally planning our wedding and shit. But, yeah, when I think about marriage *in general*—I want what my parents have."

Sophie saw the glint in Adrian's eye and remembered why she fell in love with him in the first place. He always had that boundless and innocent optimism, one that he never tried to conceal. She believed him when he said he wasn't talking about them, and though she knew it was too early and they were too young, she discovered that a part of her wanted him to be.

"So—when do you think you'll tell your power-couple model-parents about your documentary?"

Adrian groaned and covered his face. "God. Not while we're here, that's for fucking sure. Maybe not ever."

"It can't feel good, lying to everyone and getting them on camera. Your mom will get it, I think. But I don't know about your dad."

"He'd lose his shit. Not that I'm doing this to piss him off, but it's fun to think about. I never quite know where I stand with him in all this—he says he's proud of me, and he supports all my projects, but deep down, I feel like he's just humoring me. I think he really looks down on my choices, but not enough to stop me or pressure me into doing what he wants. Not enough to pressure me like Lolo did."

"That's good, I guess. Better than being openly hostile to you."

He scoffed. "Yeah, well . . . the number of times I've overheard Dad say I don't have a head for business. Or I'm not built to run an empire. I mean, it's true, but the way he says it . . . he just sounds so damn smug. Like, he doesn't say it to defend me either. He says it to put me down. And to prop himself up."

"Babe, I don't know what to say . . . that really sucks." Sophie nuzzled up to him and swung an arm over him.

"Maybe. I don't know. I could be reading into it too much. Like, I have nothing to complain about. I'm so blessed. He's a good dad. Maybe I'm just afraid of disappointing him."

"And that's completely natural. You want to make him proud. You're also smart enough to know that *Blood Relations* might make him uncomfortable. But isn't that's the goal? To ask the uncomfortable questions?"

"Wouldn't be the worst thing," Adrian said, with some confidence.

"No, the worst thing would be getting on the president's bad side," Sophie said with a chuckle. "And then getting abducted in the middle of the night, never to be seen again. Dundundunnnn."

"Hah! Are you gonna miss me when I'm gone? If I get—" Adrian said, teasing. He leaned over her, arms wide, then grabbed her around the waist. "—Taken?"

Sophie laughed, tickled. "Well, I'll have more time to spend with my other boyfriend."

Adrian peppered her neck with kisses. "Yeah, right. Who is this other boyfriend, huh?"

"Stop it, they might hear us," Sophie half whispered, stifling her giggles.

"Okay, okay, I'll stop." Adrian then lowered himself and pressed his lips against hers.

She hung onto him, lifting herself from the bed. Their breaths grew heavy as they kissed. Adrian paused, his eyes tentative and searching. Sophie leaned in and kissed him again. He moved down to her neck, and Sophie's thrill intensified as his hand crept up her leg. She took his hand and pulled it downward, between her thighs. Adrian relented. He watched her heaving and writhing under his touch. Sophie put her fist against her mouth.

Suddenly, he stopped, and when he did, Sophie gripped his

hand in protest. She'd been too overwhelmed to hear the call from the other side of the door.

"Coming, Dad," Adrian shouted back. His face was red with guilt—at not finishing the job, or at breaking the rules, Sophie didn't know. Probably both.

"One last thing before I go," he told her. "I brought you something." He took a prescription bottle from his shorts pocket and rattled the handful of pills inside it. "Xanax. So you can really get KO'd."

"Please tell me you didn't," Sophie said sternly. She had no objection to benzos in general—she'd taken them once before, to try to smooth the edge off a snowy Vegas weekend—but she knew where these pills came from. Adrian had a habit of swiping Margot's stash for the long flights to the Philippines, when weed occasionally made him more trippy than mellow.

"I only took a couple. She won't miss 'em. You, on the other hand, have barely slept. Like, really slept."

Sophie couldn't argue with that. Still, she declined. "Save them. Things might seem intense now, but this is all just the lead-up. You'll want the stronger stuff for the funeral, plus the flight back. Weed might not tide you over between now and then."

Adrian gave her a doubtful look. "No big. I have my own." He gingerly pulled her bedside drawer open and placed the bottle inside. "This is yours. Just in case."

Sophie rolled her eyes. He was always so cute when he was being stubborn. Adrian pecked a kiss goodbye.

She plopped herself down the bed, her frustration piqued. She considered the Xanax but thought better of it. She knew a better way. Adrian might have gone, but she needn't deny herself. Her tired fingers felt weighed down, as though they were filled with sand, but she gamely continued what Adrian had started. Not long after she finished herself off, Sophie fell asleep.

DSC20250313.docx
Source: A003C026_20250313_DivZoom.mov

Adrian Sepulveda: Would you like to talk about him? We haven't really gotten the chance to yet.

Divina Sepulveda-Cuesta: I was wondering when you would ask. Melchior was a foreman at the plantation, started out as one of those boys that the farmers sent up the trees with bolos to chop down the heads of coconuts, so I'd seen him around the farm since those early days. Yet he never really caught my eye until we were grown. As for him, well, he used to say it was love at first sight. He fell in love with me when he first saw me as a teenage girl.

AS1: So what happened?

DSC: Well, you see, Papa was determined to marry me off to a wealthy family so the only boys I saw were those he approved of. They were horrible matches, though. They all complained—to their parents, like the sniveling children they were!—that I was too prickly, too histrionic. Which I suppose I was, but a man should never say so of a woman. Anyway, this matchmaking went on for a longer while than anyone expected, and the next thing we knew, I was thirty-four and still single. Before this so-called family curse, people joked that I was cursed. [laughs] And then Melchior made his move.

AS1: He courted you?

DSC: In the traditional way, with gifts of flowers and serenades by my bedroom window. Some nights I can still hear him strumming his guitar. This was all done in secret, though, especially when Papa was on home leave from Camp Crame. My brother was less strict than Papa, but he still disapproved. He always warned me how Melchior was not de buena familia, how his humble origins would bring shame not only to me but to the Sepulveda clan.

AS1: That definitely sounds like Lolo.

DSC: If you think he was strict with you, well, I've got more stories to tell. I'm sorry he couldn't see you again today.

AS1: That's okay. Bad timing, but I'm patient. We'll talk when he's feeling up for it. [pause] So, your dad and kuya were against Melchior. How did that make you feel?

DSC: Do I seem the kind to respond to threats of shame? I was in love! I didn't care about any of that. Yes, I was also getting old and lonely, but so was Melchior, and he loved me, and we had found each other. That was enough.

AS1: How did you get Great-Grandlolo to agree to the marriage?

DSC: I wore him down, I suppose. You see, Raul and Olympia already had children at that point. He'd already been governor for four years. The family's lineage and status were secure. In the end, Papa thought it was better to marry me off to anyone rather than have me be a spinster. I didn't care for his reasons, as long as he let me marry the man I loved. And he did. Not only that, Papa threw us the grandest wedding the country had seen in years.

AS1: That must've cost a lot of money.

DSC: Thank God, the bride's family pays! Papa spared no expense. My unica hija deserves the best, he told everyone. Though, let's not sugarcoat things . . . the extravagance was also his way of overcompensating. He needed to save face, I know that. But again, I didn't care what he thought. I was only too happy to begin my life with Melchior.

AS1: And what was that like?

DSC: It was pure bliss. Papa gifted us with a house not too far from the farm, but Melchior moved into the manor and we lived here while that was getting built. [sighs] He didn't live long enough to step foot in it.

AS1: What happened to the house?

DSC: I had the men stop work on it, donated the plot and the unfinished structure to the parish. They use it for storage now, I think.

AS1: I'm sorry.

DSC: Don't be. We were only married a year, but it was the happiest year of my life. And since then, I've never known love or joy. Not since him.

April 13
Palm Sunday

Viewed from the east lawn, Villa Sepulveda seemed to show its age the most. This was where most of the maintenance work had been done, repairs mandated by the historical commission. To a keen eye, the signs were evident: newer wood panels where the old, storm-damaged ones had been replaced; freshly painted iron braces on the silong's crumbling brickwork; pipes that contained electrical cables and telephone lines peeking underneath the vines and trellises; the metal fixtures up on the roof by which the satellite dish used to hang. It gave a patchwork quality to the country house, but from a wide angle, the signs of old and new came together seamlessly. At least that was what Adrian said as he framed his shot, tilting his camera just so. The roof's clay tiles glowed fervidly in the sunrise.

Sophie stood behind him, watching. He'd asked her to rise early and join him, claiming he needed an assist. He didn't, not for the technical side of things, she knew that. He needed her for moral support, which she was more than happy to supply. She always admired how much of himself Adrian put into his documentary. She'd seen all the research he did, all the correspondence with martial law exiles in Europe, all the late-night video calls with journalists and activists in Manila and Ilocos and Leyte, contacts that he pursued and cultivated. He traded on the Sepulveda name to get his calls picked up, but took much care to ensure word of his project never got back to his family. "They'll find out on opening night," he'd always said.

That meant, too, that Adrian had to lie to his great-aunt Divina, the sole Sepulveda still living in the motherland. Over Zoom calls, he'd been interviewing her for months, informally, under the guise of background research for a project about his genealogy. Now, he would get to film her—and lie to her—in person.

Sophie worried about Adrian's comfort with dissembling, and about his desire to do the least damage possible to the Sepulveda name. Yet she also knew that the Sepulvedas' closeness to the Marcoses always haunted him, despite the fact that the dictatorship was half a century ago, before even his father was born. Sophie counted on that remorse to keep Adrian on the right path. He had always been firmly anti-Marcos; to him, resistance was no passing fad. Even before he had the idea for *Blood Relations*, he'd been an assiduous student of that period in Philippine history. He was the first person who explained to her the intricacies of the People Power Revolution that ousted the older Marcos from power and ended his reign of terror. Adrian understood, to an almost academic degree, the present-day fallout of two decades under authoritarian rule, and he cared about what happened to the country, even from across the ocean. Two years back, when the current President Marcos visited the Bay Area, Adrian organized the campus protest, rallying the Stanford PASU behind him. Whatever qualms Sophie may have had about his motives and methods, Adrian had at least given her more reason to believe than to doubt.

And so, on that early Sunday morning, Sophie was able to

shake off the sense of illicit subterfuge to the whole affair. It no longer seemed to matter that Adrian planned it so that everyone would still be asleep, especially Olympia, nor that he still kept up the charade about the documentary's true subject. She trusted in Adrian and the righteousness of his cause.

Blithely unaware, Divina sat for her interview in a high-backed wicker chair taken from one of the silong's storerooms and brought out specifically for the shoot. Adrian asked his questions, prompting his great-aunt to wax poetic about the history of her ancestral home. She still wore her mourning clothes, but her veil was pulled all the way back, and she bore an air of confident wistfulness as she spoke. Sophie had heard some of the details before, from Adrian's calls with Divina, but it felt different hearing them now. Through the old woman's stories, the villa came alive, as did all the figures from its far and recent past.

Divina looked back on the east lawn and extended her arm. "This right here, where we are now, is the site of the grandest party this place ever saw. My wedding." Light came on behind her eyes. "The north lawn has more space and has the view of the mountains, but we couldn't build the pavilion there, what with the pool and all. So it was here"—she pointed into the middle distance closer to the porte cochere—"where we had the gazebo, and then here"—she gestured around the space where she sat—"was where they erected the guest pavilion. We had four hundred guests coming from all over the world. Oh, you should have seen it. The lights, the flowers, the linens, the food . . . it was magical."

As the older woman went on, Sophie began to understand her more. So far, she had thought Divina very similar to Adrian's grandmother Olympia, but now Sophie saw that they couldn't be any more different. Divina spoke not with conceit, but with pride—in her lineage, in her legacy, in who she was, even in their imperfections. She'd revealed extreme emotions, but they all felt more genuine now, not for show. Divina didn't care much about how things reflected on her.

"Who was on the guest list?" Adrian asked.

"Well, the president's whole family was there, naturalmente, and the vice president's. Half the senate and the top military brass, the US ambassador . . . "

"President Marcos, you mean."

"Not only was he family, he was my godfather, and Papa's commander in chief. He got the first dance at the wedding, after Melchior and Papa. He and Imelda brought their children too, Bongbong and Imee and the others. The Romualdez clan came in full force and . . . oh, the prince of Brunei was in the country that time, he was there too. Melchior's head spun, remembering everyone's names . . . " Divina laughed. She made to speak again but seemed to have lost her train of thought.

"Oh, yes, it was a fabulous event," she continued. "The best night of my life."

"What was that like, being so close to the president?" Adrian asked. It struck Sophie how cool he was, even though she knew how nauseating he must've found the thought of his great-aunt waltzing with a dictator. However, before Divina could answer, Adrian quickly raised his hand. The video monitor flickered and died.

"Need another battery pack," he said, rummaging through his bag for a replacement. Sophie kept watching Divina, who seemed lost in her recollections. She didn't even stir when Adrian ran back to the house to find one.

"How are you finding all of this?" Divina asked once Adrian was out of earshot. "Not at all boring, is it?"

"Far from it," Sophie replied. "I love learning about these things."

"I suppose that's understandable, given your circumstances." There was no condescension in her tone, but Sophie nonetheless sensed a commiserative kind of pity. "It's human nature to want to know where one came from, how one came to be. I hope this is helping Adrian." The old woman had a twinkle in her eye as she said this last part, and Sophie was unsure if there was more to her words.

"I'm sure it is" was all she could say.

"How do you reckon?"

"Well, I . . . it's like you said. Where he came from matters to him too," Sophie replied. "It's something we bonded over, actually. This desire to know more about our families."

Divina shifted to face the villa. "Be that as it may, knowing is one thing. Making a film out of it is quite another. I still don't understand the appeal."

"Many people would find your family fascinating. I know I do."

"I meant the appeal *for him*. I think he could gain a larger audience if he focused on another subject. Something or someone more, oh, I don't know . . . relevant?"

"I don't want to speak for Adrian," Sophie began. "But your family is relevant to him, and that's the most important thing to an artist. He wants to understand himself and the world through this art, and that requires getting at the truth of the family that brought him to being. Adrian just wants the real story behind the history. And he wants to preserve it before—"

"Before it's all lost." The old woman lowered her veiled head. After a while, she said, "Well, it's not fair that he gets to have all the fun. You must have questions of your own."

"There is something I've been wondering, after listening to you speak and knowing some of the history . . . " Sophie drew out her words carefully. "It seems like there were as many good as bad things that happened here. Did you ever think of leaving this place?"

"I did, many times. It's not easy being alone, everyone dying around me or abandoning me. Leaving me with responsibilities I never asked for. I've always wondered if my brother, God rest his soul, tasked me with overseeing this place as punishment for marrying a peasant. And I've always wondered what it'd be like to start over in America. But then what would I do? This is my home. This is where my Melchior lived and died. This place is all I know and love."

"And what about the curse? You've said you believe in it. Doesn't it scare you?"

"For forty years, I didn't even think about it. I assumed it ended when Papa died, when Melchior died. When everyone left. Surely that was enough. But when Raul returned, well . . . it doesn't matter." Divina turned and looked back at the manor. "Forty years I've lived in desolation and sorrow. What else could happen to me now?"

Javier gloated more than usual because he knew something his older brother didn't know. Kai didn't know either, but Javier drew no satisfaction from having one over their youngest; Kai was never in the game, so to speak. They were in a league all their own, ignored and untouched by the eternal battle that pitted father against son, brother against brother. Eric was a different matter. Javier had always believed that his disinheritance gratified his kuya, and all week he'd been waiting to deal Eric a crushing blow.

He waited in their father's office, idly twirling an ivory-hilted letter opener from behind the former governor's desk. He surveyed the room's contents, the left side of his brain tallying how much the antiques might fetch, even as the right side of his brain overlaid these calculations with memories of his papa. Each object had a story behind it, from the standing globe that little Javier liked to spin furiously, to the leather-bound books in their glass cases that he'd been forbidden to open, to the Persian rug over which he'd once spilled a glass of chocolate milk and left a blobby stain. Against one wall stood the gun case, ancient pistols and rifles with their barrels and grips and triggers, mounted in an array that formed what looked like a peacock's fanned-out tail. *Maybe when you're older*, he could still hear his father's voice.

Javier would sell them all, every single item in this and every room.

Olympia was first to arrive, and when her two other children soon followed, her sigh betrayed a knowing exhaustion. "There's no time like the present," Javier told her, gesturing for everyone to take a seat.

Eric declined. "What's this about now?"

Javier leaned back on the tufted leather chair and glared at his mama, who refused to speak. "It's all right," he assured her. "They'll find out eventually."

"Is this about the will?" Eric asked. "C'mon, can't this wait until the lawyers arrive? Or at least until Papa's in the ground?"

"Well, we all hate lawyers," Javier answered. "Besides, I have a feeling the cat's out of the bag anyway. Right, Mama?"

Olympia sighed, turning to Eric and Kai. "Your papa made changes to his will before he died. I . . . told Javier a few days ago, but I wasn't going to keep it from you for long. I just wanted to—"

"She just wanted to give me an incentive to come to the funeral, isn't that right?" Javier interrupted. "Don't fret, Ma. I knew what you were thinking. Honestly, I wasn't sure I was coming until you told me I'd be getting something from the old man after all."

"Oh, shut up, Javi. That's not true," Kai answered.

"Isn't it?" Eric asked, his jaw clenched. "Mama's right. I've seen the changes Papa made to his will—if you could call it that. He wants to . . . he wants to disinherit everyone." He hurried out of the room and quickly returned, clutching the papers in his hand. He slammed them on the desk, their pages bleeding red with a madman's scrawls.

"What? Why? And can he do that?" Kai asked.

"As we are all keenly aware, Papa can do whatever he wants. *Did* whatever he wanted," Javier replied, the venom in his voice a mask for his confusion. "But Ma, what about what you told me?"

"This doesn't matter," Eric spat. "Everything's in the Sepulveda Family Trust—all the stocks, the business assets, the holding companies, the entire portfolio. So it doesn't matter what Papa's will says, or what it doesn't say."

Javier shook his head grudgingly. Certainly, he spurned the trust as a birthright he'd been deprived of. For his entire adult life he'd had to scrape by on his own, surviving on surreptitious doleouts from his mother and family connections who took pity on him, until he figured out how to make money talking people into buying and selling houses. He could have been a trust fund kid, and he was, for a brief, shining moment. His pride in being a self-made man never quite made him forget what could have been.

Yet more than that, he also grew to hate the family trust on principle. It was how they hoarded wealth, how they avoided paying taxes, and how they hid the taxes they stole. Its existence was further proof of his family's depravity.

"Not *everything* is in the trust," Javier countered. "Villa Sepulveda has always been passed on by will, and Papa never broke the tradition. I should know, I'd been written out of that one too."

"Right. The villa and all its contents go to the children via last will and testament," Eric said. "How do you think that helps you, huh? Look at this mess—" He jabbed the papers with his finger. "No court would find Papa lucid. And if this will gets upheld, none of us would get the villa. You're screwed either way, brother."

"No, he's not," Olympia said coolly, halting the argument. "Eric, you weren't supposed to find this. No one was. I didn't want you to see how badly your papa was . . . and these words . . . I wanted you all to remember him as he was in his prime, not like this."

Raul Sepulveda in his prime was no picnic either, Javier wanted to reply. He looked to his siblings and he imagined that they were thinking the same. None of them had been spared. Javier saw how bad it got between his kuya and their father. Eric only got an early reprieve because he knew how to fawn and obey, and because Javier took the brunt of Raul's ire. Kai was lucky; they were born a full decade after Javier, and in America too. Most of all, they hadn't been born a boy. Raul's lack of affection for Kai was a blessing, and a natural impetus for them to put as much distance from their father as possible, fleeing the nest to parts unknown as soon as they were able.

And so there Javier was. The antagonistic middle child. Raul always said that it was all a ploy for attention—Javier's disobedience, his rebellion, his gayness. The claim always had a ring of truth; after all, the world revolved around Raul Sepulveda, a great man born of a noble bloodline. All his life Javier saw how everyone craved his father's approval. How could he not do the same?

"So what about me?" Javier asked Olympia. "You said Papa left something for me. That I wasn't cut off anymore."

"I wasn't lying. Not exactly." She ran her veiny hand over the will and picked up the pages. She held them up and began to tear them lengthwise. The three siblings were stunned. "This has no legal effect, and not just because he was losing his mind at the time. He wanted to revoke his will, make sure none of us got the house."

"But that would mean it would all go to the state," Javier said, agitated. "Papa would never do that, would he?"

"He wouldn't, not if he was in his right mind," Olympia replied. "That's why I had to take certain . . . steps."

With barely concealed remorse, she explained how busy she'd been in those weeks before her husband's death. "I didn't want any of you to know, as I'm sure he himself would have wanted to keep it secret, but your papa really had gone insane. He had his lucid moments, though they became rarer toward the end. He had night terrors, yes, but the days were just as dreadful. He was obsessed with building that damn mausoleum, raving that the balbal lurked, biding its time until it could exhume his ancestors. He heard things, saw all sorts of visions—monsters and ghosts, nightmares that became waking hallucinations. You know what it was like before the treatment." She turned to her eldest. "I didn't think he could get worse."

"How much worse?" Eric asked.

"He'd hit me," Olympia continued, unaffected. "Your auntie and Remedios, too. He didn't know what he was doing. Most of the time, he didn't recognize any of us. Everything and everyone was an enemy that needed to be vanquished. He said the most hateful things about me, about each of you, things it would only break my heart to repeat."

In his mother's tale Javier identified all the classic signs of dementia, but he knew, too, that there was a kernel of truth as to his father's hatred, at least as it pertained to him. "And so he wanted to disinherit everyone, is that it?"

"He wanted to leave us with nothing," Olympia replied. "I couldn't let that happen, but he tried his damnedest. He kept asking for his lawyer, demanding to change his will. I've had to disconnect the phone line a few times. Once, he even drove to the capital. That's when we started to hide the car keys."

Kai crossed their arms, despondent. "He might have lost his wits, but he never lost his stubbornness."

"Not at all. When denying him didn't work, I used his

failing memory against him," Olympia continued. "I told him he'd already seen the lawyer or that the new will had already been drafted. But Raul saw through those plots as well. On the rare good day, he'd have perfect recall of what had and hadn't happened. It was baffling, and some part of me thought he must be faking his episodes. And so in the end, I had to resort to more direct means: I colluded with our lawyer.

"Convincing him was easy enough. The man sympathized with the story I fed him, which was mostly true: Raul sought to punish us and get rid of the villa, something he would never do if he were sane. A hefty bribe helped too. And so, we devised the plan: Instead of a new will, we made your father sign a revocation of all his prior wills. The documents were easy enough to switch around, shuffling a few pages here and there, making sure the words blurred in Raul's vision. While the lawyer kept the revocation safeguarded, he gave Raul a dummy copy of his 'will,' which was compelling enough to pacify him. I burned the decoy as soon as he passed."

"Mama, I . . . I don't know what to say," Eric said, sharing the same dumbfounded expression as his siblings. "It—it feels wrong."

Javier interjected. "And yet."

"I wanted to make sure you get part of this house, and now you do," Olympia told Javier. "Because all his prior wills are now revoked, your papa has died intestate. By law, that means all assets not in the trust shall pass to his family. Including you."

Javier didn't know where to start. He had allowed himself to hope that at the last moment, maybe his father did change his mind. He resented himself for hoping. It was too good to expect some deathbed conversion from Raul Sepulveda.

And what of his mother? Wasn't it equally foolish for him to be shocked at her deceptions? Was that outrage he felt, or gratitude?

"Well, my serious reservations aside, this is a better

outcome than where I thought this was headed," Kai said. "At least now we get to keep the villa. Or sell it, if I had my way."

Olympia shushed them. "I'm serious about what I said the other night—this place must stay in the family forever."

"And like I said, none of us have ties here, plus it doesn't make financial sense to hold on to it. I mean, we're all in agreement," Eric said, gesturing toward his siblings. "Look, Ma, we don't have to finalize anything now, but I think you have to start getting comfortable with the idea."

"Never."

Javier rose from his seat and braced himself on the desk. He should have known, and in truth, some part of him saw this coming. He turned to his mother with a vicious glare.

"You didn't do it for me. You didn't manipulate Papa so that I would get a slice of the pie. You did it so that *you* would. I've dealt with enough estate battles in my line of work to last me a lifetime, and I know this much: No will means half goes to the spouse, half split among the children. Isn't that right?"

Olympia raised her chin defiantly. "Yes. And what of it? I knew the three of you would unload the villa as soon as you could. I only did what Raul would have done if he was in his right mind. I don't regret it."

"You never fail to amaze me, Mama. Just when I think you've sunk your lowest—"

"I don't care about ownership! Nor the damn the money! I only care about this family's legacy. And you—you ingrates—what do you care about? Why are you so goddamned anxious to get rid of our home?"

"It's not *my* home," Kai groused. Eric came to his mother's side and tried to calm her, to no avail. She shuddered in anger.

Javier gave Olympia a wicked smile. "I think the real question is, why are you so goddamned anxious to keep it?" He held out his palms, daring her for a response. She'd never say it, but he so wished she would. He turned to his siblings and sneered at their dead stares. Soon enough, he thought to himself. They'd all know soon enough.

"Sure, you own half this villa now," he told her. "But don't forget, Mama—we can wait you out. I know I will."

Sophie passed by the photograph again on her way to the conservatory. She told herself it was just a case of suggestibility, nothing more. After all, the nanny did look odd, standing in the background, the lone member of the staff accidentally caught in the family photo. Alondra was yet another detail that had driven its hooks into her subconscious, just like the myths and superstitions and the various players in the Sepulveda lore.

She passed Adrian's parents' room and found the door ajar. Kai sat on a rocking chair by the foot of the bed. Margot was deep asleep. She snored loudly, a welcome sign that she was getting the rest that she needed, but one that also amused Sophie. She didn't imagine such coarse noises coming from someone so classy, not even involuntarily.

Kai patted the armchair next to them. Sophie hesitated, but she had questions. What if this woo-woo manic pixie hippie mystic was right? What if it was the ghost of Alondra that she'd seen?

"How is she?" Sophie whispered as she sat down.

Kai didn't feel the need to modulate and said, quite emphatically, "I thought I'd keep her company. She was lonely. I could sense it."

Sophie thought to indulge them. "How could you tell?"

"Vibes. And I mean literal energy vibrations. Everyone gives them off, you know. Even when they're dead to the world." They regarded Sophie from head to toe, opened their mouth to say something, but thought better of it. Sophie felt bemused. *Geez, what kind of vibes did I just give off?*

After a pause, Kai said, "Besides, it doesn't take a genius to see that she's lonely. No one's talked or asked about her all day. And I don't think anyone's come here either, except the caretaker." They gestured at the untouched breakfast plate on Margot's nightstand, covered by a mesh cloche.

"I'm sure Adrian must've been here at some point," Sophie replied. Her lukewarm defense seemed to make no difference to Kai.

"I just can't stand seeing someone so . . . neglected. Cared for by strangers. Tsk."

Remedios hadn't warmed to her or to Kai, but Sophie didn't think the Sepulvedas viewed the caretaker as a stranger, nor did Margot, who'd seen Remedios more times in the past few years than she did Kai. "They keep saying Manang Remy's part of the family."

"Yeah, they say that about all the staff," Kai answered with a resigned tone. "Papa especially. Doesn't make it true."

"There must have been some who felt just as close, though, right?"

Kai pondered this for a while. "We had an au pair at one point. Turkish, I think. I don't remember much about her, but I liked her a lot. She lived with us, in the attic. Shows you what 'being part of the family' is really like."

"I guess you didn't like being raised by nannies?"

"Oh, I wasn't." Kai explained how the Sepulvedas' nannies were mostly for the two rambunctious boys. Olympia was very hands-on in raising Kai. They looked past the open door and into empty hallway, and lowered their voice. "Mama spoiled me," they said with a hint of regret. "I was her 'little princess,' after all."

Sophie winced. "Oof. What was that like?"

"It was okay, for a while. She threw me all these princess-themed birthday parties, painted my bedroom pink, that sort of thing. My wardrobe was all tulle and taffeta and flowers and rainbows, it looked like a unicorn puked all over it. And there was gymnastics, ballet classes, and . . . " They shuddered. "The Little Miss Belvedere Yacht Club pageant."

"Oh, my."

"Yuuup. Mama was a pageant queen, did you know? She wanted me to follow in her high-heeled footsteps. She entered me every year until she stopped because I never won. Never even placed. I just hope she hasn't kept any photographic evidence."

Sophie always knew that she and Adrian were from different worlds, but this was an aspect she hadn't thought of before. What kind of childhood must he have had? And what kind would she have had if she were a Sepulveda? She had a girly-girl phase too. She coveted Bratz dolls, wore the same pink fairy costume for Halloween every year. She would have liked to have princess-themed parties. Growing up, she was lucky if her Duncan Hines cake had rainbow sprinkles.

"It doesn't sound so bad," she replied. "Except for the pageants."

"Yeah, I guess. Back then I liked all those things, or at least I thought I did. I had no reason to complain. I lived like a princess and was treated like one. But then I grew up. Grew into who I am. Middle school onwards was rough. Mama never let me pick my clothes, pick my friends, pick my nose. I had to be prim and proper at all times. Meek and obedient. Try telling that to a twelve-year-old, especially one who was all pop-punk and obsessed with Avril Lavigne. Freshman year of high school, I got an undercut without their permission and Papa locked me up in the basement. He yelled that I could only leave once my hair was long again.

"And forget about boys. Boys were never to come within ten feet of me. Not that they did, and besides, I wasn't into boys back then. High school was my lesbian phase, which, you know, probably sucked for Ma and Pa, since Javi also just came out and they haven't even fully dealt with that yet. And now their little princess was a lesbian, too?" Kai laughed. "Papa fully lost his shit."

"But at least you and Javier had each other."

"Well, he took the heat for me, that's for sure. He's eleven years older and so Papa blamed him. Said it's his bad influence that made me who I am. Javi wasn't even home around then; he was already at NYU. And really, I didn't have to be led to the land of queer, I found the way myself," they said, biting their lip. "So no, Javi and I didn't 'have each other' back then, but I kinda owe him for being the scapegoat."

Sophie suspected that Raul never would have treated Kai as harshly as Javier, even if their ages were reversed. No matter who turned queer first, no matter who influenced whom, Raul seemed the kind of father who cared more about how his sons reflected on him. The fact that Kai was the youngest child also made them easier to disregard.

"And then I left home when I was sixteen," Kai went on. "Thank Goddess I got into this accelerated program in Heidelberg. Even if I didn't, I still would've gone away. It's not like I needed college as an excuse. And I haven't been home since."

"Not once?"

"I'd pop in at Belvedere if I was passing through the West Coast, but I never stayed long. Never did stay long in any one place, anyway."

"Now I get why your mom was so happy to see you again."

Kai's lips curled. "I just wish it didn't have to be *here*. All my alarm bells are ringing. Have been since I got here. And now look at her." They lifted their chin toward Margot.

"It's just a stomach bug from the shrimp," Sophie said.

"It's not. She's trembling, don't you see? I had to bring in an extra blanket for her."

She'd assumed it was just from the heavy snoring, but Sophie noticed the tremors now. "She's taken medicine, right?"

"Remy said she did this morning," Kai answered. "But it's not gonna be enough. Margot's feeling it too. Not that bullshit gaba, but something else. She doesn't recognize it consciously, but her body does, and it is rejecting this place."

"Yeah, but the rest of us are fine . . . "

"Are you?" Kai asked pointedly. They held her arm. "Or do you feel it now, that cold aura?"

Something about their manner made Sophie nod, almost involuntarily. Too many odd things had transpired in the few days since and she wasn't sure she could so easily dismiss them anymore.

"I'm telling you, something is coming." Kai leaned back and rocked in their chair, fidgeting with their black crystal pendant. "Margot's been here before, but she's not from here. Neither am I and neither are you. And I'm worried for all of us."

"I can't believe you did this," Sophie told Adrian as he gently offered her mud-crusted iPhone, wrapped in a hand towel. "And all by yourself? I thought we had a plan."

"I wanted to surprise you—and spare you a couple hours hunched over the thickets." He explained how he'd sneaked off to scour the cogon and the groves near where she'd said she dropped it. "Find My iPhone is completely useless, by the way."

Sophie showered him with kisses. Her phone was still dead, but it should be back to functional after some time in a bag of rice. She placed the bag in one of the side altars of the oratorio, where she hoped the ambient heat from all the candles, if not the supposed blessing of the saints, might speed up the process.

It began to drizzle shortly after lunch. The breeze splattered rainwater into the conservatory, where she and Adrian decided to forego their siestas and instead read books next to each other. He rose to shut the windows. Not long after he did, Sophie noticed a sharp, bleachy smell, like a cleaning agent had been spilled somewhere close. It also had a more unpleasant base note, the stench of decomposing meat. It reminded her of that hot summer when she held down a waitressing job at the only diner in Ruskin, where she'd worked the night shift and done trash duty at the end of the night. Sophie thought she'd been imagining it until Adrian inhaled and confirmed it with a wince.

"What the fuck is that?" He flung the windows open again, though not as wide as usual. The air flow scarcely helped.

"I think it's coming from the kitchen," Sophie answered. "The generator going on and off every day can't be good for the box freezer." She stepped into the hallway, where she was hit harder with the putrefaction. It was strongest down toward the sala mayor. She pointed at the open casket. "That smell is coming from there, I think."

"Oh, jeez, you're right." Adrian waved his hand over his nose. "So much for formaldehyde."

All afternoon, someone or another made a stray mention about the foul air, but it was courteously dismissed, denied, or ignored, the same way people do when someone passes gas. Dinner came and went, uneventful and quite rushed. Everyone wanted to avoid the smell as much as they avoided acknowledging it. Remedios didn't bother bringing out dessert, seeing how quickly the table cleared out.

Retiring after the meal, Sophie was relieved that the smell wasn't too strong in her room, situated at the end of the hallway farthest from the sala. She left her window open to let some fresh air in, but drew the sheer curtains over it.

She unearthed her phone from the bag of rice and squealed when it turned on. Finally, some good news. The icon still showed *SOS* instead of signal bars, but she'd won half the battle. Maybe they could trek downhill again tomorrow.

She took a gummy before bed, green for good luck. To be sure, she'd also eaten a banana for dessert. She hoped that tonight, she wouldn't be paralyzed, dreaming of long-dead nannies or dark monsters hiding in the tall grass.

Yet Alondra did visit her again. It was her, Sophie was sure of it. There was a shimmery quality to her, and the entire dreamscape looked ethereal, as though Sophie saw everything through a layer of frost.

Alondra wore her belted gray dress, her long hair tied neatly behind her. As in the picture, she stood under the veranda's awning, waving at two boys running on the back lawn. The taller one was about nine or ten. He made a running jump and launched himself into a cannonball, splashing into a swimming pool. The slightly younger one followed him.

They splashed around gaily, but as Sophie drew closer she saw that the water was a thick, dark sludge, almost like tar. It coated the boys completely and weighed down their arms as they flailed. Sophie ran toward them, panicked, but when she reached the edge of the pool, she saw that the boys weren't screaming for help at all. They were frolicking, shrieking as children do in their excitement.

Alondra stood next to Sophie, smiling. Sophie turned to her and said, "They'll drown."

The woman remained still, as though she didn't hear.

Then, Alondra turned to her, lips curled in a devilish rictus. She raised a finger and pointed at the abyssal pool.

"Witness."

A hand rose from the sludge and pulled Sophie by her left

ankle. Sophie slipped and felt several hands dragging her deep into the murk.

The ooze was thick and heavy. It blanketed her hair and streamed down her face. When she opened her mouth to scream, the sludge went into her mouth and choked her.

Sophie jolted awake in a cold sweat, her heart palpitating. She tried to raise herself off the bed, but her body did not respond to her will, as though she was still held down in that sludge. Her limbs were unmoving and only her eyelids felt alive, fluttering wildly, her gaze darting around in the dark.

Above her, she saw that the pendulous linen canopy of her four-post bed was shaking, straining against something heavy. The cloth came apart with a high-pitched rrrrip!

A cascade of brown, husked coconuts rained down on her. They pelted her body and their rough hairs scratched her skin. Sophie screamed in agony, the shock shaking her muscles loose of the nightmare's grip. Smothered and struggling to breathe, she clawed her way out from under the pile that continued to fall on her.

In the faint light she saw that the coconuts' usual spots were not spots at all. They were holes. These were no ordinary fruit. They were brown, rounded skulls. Sophie flung them away from her and one cracked open. The smell of decay filled the room. Inside, the fruit's flesh was gray and rotting, and instead of white milky juice, what flowed out from the broken shell was blood.

Sophie rolled and flailed and fell off the bed. Every part of her radiated with pain. She rose to her feet and ran out the door, limping. The hall was illuminated by a single sconce, and right by it, she saw Adrian standing by his bedroom.

"I heard screaming. Are you okay?"

She rushed toward him and cried into his arms. He tried to hush her, soothing her with gentle strokes on her back. When her eyes adjusted to the light, she realized that she was in fact in the arms of Adrian's father.

She pulled herself away from him. "I—I—don't know what happened—" she said, panting. "There was that woman, and the coconuts, and they were skulls and there was blood—"

"Sophie, breathe. What are you talking about?"

"It was real, wasn't it?" She nervously looked back to her bedroom, half expecting bloodied heads to roll out the door.

"Why don't we get you a glass of water, huh? Would you like that?" Eric held her by her biceps. She quaked, as though her flesh was still tender after being bludgeoned by a mountain of coconuts.

"No," she said, wresting away from him.

Her body thudded against a wall, which shook some sense into her. She instantly became aware of how crazed she must seem, yelling about imaginary dangers. Eric looked at her with worry and repeated himself. He extended his hand.

Dazed, Sophie took it and let him lead her down the corridor. Her head felt light and her vision still swam with the surreal shimmer of her nightmare. Her feet were unsteady too, and she clung onto Eric as he guided her steadily and in silence.

As they turned the hall, a door opened ahead of them. Doña Olympia emerged from her bedroom wearing a black robe, her hair wrapped in a silk turban.

"What in God's name is going on here?"

"Sophie had a nightmare. She needs some water, or maybe tea to calm her nerves."

"What happened?"

Sophie tried but couldn't respond coherently, her faculties still reconstituting. She mostly repeated Eric's explanation.

"You poor thing," the older woman replied. She wiped Sophie's damp brow with the sleeve of her robe. "Enrique, why don't you go back to your room? You must be tired."

"Ah, you know me. I'm used to it," he answered, then turned to Sophie. "I'm such a light sleeper, I get woken up by any bump in the night. And you're the one who should be getting rest, Mama."

"I was up anyway," she answered tersely. "I'll take care of the girl."

Eric succumbed to the command and handed the shivering Sophie to his mother.

Olympia sat Sophie on the kitchen table and handed her a glass of water. She then scooped some tea leaves into a cup and saucer and put on a kettle. Sophie stared at the flame, waiting for the shock to subside.

"I'm so sorry, I don't know what came over me," Sophie said. She felt some relief to know that her racket hadn't woken Olympia, though she still worried how noisy she'd been. "It was a really bad nightmare."

"There's been a lot of that going around, it seems." Olympia peered into Sophie's bloodshot eyes, and she hoped they didn't betray her.

"It felt like what we were talking about the other day. The bangungot. I couldn't move and I couldn't breathe."

"What did you see, in this . . . bangungot?"

"It's hard to describe. Just images and stories from the past few days. You'll think it's silly."

Olympia pursed her lips, folding her arms together. "Oh, I can tell from silly. So, what was it? What did you dream of?"

Sophie thought of Alondra again, the young nanny with the long black hair, and wondered whether she should tell Olympia. But what was there to say? That she saw someone in an old picture and the image had seeped into her subconscious? And what about the falling coconuts, wouldn't that raise a sore subject?

A faint whistle issued from the pot.

"Who came to visit you, Sophie?"

"It was nothing, really. It wasn't that the dream was scary so much as me scaring myself. The jet lag hasn't completely passed either, so my body's out of whack." Sophie tried to seem nonchalant, but the woman was not buying it. "Should we get the—"

"Remedios told me your sleep has been fitful. And there was a fuss about the peepholes too, wasn't there? You wanted them covered?"

"Uh—yes. I felt a bit uncomfortable, and Adrian—"

The whistle grew louder but neither of them moved.

"You've been tossing and turning these past few nights then?"

The kettle wailed, its plume of steam frantic. "I think the water's ready."

Olympia rose and silently strode to shut the stove. Relief washed over Sophie as the shrieking came to a hush. She thanked the older woman for the tea, her voice soft and her head low. An awkward silence hung between them, both waiting for the tea to sufficiently steep, but at least Olympia seemed to have quit asking about her nightmares.

"You and I have never had any time to get to know each other, just the two of us," Olympia said after a while. "All I've heard are stories. Sad as this occasion is, I'm glad I finally get to meet you. See the real you."

"Yes. Me too."

"Now that my husband is gone, it all falls to me to keep the family together. I'm the only one. I have to keep them safe. Happy. Is Adrian happy?"

"I think so. I try to. Make him happy, that is."

Olympia reached out to tuck a stray strand of hair behind Sophie's ear. Sophie flinched at the invasion of her space. The reaction merited a quick flash of indignation from the old woman. Her veiny hand moved across Sophie's cheek before lifting her chin, assessing her.

"It's hard being a grandmother. Adrian grew up with me and Raul in the same household, but we could only do so much. He has his parents to provide for him, mold him, love him. As his lola, I've had to . . . take a back seat, I guess you could say." There was a hardened kind of melancholy in her voice, a refusal to accept.

Sophie carefully turned her head away. "Adrian adores you. I can tell. He talks about you a lot."

"We don't talk much, you know, so that's a nice reminder. He's quite hard to read. You never know what he's thinking. But I would do anything for that boy. Anything." Olympia motioned toward the cup and Sophie felt compelled to take a sip. "It's different with my children, naturally."

"You must be so happy to see them all again," Sophie replied.

"Motherhood is a wondrous gift. That bond between mother and child cannot be overstated, don't you agree?" Olympia asked, and from her tone it seemed that the older woman hadn't merely forgotten Sophie's complicated history with her parentage.

"I feel this pinch, here in my chest," Olympia went on, pointing. "Every time something bad happens to Kai. Like when they broke a rib while skiing, or when they picked up a nasty virus in Brazil and ended up in a hospital for a month. They never call—they say they don't want to worry me—but I always know. Several times it's happened. They think it's a telepathic bond or some such mystical nonsense."

"It's a mother's intuition."

"More than intuition," Olympia corrected. "I knew what Javier was, even before he did. That's not something I intuited. I saw what he was because I saw him, all of him, for who he was. For who he is. And I have the benefit of age—decades of knowing how to live in a man's world, how to cope with . . . shame."

Olympia leaned in and placed her hands over Sophie's. They were almost translucent, but they were smooth and warm. She enfolded Sophie in her palms, and Sophie jolted when the older woman's grip grew tight.

"And Enrique," she continued. "My firstborn. I know him most of all. For his own ends, Raul played favorites with our children, but I know he didn't have one. I'm not ashamed to say that I do."

Sophie's pulse quickened. She tried to extricate her hand, but Olympia resisted. "Could I please . . . "

"Enrique is good-looking. Smart, accomplished. Rich. Most of all, he has an unselfish heart. It's his best quality but it tends to be exploited by so-called friends, opportunists . . . and nymphets like you."

"I'm sorry?"

"Nightmares . . . Psh! You must think you're so clever. I know exactly what you were trying to pull, little girl," Olympia said, seething. "And it will not work. I won't let it happen."

"What are you—?"

"Don't even deny it. That whole damsel-in-distress act did not fool me. I am warning you: Stay *the hell* away from my son."

"What? No, that wasn't what—"

"Save your breath. I've seen too many of your type. Malandi. Girls with no virtue. Temptresses, just like the snake in the garden. I saw from the moment you arrived how you've bewitched my boy. He's become this timid, subservient weakling, and I can only see one reason why."

Olympia's nails dug into Sophie's skin. She winced, quaking as she answered. "No, no, that's not true. This is all just a big misunderstanding. Eric heard me screaming and he was trying to help and I really did have a nightmare, about the nanny and the dead farmers and the boys in the . . . "

"Lies, all lies!"

“I swear, I would never do anything like that. You could ask him, too, and he’d say the same thing. Ask anyone, they must’ve heard me scream,” Sophie continued, insistent. “Please, I would never hurt Adrian, I would never disrespect you or Eric or Margot like that, I swear.”

“As I said—a mother knows.” Olympia released her and stood before her imperiously. “Now then, it’s been a terrible week and I don’t want to cause my family any more distress,” the old woman said. “So you will keep this between us and you will be on your *best* behavior. I will be watching your every move. One misstep and I’ll cast you out into the mountains. Do you understand?”

Sophie nodded, even as her entire being wanted to protest.

“And after Raul is finally laid to rest, you will leave and you will end things with Adrian,” Olympia commanded, not even seeking a reply. “You will forget you ever met this family and we will never see your face ever again.”

APRIL 14

HOLY MONDAY

THAT MORNING, THE PALASPAS NEEDED TO BE gathered for burning. The woven palms—painstakingly stripped and braided, tied with twine and ribbon, displayed to usher in Christ's return and eventual death—were to last only a few days before being thrown to the fire. Javier had been taught why they needed to be burned, both in Catholic school and by his mother, but he'd long forgotten. All he knew was that the task of going around the manor and taking the palms down from their hangings would give him the opportunity to see Dante again.

He couldn't get enough of the boy after last night. After everyone had retired, the two of them rendezvoused in the silong, finding their way past vaulted stone ceilings that looked like a dungeon's, through a maze of chambers for grain storage or laundry, long-emptied maids' quarters, and storerooms filled with old furniture—broken chairs, scuffed end tables, bureaus and artwork in outmoded styles, idols on pedestals, all covered in thick beige drop cloths. All the things a great house would want to keep out of sight.

The two men fumbled around in the dark of one of these storerooms. They didn't bother to uncover what looked like a divan before they fell into it, enfolded in each other's arms, their wine-laced breaths heavy in anticipation.

"It's all right," Javier said as he cupped Dante's chin, his reluctance visible in the faint moonlight streaming through a barred window. "Connor and I aren't together anymore."

"You're still married, though. I don't . . . it doesn't feel right."

Javier stifled a laugh. There he was, twice the other's age, and master of the house, too. There they were, in his ancestral home, with his entire family right above them, gathered on the occasion of his father's funeral, about to engage in acts that any dyed-in-the-wool Catholic household would find profane. The fact that he was married was, in his mind, the least objectionable thing about what they intended to do. Why did this kid think marriage had anything to do with fucking?

"I told you, we're separated. And he's the one who left me," Javier answered patiently. "Believe me, he doesn't care what I do. Or who I do it with."

Javier disrobed Dante and saw that he was fitter than he appeared through his work clothes. He was smooth too, and his youth seemed more pronounced by the way he quivered as they kissed, and then in the way he writhed as Javier took him in his mouth, the way he moaned faintly, suppressing his pleasure.

There, too, had been a tentativeness to the way Dante took control when it was his turn, an almost virginal vacillation. Javier had not seen that in ages, and it thrilled him. Sex with Connor had long grown old and predictable. That was the reason Javier strayed. He traded the security of his marriage for that thrill: the push and pull, the risk of failure, the unexpected surprise. He craved the transgression, the sense that he was taking something he rightfully shouldn't. That he was getting more than he deserved, and getting away with it.

Even after they both were completely spent, lying in the

dark, guarded by hooded saints, Javier craved more, and he wanted it as soon as humanly possible. Yet the driver had other duties, and he'd been absent all morning. Javier roamed the manor, picking off one palaspas after another and gathering them in a canvas sack, but he had no luck bumping into Dante.

Javier saved the sala mayor for the end of his circuit. It wasn't just because of the putrescent air, though that certainly didn't help matters; at least it hadn't gotten worse overnight. He had been avoiding the room since he arrived, unable to gaze upon his father's pale face without reeling in disgust. Each time Javier caught a glimpse of him, he felt the sharp stab of mortality, of old age and decrepitude and senility, things he wasn't yet ready to confront. Both in his life and in his father's unexpected death, too much had been left unresolved.

The old ladies prayed the rosary at the corner of the sala farthest from the casket. They flapped their fans furiously; Divina wore a thicker veil too. Javier bowed his head as he walked past them, covering his nose. The lilies had wilted and needed to be replaced. He held his breath as a breeze blew in, snuffing one of the candles. His mother asked him to relight it, once more ignoring his repeated suggestion to move the entire candelabra away from the window.

A palaspas had been hung on the wall above the open lid of the casket. Javier tiptoed to reach it and undid the knot that tied it to an ornate hook. His hand slipped. The palm fell onto his father's face, eliciting a gasp from his auntie. Javier himself was startled, then distressed: The fanned end of the palaspas had stabbed his father's cheek.

He slowly extracted the blades of the palm, fearing the damage. His father's skin looked taut and thin. Too thin.

Olympia came up to the casket and found three slashes marring his husband's jaw. "What in God's name? Look what you've done! Why can't you be more careful?"

Divina joined her and crossed herself. "Dios mio, his face! We need to fix him!" Her head turned frantically, searching the room for some sort of solution.

"I'm sorry, I'm sorry," Javier said, fending off Olympia's slaps at his arm. "I think—we might be able to—"

He didn't get the chance to finish his thought. He fell silent, and so did the two women, struck with dread. The dead man's cheek appeared as though it was moving. Its ashen surface seemed to ripple around the fresh punctures.

Javier blanched.

Raul's skin began to stretch. Then, from underneath, sharp, black barbs emerged. Legs and antennae and horns strained the slashes, which grew wider and wider until they formed one big hole, exposing what was beneath: a wriggling nest of tiny, horned beetles. They crawled all over Raul's yellowed teeth, his blackened gums, the gray flesh and the flaps of skin hanging on to bone. The cadaver was rotting, more quickly than it should have been; indeed, as though the body had never been embalmed at all.

"My husband!" A moan came from Olympia's throat, ending in a wretched cough as she sank to her knees. Her eyes rolled toward the back of her head.

The beetles crawled all over Raul's pale face, down his collar and the casket's satin lining. The stench of decomposition overwhelmed the room. Olympia crumpled limply to the floor, Divina herself struggling to keep upright.

"Holy fuck!" Javier yelled. He dropped the palms he held and slammed the lid shut. The loud thump echoed, and a gust of miasma issued from the casket. Javier stumbled backward, disoriented, fighting and failing to calm his gut. He retched violently, spewing last night's dinner onto the floor.

Sophie stayed locked up in her room, leaving only to use the bathroom. She told Adrian that the odor made her feel like vomiting any moment. It was half true: The events of the night before made her sick to her stomach. When he reported that his lola would no longer wait to bury his lolo, all she said was "That means we can leave sooner."

Adrian recoiled in shocked dismay. Sophie apologized, but never went as far as to explain herself.

But for once, the Sepulvedas were in agreement. The grisly sight of Raul's rotted face outweighed any need for a priest to sanctify him. The pit had been ready for days, Javier reported, before reiterating that a subsequent service, though not ideal, was completely acceptable under Catholic tradition. No matter; Olympia herself didn't need convincing. Once she recovered from her fainting spell, she readily said yes to the plan, rain or shine, guests be damned. Her husband had to be laid to rest, the sooner the better. She so declared with a pained resistance in her voice, and not a small amount of terror. There could be no clearer reminder of the family curse than the devil's beetles, and now they had invaded the family home.

The casket was shut, as were most of the windows, to keep out the smoke from the fire that the groundskeeper had started in the yard. That was what the farmhands did to keep pests at bay. Eric remarked it was too little, too late, but allowed Tiago anyway; the smoke might at least help with the smell.

Along with the news, Adrian brought Sophie a light lunch of scrambled eggs and pan de sal. Sophie barely touched them. Adrian worried that it might be more than the malodorous air causing her nausea and suggested she wear a face mask, as he and some of the family had begun doing since Margot fell ill. Sophie told him no. It would only worsen how she felt: trapped.

"How's your mom doing?"

"All right, I think," he answered. "I should check on her.

But Dad says she's gonna be fine. She's a real trooper, plus we have enough meds."

Adrian's mention of his father only increased Sophie's paranoia. Sophie considered uncovering the peephole and using it herself, to see if Olympia was around. Was she coming? Was she listening in at this very moment? She did say she'd be watching every move.

Adrian wiped the sweat off Sophie's brow. She swore she sensed a tremor of hesitation in his touch. Did his lola tell him about last night? What did she say? Sophie reminded herself that he'd never been the kind to avoid difficult conversations. That was more her style. Unlike her, Adrian would've brought it up if Olympia had repeated her accusations to him. He would have started a *conversation*. Besides, he could never hide his feelings well. For better or worse, his face always made them plain.

It had been impossible, for example, to hide how heartbroken he still was when the two of them first started seeing each other. Sophie hadn't had enough experience with boys to know how someone on the rebound acted, but if she had to guess, it would be exactly the way Adrian carried himself on their third date. He danced around the topic of exes, waxing philosophical about the fleeting nature of young love. Still, from the way he gulped down his Shiner Bock at the end of his sentences, Sophie detected that he hid some fresh wounds.

As he escorted her through the main quad back to her dorm, Adrian told her he was "on the precipice" of getting over his ex. He'd been cheated on, and apparently not once, but every time he'd been in a relationship, so the wounds were not only fresh but deep. He told her he'd understand if she didn't want to date someone with some baggage, and he didn't want to withhold it from her either. The disclosures only endeared him more to her, and they invited Sophie to share her own string of disappointments. High school sweethearts who toyed with her feelings, boys who didn't know what they wanted. Boys who didn't quite show their emotions or share their thoughts the way Adrian did. That night, they discovered that as much as she was able to read him, Adrian also read Sophie. He could tell there was something she wanted to know, but she let him keep it to himself for a while longer. He found it overwhelmingly generous and kind.

That was the moment he began falling for her, Adrian had told her much later.

"Do you regret bringing me here?" Sophie asked him now.

"What kind of question is that?" he said, nonplussed. "Babe, you're the only reason I haven't gone insane with everything going on. What's this about?"

"It's just that . . . we haven't talked about the fight since, well, since it happened."

Sophie regretted dredging the issue as soon as the words left her lips. "It's settled," that was what they'd both said as they boarded the Gulfstream. "We're not bringing this with us halfway around the world." Now here she was bringing it up again.

She already said she'd forgiven his insensitivity, his refusal to ease a longstanding insecurity, let alone talk about it. He should have known how rejected his choices made her feel, but he'd kept brushing her off and delaying her with promises. Worse, he hadn't said an honest word about why. She had her guesses: She was not rich nor "de buena familia," she was adopted, she was Filipina, maybe all of the above. When the bouts of insecurity were at their strongest, her suspicions became less attuned with reality: Maybe she wasn't smart, pretty, tall, slim, shapely, cultured enough. By omission, he had let her feel all these inadequacies. He let her feel unworthy of his family's approval, and instead of assuring her, he evaded and made excuse after excuse. She'd forgiven his lies, but only after a knock-down, drag-out shouting match.

He, too, had already said he'd forgiven her, though not

without throwing his grievances in her face. How she'd kept her resentment from him and let it simmer for months. How she'd claimed she understood his reasons whenever he declined her entreaties to spend time with his family, who lived not too far from campus, one bridge away from the city. She'd pretended to be fine with separate holidays, vacations, breaks, and she had never pressed the issue, claiming that one short afternoon during Stanford Family Weekend was enough for her. It was almost saintly, she admitted, the way he handled the whole thing.

He'd only just heard about his lolo's death. He was to drive up to Belvedere ASAP and pack for a funeral halfway around the world. She couldn't have picked a fight at a worse time, and a lesser man wouldn't have indulged what she now viewed as a child's tantrum. Still, in the end, the tactic worked. She was in the Philippines. She was with the Sepulvedas. She got what she wanted.

"Babe, I put it behind me the second our plane got off the ground," Adrian assured her. "I want you here. I *need* you here. And yes, I messed up. I should have brought you to meet the family sooner. Is that what's still bothering you?"

The question came without a hint of frustration. It was an invitation to open up. Yet there was no right way to tell him how unhinged his grandmother was, especially now.

Sophie hung her head low. "Ignore me. I'm being silly, worrying for no reason. It's nothing, really. I'm just a little loopy from basically being asphyxiated by the stink."

"Babe, I'm so proud of you and I'm so proud to be with you. I'm sorry I made you think I was keeping you away from my family. And I'm sorry I made you feel like I was ashamed of you," he said, then took a sharp breath. "If anything, the way they've been acting, it's them I should be ashamed of."

She couldn't argue there.

Adrian kissed her forehead. "I love you. You know that, right?"

Sophie nodded. His words were a balm. It didn't matter what Olympia thought. She was mistaken, and besides, Adrian needed her. He loved her. That was all that mattered. She felt sanguine, so eager to forget and move on, that she decided in that moment never to tell Adrian about the night before.

Tiredness soon overcame Sophie, and Adrian tucked her in for a siesta. She needed rest to fend off whatever she was coming down with, he said, plus she had to muster her strength for the funeral tomorrow. The reminder that she'd have to dress up, partake in a somber ritual, endure the outpouring of grief, and stand in Olympia's presence didn't faze Sophie at all. She fell asleep easily, and had the most restful nap she'd had in ages.

The smell of burning leaves wafted throughout the manor, mingling with the fetid air. It roused Sophie, and when she opened her window, she saw Tiago and Dante feeding dead leaves and twigs into the fires of a steel drum. Farther off, Remedios stood by her thatched roof cottage, doing the same. Unlike her son and spouse, she held green leaves, not dead. She dropped them into the drum with an air of ceremony. The curious display impelled Sophie to leave her room and sneak down the back stairs leading to the veranda, hoping no one spotted her as she went.

Once she'd crossed the lawn and gotten closer, she saw that the caretaker was in fact burning the palaspas. Remedios pulled her shawl more closely around herself, tossing one of the woven palms into the fire, which burned as red as the sunset sky.

"Why are you doing that?" Sophie asked, peering into the drum. It contained a wire mesh and some sort of pan that collected debris.

"You know Ash Wednesday? This is where the ash comes from," Remedios said. "The parish will use this for Lent next year."

"Oh, yes. I remember that from church," Sophie replied, making a crossing motion with her thumb.

Remedios took a palaspas from the basket by her feet. Sophie bent down and took one for herself. She threw the thing into the drum and watched as the flames licked its shiny green blades.

The caretaker regarded Sophie approvingly. "Ashes to ashes, dust to dust."

Sophie thought back to what her parents had taught her about Lent, about this time of suffering through reflection. She recalled how old Reverend Hansen's spastic thumb branded her forehead with a thick, black smudge that barely resembled a cross. It made her and all the other churchgoers look like they were member of some sinister cult. *It is a reminder of our death*, her mom had told her. *How we are all mortal*. "For we are dust and to dust we shall return."

Even the palms themselves were part of the cycle: heralding the end of one Lenten season, to be destroyed and used for the next one. When all the palms had been cast into the fire, the two women stood there, waiting for them to turn to ash.

"You should leave this place," Remedios told her, breaking the silence. Her tone had an evenness and certitude, as though the remark was not a matter of dispute.

"What? Why?"

The caretaker looked up at the villa, at the shadows of the people who moved around its rooms. "I know what happened last night. With you and Doña Olympia." She made a circle with her fingers and put it over her eye. The peepholes. "There's one in the kitchen."

"No, you have to understand—what she said isn't true. I wasn't trying to—"

Remedios waved her off stiffly. "And you've been seeing Alondra?"

"Yes," Sophie answered, confused. "I thought you said . . . "

"That is not a good sign. The storm, the beetles, Ma'am Margot getting sick . . . what happened to Don Raul's face . . . " The old woman crossed herself somberly. "And now Doña Olympia has it out for you. As if the curse was not enough."

Sophie insisted on her innocence, denying she had designs on Eric. Olympia had gotten it all wrong. Eric was trying to help her, and not a minute had even passed before Olympia came upon them. Remedios took in the explanations, and the smoke began to sting her eyes. After Sophie had gone on for some time, Remedios finally spoke.

"I believe you."

The doña had always had a darkness to her, the caretaker explained, one Olympia took pains to hide from everyone, even herself. Remedios knew it and had seen it most of all. She had always been loyal to the Sepulvedas, and her gratitude could never expire. The Sepulvedas had fed and sheltered her and her family for generations. "But they did other things too," she said. "Things that outweigh a lifelong debt of gratitude."

"What do you mean?"

"Tell me what you saw last night."

Sophie described her nightmare: Alondra looking like she did in the photograph, the boys and the sludge and the heads of coconuts. She also recounted how Alondra had appeared to her on previous nights, a dark specter stalking her. Remedios grew more concerned with every detail.

"What they've told you about the curse—they didn't explain it correctly." Remedios massaged her palm with her thumb. Her eyes glistened in the firelight. "Doña Divina said it was because of a coconut tax that they had nothing to do with. Well, that's not the end of the story. To the contrary, that was only the beginning."

OCTOBER 1985

SINCE VILLA SEPULVEDA'S RESTORATION FOR THE grand wedding, Remedios always took the long way. Down the east lawn, around the gazebo, and past the stone fountain. From the front, she could admire the manor fully: the roof that shone as vibrant as the flesh of those tangerines that her amo adored; the twinkling capiz, each square individually buffed; the double doors freshly stained, no longer weathered, their angelic carvings looking sharper and more lifelike. The adobe masonry looked sturdy, too, and where there was brickwork, each block looked fresh from the kiln. What was old seemed young again. Or was she merely gazing upon her beloved villa with new eyes?

With a lightness of spirit, she went in through the zaguan and made her way into the supply room. She set aside the feather duster, the brooms (walis tingting and tambo), the bunot for polishing the veranda's azulejos, the bars of red and clear wax, the piles of rags. She had a longer than usual to-do list that day, but that didn't faze her. A party in Villa Sepulveda was its own cause for celebration, even for a maid. After all the dusting and waxing and sweeping, there'd be music and dancing. Not with the Sepulvedas, of course, but the sound from the upstairs speakers would reach the silong, where the help had their own party. The beer and tuba were freely shared between upstairs and down, and the family let them have some of the leftovers too. They were generous that way.

So lost in her daydreams, Remedios didn't notice the man that crept behind her until he grabbed her by the waist, his tickles sending her into peals of laughter. Tiago spun her around and raised her arm, swung it around his neck.

"Huh huh huh huuuh-hi . . ." he sang as he slow danced with her. They'd danced to Spandau Ballet at their wedding not a season past. It was a modest one, infinitely so compared to Señorita Divina's, but to Remedios, it was no less romantic.

"Stop it," she said, her swaying hips belying her protest. "We have a lot of work to do and I'm already running behind. Nanay is gonna be mad."

"Oh, my wife. My beautiful, worrisome wife," Tiago said, still humming. She wiped the sweat from her husband's brow, in awe of her fortune. How was she blessed with such a handsome, caring, hardworking man? The maid and the gardener. It was a tale as old as time. "She won't even notice. She's too busy yelling at the others."

"You know, Lena still doesn't know how to cook rice without the bottom getting burnt? And Nieves, well, she just moves too slow."

"Everyone's slow compared to your nanay."

Remedios giggled. As far as mayordomas went, no one worked harder, faster, and better than Trining. No one yelled louder either, and not even being her daughter spared Remedios from her sermons. If anything, she got it worse than the rest of the staff under her mother's command.

"These new ones aren't so bad. Nice girls," Remedios said,

despite herself being years their junior. She'd grown up in the cottage in the shadow of the villa, raised by its caretaker; that history, coupled with youthful arrogance, made Remedios feel as though she were their equal, if not above them, at least in experience. "Easy to talk to, which makes for lighter work. They spook easily, though."

"Nanay Trining still scares me too, and I live with her. Or did you mean our new boarders?" Tiago smirked.

For the past two weeks, the silong had become a sort of barracks for Don Claudio Sepulveda's men. The general had home leave from Camp Crame and descended on the villa with six of his trusted underlings. Caught unaware of the additional arrivals, the Sepulvedas made space by asking the more senior staffers—the driver, the nanny, the groundskeeper—to vacate their quarters and stay with their families in town for the month, paying them extra for the inconvenience. There were more than enough empty rooms in the upper level, but Olympia wouldn't cede them to the invasion of boisterous soldiers. The men lazed during the day, saving their energies for their nightly drinking sessions on the veranda. They liked to tease the help, but it was all in harmless fun, at least thought Remedios, whom the men mostly left alone.

"Can't be easy having to share the silong with the army," her husband continued. "They must be terrified."

Remedios nodded. Lena and Nieves did complain about the snoring and the smells and horseplay, but that wasn't what she meant. It was Don Claudio that had struck the fear of God in her coworkers from the very moment he arrived, and they'd been terrified of him since.

The three maids had been present when the general marched up the grand staircase in his regalia, incandescent with rage. As soon as Raul came to greet him, Don Claudio berated him, ranting about the farmers' blockade on the highway into town. He'd heard rumblings, and the rumors had reached Manila, but he couldn't believe that his son had allowed the protest to get so out of hand.

"What the hell kind of place are you running here? Have I taught you nothing?" Don Claudio had yelled, smacking Raul upside the head. The soldiers laughed, too comfortable in the presence of their superior. "Never in our entire history have we had a strike!"

News traveled slow on an archipelago, especially as the president and his friends had control of major media outlets. However, what happened in Escalante did reach the villa swiftly; the island of Negros Occidental was nearby, and the sugar farmers' protest was massive. Remedios couldn't imagine that there could be five thousand people who hated the president that much; every time he visited with the Sepulvedas, he always seemed so courtly and benevolent. She'd also never heard the terms "tear gas" or "casualty" before.

The flames of dissent jumped two narrow straits and reached her island in short order. They saw Escalante's bloody end, and despite it, or perhaps because of it, the peasants at Sepulveda Farms rose up as well. *We suffer just as much as the sugar workers of Escalante*, they protested. Worse, they'd also been bamboozled: Years after thousands of farmers paid millions of pesos, they saw none of the promised benefits of the coconut levy and its fabled fund. None of them were any closer to owning their own plots of land. The peasants at Sepulveda Farms never had any proof, but they knew the fund was a large-scale scam that went all the way to Malacañang Palace, and they were certain the Sepulvedas were part of it. The placards that lined the highway, written in black and red ink, charged both families equally: *Marcos diktador! Sepulveda kurakot! Nasaan ang coco levy? Justice for Escalante!* A lengthy poster listed the names of corporations that got capital infusions from the fund, all of them owned by Marcos cronies:

San Miguel, Purefoods, Shell, Planters Bank, Clear Mineral, Marcopper Mining. In block letters and underlined on the bottom: Sepulveda Holdings.

Remedios didn't know whether her amos stole from the fund or not. She didn't want to know. The matter was between the family, the farmers, and the law.

With a maddening sort of helplessness, she'd watched Raul's father call him names. *Spineless! No-balls! Inutil!* At the time, Raul might have been a tad young to use the title "Don," but he was in fact the master of the villa and the farm. He also happened to be the provincial governor, on whose shoulders it fell to resolve the strike that jeopardized his personal and political life. To Remedios, however, he was her kind and gentle amo, and even as the other maids had fled the sala in terror, she couldn't pry herself away. Raul's humiliation tore at her. She'd wanted to help him, to protect him, but all she could do was watch.

It was hard to explain why she felt the way she did, and so she didn't bother correcting Tiago. Anyway, he was partly right: Lena and Nieves feared a military man.

Remedios collected her cleaning supplies and placed them in a basket, holding the brooms and the duster under the crook of her arm. She looked out the window. "I think I'll start with the guest rooms today."

"I thought they didn't need tidying?"

"Exactly."

"Hiding from her, I see."

Remedios winked. "Just until after lunch is served. She'll probably cool down by then."

Tiago pecked her on the cheek before heading out of the zaguan. "Yeah, good luck with that."

It was shortly after his father's arrival that Raul decided to invite the strike leaders to Villa Sepulveda for a parley. He sent word through Melchior, his new brother-in-law, who still worked as an overseer on the farm: The governor is open to granting the farmers' demands in exchange for specific, but very minor, concessions. He makes no promises, but he asks for an opportunity to be heard. The strike has gone on long enough.

When they came down the mountain and passed through the town to pick up supplies, the labor leaders still deigned to speak with Remedios. She had denied any knowledge about the governor's proposed deal, which was accurate enough, and she most definitely had no clue whether the offer of truce was a ploy. Yet she also didn't hesitate to express her confidence, her almost instinctual readiness to believe what her amo said. When she heard that the parley would be more of a feast, well, that only cemented her belief. Whether it was to pay fealty to the president or to impress a new business partner, the Sepulvedas threw parties as much to celebrate as to win their guests over.

Not everyone seemed as enthusiastic as Raul, however, especially not the lady of the house. Yes, the banquet table would be overflowing, as at any other party Olympia had thrown. Even as she changed the sheets in one of the guest rooms, Remedios could hear the pig getting slaughtered in the dirty kitchen. One of the plantation's trucks had only just pulled in with crates of fresh produce and tuba. However, Olympia didn't drive the maids as hard with the cleaning, nor did she place an order for flower arrangements and centerpieces. Perhaps most tellingly, she didn't summon her favorite beautician from the capital. Between her and Divina, there'd been no excited tittering about dresses and jewelry. Olympia picked an ivory frock to wear; it was studded with sequins from head to toe, and its lush creaminess complimented the warmth of her amo's skin, but Remedios thought it was the least exciting thing in the lady's wardrobe.

It was going to be a different kind of party, and Remedios supposed that was to be expected. After all, Olympia was the governor's wife, and Miss Philippines 1972 before that. Divina was an heiress descended from a noble bloodline. No matter how much Raul emphasized the night's importance, one couldn't expect those women to welcome peasants in their home, let alone mingle with them. These particular peasants most of all.

"Liars, all of them," Remedios had heard Olympia tell Trining. "And crooks too, most likely. Remember to lock up the rooms until they leave."

Remedios didn't know lies from truth, and she didn't much care. She had other concerns, and besides, she'd heard too many stories about her amos and the Marcoses. They were all she knew. She was eighteen, born within president's long reign; she lived in Leyte, where the First Lady came from; indeed, she worked for a family that was related to the First Lady. Most of all, Remedios came from a family of loyalists. "He brought prosperity to our country," her mother never failed to remind her. No one told her the bad stories; all she ever heard were the good—good enough for those who didn't look too close or ask too many questions, good enough for those who didn't suffer, who were nourished by the administration. She had only just gotten married. She had a home and a future to think about.

The door slammed open and little Javier barged into the guest room, rushing around Remedios in search of something. He decided on a large chest in the corner, in which the linens were kept. He climbed into it, closing the lid on himself with effort. Remedios rolled her eyes, thinking of the sheets she'd have to refold, even rewash, if the kid's shoes got dirt on them.

"Ate Remy, could you close the door, please?" asked the muffled voice from the chest.

"You'll run out of air in there," she warned. Javier shushed her.

Once the door clicked closed, he whined, "Augh. It stinks in here."

"That'll be the mothballs."

Javier didn't reply. Remedios fluffed the pillows, counting down the seconds until the boy gave up and quit his hiding place. He and his kuya were adorable, but their antics could be so out of control, enough to give her pause about having a child of her own any time soon.

A knock came. "Oh, no, Señorito Eric, there's no one in here but me . . . " Remedios answered in a singsongy voice. Her mood soured when she turned to the open door.

Alondra.

"Sorry to bother," the nanny said in greeting. She raised her voice a little. "Javiiii . . . where are you . . . ?"

"Like I said, it's just me in here."

Alondra crouched and peeked under the bed. She whispered to Remedios, "Their mama wants them bathed before lunchtime."

"You better find him, then. Clock's ticking."

The chilly tone didn't deter Alondra, who searched the room, carefully stepping around Remedios as the latter went about her duties. To her credit, Alondra seemed genuinely enthusiastic about this game of hide-and-seek, the bathtime deadline notwithstanding. She'd always been so attentive with the kids, much more than Olympia, whom Remedios had never once seen pick up a ball or read a bedtime story. Alondra had only just turned twenty, and she was single besides, but she cared for Eric and Javier with a dedication that was almost maternal. Whenever Remedios considered the mothers she'd seen and known, something she did often of late, she recognized how they all fell short of the Sepulvedas' nanny. That secret admiration was enough for Remedios to tolerate her.

It, too, was enough for her to forget, however shortly, what Alondra was.

Unlike the rest of the staff, Remedios knew Alondra Duran outside of the villa. She'd been a couple of years ahead of Remedios at Maalin Elementary and then all the way through high school. They were never friends, and in truth, it was unfathomable that they could ever have been. Alondra was beautiful, smart, tenacious, and kind. Any girl would resent her, would resent the heavens themselves for showering another with so many gifts. Alondra was supposed to be ignorant; she was supposed to be ugly. She was supposed to be shunned. Instead, the opposite happened; her beauty and her open heart endeared her to all. Remedios struggled to compete for the boys' attention, which she considered more than enough justification for her dislike. Yet Remedios had another reason: Alondra came from a long line of mambabarangs.

She was a witch.

She lived with her parents and a teenage brother at the foot of the mountains. They all kept to themselves, which didn't help the family's reputation. The townsfolk claimed the Durans communed with spirits, with dark creatures that lurked in the forests, and though they showed their faces at San Isidro every Sunday, their churchgoing was viewed as no more than a cover for their vile deeds. Whenever some tragedy struck Maalin, it was blamed on the Durans as much as God's wrath. Remedios knew that not all witches were evil, but her teenage envy of Alondra's long and lustrous hair, clear complexion, and classic Filipina features only convinced the maid that Alondra was a demonya in disguise.

Alondra wanted to become a nurse, but her family was dirt-poor, more than most in that poor town in the poorest region of the country. Her grades weren't enough to lift her out of poverty, but the Sepulvedas were. At least their high school principal thought so when he recommended her to Olympia as a nanny for her two boys. At first, Alondra only worked at the villa in the summer. After she graduated high school, she lived in the villa full-time. She was assigned one of the maid's quarters in the silong, the one near the back stairs so she could quickly come up in case one of the boys had a nightmare and needed calming. She'd always planned to stay for a short time, only until she saved enough for college. She wanted to study in Cebu, at the University of the Visayas. Saving took longer than she'd thought, as she also supported her family, who, without her, could only afford to subsist on the crops they grew or foraged. And so, two years in, Alondra found herself still tending to the little princes Eric and Javier, chasing them around the villa and getting them out of trouble.

"Okay, I give up," the nanny declared after some time. "I guess Javi isn't here after all!"

A laugh-cough came from the chest and Javier sprang out of it, his head shrouded in a white sheet. "Boo!" he shouted at Alondra, who feigned utter shock. The boy then ran out the door, screaming and flailing his hands, throwing the sheet behind him.

"It's bath time, Javi," she yelled back. To the maid's surprise, Alondra didn't go after him. Instead, she bent down on the chest and started folding the linens Javier had left in disarray. "I'm sorry about this."

"It's fine, leave it."

Alondra kept folding, waving pillowcases in the air to straighten them. Remedios felt compelled to join her, if only to speed her departure along.

"The kitchen smells so good," Alondra said. "It's going to be quite the spread tonight, huh?"

"What, are you thinking of sticking around for it?"

"Well, your nanay's cooking is so good . . . "

"She said she'll set some trays aside for us in the silong." Remedios smiled, despite herself. "And it won't be just the live-ins. Everyone's staying late, I hear. That's what they said anyway."

"I can't. I'm needed at home before sundown." Though Alondra said it matter-of-factly, her words conjured in Remedios some sinister ideas about arcane rituals in the witches' shack. "But maybe there'll still be lechon left over when I come back Monday."

"Dream on."

"I do hope you have a fun time tonight."

The remark struck Remedios as condescension, like Alondra thought herself above such festivity. Above such company. She swiped the last of the sheets and folded it herself. "Yeah, well, it's sure to be fun now that you're not coming."

After a split-second look of surprise, Alondra left her with only a smile. That smile, sweet and unassuming like the ones she gave her wards, was just another one of her guises—and Remedios could see right through it.

That first Friday night in October, the Sepulvedas put out a banquet on the veranda: pancit, inihaw, lechon both baboy and baka, kaldereta, kare-kare, and many more dishes, much more than their twenty-odd guests could finish in an entire weekend. And of course, there was tuba. Jugs and jugs of coconut wine to lubricate the grub and loosen the tension on both sides of the bargaining table.

Remedios helped with service, laying out the platters that seemed to stretch from one side of the villa to the other. She attended to the guests with a smile, all the while thinking how ungrateful they were. She listened in on the conversations, the farmers' repetitive complaints, always asking for more, more, more. They claimed to receive so little after giving so much. They complained about the harvesting and the husking and the hauling. She knew those men and women; a few grew up in Maalin with her. She knew how they exaggerated, and she disdained it. They puffed up their chests and used harsh words, but in truth, they had come here to beg. Raul seemed accommodating toward them, almost obsequious, and Remedios disdained that too.

"No problem—we'll get new carts and trucks. Whatever needs upgrading," he offered the peasants.

"Carabaos, too? For those who are still hauling manually?" asked the weathered, bald man they called Ka Miroy, who dominated the conversation from the farmers' side of the aisle. "What about fertilizers, pest control?"

"The farm needs all those things, so you won't get any resistance from me. No delay either. We'll get on it as soon as the new year rolls around. And we'll build a brand-new warehouse, once we're past typhoon season."

The murmurs of assent signaled an auspicious start. Then came grousing about the income share, the sakadas stating that times were getting tougher under Marcos, and that the 60–40 standard was unconscionable. After some back and forth, Raul asked, "What numbers would you be happy with?"

"A hundred sounds nice," someone from the end of the table shouted, to a few laughs.

"40–60," Ka Miroy answered. Don Claudio, who'd been silent for the most part, snorted.

"Ah, Ka Miroy, you've been to the mercado. It's not like this is your first time haggling," Melchior answered, clicking his tongue. "Be more realistic. Didn't you tell me you'd die a happy man if you ever saw 50–50? An equal share . . . "

"Equal aside," Raul interrupted. "The farm will have a hard time meeting your other demands if it has less money coming in. I'm not saying no, but we need to consider these things."

"After everything's tallied up, we only get to take home a few hundred. A thousand if we're lucky. That's barely enough to buy rice and vegetables, not even meat," replied another sakada, grimacing at the chops and steaks in front of her. "And *we* need to consider those things."

More murmurs of agreement. One of the senior peasants spoke about his unpaid doctor's bills and having to rely on herbal tea for his pneumonia that never seemed to go away, followed by another talking about a missing brother. Raul listened patiently as the sob stories grew more melodramatic, and even the stone-faced Olympia looked affected, but Remedios tired of them quickly. Life's not fair. Everyone suffers in one way or another. They're not special, and they sure didn't deserve special treatment.

"Yes, all that, and we haven't even talked about the coco levy."

A hush settled on the table and everyone turned to the sakada who spoke.

"We don't have to dance around it. That's really what this night is about."

Remedios craned her neck from behind the column where she'd been eavesdropping. She knew that man. She'd seen him outside the villa dozens of times, usually around dusk, in the short lull between the end of the afternoon's labors and dinner time. He always came by riding his dinky motorbike that ran on crude oil and spewed ink-black smoke, waiting for a tryst with his lover. She knew exactly three things about him: His name was Hugo, he worked at the farm, and he was bewitched by Alondra.

Remedios was surprised to see him mixed up in this, and so vocal, too. He always looked so sheepish when he hung about the iron gate, expectant, and so childlike in his excitement whenever he saw Alondra coming down the driveway. Remedios had spied on the couple enough times to gain some measure of the man who blushed at every kiss and stared longingly at every goodbye; she never imagined he'd have another side to him. It felt like trickery, this new face he showed, and it made her mistrust him almost as much as she mistrusted Alondra.

"Look, I've been a sakada since I was old enough to swing a bolo," Hugo started. "I've been to Davao and Bukidnon and Samar, and I've worked for enough scheming hacienderos and sadistic overseers. Once, when I worked the pineapple farms, I spent a month locked up in the cellar after my amo heard that us peasants were planning a strike. They put eight of us in a tight room, with hardly any food and water and nowhere to relieve ourselves. That's where I'm coming from. These past two years working for the Sepulvedas were better than I've ever seen, but now I know it's all a lie." He raised his chin at the governor with disgust. "Even . . . this."

"Now, come on. We're giving you most of your demands."

"More empty promises. Isn't that how this all started?" Hugo turned to his comrades. "What was it Melchior said when he came to us, hat in hand? 'The governor wants to rebuild trust.' Well, you can't just do that by giving us more of the same."

"Tell me, then. How can I regain your trust?" Raul asked calmly.

"We want to see the books. New trucks and a slightly bigger cut don't matter, not if we're being taxed to fund your family's caprices." Hugo looked up at the manor, its columns and string lights. "These men and women here, we are the ones who work the land. We know how much it produces. We know the farm's profits couldn't possibly cover your lifestyle. Why, we all witnessed the 'wedding of the century,' didn't we, folks?" The other sakadas nodded, grunted their agreement.

"I heard you spilled eighty cases of champagne and slaughtered thirty of heads of cattle. Sixteen million pesos for a party, is that right? Did that feel like enough for the noble family to save face?" Hugo laughed. Divina looked like she might choke on her wine, and Melchior glared at the sakada, which only egged him on. "And didn't you just buy a mansion . . . in California? Thought you might hide your loot overseas, huh? Tell us, how can you afford all of that—all of this—after last year's harvest? All the workers are thinking it, not just the ones here present: You are thieves. Every single Sepulveda. And we don't want to deal with thieves no more."

"The books! Do you even know how to read, you piece of shit?" Don Claudio erupted. "Raul, you're not going to sit there and let this loko insult us, are you?"

"Papa, please—"

"I was the one who built that wealth. Me—and my late wife! That money is legitimate," Don Claudio said, jabbing a finger toward Hugo. "And you lowlifes can fuck off. Get up and get out of here!"

"No one's leaving. We are not done," Raul answered firmly. After a long pause, he turned to Hugo and Ka Miroy. "Fine. You can examine the books. We have nothing to hide."

"Tomorrow," Hugo quickly added.

"Whenever you want."

"And we want tenancy agreements too. In writing," Ka Miroy said, and he was met with groans from the Sepulveda side.

"What did I tell you about these people?" Don Claudio told Raul, rising from his seat. "You give them a finger and they'll take the whole damn arm! Come on, son, this whole meeting was a mistake. Let's cut our losses before I really get pissed off."

"Sit down, Papa! I'm the one making the decisions here. Not you."

To everyone's surprise, the general yielded. No one spoke for a while, and Hugo took the chance. With restraint, he explained, "The books are to regain our trust. The contracts are to correct a wrong. Like we said, this all comes down to the coco levy. We've been taxed for years with nothing to show for it but coupons and receipts. If you truly aren't stealing from the fund, that's one thing sorted. But Don Raul," the sakada said, gently, "You're the only person who can give your workers a better life. It won't be this government, we're sure of it. And we're not asking you to give up your land. We're just asking for a chance. For something we can hold onto that's real, not like those worthless IOUs that will never get settled. You keep saying you care for the people. You campaigned on it. And once upon a time, I believed you. Make me—make us—believe you again."

Hugo's conviction stirred sympathy, even inspiration, in Remedios, and by the time Raul stood and extended his hand, she was convinced. This was the right thing to do.

The governor shook with Hugo, then with Ka Miroy and the other leaders, who seemed just as stunned as the Sepulvedas sitting opposite them. "Have your inspectors come by my office tomorrow and I'll show you the accounts myself," he said. "Afterward, we can discuss the details of these tenancy agreements. You'll want to do it in order of seniority, I assume?"

Ka Miroy chuckled, wiping the sweat off his shiny pate. "Only seems fair."

"And the strike?"

"We'll report back to work after we see the books," Hugo told Raul, his tone no softer. "But if anything goes south, we're back on the streets quicker than lightning. In bigger numbers, too."

Melchior wedged overflowing tumblers of tuba between the two, spilling on the grilled shrimp. "Enough of that—I think it's time for a toast, no?"

The mood instantly turned celebratory. The Sepulvedas and Don Claudio's men feasted, swapped stories and commiserations. Kuratsa music played, and the inebriated soldiers danced with each other and the sakadas. Remedios caught sight of Hugo, who gave her a lopsided smile of recognition.

For a flash, she again saw the Hugo she'd grown to recognize, the shy yet devoted suitor who apparently knew how to win both hearts and minds.

She hung around in the silong for a while, partaking with Tiago and the rest of the staff, while Lena and Nieves did double duty: The new maids shuttled between parties, heading up to the kitchen and down, out the screen doors into the veranda and back into the silong, refilling plates and trays and cups and jugs of tuba. They still managed to enjoy themselves, swaying and cha-cha-cha-ing as they weaved between the guests, and thankfully, their duties got lighter the later it got. Remedios would have helped, but being the caretaker's daughter and newly married too, she earned the privilege of being dismissed early.

Midnight passed and the party showed no signs of abating. The farmers and the soldiers played a drinking game that involved balancing a copita on one's forehead, while the old-timers talked about the next year's elections. The general's spirits seemed to have lifted too, red-faced not out of his usual rage, trading cockfighting tips with Ka Miroy.

In time, fatigue caught up with Trining, and after she retired, the silong party started to dwindle. The help who'd been temporarily kicked out of their quarters tipsily loaded onto a tricycle back to town, and even Tiago, who could drink anyone under the table despite his lanky frame, soon sought his bed as well. Arm in arm, he and Remedios ambled up the north lawn, humming along to the fading music as they entered their cottage.

That night, Remedios crawled into bed with a full belly and a full heart. She didn't think tonight's party would be so unlike the ones she'd seen before. The usual trappings and merriment aside, there was an infectious sense of relief, like a lid had been lifted off a wildly boiling pot. There, too, was the sense of hope: of things getting better for the farmers, of things returning to normalcy for the Sepulvedas. Everybody happy. She let that feeling carry her off to sleep, nestling herself in the arms of her Tiago.

It wasn't long until she found herself awake again. The sound could have been easy to misplace, especially that night. There'd been bottles of champagne next to the whiskeys and the tuba. Corks had been popped, startling the maids giddy. Yet Remedios recognized it, even from the depths of slumber. She'd grown up in that villa. Before the general got promoted to Camp Crame, she'd seen and heard his weekly target practice.

She roused Tiago, who rose when more gunshots rang out. They both peeked out the window.

The music had stopped but the lights were still on. Figures paced the veranda, much fewer than when the couple left the party. Even from afar, Remedios spotted the glint off the sequins from Olympia's gown. She stood next to Raul. Remedios sighed in relief. "They're safe," she told her husband.

"Someone else might be hurt."

Remedios scampered to her nanay's room. Trining was fast asleep. So assured, Remedios and Tiago left the cottage and went across the lawn buzzing with trepidation.

Her mind raced with possibilities, possibilities that narrowed the closer they got to their destination. Once it became clear what had happened, it was too late. Raul and Olympia had spotted them; so did Don Claudio, flanked by his men.

With a vexed look on his face, the general beckoned the couple to approach. They both cowered in fear. Remedios had the thought to run.

"Don't make me ask again," Don Claudio barked.

Fearing for their lives, the maid and the gardener stepped

onto the veranda and into the middle of a massacre. Sakadas were slumped across the table, over chairs, on the steps, and on the green. Their mouths frothed. The darks of their eyes rolled into their heads as they convulsed on the cold of the azulejos. A few moaned for help, but their sputtering pleas died in the open vast. A cadet walked over to one of them and shot the peasant in the head. Hugo. Remedios buried her face in her husband's chest.

"What have you done?" she heard Tiago say.

"You're here, and you already know, so you might as well get to work," the general answered. Behind him, two soldiers carried jugs of tuba in each hand, pouring their contents on the grass. The peasants never stood a chance. Their bolos were still slung on their sides. They'd kept them close as they ate and drank and got lulled into complacency, but they couldn't have known, nor could they have resisted the drink.

By the soldier's feet, Remedios saw the hem of a maid's uniform. Lena. Right next to her lay Nieves. Both were riddled with bullet holes. Remedios wailed.

"Remy, tahan na muna," Olympia said in the soothing tone she usually deployed on her boys when they acted up. "We can cry later. Right now, we need flashlights. Do you think you could go get them from the silong, please?"

Remedios shook her head violently. "We won't say anything, we promise. Just let us go back home. Please don't make us—oh, God, please don't . . . "

"What's done is done," Don Claudio said, twisting the maid's wrist. "Now, do as you're told."

Tiago pulled the general away from Remedios. One of the soldiers approached, gun drawn, and with its butt he hit the groundskeeper. Tiago staggered back, blood gushing from the side of his head. He fell half kneeling to the floor. The soldier pointed the gun at him and asked Don Claudio, "Should I finish him off?"

Stop!" Raul yelled. "No one else needs to die."

He then came upon the general and asked him to release his grip on Remedios. Raul then took her aside, away from the commotion. "Remy, I don't want you to suffer the same fate as the others." He spoke with a gentle voice unbefitting the circumstances, and she took the words not as a threat, but as an expression of his loving concern.

"I can't . . . Please, don't ask me to . . . They're dead, they're dead and you all . . ." she said, her glance landing on the fresh bullet holes in Lena's gut.

"Nothing bad will happen to you, I swear on my life." He placed his hand on the small of her back, steering her into the silong. "Remy, I'm begging you. If not for yourself, do it for Tiago. Do it for me. *I* need your help."

She didn't nod or shake her head, and she didn't say anything. She didn't need to. All she needed was that plea, and a little push. Her feet took her the rest of the way.

When Remedios returned with the torches, Don Claudio was kicking the bodies, trying to confirm they were dead. He cursed as he went, decrying the lack of a more direct confrontation. He sneered at the use of poison. "Such a feminine way to kill," he told his soldiers. Still, he seemed satisfied with his son's accomplishment. He also seemed particularly proud of the manner by which Raul planned to dispose of the bodies, asking with some vigor, "Okay, anak, how do you want us to do this?"

Raul gazed out onto the lawn.

The swimming pool had been a balm for everyone in the villa, even the ones who were denied its use: the cooks, the driver, the nanny, the maids, and the landscapers. It exhilarated the farm workers too. The pool was visible from beyond the stone wall that separated the plantation, and the mere sight of its cool blue waters relieved their aching arms and broken backs. Remedios herself had often prattled with the other maids about dipping their toes into the water, as though it had some healing property. Skimming the surface was a taste of affluence, which was healing in its own right.

Still, part of her viewed the pool as an absurd extravagance, as preposterous as most things the Sepulvedas wasted their money on. The furniture, the artwork, the fancy clothes that were only worn once and never again.

She'd forgotten whose idea it was to build the pool, but if it was Olympia, well, she soon lived to regret it. Her sons had a knack for roughhousing and evading supervision. Drowning was a likely scenario and it wasn't worth the risk, her luaus and the magazine spreads be damned. It wasn't worth the expense either. The upkeep was costly given the villa's remoteness from any major city that had pool servicers. Plus, whenever typhoon season came, which lasted almost half the year, the pool inevitably got filled with muck. After the novelty had passed and all that remained were the burdens, Olympia demanded that it be emptied.

When the general came to the villa with his men, pushing his son to take charge of his "peasant problem," Raul found the perfect excuse to finally get around to the chore he'd been putting off for months.

The waxing moon hid behind a thick blanket of clouds. No one could see far past the veranda. The farmers couldn't have noticed that the blue waters they once admired were no longer there. Even if they did, they might not have thought anything of it. Remedios herself didn't, nor did she imagine what the pool had turned into.

The night also obscured what she had turned into.

Melchior stood next to her carrying a kerosene lantern. Remedios hadn't registered his presence until then; he seamlessly blended in with the soldiers and the Sepulvedas. He told Remedios to walk ahead of them, then told Tiago to help lift one of the bodies. Even out of the plantation, Melchior still played the part of foreman.

Remedios watched him intently. There was no ease in his manner—unlike the soldiers, for whom death and destruction were routine—but unlike Remedios, he also didn't act out of survival or servile piety. The grisly task was just another thing that needed doing to advance his interest, just like everything else he'd done that night, just like his marriage.

The women showed the way from the bloody veranda to the void in the north lawn as the soldiers, the governor, the general, the overseer, and the young groundskeeper hauled the dead by their limbs and flung them into the pit. Remedios shone the torch, her hands trembling as she stood right next to Olympia, who held her light steadily. Two sakadas were belatedly discovered to still be breathing, though barely. The soldiers saved their bullets and threw those bodies in too. Once done, everyone headed back to fetch the next batch.

As they lifted and hauled and marched and flung, the soldiers sang their cadences, tipsy with tuba and murderous glee. *Left, left, left right left . . . Ang panukat ng 'kano ay numero sais . . . and panukat ng Pinoy, tama na ang tres . . . Left, left, left right left.* The general led his men; Raul, notably, did not sing along. The men also remarked upon Lena and Nieves—the curves of their lifeless bodies, the peaceful, docile way they looked. They sang, laughed, made lewd retorts. Tiago tried to hide his mewling. Blood still dripped down his cheek. Melchior, not unkindly, assured the younger man that it was almost over.

After the bodies were cast into their gleaming white grave, they were covered in a mountain of dirt. Raul himself drove the dump truck. This was his design, and he saw it to completion. Melchior and the soldiers then leveled the ground, pounding the soil with shovels like hammering nails on a coffin.

By daybreak, the pool was no longer there, and neither were any signs of the prior night's carnage.

Still, Remedios had seen it all. It was her job to see and

make sure everyone saw. She saw the skulls crack as they hit tile; she saw bones break skin, crushed by the weight of their brothers- and sisters-in-arms. Their blood gushed and thinned in the remnant pool water, and the metallic smell commingled with chlorine. Her own limbs ached at the sight of disjointed legs and dislocated shoulders, the tangle of bodies that seemed to reach out from the pit of hell itself, reaching for the hand of salvation. It would never come for them, or for her.

The days that followed were a jittery blur. Remedios took on the bulk of the cleaning now that the manor was understaffed, and she ran on only the few hours of sleep that her nervous mind would grant her. The lying made things worse; as she did her chores, she needed to avoid her mother. Trining seemed to buy her daughter's story, especially after it was backed up by Melchior, that the new maids were abruptly fired after making a drunken scene at the feast, but somehow it didn't stop the caretaker's prying looks.

The dusting and the sweeping took longer, and Remedios's thoughts pulled her to the past and the future in turns. *What have I done? How could I? What will happen to me now? People will be looking. What if someone finds out?* She cut herself preparing the lemongrass, the stalk slipping from her trembling fingers as she peeled off the tough outer leaves. The sight of blood made her vomit.

It brought little comfort that the rest of the family seemed equally tormented. Olympia was more withdrawn from her sons than usual, and Divina overcompensated for her sister-in-law as a means of distraction. Raul, whom Remedios had never once seen angry, marched up and down and all over the house, snapping at his wife, arguing with his father or his men, barking at his staffer on the phone. Everything seemed to get on his nerves. Eventually he withdrew to his office and forbade everyone from bothering him, his kids included. He also forbade anyone from coming to the villa.

Tiago was the one refuge in the storm. He and Remedios didn't talk about the feast, but he shared the same look of suffering in his eyes. He hid it behind his usual playful smile. He was gentle when he spoke with her, and he gave her space as they went about their work in the manor. But at night, as they lay next to each other, Remedios couldn't help inching away from him. How could he stand her after what she'd done? It never crossed her mind that he might have the same fears as her.

She had never missed church in her life, except that Sunday.

On the third day, Alondra returned to the manor as expected. Yet she didn't come to tend to the boys. She came to Villa Sepulveda screaming bloody murder.

"Let me in," she yelled as she rattled the gate. "I know what you did!"

Tiago was the first to see her. He tried to calm her down, but the woman couldn't be appeased. Despite his refusal, she begged Tiago to let her in. Soon, Remedios came down the stairs, drawn by the racket. Fear struck her as she made out Alondra's words, and once she reached the gate, she saw the tender, pitiful way that her new husband looked at Alondra, and an instinctual jealousy burned in her breast.

"What are you talking about, you madwoman?"

"The sakadas. I know something is wrong, and it's their doing." She pointed an accusing hand at the manor.

"Would you please keep it down?" Tiago asked, looking behind him.

"Please, where is Hugo? Where is everyone? I just want to talk to them."

"They all left here at dawn. Drunk off their minds," Remedios answered. "We don't know where they are."

"Then why can't I come in?" Alondra spat, shaking the

gate with unusual strength. "I know you're lying. Hugo hasn't been home since Friday. None of them have. The Sepulvedas are keeping them prisoners, aren't they? Are they torturing them?" She screamed toward the manor, "They won't give up, you know!"

Remedios pried Alondra's fingers from the iron grills, kicking her through the gaps. Through the struggle, none of them noticed the man coming down the driveway.

"What the hell are you doing?" Raul asked Tiago and Remedios. To their surprise, the governor unlocked the gate and uncoiled the chain. "Why haven't you let her in?"

"But you said . . ."

"—not to let outsiders in. Alondra isn't an outsider," Raul scolded them. "And she's always welcome here."

Warily, the nanny stepped through the gate. Raul escorted her inside, patiently listening to her barrage of questions. Remedios trailed after them.

"Please, sir, I need to speak with Hugo. Is he here? This is the last place he went . . . What time did he leave?"

Alondra's agitation grew with each step, further stoked by Raul's glib nonanswers. *They left, I don't know, must have been after I fell asleep, it went late*, all the same lines Tiago and Remedios tried feeding her. By the time she reached the front door, Alondra was convinced the governor was lying too. She stormed into the manor, yelling all sorts of accusations.

Divina came out of her bedroom, her nephews in tow. "Do you know where they are? Where is your kuya holding them?" Alondra asked her as they reached the sala. "What did he do to them?" Divina was stunned silent, and Alondra grabbed Eric, all of nine years old.

"Where is Hugo? You've seen him, right? You know, the people who were here at the party?" The boy shook his head anxiously. His younger brother bawled, fearful and confused.

Don Claudio intervened, wresting his grandson away

from her. He turned to Raul and gave him an imposing look: *This one is going to be trouble.* Alondra missed it, but the look struck Remedios with terror.

"For the love of God," Remedios willed under her breath. "Stop making a scene."

"Don't worry about this, Papa," Raul said, now needing to placate him too. "She's just a little heated. And confused. She's not usually this way." He then turned to Alondra. "Can we please take a breath? Look, you're scaring the kids."

The plea worked. Alondra seemed to compose herself, the fire behind her eyes contained for now. She then declared evenly, "I'd like to search the house."

"Go ahead," Don Claudio taunted, not a little impressed by the nanny's audacity.

"If you must," Raul said. "I'll go with you."

Alondra went through every room. Raul opened each door, closet, and crawlspace for her. In the silong, he unlocked the maids' empty rooms and the soldiers' temporary quarters. He even asked Remedios to let Alondra search her home, much to the maid's vexation. Alondra found nothing.

After they left the cottage, Alondra didn't ask to search any other places. She looked defeated, and despite her relief that this episode was over, Remedios herself felt a sense of loss. Part of her had wanted Alondra to find her answers. So what if it all came out? She was young, and she'd been forced into it. Maybe the consequences would be easier to bear than the secret.

Raul and Remedios led Alondra back into the manor. When they walked past the north lawn, Alondra froze in her tracks. She paced toward a patch of fresh soil. The pool had been there; Alondra knew it all too well. It had only been a few weeks since she'd been pranked into "saving" Eric from drowning.

"When was it filled in?"

Met with silence, Alondra repeated herself. "When did you

fill it in? And why?" Her voice grew more frantic as her imagination seemed to run rampant. "What have you done? What have you bastards done?"

Alondra dropped to the grass and dug her fingers into the soil. Raul snatched her by the crook of her arm and tried to pull her up, but she was undeterred. Once again, he asked Remedios for help.

For too long a pause, the maid just stood there, looking on with distress and expectation. Alondra formed a hole in the ground, and as her digging went deeper, Remedios imagined it filling in with blood. She could hear it rushing from underground, feel the pressure building, raring to explode like a grisly volcano. By the time she snapped out of her vision, Don Claudio's men were already coming down on them.

Raul handed Alondra off, and the soldiers dragged her away kicking and screaming. He marched them all toward the west side of the manor. "Throw her out the gate," he said with a fraction of the command that his father would have had, "and make sure she never steps foot here ever again."

Remedios couldn't bear to watch. Her feelings about Alondra and her fear of getting caught didn't matter; she'd seen enough violence for one lifetime. She ran back toward the manor, heartsick.

On the veranda stood Eric, shaken but no less curious about what was happening. Remedios gathered him in her arms and tried to shield him from the sight, but the boy wriggled away. He hadn't warmed to her the way he had to Alondra, and his refusal felt like a verdict of the worst kind, since it had come from an innocent. It felt like he blamed Remedios for his nanny getting taken away. Getting hurt. He only took his eyes off Alondra to stare at Remedios bitterly, and then he ran off. The maid fled to the kitchen in tears, hiding, hoping to lose herself in her chores.

She saw Eric again much later, looking more shaken than

before. He stared out the window by the top of the grand staircase with a hollow look in his eyes. No, not hollow—haunted. Remedios called to him, asking where Javi was, as lunch would be ready soon, but the boy made no reply. She came closer, placing a hand on his shoulder, and this time, he didn't flinch from her.

"She's leaving," he said in a monotone. He pointed out the window. "Alondra's going away now."

Tears dampened his cheek. It took Remedios a long time to understand why the boy cried. She assumed it was because he would miss his nanny. He was very fond of her, yes, and Alondra mothered him more than Olympia herself, but a sense of disquiet told Remedios that there was more to it. His crying grew the farther Alondra went, and with his tears came a swell of foreboding in the maid's chest.

It also took Remedios a long time to understand why Alondra was only just then starting down the driveway, limping in the shadow of the fountain and the angel's broad wings.

"What happened?" Remedios asked the boy. "What did you see?"

She looked out the window again. Alondra was alone.

Remedios rushed down the stairs and chased after her. By the time Remedios reached Alondra at the gate, she still hadn't found the words. She held Alondra's hands, cold and clammy, and looked past the long, black hair framing her wan face, into her red-rimmed eyes that twitched like the weak, flickering light of a dying fire.

For the first time in their short lives, she felt a kinship with Alondra. There they both stood, on the villa's threshold, broken. Remedios cradled the woman in her arms. Alondra remained still, stiff, and her bones jabbed at Remedios as she tried to comfort her.

"Where are they, Remy?" Alondra asked, whispering.

Remedios hugged her tighter as though drawing strength from her. "Alondra, I . . . "

"What did *they* do to them?"

Remedios felt truth's insistence recede. Gravel crackled underneath approaching footsteps. "Nothing," she whispered back. "They didn't do anything. The sakadas aren't here. No one's here."

Alondra untangled from her and shoved her away. Remedios repeated herself, pleading. "I swear, they're not here."

Two cadets came toward them. Alondra retreated through the gate and tripped on the curb. Remedios rushed to help, but Alondra gestured for her to stop. She held herself upright on the asphalt and looked up at the villa, at the massive iron gate that slowly closed before her. Through spiked bars and rage-filled tears, she glared at Remedios in judgment.

Alondra crawled to the roadside and grabbed a handful of gravel. She flung it toward the villa. The pebbles clinked against the iron, and the sound was the sound of Remedios's own heart breaking.

"Gabaan kamo!" Alondra yelled as the gate clanged shut. "Gabaan kamo, mga putang ina!" *Gaba fall upon you!* She kept repeating it like an angry, anguished chant, the kind of chant that reverberated on stone walls, echoing through time.

Curse you all, you sons of bitches!

April 14

Holy Monday

Remedios clutched the scapular that hung from her neck, holding the icon of the Sacred Heart close to her breast. Then, she cried. For the last forty years, she cried and lit candles and said prayers for the eternal repose of those people's souls, all the while assuring herself she'd needed to comply. Resisting wouldn't have saved any of them. Resisting would have meant seeing the bottom of that mass grave herself. In the time since, she'd become less troubled by the selfishness of that notion. Still, she cried and begged forgiveness, from those whose names she knew by heart and those whom she never met until that night, her so-called grief as useful as a parasol in a storm. It didn't ease the burdens that those farmers carried in their lives and the next. It didn't bring them justice. By her hand, they'd become part of the desaparecidos, the unfortunates disappeared by the dictatorship and its legions.

She didn't know then, but even before that fateful night, the desaparecidos had already numbered thousands. The tales were that many of those people were not dead, as the Marcos loyalists claimed; they had decamped to the mountains to join the communist rebels, the New People's Army. There were rumors, too, that some had intentionally made themselves disappear, fleeing to other towns and countries, waiting for the president's death. These people were enemies of the administration; no doubt they were hiding from his wrath.

Most of the country was not so naïve as the young Remedios. It wasn't until after the People Power Revolution that she learned of the hundreds of eyewitness accounts of someone being snatched into an unmarked van, a canvas sack placed over their head, muffling their cries for help. Labor leaders, campus activists, journalists, protestors vanished without a trace. Every province had legends about this dilapidated warehouse or that remote cave system where the desaparecidos were taken and tortured as insurgents. The bed of every river was the alleged resting place of waterlogged bodies, mouths gagged, hands tied, feet shackled and weighed down with cinder blocks.

These were not far from the tales that would be told about the missing peasants of Maalin, Leyte. They were sick and tired of corruption and so they joined the NPA. They were still alive and plotting their return. This was easy enough to believe if one hadn't been paying close enough attention.

The sad truth was that the Sepulvedas' victims weren't desaparecidos at all. For decades, Remedios held on to this as much as her remorse. They had come to Leyte from all over the country. They were sakadas who went where there was work to be had, following the harvest and typhoon seasons. They were single and didn't have families, nor did they live in one place long enough to make friends, aside from the temporary bonds that formed in the workers' quarters they shared with a rotating cast who came and went, just as they all did. They were transient. No one missed them.

How could someone be disappeared when no one was looking for them?

How could they be disappeared when she knew where they were?

"Everyone always imagines they would have done better," Remedios told Sophie, her voice thin and reedy. She took the corner of her shawl and wiped her face dry. "That if they came face-to-face with evil, they would fight it with no reservations, even when that face turned out to be familiar. *Especially when*. But people are never as strong as their convictions."

"Alondra was. She had every right to curse this place."

The caretaker bowed her head. "Typhoon Saling came two nights after. Then came the pestilence, and the crocodiles, and the plague of malaria. After Melchior got crushed by coconuts, and after Don Claudio bled out of every hole in his head, Don Raul decided they should all flee to the States before the worst of the curse took more of them. I still remember when they left, exactly a week after People Power. The gaba yielded after that."

"What about Alondra? Did she really die like you said?"

"No one had seen or heard from her in months, but we felt her presence in every tragedy. Little did we know she was suffering a tragedy of her own. She was pregnant."

The caretaker paused, unsure. She allowed herself to be mesmerized by the fire while she decided. What the boy saw, what Remedios thought had happened—these would only stain the memory of an already tragic figure. Alondra deserved more than that. She deserved more from Remedios, then and now.

"Alondra was pregnant and always seemed on the verge of miscarriage, the parish priest told us. She bled constantly and grew weaker every day. She endured this for four months until her body gave out and she lost her life, as well as her child's. It was a boy."

The flames glinted in the damp of the girl's eye.

"They were buried in the mountains, near the Durans' old shack. The family wasn't allowed to do that, but Father Tomas took pity and still blessed the bodies. Her parents and brother moved to Biliran shortly after that."

Some days, Remedios looked out of the veranda onto the mountains and thought she still saw the thin plume of smoke from the day the farmhands burned down the witches' empty shack. She glanced that way now and crossed herself. "I was so cruel to Alondra the last time I saw her. I've regretted that day ever since. But the news of her death also meant the curse was gone for good. All this time, I'd been sure of it. How wrong I was."

"Because Raul came back," Sophie answered. "Everything that's happened . . . his bangungot, the typhoon, the beetles . . ."

"Yes, history is repeating itself. Gaba came for the Sepulvedas before, and it comes for them now."

"But Raul's dead. Shouldn't that be the end of it?"

"Gaba takes everyone in its wake. You've seen how it does not care. Townspeople and sakadas died back then too. But the Sepulvedas will suffer the most. And that's why you must leave as soon as you can. Especially now with that corpse. The balbal is sure to follow now."

The corpse eater. The one that swallows death whole.

"Don Raul said he saw it lurking among the trees," Remedios went on. "That's why he wanted to build the mausoleum. He needed to shield his family's bodies. I told him the balbal only eats the newly dead, but he couldn't be stopped. He heard the monster too, and when it wasn't nightmares, it was that sound that shook him awake." She placed her palms against the heat coming off of the drum. The flame had grown smaller, the wood in its bottom turning to embers. "And now, his foul odor calls to it like shit calls to the flies. The balbal is coming. Keep your ears open for it. You will know it by its cry. *Eeeeek eeeeek eeeek*, shrill and grating, like a rabid bat."

"If it's coming, then shouldn't we all leave?"

"I can never leave this place. This has been my family's home for generations. We will stay," she said, her tone conveying that Sophie was not part of that *we*. "And we will fight."

"Fight how?"

"With fire. The legend says that's the best way. It fears the spark of life."

After a while, Sophie said, "It's not right. What about those who had nothing to do with the massacre? Adrian shouldn't be a victim of this . . . this curse. This isn't his fight. It's not his dad's either; he was just a kid when it all happened, and so was Javier. Kai wasn't even born yet, and . . . if anything, only Olympia and . . . "

The caretaker took Sophie by the arm. "Girl, have you not been listening? As much as I love them, this family is its own curse. From the great-great-great-grandfathers down to Sir Adrian. They will take you down with them, when the time comes. You need to save yourself. These nightmares you've been having . . . why in God's name do you think Alondra visits you? Take them for the warning that they are."

"I can't just leave. I won't."

"Those poor souls taken by plague or eaten by crocodiles, the ones crushed by coconuts—they were the lucky ones. They were killed by the curse. They have headstones. But the ones who die at the hands of the Sepulvedas"—here, the caretaker's voice cracked—"those are the unlucky ones. Their families will never know whether their father, sister, friend, lover was still alive. They will never know where they are. Eventually, they might believe they're dead, and though that might be true, belief is a far cry from certainty."

Remedios turned toward the lawn. She recalled the faces of those people she'd helped consign to their unmarked grave. They were called desaparecidos, but they hadn't disappeared, not in the truest sense of the word. They'd always been here, and they always would be.

April 15

HOLY TUESDAY

There was no bishop nor hearse. The procession would last only from the manor's front steps to the graveyard on the hilltop west of the property, instead of taking a journey to Maalin, to the nave of its small parish, to be gawked at by the entire town. The cortège was sparse and did not see any of the personages on the doña's lengthy guest list. The president and the current governor did not stand as pallbearers, thus replaced by the groundskeeper and the driver. Kai needed to escort their mother, and so Olympia's sons, her grandson, and the male staff made an odd number. The golden casket shifted and skewed as the men walked on uneven ground, straining under the heat of the noon sun.

The rest of the family followed from farther back. The lilies atop it were limp, gathered from vases around the manor. Yet the smell of decay lingered, even with the lilies, the closed lid, the open air. The widow and the sister of the deceased, all in black, fanned themselves wildly.

Margot was still too weak, her consciousness coming and going in brief flashes, and so she had been left in the manor to rest. Sophie felt a perverse kind of envy toward her as she struggled to maintain her composure. She didn't want to play the part of a mourner. Not after learning what she now knew.

As they all came around back, she turned away from the veranda, from its welcoming shade and its intricate blue tiles, from the bulbs of the string lights that glittered like daylight fireflies. She wanted to unsee the slaughter on the banquet table that once lay there. All those men and women, their mouths frothing in agony. Her insides turned as though she herself had drunk Raul's poisoned wine, and her pulse quickened again. Despite the heat, the sweat on her brow was cold.

Her body's sympathetic response to the caretaker's revelations had been as strong as it was relentless, driving Sophie to finally take a couple Xanax before bed the night prior. Complete oblivion was the only thing that could stop her heart from racing, her mind from replaying the bloodbath like a sadistic film reel. And it did. She'd woken up feeling as though she was asleep one second and steadily waking the next, with no recollection of a dream. No visions haunted her. No demons, no beetles, no Alondra. No paralysis either.

Her relief proved short-lived, however, when the morning light revealed what she'd done to her arms. She felt the sting as soon as she saw the scratches. While she slept, she'd clawed at her own flesh, her forearms and biceps raw to the touch. Dried blood stained the edges of her fingernails. The marks reached her neck too, her chest only spared by a ratty T-shirt. She freaked out, but once the panic subsided, she understood. Her subconscious wanted to excoriate her. She knew what she knew. It had burrowed into her deepest recesses, and she wanted to tear it out of herself.

Sophie pulled down the sleeves of her black dress, gathering the lace shawl around her for good measure.

As their cortège crossed the lawn, she slowed her stride, feeling the give of the soft grass beneath her shoes. Was this the spot, she wondered. Is this where this man—this murderous, evil man—buried those poor people? Was she treading above the bones of his victims? She caught sight of bamboo stakes that bounded the patch of land where the mausoleum would have been built. She imagined the opulent marble structure, the encasement of the family's forebears, weighing down on all those bodies. Crushing them more than they already had been. Her chest tightened, looking around at the mournful faces of the Sepulvedas.

At the top of the hill, she saw the entire length and breadth of the villa. It looked larger on the outside, and its chambers seemed as though they should only fill half the manor's footprint. She envisioned its contents: the four-poster beds, the jewelry, the Renaissance paintings, the marble statutes, the fine china and heirloom glassware, the antique mirrors, chairs, credenzas, armoires filled with designer clothing. Spoils bought with the coconut fund, languishing and collecting dust in the silong's storerooms. Relics of a stolen lifestyle. Luxuries that good, hardworking people were slaughtered for.

Raul's sons cried as the empty grave came into view. A rectangular valley between mountains of dug dirt. Adrian's hold on the casket wavered as he sniffled and wiped himself dry. The doñas wailed, Remedios too.

Sophie allowed herself to cry. At least to the Sepulvedas, the display would seem appropriate, even expected. She watched the family, tears overflowing, but in that chorus of sorrow, she wept alone, mourning a different tragedy altogether.

From the moment she arrived, Sophie had felt like an outsider, an interloper. An intruder. She'd insinuated herself into these proceedings, her need to belong so blindingly undeniable. She fought for it with Adrian. In every way she could, she groveled for it with his family. She comported, contorted, minimized, and questioned herself, for she couldn't stand to impose any more than she already had. *Don't mind me.*

Pretend I'm not here. Yes, I agree, of course, you're right, excuse me, I'm so sorry, I'm so grateful, please and thank you. The Sepulvedas never demanded it, not in so many words, but in advance and with no expectation of return, Sophie gave them her compliance.

She understood now what Alondra had been trying to tell her. As much as it conflicted with her own sense of justice, Sophie began to feel that Alondra's vengeance—her curse—was justified. Sophie wished to spare Adrian and anyone else who wasn't involved in the massacre, but the rest of the Sepulvedas had to answer somehow. If not by the laws of men, then by whatever it was that governed the unseen. Sophie herself hadn't been in harm's way, but she had been asked to bear witness. Decades too late, but now she had. She didn't know what she was expected to do hence, but she knew one thing. She couldn't stand to be here any longer. She would leave the villa tonight.

The site did not befit a man of Don Raul Sepulveda's stature. Instead of a headstone, there stood only a cross made of two bamboo sticks lashed together with twine. If his family hadn't gathered there in their fine black mourning clothes, one might think that the deceased was a pauper and this was a potter's field.

The hole was deep, but its sides were not cleanly straight. The trunks of young coconut trees flanked the long sides and three thick cords of abaca were hung across the hole and over the logs, each length tied to wooden stakes driven into the soft ground. The pallbearers set the gold casket down like a baby in a cradle. The ropes held.

The men assumed their positions by each stake. Kai joined to fill the gap and stood on the opposite end of Javier's rope.

On the groundskeeper's count, they all undid the knots and slowly lowered the casket into the ground. "Steady . . . steady . . . " Tiago said evenly, directing his son as much as the other pairs. The soil was soft, and Javier felt himself getting pulled in. The rope burned his palms as he pulled back, keeping pace with the others. Soon, the rope slackened, the casket having reached rock bottom.

Javier looked down at his father's casket and a surge of emotion overcame him. He covered his mouth with his fist, trying to hold himself together. His job was not yet done; the ropes needed to be pulled. He wrapped his end around his wrist and gripped with both hands. He tugged, but the rope did not budge. He tried again, planting his feet firmly and using the weight of his entire body. His foot skidded in the soil and he lost his balance, landing on his back. His mother squealed in shock.

For a long while, Javier stayed lying in the mud, laugh-crying at the heavens.

When his laughter quieted, his kuya helped lift him off the ground. Eric tried pulling the rope himself, but it was still stuck. In the end, they decided to throw the rope in. Javier lowered it slowly, careful to avoid hitting the face of the casket.

The bereaved gathered around the grave, Eric standing in the place of honor. He looked like he might no sooner jump in himself. After Remedios handed out the booklets, he began to lead everyone in prayer. He stammered through his Our Fathers and Glory Bes, his words interrupted by incoherent cries that drowned everyone else's, even their mama's. It seemed to Javier that the rest of the family restrained their emotion out of respect for Eric; Javier certainly felt obligated to.

Javier watched his mama clinging onto the framed photo of his papa, hugging it close to her bosom. She'd carried it from the sala mayor to the top of the hill, stroking Raul's face as though she tried to draw courage from it. The old man now glared at Javier from across the grave. He could not deny it, not even now. Especially now. He was his father's carbon copy. Never before had he felt so close to death as he did in that moment, not even when he first saw his father's corpse, not even when he accidentally mutilated its face and revealed the rot within.

"Lord, have mercy," Eric cried.

"Lord, have mercy," they all cried back.

"Christ, have mercy,"

"Christ, have mercy."

"God, the Father of heaven,"

"Have mercy on us."

"God the Son, Redeemer of the world,"

"Have mercy on us."

"Eternal rest grant unto him, O Lord,"

"And let perpetual light shine upon him,"

"May he rest in peace."

"Amen."

The words taunted Javier. Was Papa at peace? Had he been, in his final hours? Should he be? Javier bit the inside of his mouth, tasting blood. He was the one who wanted to remember, and who wanted his father to remember. He felt a maddening sense of irony that Raul got diagnosed with Alzheimer's just as the younger Marcos was elected president. He forced his father into that treatment program, paying a hefty price to ensure the old man never forgot what he'd done, especially not when the country seemed to have forgotten what the Marcoses had done. And when Raul decided to return home, Javier felt a sense of possibility, of potential vindication. It came back to him, finally. Papa remembered that night, and now, maybe he could face some sort of personal reckoning.

If only he hadn't died too soon.

Some days, Javier still heard the gunfire. Real, live rounds discharged from a weapon. He was seven. He'd been awoken by the sound in the middle of the night. His kuya had slept through it; Eric had always been a deep sleeper, and he only turned and grumbled even when Javier cried to him for help.

Javier remembered his surprise at finding his Auntie Divina in the bedroom, sitting on a rocking chair, watching over them. He thought she was a ghost. She tried to hush Javier, who insisted he heard gunshots. She insisted he'd had a nightmare. Or it might be the music, she added. His parents' party was still going strong. Voices, booming and jubilant, carried in from the veranda. But Javier knew what he heard. He pretended to sleep, puzzling out the snatches of conversation that he caught, all the yelling. His lolo, his papa. The soldiers chanting. The later the night drew on, the more he was convinced that something bad had happened. Then, he heard the truck. The next morning, Javier saw that their empty pool had been filled overnight.

In the days that followed, people came by the villa asking about missing farmhands. He remembered their nanny Alondra crying and screaming down the hall searching for someone. His memories of that time came and went, but the sense of dread never left him, following him through life like a specter. As a child he didn't know how to make sense of it, didn't even know if there was something to make sense of. But when he grew older, he could no longer ignore the suspicion that gnawed at him.

Obviously, he knew how close the Sepulvedas and Marcoses were. Javier knew his father's cousin Imelda. He was that curious boy who sat through dinners where his parents and their friends traded hushed stories. He overheard late-night calls between his papa and the president. Their Belvedere home played host to the Marcos children when they visited the Bay. What he didn't learn firsthand, he studied in school—not in the history classes, but on his own, as he began to develop his sense of identity. At NYU, when he was supposed to be majoring in business, Javier took classes in Southeast Asian history. And he read as much as he could. Books, memoirs, old news articles, current ones from the motherland. He watched the documentaries. He could trace the timeline of martial law. He knew the exact figures of the dictatorship's excesses: the billions of dollars of plundered wealth, and the islands and skyscrapers and corporations and vintage automobiles and jewels and fine art purchased with said billions. He learned about those who were detained, tortured, disappeared, executed in methods of varying cruelty: activists, students, organizers, citizens who opposed the dictator's rule and refused to fall in line. He knew those numbers too: the thousands of extrajudicial killings, the tens of thousands of tortures and incarcerations.

Most of all, he knew of the mass murders: in Culasi and Pulilan and Daet and Escalante and many other places, rural towns in provinces near and far. Deep in his heart, Javier believed that another massacre had occurred too, on that one night in Maalin, Leyte. In the guise of a celebration, Raul Sepulveda, the First Lady's cousin and a governor from the ruling party, and Claudio Sepulveda, a general in the dictator's army, had gunned down farmers and then made them disappear.

Javier held on to this belief for years, nursing it in that prolonged way he nursed a drink. He bore the guilt even though he didn't know for sure, even though he never pulled the trigger. He spent countless evenings looking out at the lights of San Francisco from the fancy penthouse the Sepulvedas had owned since the seventies. One of his papa's overseas investment properties until the big move, when he took the family to the States, the same week Marcos was ousted. Javier had checked the dates. It was a coordinated escape. He sipped his whiskeys night after night, wrestling with the possibility that everything he had—everything since he was born—had been paid for with the sweat and blood of the Filipino people.

There were things he had yet to do. He didn't obsess over the country's dark history, or his family's, without gaining a sense of responsibility. For it wasn't history, wasn't it? All was in the here and now, happening again, happening continuously, because it never stopped. Not the plunder, not the atrocities, not the constant evasion of consequences and denial of justice. He should do something. Still, as he cried over his father's golden casket, looking out onto their ancestral manor, Javier doubted that he could do anything at all.

After the last amen was spoken, the groundskeeper handed Eric a spade. He scooped a mound of dirt and flung it down the grave. He then passed the tool to his son, who did the same before passing it to Javier.

He crouched low onto the ground. His hand trembled as he dug. His tears dampened the dirt. Perhaps it was for the best that they forewent eulogies. He wouldn't have been able to contain himself. He stared at his papa's photograph and then at his mama, an anguished avatar of devotion. With ceremony, Javier straightened himself and stretched out his hand above the pit. He upturned the spade and watched the dirt fall atop the casket with a thud. His father buried a lot of secrets, and those secrets were the legacy Javier would have to live with for the rest of his life.

Afterward, the family made another procession, this time led by the groundskeeper and his son. Down the hill, then past the fence and through the lawn, toward their cottage. Sophie didn't understand why they all didn't go back into the manor right away, especially since Margot had been unattended for some time now. Her condition could take a turn any minute.

She might be thirsty or cold or convulsing while the family gathered in the Ilagans' small yard.

Tiago went behind the cottage and the Sepulvedas waited in silence as though they all knew what to expect. Sotto voce, Sophie asked Kai what was going on. They explained that no one was allowed to go home right away because of pagpag. A local superstition, one that Kai happened to share, about how the spirit of the departed followed their loved ones back home after a burial. A short detour was needed to confuse it. "Pagpag literally means to shake dust off," they explained. "And that's why we need to stop here." They spoke with such finality that Sophie didn't press further. If the goal was to shake off Raul's spirit by making a detour, then by that logic, why should they lead him to haunt the cottage? Hadn't he done enough to his servants?

Tiago returned and called the Sepulvedas to follow him. He led them to gather around the steel drum in which a fire burned high. The smell of kerosene was suffocating. Into the flames Remedios and Dante threw dead leaves and twigs, more debris from the typhoon. Black smoke billowed around them all, stinging their already reddened eyes. Kai leaned in to whisper, "This part, though, is bullshit. Spirits can't be smoked out like pests. Not with dead coconut palms. Now, if we had some goddamn sage . . . "

The groundskeeper's dog Askal weaved between the mourners, sniffing the ground in search of something. Javier shooed it away and the dog settled next to Adrian, curling up by his feet and licking its paw.

Sophie watched him from the other side of the fire, his arm around his dad. Adrian stood strong while Eric bawled into his chest, but when Adrian caught her gaze, his tears fell in earnest, as though she'd granted him permission for a moment of weakness. She cried too, herself feeling Adrian's anguish. Who was taking care of him? The peepholes, the missing cell phone, the awkward family dynamics, the visions, and the nightmares. Sophie could take care of herself just fine, even counting her confrontation with Olympia, but Adrian felt responsible for her. She cried knowing how difficult it had been for him, remorseful that she'd failed to do more for him in kind.

They all returned to the villa. The air was noticeably fresher, even fragrant. Remedios put out a merienda spread of coffees, teas, biscuits and crackers, and tuna salad sandwiches with the crusts cut off. No one touched the food. Everyone was too sapped to replenish their energy.

Once Adrian had settled his father with a cup of coffee, he and Sophie went to his mother's bedside. Olympia had ordered that a kulambo be installed in each bedroom, and despite Margot already being sick, one had been hung over her bed. Through the diaphanous curtain of the mosquito net, the woman looked deathly white.

Sophie gasped. It'd been, what, two days since she last came into this room? Adrian was as shocked as she was. His mother's cheeks had sunk and lost all color. Even as she slept her breathing was labored, syncopated and shallow. She wasn't snoring loudly anymore; it sounded more like damp air sputtered out of her.

Adrian refilled the glass of water on the end table, then took a washcloth to wipe the sweat off his mother's forehead. When he was done, he fell onto the bench at the foot of the bed. He cursed, trying to muffle his sound. "Manang Remy thinks it's malaria, what with the chills and the vomiting," he said. "She hasn't been eating, apparently. I figured I'd come in here and try to coax her, but . . . "

They kept their masks on just in case it was something else airborne, but this didn't strike Sophie as malaria, and it was definitely not just a case of the flu. "We need a doctor, and fast," she said. "Flu medicine isn't enough. Has anyone tried checking the roads? I could also go and see if I can get reception."

"Dad says he'll go. He needs to be the one who calls the governor or whoever can send a chopper over." He dropped his head on her shoulder and heaved a sigh. She held him close and stroked his hair. "I'm so tired, Soph. And I'm sorry I haven't been there for you much. But between the funeral and how Dad's been a fucking wreck, plus Mom being like this—"

Sophie hushed him. "I understand. It's all good."

No, she couldn't add to his burdens, not now. There was no way she could tell him about his family's gruesome secret. Every part of her wanted to scream about it, wanted him to join her in the knowledge and the screaming as she knew he would. But this was not the time. The revelations would break him.

"I'm starting to believe this curse bullshit," Adrian continued. "Sorry I was such a jerk about it when you first told me about the beetles."

"I couldn't believe it myself."

"It's just that . . . I've spent so many summers in this house. This is one of my happy places. Nothing bad ever happens here. Now, it's just a place of misery and death."

She would wait to tell him how true that was, and how the misery and death stretched beyond the present. How he'd been kept in the comforting cradle of ignorance. Adrian deserved to know, and though she struggled to find the right time, Sophie would make sure he was saved.

Once more, Javier found himself lurking in the maze of the villa's silong. He waited behind the landing to the grand staircase, hoping to chance upon Dante, who assisted with kitchen duties. The afternoon merienda had only just been served, and soon it would be dinner. On any other occasion, Javier might have waited until nightfall to whisk the boy away for another tryst in the storerooms, but he needed relief now, and he needed it fast. The day's events had made him feel like a coil pressed to its limit, crying to be unwound, at risk of breaking.

It was then that he saw Adrian's girlfriend sneak into the zaguan. From behind a row of foundations, he watched Sophie lurk around the parked Bentleys, peering into their windows. She scurried around in search of something. The clinking of metal, hammers on wrenches on screws on who knew what else, reverberated in the vaulted stone chamber. She rifled through the key hooks, then a tool cabinet's drawers and trays, completely unaware of his presence.

"What are you doing?"

Javier's voice boomed through the silong and gave the girl a shock. She recovered easily enough. "I need to start making my way back home. I've been gone so long and I've missed so much at school. Plus I haven't been able to reach anyone and . . . my parents are worried sick, I'm sure of it."

She didn't seem half-convinced herself, and Javier saw no need to press it. "Well, the main event is over, so I suppose you've done your duty. But what's the plan here, exactly? The roads are impassable, haven't you heard?"

"I—I know. But there must be a way. I'll go on foot if I have to. Through the mountains, or rocks, whatever. I just can't stay here anymore. This place . . . "

Her hesitation intrigued Javier. Like him, she seemed close to breaking too. Why, he couldn't tell. She surely wasn't running toward home or school. Neither was she running away from the villa out of worry or boredom, given the tinge of antipathy in her voice. *This place*. Yes, Javier knew what this place truly was, and he recognized what Sophie was doing. This flight was an act of renunciation. She was as done with Villa Sepulveda as he was.

"What about this place?" he asked with a nervy tone that might be mistaken for arrogance. "Do you think something bad's gonna happen to you here?"

"Something worse, you mean." She appraised him head to toe, and Javier felt exposed, naked. "I mean, look at what's been happening. The curse. Doesn't it terrify you? Doesn't it make you want to leave too?"

"This is my home," he snapped. "My father just died. I can't just leave."

He glared at the girl. The stranger. She knew something. She must, by the way she acted. She wasn't just talking about the myriad miseries that beset the manor in recent days. He could tell her. He could unburden himself with her and, in doing so, start setting things right.

"You can't run away from family," he told her, a wave of bitterness washing over him.

Right then, footsteps came down the stairs. Someone called out his name, and for a second it sounded like his father's echo. Javier immediately felt as though he'd been caught in some illicit act.

"There you are. You're needed upstairs," Eric said. He seemed taken aback upon seeing the girl by the car. "What's going on here? Are you headed somewhere?"

"Where could we possibly go?" Javier answered.

Sophie's lips tightened, her glance darting between the two brothers before landing on Javier. He saw a flash of defiance in her eyes. She wasn't going to say anything. She didn't want to. She expected him to deal with Eric.

"What are you doing here, then?"

The girl stiffened as Eric came closer. It was subtle, almost imperceptible, but Javier saw it. Her hackles were raised. He had no intention of telling on her, but he supposed he'd given her no reason to trust him.

"Oh, just chatting," he told his kuya.

"About what?"

"The weather. Wanna join in? You got opinions you wanna share?"

"I'm sure talking to Javi is fascinating," Eric told Sophie sarcastically, "but Mama's looking for him." She lowered her head, a nod but not quite.

"What does she need now?" Javier asked.

"Oh, I don't know, man. Did you think maybe a grieving widow would want to be with her kids after burying their father?"

"Isn't that what you're there for?"

Eric was dumbstruck. His aspect softened as he said, "I'm sorry about this, Sophie. You have to excuse us. It's been an emotional day, you understand." She said yes, almost in a whisper. Eric then turned to his younger brother, imploring. "It won't take long. Please? She needs you."

Javier, surprised at the sudden shift, replied just as meekly, "I'll be right there." Still stunned, he turned to Sophie once his kuya was out of sight.

"I'm gonna go, but don't do anything stupid," he told her. "You don't wanna leave under these conditions and risk running into another landslide. And nightfall's coming. Better to do it early tomorrow, before everyone wakes up. It'll be easier to nick the keys too."

Sophie gave him a skeptical look. "You're serious?"

"Wait out the night. First thing tomorrow, if you're still up for it, come find me and we'll figure it out. I don't know how far you'll get," Javier said with some kindness. "But just because I can't leave doesn't mean you don't get to."

Suddenly, they heard the dog's yapping, urgent and incessant. The sound carried into the silong, but it came from outside, right near the zaguan's entry. Then, a sharp crack broke in the distance. Javier went out the garage to see, and Sophie followed.

The dog ran out onto the west lawn toward the flower garden. Beyond the villa's boundary wall, a clump of dwarf coconuts shook. The cogon grass trembled. Another loud crack. This time Javier heard it more clearly. It was a long ripping sound, creaking like wood being broken apart when a tree is felled.

"What is going on?" Sophie asked with a quaver in her voice.

The trees stopped rustling but Askal kept barking. Javier went to get a closer look. He saw movement, someone—or something—trudged through the tall grass. A dark, lumbering figure. He turned back and took Sophie into the zaguan, barring the door behind them.

"Couldn't see anything. Probably just a fallen tree," he said, trying to assure her and himself.

"That wasn't a tree, that was a living thing. It sounded like an animal. Like a, like a . . . " She was at a loss for words, clearly anxious. Javier gave her a searching look. She grew still, as though recalling something, then spoke softly.

"Like a rabid bat."

Tomorrow, she would be rid of this place.

Details were unimportant. Javier had made a promise, such as it was. Hesitant, ambiguous, but it was enough. She had good cause and she had a way forward. Once she had the car key, the rest would fall into place. Adrian would come with, surely, and they'd find a way to bring Margot too. Maybe Kai, if they were up for it. They'd go as far as the road would let them, and then . . . Then, the next part of the plan, based on the conditions on the ground. Through the jungle, or down a ravine, landslide be damned. Not even the threat of a corpse eater would stop her.

She'd been pushing the thought out of her mind since the afternoon. The encounter unnerved her, and when snatches of it returned to her, she could swear she'd seen a figure stalking behind the thick tree trunks. Listening, lying in wait. She recalled the caretaker's warnings, and when darkness fell, she could hear aberrant screeches, blending into the background of the crickets' song, almost taunting her.

Stay, for I am out here.

Leave, for I am coming.

Sophie assured herself it was all in her head.

She hoped to sleep soundly, same as she did the night prior. It had been a dreamless sleep, a welcome surprise—notwithstanding her scratching her arms. Still, she didn't want to risk further injury, and so before she lay down to bed, she put away the pill bottle pilfered from Adrian's mother. The day's stresses were enough to knock her out in short order, and they did.

When it came, the sound was clear enough to rouse her awake. It was as Remedios had described, and as Sophie herself had heard only hours before: *eeeek eeeeeeek*. It was close, as though just beyond her bedroom wall. Half-conscious, she turned to the wide-open window. The gossamer cocoon of the mosquito net swayed in the soft breeze.

She didn't glimpse the thin band of light that came in from the hallway. The hinges of the bedroom door creaked as it opened and then gently shut. *Eeeek eeeeeeek.*

The tall, dark specter had returned. But that sound . . . that was the balbal's cry, wasn't it? Her vision was hazy, turned iridescent by the veil over her bed. Whatever had visited her, it appeared to be both and neither of them at once.

The creaking grew louder. She took a sharp breath and stayed still. She was alive, she assured herself; the corpse eater wouldn't want her. *The dead man's body is deep underground on that hilltop; nothing here rots for the balbal.*

Yet here it was, creeping closer, grazing its claw across the mosquito net. When it reached her side, the monster's face caught the light.

The monster wore the dead man's face. No—Adrian's.

No—his father's.

With ravenous eyes, he lifted the thin sieve that served as her only barrier of protection. The dreamlike haze dissipated. All was stark and vital, figures casting crisp shadows.

The realization left her frozen in fear. She could not move. Her limbs were locked in place. Every fiber of her body could only manage to twitch in response to her commands. Her eyelids were active, a blessing and a curse, and they flitted wildly. Her gaze darted around the room: at the canopy above her, at the bedposts, the curtains, the armoire, the mirror, anything and anywhere but the man looming over her, creeping onto the bed.

She heard herself screaming, cursing, but her voice echoed only in her head. She saw herself kicking and pushing him off her. She willed it all so fiercely that for a moment she did see her hands finally rise. They reached for his face, rough fingers clawing into his cheeks. Yet those were not her hands. Hers remained petrified by her side. Those were someone else's. The gray pallor, the veiny surface covered with dirt. There was another in this room.

Alondra.

Her sharp nails dug into the man's head and pulled him away from the bed. He stumbled and fell to the floor, himself frozen in fright.

She hovered toward him, her gray skirt fluttering in midair, billowing like a storm cloud. She began to float toward the ceiling and the room was eclipsed in darkness. Even the moon in its fullness dimmed dead.

The man spoke, mouth aquiver. He was begging, but his words were muffled. She raised an accusing finger at him and then opened her mouth. All the air seemed to have been sucked out of the room. She said in a low and bitter rasp, "*Never again.*" She swooped down from her height like a vicious bird of prey, her hand still pointed at the cowering man. He scrambled on all fours and reached the door, slamming it closed behind him.

The sound felt like a fracturing of the universe.

The wan light returned. The specter vanished, and soon, so did the grasp that terrorized Sophie's body. She lifted her head. The breeze cooled her skin and the mosquito net resumed its listless dance. The crickets chirped. The door was closed. All appeared as it had been, but how many times had her mind betrayed her since she came here?

Yet there were her heaving breaths, her wild heartbeat, the sweat on her brow. There was Alondra's voice. Those two words still rang in her ear. And then there were the tears that streamed down her face. Those were real, Sophie knew. All of it was real.

April 16

SPY WEDNESDAY

NOT ALL THE UNATTENDED CHILDREN THAT roamed the plaza of the Church of San Isidro were urchins. A few were merchants forced by their parents to peddle garlands of sampaguita blossoms for the parishioners to hang on the necks of their patrons' statues. Remedios would have bought from those children as was her custom. She would have hung the flowers on San Isidro before circuiting the nave for the Stations of the Cross: fourteen murals depicting Christ's passion and death, fourteen episodes from his condemnation to his entombment. Alas, the roads were still impassable, and she would not do her circuit this year. She would not do the prayers at each of the Stations, but she would make her offering. She plucked the sampaguita from her backyard garden, thankful that her bushes hadn't been ravaged in the storm. She pierced the fragrant white flowers with needle and thread to make a garland. When she was done, she gathered shawl and rosary and made a different trip altogether: up the hill to where the Sepulvedas were laid.

Remedios walked the path that she'd trod just the day prior. The light of dawn still fought the darkness, yet the way was clear to her. After all, she'd gone up that hill more times than she'd visited her own parents in the town churchyard, a fact that never sat well with her but one she never felt compelled to rectify. Her tatay wouldn't mind; he barely knew her, having died when she was three. Her nanay, however, might have some feelings about it. Remedios often imagined the disappointed face of her mother's ghost, arms crossed as she stood by her tombstone on the rare occasion her daughter came to visit. Remedios tried to convinced herself that Trinidad Ilagan would understand: The trip to town detracted from her duties to Villa Sepulveda. Trining would have acted the same; she was loyal that way.

As with the job Remedios performed now, she'd inherited that trait from her mother, the way she learned how to polish the manor's wood floors, how to make the oyster windows gleam, how to save the silverware from tarnish. She was as devoted as her mother that even after the old woman died, the Sepulvedas felt the villa was still under the care of the same untiring woman.

Those who knew Remedios—the house staff, the townsfolk, the plantation hands, lumberjacks, and millworkers—all wondered if she would be this dedicated to the family if the rumor wasn't true. It was a rumor that had hounded her since birth. Some had more tact than others, and occasionally one would slip and make a crude joke. If not that, it would be a snide remark about special treatment. Trining and her child lived on the property, were paid more, and reaped privileges the rest of the help never enjoyed. Surely that was a sign.

As a child, Remedios decided the best course was to deflect and ignore. However, Trining was never the type to brush off a slight, and she vehemently denied the rumor each time it reared its ugly head. She guarded her reputation, and whenever she gave the offenders a tongue-lashing, they invariably backed off, chastened and apparently convinced. They would say, afterwards, that Trining was a very devoted wife (and later, widow), that she was so religious she wouldn't risk the flames of hell for any man. Besides, she was the help. Don Claudio would never have lain with her, his womanizing reputation notwithstanding.

And look at this girl, they would say of Remedios, pointing out her dark skin, her button nose, her peasant features. *How could she be a Sepulveda?*

That she took after her mother was in fact a great relief to Remedios. It eased her concerns and made lying to herself come easier. Surely her nanay would have spurned the general's advances, if they came at all.

She also often reminded herself of an incident when she was fourteen. She'd recently started working in the manor and was alone in the kitchen one afternoon, descaling pompano for dinner. The general came upon her and caressed her shoulders. *Dalaga na si Remy*, he'd said, his eyes hungry. *My, how you've grown*. He praised the roundness of her cheeks, her shapely figure. He wouldn't have acted that way, she would tell herself, if she was really his daughter.

This was how Remedios convinced herself that she was not a Sepulveda, and this was how she convinced Tiago too, when he'd asked. He believed her, seeing how firm she'd been about it.

The only time his belief seemed to have wavered was the night of the massacre. In the furor, he'd asked Remedios to stop and think about what they'd been asked to do. She didn't tell him that she was afraid for their lives, though that much was clear, nor did she make a case about their generations-long indebtedness to the Sepulvedas. When Tiago asked why she'd so easily take part in this savagery, all Remedios said was "I can't turn my back on my family."

It was a slip of the tongue, she told herself, later. She told herself a lot of lies after that night.

She lied to her nanay, who always wondered what happened at the feast, who asked about the missing farmers when people came around the villa looking for their son, their father, their sister who last said they'd been working for the Sepulvedas. She repeated the story Raul had crafted, the same one Melchior and Tiago agreed to repeat. Negotiations broke down. The farmers regrouped in the mountains with the NPA, swearing they'd return with a vengeance. She maintained the lie for years, and when Trining died, Remedios was racked with shame. *Now she knows*.

In her solitary moments, Remedios developed a habit of talking out loud to her mother. She'd asked her nanay countless times before, and she asked her again now, as she weaved past coconut trees on her way to the Sepulveda plots. "Would you have done the same?" The asking brought her some comfort because it allowed her to lie to herself once more. "Yes, you would have done the same." Trining would have put those men and women in the grave too. She might even have served the wine. And she would have kept the secret, defending the Sepulvedas' reputation the way she'd defended her own. This propensity for silence, unwavering in the face of overwhelming guilt, was another trait that Remedios inherited from her mother, one that she easily mastered. She herself was a secret, after all.

Dark marble tombstones stood at attention on the top of the hill, the row punctuated by the makeshift bamboo cross that marked the fresh grave. Remedios inspected her garland, the scent of its pearly white blossoms suffusing the wet air. From a distance she didn't notice how the ground had been disturbed. The dirt was furrowed, not flattened the way it should've been after her Tiago and Dante had filled the pit. Mounds bordered the grave as though the casket was yet to be entombed.

No—as though the casket had been unearthed.

Remedios ran closer, dropping her sampaguitas and her rosary beads. She screamed when she saw what lay on the shallow pit: The casket had been dug up from the ground, its lid fully ajar. The smell of death emanated from it.

Raul had disappeared.

True to the legend, in place of his body was the rotting trunk of a coconut tree. It lay in the very center, nestled between smooth folds of satin lining. The trunk's ends were ragged, as though it had been chopped down with a rusty saw. Maggots wriggled in the wood's putrid flesh, and in places where they'd bored rough holes, horned black beetles gathered in clumps, clicking and hissing and climbing on top of each other.

Remedios ran down the hill, crying and screaming. She summoned her husband and her son, called for Christ the Redeemer, the Virgin Mother. She must have seemed like a lunatic, but her mind had the clarity of a single horrifying thought repeating itself over and over.

The balbal has taken him. The balbal has taken her brother.

This was what it was known to do: dig up the newly dead and put a dead tree trunk in the place of its victim. "And that is what happened," the caretaker swore in short, panting breaths. "It was the balbal."

Remedios repeated the monster's name and it earned her a slap in the face.

"Maghulos-dili ka!" Olympia commanded her servant to calm down, though it was clear the widow was the one who needed calming. Her hands quaked and she'd lost all color to her face. She paced nervously around the sala, where the rest of the household had gathered. "This can't be. This cannot be happening."

Javier thought the same, but he didn't know whether he was truly in disbelief or merely in denial. "Manang Remy, there must be some other explanation," he said. Seeing how agitated everyone was, he withheld the sarcasm he ordinarily would have delivered. "Like a wild animal or something?"

The groundskeeper shrugged tentatively. "There are wild dogs up in the mountains, wild boars, too, but they keep away from the villa. They don't roam our groves either, even on the outskirts."

"Dogs and boars? With what, shovels?" Eric said, flustered. "*Someone* did this. Papa's enemies, perhaps. I don't know who, but this was a human act."

Kai piped up. "I feel we're missing an obvious fact, Kuya. The landslide. If a person dug up Papa's grave, then it would have to be one of us, right? Who else even knew that he was buried yesterday?"

A new kind of tension settled over the room. Suspicion. Olympia's fevered stare flitted from one face to the next before landing on Javier's. "No one here would do such a thing," he answered defensively. "Besides, it would have taken more than one person working through the night to do that. We would've noticed."

"Maybe there are people on the property that we don't know about," Eric added. "Someone in the mills or warehouses. Maybe even people who live in huts up in the mountain."

"What, the rebels?" Divina sneered. "They've been wiped out for decades. No one's up there. And no one could possibly be on our property, stranded for a week without food. They would've already come to the manor for help." She crossed herself, then kissed her hand. "It is the balbal. I know it, and the sooner we all accept it, the better we can protect ourselves."

"No, I shall not accept it. He hasn't been eaten by some *demon*," Olympia answered. She turned to her eldest, plaintive.

"You must look for him, hijo. He should still be around here somewhere. Whatever or whoever did this, he couldn't have been taken far."

"Ma, we have acres of farmland. How are we going to find him?" Javier replied, encouraged by apprehension on his kuya's face.

"Punyeta, I don't care how! Just find my husband!"

Cowed into obedience, Eric gathered the men by the exhumed casket at the top of the hill. Javier gagged at the sight of the rotten trunk covered in maggots and beetles. He kicked the lid shut, sparing them all from the reek of death.

Eric gave out the assignments: He would set off with his son and search north of the hilltop, while Javier and Dante were to go east. Tiago would go west and past the gates. The task was daunting, even more so when they saw the green expanse surrounding them, the thick groves that stretched for miles in every direction, but Eric seemed determined as he gave directions. Javier knew better; his kuya was faking it, and for good reason.

"We'll find him," Dante assured Javier as they descended the hill. The morning fog hadn't lifted, enveloping the land in a gelid mist. "At least the skies are clear. We should be able to cover a lot of ground before we break at noon." He gave Javier an encouraging smile, but it failed to do the trick.

"I don't intend on doing this till then."

After an hour of aimless and mostly silent searching, Javier lost any semblance of hope. Dante was the total opposite. Every few paces, he crouched low to the ground. He pointed out broken branches, trampled grass, muddy indentations that could be hoofprints. Each time he did, Javier only grunted in response, and the longer their task wore on, the more scorn he felt toward the younger man. Didn't he see there was no reward at the end of this quest? They wouldn't find the cadaver. Even if they did (a vanishingly slight possibility) it would be mangled and torn by beasts, its rotten insides flayed open in full view. The sight wouldn't bring comfort to Olympia, nor to Javier, not that he sought it.

"He's gone, Dante. Let's head back. There's no use."

"How can you say that?" he asked with a slight whine in his voice. "He's your papa. He needs to be laid to rest, properly, otherwise his soul will never reach heaven."

Javier assessed him curiously. Dante was dead serious. It took all Javier's strength not to laugh. "You think he's got a shot at heaven? The gates are closed to him, trust me."

"Not if enough people pray for him."

"Hah! There aren't enough people in the world! Heaven, hell—the only hell I know is the one Papa inflicted on other people. If it is real, well, he's bought a one-way ticket southbound. Bought it way before you were even born."

Dante's eyes narrowed. He trudged ahead, leaving Javier behind.

"You really believe all that Sunday school crap, don't you?" Javier continued. "Wait, wait, don't tell me—are you one of those good Catholic fags who do confession after sucking dick? How many Hail Marys does it take to wash away your sins? I bet you abstain from taking it up the ass on high holy days too."

"You don't have to agree with me, but you don't have to make me feel stupid."

The remark stabbed Javier with a pang of guilt. He pulled on Dante's arm. "I'm sorry, I didn't mean that."

"Yes, you did, you asshole."

"Cut me some slack. It's been a hell of a day, okay? I'm tired, and you saw how crazy Mama's been acting and—"

"You do that a lot, don't you?" Dante snapped with startling belligerence. "Blame your bad attitude on your parents? Nothing's ever your fault, is it?"

"Oh, fuck you." It was Javier's turn to march away, but Dante gripped his forearm.

"What, you can't handle the truth? Are you gonna blame that on them too?"

"If your dad fucked you up the way mine did, you might not be so quick to judge. Now quit being a brat and let me go." Javier shrugged his arm away, but Dante held fast.

"I'm a brat? You're the one who can't take any responsibility. 'Papa did this,' 'Mama did that,' blah blah blah. You already got everything and you still can't be happy. You're a grown man and you don't act like it. Do you know how pathetic that is?"

Javier shoved him away but Dante only pulled him in closer. The younger man's eyes were filled with self-righteousness. His grasp tightened. His breath felt warm on Javier's face. Javier inched closer for a kiss, but Dante turned his head and released his grasp. He unzipped himself and leaned back against a coconut tree.

Javier scanned the grove but he couldn't see more than a few yards. Everything looked hazy in the fog. Dante, his manhood throbbing, did not share Javier's fear of getting caught. Emboldened, Javier reached for him, but Dante seized him by the shoulders and shoved him down to his knees. He towered over Javier and took his shirt off, his body tight and smooth. Javier had been craving that newness, that innocence, since he first saw the boy half his age, the one who now stared him down with revulsion.

"Go ahead," Dante commanded. "I know you want it."

Sophie's heart thumped wildly upon hearing the bedroom door. It was daytime, and Adrian's voice greeted her, yet the creak still transported her to the night before. She crawled under the sheets, pretending to be asleep. He came to rouse her anyway.

"Don't come any closer," she said, trembling. "I'm sick."

"Oh, no. Sick how?"

"I think I caught what your mom has. You should stay away. I don't want you to get infected." She tried to sound stronger than she felt, but each word out of her mouth betrayed frailty. A dull ache throbbed in her chest.

"Do you have chills? Let me feel you for a fever . . . "

"No! Just leave me, please."

"I'll be fine," he answered. "I just want to make sure."

Through the sieve of the mosquito net, Sophie looked at Adrian with trepidation. He didn't seem to notice. He held out his palm and she reluctantly placed her forehead against it, feeling his warmth through the barrier. Sophie exhaled. A wave of comfort came over her, as though his touch promised to heal whatever had broken inside of her. It crested swiftly, relief replaced by revulsion, and she withdrew from him, shivering.

"Not too hot, which is a good sign."

Adrian left the room and came back with water and flu medicine. It took some persuasion for Sophie to lift the net and take the pills. She felt a gnawing need to tell him, but she didn't know how. She still struggled to tell herself what had happened. She couldn't trust anyone, not even her own body, her own senses, and it tortured her. In that moment, the one thing she craved was Adrian's protection, but she couldn't find the words to ask. And where should she begin? With the more immediate depravity of his father's attempt, or with the ancient depravity that remained buried in his family's backyard? She knew too much, saw too much, and for the first time she understood what it meant for something to be so unspeakable.

"I'd like to go back to sleep now." She reclined and turned her back to Adrian, wrapping herself with the blanket.

Silence. After what felt like eternity, he spoke, his voice cracking. "Something's happened. Lolo's body is . . . gone."

He explained the disappearance, the alleged thievery by the balbal, the theories thrown about by his family. Sophie shook as Adrian mentioned his father, saying how the men were soon setting off to search for the missing cadaver. He sounded so tired, so helpless.

"Be careful out there" was all she managed to say.

With palpable gloom, he left her to rest, promising he'd return to care for her in a couple hours. His words sounded distant, a ghost of an echo, and their meaning felt just as unreachable. A demon and a desecrated grave, the rotted, hollowed-out trunk . . . Had Adrian spoken with less calm, she would have called him mad. But what was mad anymore? From the moment she crossed the villa's iron gate, nothing had made sense. This whole place was mad. Mad and malevolent.

She'd been warned that misfortune would befall the villa, and it did. Maybe she'd been warned too late. Maybe she didn't act quickly enough. But now the family was gone, most of them anyway, scouring their cursed land. She could act now. Alondra had saved her from the worst; she couldn't allow the woman's intercession to be in vain.

With great effort she peeled herself off the bed. She skulked out of her room and down the hallway, listening. The two old women argued in the sala, their voices raised. These words, too, made little sense. Everything was meaningless noise, drowned by her heartbeat and the rush of blood in her body.

She headed into the kitchen, toward the back staircase that led into the veranda through the silong. The sound of flip-flops clacked on the wood floor, approaching her. She hid in a corner behind the china cabinet, but to her relief, Kai emerged from the hall.

Sophie grabbed their arm. "The roads—are they clear, do you know?"

"Jeez, you fucking scared me—"

"I need to get out of here. Can you help me?"

"Oh, I see you've heard about Papa. I'm freaking out too," Kai said, conspiratorial. "I knew the vibes were off here, but I didn't expect . . . this."

"Answer the damn question—can you help me?" Sophie asked, her eyes wild.

"Are you okay? You look so pale." They reached out to stroke her face and she flinched away.

"I'll be fine as soon as I'm out of here. Please, listen. How about the mountains? Do you think there's a way through there?"

"How should I know? The landslide was huge. In all likelihood, it'll be too far to go around. And mountains are dangerous, these ones even more so." Kai fell silent and cast a faraway look out the window. A flock of sparrows scattered from the treetops.

"There's gotta be a way. Come on—think. Maybe we take one of the cars, what do you say?"

"Sophie, you're scaring me. What the hell happened?"

Eric happened. This fucking family happened. Sophie wanted to lash out, but she knew she had to keep it together, even as that became increasingly impossible. "Look, nothing happened, all right? I just need to leave. Now. You've been saying so since you got here: This place isn't safe. I finally agree. I believe you, Kai. You were right. So, help me. Please? I'm begging you."

"I don't know how . . . with the landslide and all . . . we could try to call for help again, but I—well, I don't know what that would do, really . . . Trust me, I wanna get outta here too. This is all getting to be a bit much. And I do wanna help you, Sophie. But you can't expect me to go while my dad's missing, y'know? Maybe when they find him, or when the guys come back, we can ask Tiago to—"

"No, that'll be too late!" Sophie said with gritted teeth. "Jesus Christ! Can't you come up with something? Leaving's the one thing you're supposed to be good at!"

The remark landed like a slap, and Kai turned red in chagrin.

Just then, Divina called out for Kai about tea, her voice drawing closer. Sophie shot Kai the coldest of glares. She thought they were different. They should have understood, even without explanation. What a fool she was.

Sophie skittered away, back down the hall and into her room. She shut the door quietly and locked it. She then took the chair by the desk and used its back to hold the doorknob in place. She drew the windows and the curtains closed. She reached for her phone. Her dumb, useless phone. She cradled it like a talisman while she hid under the covers, pulling them tight around her. She would stay here in this tiny, suffocating room, goddamn it. She'd stay until a plan came to her. Here at least she had a chance of being safe. For if she had no way of leaving, then she sure as hell wouldn't let anyone get in either.

The manor no longer stank of rotting meat; instead, the sharp smell of wilted flowers pervaded the air. A single vase of droopy, white roses had been left behind, spared from the grave. Doña Olympia picked a petal off the parquet and rubbed it with her thumb and forefinger. Better than the smell of death.

She caught a glimpse of the family portrait: she in a powder blue terno, her late husband in a piña barong not unlike the one in which he'd been interred. He looked vital, almost lifelike, and the sheen of the oils seemed like the sweat that glistened on his brow on humid days like this. "Where are you?" she asked the image with the sharpness that had lingered from her earlier conversation. She massaged her palm, stinging from when she hit the caretaker's cheek.

It was unlike her to lose her temper like that. The lady was a renowned terror, but the renown came from the way she inflicted it: with a calm, genteel manner, like a keen blade, whose injury is felt too late, when it has already stabbed too deep. Olympia imposed her will this way, much the same way in which she exercised her other virtues. She had a quiet vanity that did not call attention to itself; she had an intelligent passion that smoldered, rather than burned in a conflagration. She possessed an inexhaustible love for her children that she maintained at a distance that did not smother them, or her. Even in that role as a mother, she did not allow herself womanly emotional extremes. She built the perfect life that way. In perfect, curated balance.

She stepped back from the portrait as though imbibing her family, seeking to rejuvenate herself with their immortal miens. She failed miserably. Raul was gone, twice over. His death had almost been enough to cause her own; his disappearance threatened to finally do her in. And her children—how she tired of them. All week she'd needed to fight them on everything. Was it too much to expect some reverence? Didn't they know how much she suffered? She hadn't found a moment's peace to sit with her grief; she'd been the one to make arrangements, to draw up contingencies, to make every decision, big and small. To plan for the future of this great and crumbling house, which her ungrateful brood would be so quick to forsake.

She'd come so close to telling them too. Selling the villa meant more than giving up a centuries-long legacy. It meant utter, irreparable ruin. The end of the Sepulvedas and everything they'd built. True, it might help if her children understood the consequences of the villa changing hands; maybe then she wouldn't have needed to swindle their unbalanced father. Yet her maternal impulses compelled her to spare them from that terrible burden, even if it meant deceiving them.

The grandfather clock told her it was almost time for the novena. She should summon everyone. No one could be late for the ninth and final day.

As she rose from her high-backed chair, still holding the crushed rose petal by her nose, a call came on the wind and beckoned her to the window.

Out on the lawn, she saw a figure floating away from her, heading north of the manor. It was a woman in a gray dress, her long jet-black hair flowing freely down her back. She carried something in front of her. Raul. As though weightless, his body draped across the woman's outstretched arms, head lolled to one side, the decomposing gash on his cheek exposed.

Olympia yelled for the woman to stop, but she kept walking. She didn't look back. The widow called for Divina, then Remedios, but no one heeded her. The manor felt deserted and her voice seemed to bounce off its walls.

She sped down the grand staircase in pursuit. By the time she reached the lawn, the woman absconding with Raul's corpse was gone. Olympia scanned the area, calling out her husband's name as though he could reply. She ran north, toward the mountains. They couldn't have gotten far.

Soon, she saw the figure again, as though it blinked into existence. The woman was almost at the stone fence, having gone much farther than she should have been able to in such short order. She'd almost reached Remedios's home. Olympia ran, her mourning gown dragging through the mud, not letting the woman out of her sight until she turned and disappeared behind the cottage.

The hedges around the cottage had grown thick. Their lush leaves and pointy branches scratched Olympia as she passed. It felt as though the tendrils reached for her deliberately, grasping at her, trying to enfold her in their prickly embrace. She swatted the vines away, pricking herself on thorns of hyacinths and yellow roses. A branch sprang and slapped her face. It left a bleeding slice on her cheek, right where her beauty mark lay. The hedges seemed impossibly tall and endless; she couldn't see the end of the brambly, verdant tunnel. One thought drove her through the morass: She would not let this woman get away.

When the vegetation finally disgorged her, Olympia found herself deep in the plantation's groves. The stone fence was far behind her. The gray woman was out of sight, lost in the striped trunks of the coconut trees, shrouded by the fog and the tall grass. The damp air stung the fresh scratches on Olympia's skin, but she was on a mission. "Come back here," she yelled. She gathered her skirt about her and trudged forward, determined to recover her Raul.

She'd always been this willful, though she'd never let her doggedness and ambition be seen so nakedly. She left all of that to her husband; she would be the blessed recipient of his efforts as though she had no hand in his successes. In truth, Raul had never been as headstrong as her. The latter stages of his life only cemented this belief. She wasn't the one who'd lost her faculties. She doubted Raul would do the same if the roles were reversed: would he hunt down this woman, or would he cower in the face of unreality? Would he be the blubbering idiot he'd been when he had Alzheimer's? Or would he be the cowardly, miserable wreck plagued by visions and nightmares?

Olympia forged ahead, her sense of direction governed only by intuition. The mist grew thicker. A gust of wind shook the palms, enveloping her in the susurrus of their blades. The hissing crescendoed until it became deafening. She put her hands over her ears and shut her eyes.

A tap fell on her shoulder. She spun around. No one was there. Another tap, then another, falling on her back, and then on the top of her head. Black beetles. Olympia gasped in horror.

They showered onto her, from the treetops that sagged under the weight of the infestation. She swatted them away, flailed and spun to get them off her. She crushed one with an open palm, and the bug's horn pierced her skin. She howled and ran past more and more pillars of pestilence, but everywhere she turned, the trees were covered with shiny black carapaces, with sharp, barbed horns. The horned devils buzzed and clicked and hissed, the sound beating her senseless. Her legs gave and she fell to the ground.

The beetles kept raining down on her, clambering on top of her, their rough legs and claws and horns making new marks on her already scratched skin. They were so heavy, and lifting her limbs came close to impossible. They tangled in her undone hair, climbed on her painted face. Every fiber of her wanted to, but she resisted screaming for fear of them getting in her mouth. They bit down on her, their mandibles as piercing as the sound they made. They bored holes into her flesh.

Olympia rolled and turned and spasmed, both in agony and in an effort to get them off her. Barbs dug into her, but the scarab's shells gave a satisfying crunch. She kept going until she could see again, lift her limbs again.

The cacophony quieted. Her eyes adjusted, and she saw the trees were no longer overrun by the devil's beetles. Not a single one was in sight. Even their gouges on her skin were gone. She crawled on all fours and allowed herself to collapse against a tree trunk. When she caught her breath, she yelled again.

"Where the fuck are you, you fucking bitch?"

For Olympia knew now what was happening. She understood what this was. She was not in the groves. She was in a living hell. This was gaba. This was Alondra.

The doña had never been in denial about it. She'd been able

to justify her sins; she only did what needed to be done. She'd been able to forget those sins, too, when she and Raul sought refuge in America, the country that sheltered their allies and their masters. The Marcoses had Hawaii; the Sepulvedas had the Bay Area. She'd even been able to mythologize those sins, make them part of the family lore, of town legend, a point of cultural interest that concealed the ugly truth. No one talked about retribution and reparation when a ghost story was on offer. Yet Olympia, for all her efforts, had never been able to disbelieve the curse.

"Show yourself, Alondra!"

The widow's voice was hoarse, but she kept screaming. It was all she could do. She wouldn't get Raul back. That vision was not him, not his body. She would at least come face-to-face with that blasted woman, that spawn of mountain witches, and show her that Olympia Sepulveda was not afraid of anyone, not even the dead.

Thus challenged, Alondra showed herself in the distance, barely visible through the lifting fog. She looked as she did that last day Olympia saw her: eyes sunken, hair running wild like the madwoman she was, barging into every room of the manor in search of her beloved.

Alondra cradled Raul's corpse with preternatural strength. She lifted him toward Olympia, who took the gesture as a sick dare.

Here.

The widow rose to her feet and slogged through the cogon. Her pulse beat wildly, her blood boiling with every step. Alondra remained impassive, a statue waiting for a supplicant, and her aspect further incensed Olympia. The widow stumbled as she quickened her pace. The vision disappeared once more.

Alondra's voice came clear on the breeze.

Come on. Keep going.

Olympia searched frantically, turning every which way. She

couldn't see where she was going but still she ran as fast as she could, even after she'd lost one chinela, then the other, oblivious to the pain from the twigs and pebbles underfoot.

Yes, yes, that's it.

Her prodding was as unbearable as it was unnecessary. Olympia would never give up. In any case, Alondra wouldn't let her quit. This was a woman who bided her time and waited for decades; she would never leave Olympia in peace, and so one way or another, this had to end now.

Almost there. So close.

Olympia pushed out of a thick growth of cogon and reached a small clearing. The view before her opened up, revealing another phantasm. Not her tormentor nor her dead husband, but something else. Something darker and more terrifying, straight out of her visions of hell.

Two large, hirsute demons with cloven hooves leaned against a coconut tree, writhing against its trunk in a fitful and deranged dance. Their tails flicked back and forth and the spires of their twisted horns locked against each other's. Their intertwined arms, carpeted with dark, bristly coats, pulled this way and that, their legs shifting and spasming in time with their guttural roars. Spit dripped from the tips of their teeth, mingling with the sweat that pooled and ran down their sinews.

It took a while for her to understand, but she soon heard the pleasure in their panting breaths, saw the cadence of their movement, and she recognized the crazed yet ecstatic look in the demons' bloodred eyes.

She, too, recognized one demon's eyes as those of her younger son.

She cried out, first in shock, then in revulsion. She dropped to her knees, breathlessly clutching her breast. The demon, her demon son, unhitched himself from the other and loped toward her on all fours. He hovered over her, blood and sweat and sex trickling from the matted fur that covered his entire body. The other demon followed suit. She recognized this one too. Beneath the dark-furred face was Remedios's boy.

Oh, God. No, not him.

The widow screamed and collapsed to the ground.

The boy crouched beside her, braying. Her son brayed too, more loudly. He howled as he placed his rough, clawed hands over hers. The two demons bleated and brayed at each other and at the darkening sky.

She heard a pop in her ear, a rush of blood. Her chest tightened as though the demon's hand itself had gripped her heart and squeezed. Her vision blurred. Past the demons' forms Olympia could see her son Javier, and Dante, his lover. His cousin. Their naked bodies were the last thing the doña saw as she drew her final breath.

APRIL 17

MAUNDY THURSDAY

THE BANQUET TABLE HAD A STORIED PAST, MUCH like most objects in Villa Sepulveda. It was made of narra, a redwood that grew in the north of the country, known for sturdiness that not even the sharpest termite fangs could damage. See the grain on its surface, the rings it had before it was felled. Its color was a luscious shade of umber, with a subtle varnish that didn't overpower the wood's natural rosy scent. The passage of time had smoothed them out, but the mahogany's intricate carvings, depicting laurel leaves and aster blossoms, still looked lifelike. It had once belonged to the governor-general, claimed Don Oscar, who bought it at an auction after Spain had sold the islands to America. He could have easily commissioned the same artisans from Paete who had crafted it for the governor-general, but Oscar, like his father and his descendants, had always wished to fill the manor with conversation pieces. The crystal chandelier that hung above had its own colorful history too, but that had been lost to time. Suffice to say the fixture only emphasized the majesty of the banquet table, which had seen hundreds of feasts through the years. It served celebrities, politicians, two archbishops, and four presidents, including the current one and his father, when he was in power those two-odd decades. How often did Ferdie, as the family affectionately called him, visit his wife Imelda's province, making sure to stop at Villa Sepulveda for a night of revelry? How often did he dine with the family during his bloody reign? The banquet table served every Sepulveda since the last century, saw hundreds of celebrations, arguments too, and it had served to absorb Don Claudio's renowned fits of anger, bearing nicks and cuts from whenever he stabbed its surface with his dinner knife.

The table, however, had never served a corpse before.

With a stunned somberness, Javier brought his mother's body up into the manor and laid her out on the narra. Divina and Remedios were first to see them, and while the women wailed, Javier remained completely silent. Even in the commotion when his kuya returned with Adrian, Javier was a mute sentry. It took Eric shaking him aggressively before he blurted out what had happened.

"She was delirious," Javier started. He described how Olympia came into the clearing with a dazed expression on her face, blubbering incoherently before collapsing. He offered no explanation for the cuts that covered her body, the mud that caked her feet, the sludge of squished insects on her neck and arms. The doña, typically so stately and beautiful, now looked like a mountain woman in her shredded mourning clothes, her veil hanging on to her unkempt hair by a single pin.

He likewise omitted what his mother had witnessed in her last moments. He had sworn himself and Dante to secrecy.

As he gently laid his mother on the banquet table, Javier hoped he was wrong. Yet despite her delirium and incomprehensible state, despite a host of other causes—her own age and health, grief over Raul's death, the stresses of the past week, and the curse, that godforsaken curse—Javier had no doubt that he had killed her.

The women placed a sheet underneath Olympia and began the work of cleaning her body. Once, the table had performed a similar function for Javier, when he'd fallen from race-climbing a coconut tree with his brother and some of the younger farmhands. He got a huge gash on his left bicep, and Olympia had dressed his arm on that same dinner table. She set down bowls of water and some soap and cleaned the wound intently, her face lined with misery. As he watched Divina and Remedios do the same, Javier finally wept for his dead mother.

Kai suggested moving Olympia to her bed, but the brothers shot it down. "We'll hold vigil here, for now," Eric said. "Until we can get the funeraria to come over." No one knew the state of the roads, not even Tiago, who'd been too busy with the search for Raul. Once the women had washed Olympia, they straightened out her dress and brushed her hair, pinned her veil and put blush on her cheek. Divina made sure to have Olympia clasp her favorite rosary beads before her fingers hardened in rigor mortis.

Javier relit the candelabras they'd extinguished only two days ago, then moved some of the wilted flowers from the sala. He knew all this was far less than his mama deserved, and far less than she would find acceptable. "I'm sorry this was all I could do," he told her. He gently stroked his mother's hair, lamenting the fact that in a span of days, he had become an orphan.

The clock struck midnight on Maundy Thursday.

The three siblings kept watch over their mother. Kai took to their vape pen. Propriety be damned, they said. Eric didn't have the energy to reproach them. He watched them pace the room, languorous and glassy-eyed. Kai offered the pen to Javier. "This'll do for now, but it'll take something a lot stronger if you're trying to cope."

"Self-medicating isn't my style."

Eric surprised the other two when he reached out his hand instead. He took one long drag. "This," he said as he flourished the pen toward Javier, " . . . is not my style either. But it's better than nothing."

Javier reached over their mother's body, put the pen to his lips, and puffed.

"You were her favorite, you know," Eric said mawkishly, with no hint of ill will.

"Not me—Kai," Javier answered.

Kai waved him off as though repulsed by the idea. "She didn't play favorites, but if she did, it would be you."

Javier found it amusing how three children raised together could have such divergent views of the same parents and the same events. Had he just been more sensitive, more attuned to what roiled beneath their father's words, their mother's smiles? He never questioned Olympia's love, but he knew she never much liked him. Not as an adult, certainly, and not even as a child. There'd been concern, there'd been worry and care, but not fondness. She protected him because it was her duty; she sought the best for him because it cast her in a virtuous light. He and his siblings were mere reflections on her. Whatever maternal gestures Javier received over the other two were gained only because he fought for more attention. Olympia didn't lavish them on him out of favor, nor did she grant them willingly.

"Out of us three, I disappointed her the most," Javier replied. "Moving out, cutting off ties . . . the constant arguments with her and Papa. Even now, you've seen how she and I fought."

"And she forgave you the most," Eric said.

"You think she'll forgive me for selling the house? Forgive us?"

Eric and Kai fell quiet. "She did everything to make sure the villa stayed in the family," Javier continued. "And it was the last thing she asked of us."

"We don't have to talk about it right now," Eric answered.

"I know I was the most vocal about it, but now that she's gone . . . " Javier grew teary-eyed.

"Wait, are you sure?" Kai asked. "Or is this the weed talking?"

Javier hung his head low. His career had taught him how one's home spoke volumes about who one was. From the threshold, he could tell whether the homeowner was generous or miserly, whether they preferred high or low humor, whether they voted in the last election and for whom. He could tell how they liked to spend their time, how they viewed modernity, what kind of friends they kept, what secrets they hid. How many estates had he sold with hidden bedrooms, contraband storage, underground tunnels, sex dungeons, slave quarters? The bigger the house the greater the secrets. A mansion held by the same family for generations might not know about their ancestors' lurid past, but it would all come out in the end, when the for-sale sign goes up and the inspectors come in and the surveyors take out their tools. Things would get unearthed. Sometimes, the discovery made the property value go up—like when he once found a historic speakeasy behind a hollow basement wall in a client's Harlem brownstone—but, of course, that depended on the nature of the secret.

He never really made up his mind, if he was being honest with himself. His bluster notwithstanding, he did worry about the revelations that would follow the villa's sale. This worry came from his more craven side, the Javier raised in luxury, the one who felt just enough guilt about what he knew, but not enough to do anything about it.

The other side of Javier held on to what was right and just.

If his family's crimes would ever come out, it would have to be now. Selling meant the revelation wouldn't be forced out from anyone in the family, especially not from Javier himself. For a time, this side of him had won out. He was done with this place. He was willing to let the chips fall where they may. He became even more determined seeing how his mother went to great lengths to keep the villa and its secret.

But now she was dead. And in one of their last conversations, didn't he practically wish her dead? Wasn't her last vision that of his transgression? Didn't he see the disappointment in her eyes, feel her rejection in her gasping breaths?

"Yes, I'm sure," Javier told his siblings. "I don't want to sell. And I won't let either of you sell either."

He was no better than his father. He accepted it now. He would keep the villa within the family, as his father wanted, as his mother wanted. The truth would out eventually, but it didn't have to come out now, and not by his doing. He would keep the secret at the cost of his own soul. Already he had killed his mama; he could not fail her in this too.

The siblings settled into an agreeable silence after Javier's decision. Once in a while, Kai chortled, recalling a bittersweet memory about their mama, but didn't say much more than that. Eric mostly rested his head on his interlaced hands, fighting the urge to nod off. The eldest wouldn't let himself be the first to tap out, Javier knew, and when he offered to make some coffee, his kuya volunteered instead, leaping to his feet as though to shake off his lassitude.

Eric returned from the kitchen carrying a laden tray. He poured, sugared, and stirred with care, the same way he fussed over their mother while she was being cleaned. He told his siblings to mind her dress, to make sure they didn't splatter or spill. He sounded so matter-of-fact about it that Javier momentarily forgot the surrealness of the scene. *The three of us are sharing a late-night coffee, that's all. Mama's cold body isn't laid out on the dinner table in front of us.* He almost laughed, but the moment was broken by the sound of a coffee cup crashing to the floor.

His kuya stood by the head of the banquet table, shaking. His mouth hung open and he fixed a terrified stare at the threshold of the dining room.

"No! Leave me alone!" he yelled, dashing behind the high-backed chairs to shield himself. "Get away from me!"

The other two sprang from their seats, startled and confused. "Kuya, what's going on with you?" Kai asked. Eric breathlessly pointed into empty space as he ran circles around the room, trying to evade an unseen pursuer.

"That's not true! It wasn't my fault!"

"Who are you talking to?" Javier asked, pulling on Eric's forearm. Eric shook him loose and ran to a corner of the room by the liquor cabinet. He curled into a ball, repeating his denials.

"I was just a kid! I was only just a kid! They made me watch!"

Javier and Kai steadily approached their brother with worried pleas. Eric didn't see or hear them. He began mumbling a prayer but he was so gripped with fright he couldn't get past the first lines. "Our Father, who art in heaven, hallowed be thy name, your kingdom come, your kingdom come, our Father, who art in heaven . . . our Father, please . . . "

He covered his ears with his hands and rocked in place. "Yes! Never again! I promise! I'm sorry, please forgive me . . . " He repeated himself over and over, apologies replacing his prayer. "Please forgive me! I'm sorry . . . forgive me . . . "

Suddenly, Eric peeked behind the arm that covered his face and caught Javier's gaze. He lifted his head and unfurled himself from the corner.

"What is happening to you?" Javier asked. Eric desperately

held onto his brother's arm and raised himself off the floor. The beginnings of words sputtered from his mouth, but none of them made sense.

Kai pulled him into their arms and hugged him tight. They ran their hand up and down his back. They scanned the room, then whispered sharply at Javier. "I keep telling you, the energies in this house are fucking vile."

They took off their black tourmaline necklace and slipped it onto Eric's neck. He didn't put up a fight. "Don't worry, I have another. This'll keep them away, all right? Whoever it was, they can't hurt you now."

Eric peeled away from his siblings and stared at them both. Javier felt a pang of unease. His brother still had that look of fear, but there was something else behind it. Despair, as though he'd suffered a terrible defeat and his life was over. Eric shuffled away without saying a single word.

After the shock subsided, Javier told himself his brother merely had a bad trip (he was old, and when was the last time he smoked, anyway?). It was only as he was picking up the broken shards of painted porcelain that he recognized the look for what it was. He should have known sooner, for he had felt it too. That wasn't fear, or despair; that was the look of self-loathing.

Remedios watched in silence as Sophie slurped down a bowl of chicken tinola. Her guest was voracious and unapologetic about it. "I'm starving," she'd said at the door, her voice faint. She looked pale and her gait was unsteady. The caretaker was confused and not a little bit miffed—it was two in the morning and she'd had a long and trying day—but worry predominated her less generous emotions and so she ushered Sophie in. The girl hadn't spoken a word since.

"There's food in the house, you know," Remedios said when Sophie finished her bowl.

"I know."

"Have you had another nightmare?"

"You were right. That house is cursed. I thought I could last another night, but death stalks that house and I— His lolo's missing, his lola's dead, his mom's dying. And his dad . . ." Sophie's face hardened. "It's all so fucked up. Please, can I stay here until the morning? I wanna get out of here as soon as it's light out."

Remedios reached across the dinette and held Sophie's hand. "What happened to you? And go where? The landslide won't be cleared by tomorrow. No one works on Holy Week."

"Yeah, because God is fucking dead, right? God is dead and there is a balbal on the loose and that damned house has another corpse for it to feed on."

"Is that what you're afraid of? I told you, hija . . . the balbal doesn't kill for food. It craves rotten flesh."

"Well, I don't want to be there when it comes for Olympia. And it will come. I believe that now. You were right about everything. The curse, the monster, all of it is real. Alondra too," Sophie said with conviction. "I saw her."

"What do you mean? Saw her when?"

"Last night." Sophie's eyes welled up in tears. "In my room. She was there . . . she— It wasn't just another nightmare. It was real, I wasn't— It was like you said. She's trying to warn me. She wants me to leave."

There was a desperate hardness in her words. In another place and time, Remedios might have thought Sophie unbalanced, but she'd since learned how to tell the difference between paranoia and well-founded fear. "What happened to you?"

Sophie shook her head emphatically.

"'Never again.' That's what she said. Why would she say

that? What happened *to her*?" The tears she held back finally fell.

Remedios pulled her close. She'd already told the girl what happened, the litany of horrors the Sepulvedas inflicted on Alondra. Yet she sensed that Sophie meant something else entirely. Remedios did leave something out, and one way or another, Sophie knew. She searched the girl's face for confirmation. All she found was anguish.

"It won't help repeating. I've already told you," Remedios stated. "Now, won't you please let me help you and tell me what happened?"

Her answer had made the girl withdraw inward. She looked hollowed out, like a husk of a human. For a long while she seemed on the verge of speaking, then finally said, "Alondra came to me in a vision and saved me—was trying to save me. She wants me to flee this place, and I will. Please let me stay here. I'll be gone by daybreak, I swear."

Remorse left Remedios no choice but to let the girl stay the night. She watched over Sophie as she snored the deep, sibilant snore of the soul-weary. Sophie had withheld just as she had, but the caretaker couldn't fault her. Remedios wouldn't pry any further. No good would come from telling, she assured herself. She'd told too much, or maybe not enough, but either way, Sophie and Alondra were each entitled to their silence.

A gentle shake roused Sophie awake. Adrian sat next to her on the couch, smiling in relief. He missed the dread on Sophie's face, which to him might have registered as the disorientation of waking up in a strange place. She tucked in her knees and wrapped the blanket tightly around her, placing as much distance from him as she could.

"How are you feeling?"

"Fine," Sophie replied on instinct. "I mean, not fine. Not worse, but still sick. You should go back to the villa. I might be contagious. Where's Manang Remy?"

"She's at home. They all are. Novenas," he answered with a crack in his voice. He was trying to sound strong. "It's the first day for Lola."

She thought about consoling him. Pulling him into her arms, telling him to let it out, the way she'd been doing days before. Instead, she remained motionless. She couldn't stand him crying for Olympia, the harpy who accused her of seducing her son, disbelieving her protests and turning the tables on her so easily, like it was second nature. That was denial, Sophie realized now. Olympia knew what her son was; she said so herself. And she enabled him.

"You should take this. It'll help with your fever," Adrian said, noticing her quiver. A glass of water had been set on the table, next to a bottle of flu medicine. Sophie obliged. She sighed and closed her tired eyes, hoping he would be gone when she opened them again. She waited in silence, and so did he.

Adrian looked around at the caretaker's humble sala. "Why did you come here, Soph? Are you mad at me? Did I do something wrong?"

Everything is wrong. This villa is a nightmare and I need to wake the fuck up.

"No, I'm not mad at you . . . I just needed to stay away from the rest of the house. It's for your own sake." She felt wretched, she added, just like his mom. Her mystery illness was very likely contagious, since Sophie'd contracted it too. Sophie surprised herself how easily the lies came.

"Please come back home with me," he asked. "It'll be easier for me to look after you. Besides, I've checked in on Mom a couple times and I'm still fine."

"I'd really like to stay here. Only until I feel a bit better, I promise. I'm just across the lawn." *Right by the mass grave.*

"I don't want to be away from you."

"You could stay." *Because I'm sure as hell never going back to that house.*

"Babe, I'm needed at home too. If I'm here with you, then what about Mom? And Dad . . . "

Don't you fucking mention him. "I understand. But I'll be fine right here, I promise."

"I need you," he pleaded now. "Everything is fucked up and you're the only one who can help me get through this." He cowered into the couch, pulling at the ends of her blanket. Sophie's heart ached in sympathy and guilt.

"I can't."

"Why? What's going on, babe? What's this really about?"

"It's the curse."

Adrian looked incredulous, as though she spoke in gibberish. Before he could reply, she continued. "You need to know the whole story. You need to know everything."

The part about the coconut levy was as good a place to start as any. Sophie told him about the farmers' strikes, the protests that erupted after years of exploitation. Adrian listened, horrified, as she spoke of the millions his family stole from their laborers, the billions the system stole from farmers all over the country. Sophie recounted the details as she'd heard them from Remedios, leaving no detail out, even as she reached the night of the massacre.

"Your lolo invited them to a feast. It was supposed to be a truce, but it was a trap." She told him about the poisoned tuba, the gunshots, the pool that was turned into a pit.

Anger rose inside her with every horrid detail, and her ire was only compounded by Adrian's reaction. Tears filled his eyes and yet he turned away, mouthing words of rejection, of denial.

"People were killed, Adrian. You know it's true. You've read the books. And you know your family. In your heart, you know what they're capable of."

"I've always felt that something was wrong with us," he said with disgust. "That there must have been some evil bargain that my family made. But I never thought it would be . . . this." He was silent for a long time. He looked out the window, at the plot of grass where the bamboo stakes still stood. "They killed for this. For everything that we have. That I have."

"It's not your fault."

Sophie felt a tinge of revulsion at her words. *She* was always reassuring *him*, offering her forgiveness, her comfort, her solace to the always blameless Adrian.

"This is fucking mass murder," he replied, sniffling. "And those people . . . they're still out there. Jesus, fuck. Their families never knew. I gotta do something."

"As soon as we get out of this place . . . "

Adrian turned to Sophie as though he'd forgotten she was even there. "I'm kinda . . . glad they're gone now. Lolo and Lola. And Great-Grandlolo too. Everyone responsible for it. I get why you'd want to leave after hearing all that, but you don't have to stay here. Come back to the house with me. We'll get through this. Together."

His response heartened her. Adrian was a good man and he would do the right thing. Sophie needed that assurance for what she had to say next.

"I can't go back, Adrian, because there's more."

She could have stopped. She could have waited for another time, after she herself had processed what happened to her. After she'd decided what she wanted to do. After she felt strong enough. After Adrian had less to deal with. Yet if there was some lesson to be derived from her time here, it was that there might not be an after. Her chest tightened as if a great serpent had coiled around her. Her tongue felt heavy, and every word sapped her vitality.

"Two nights ago, the night of your lolo's funeral . . . something happened."

It was like a dam had broken open. She told him about her nightmares, the sleep paralysis that had never troubled her until she stepped foot in the manor. She described the visions she thought were real, and the reality she thought was mere delusion.

"It's your dad. I was sleeping and . . . he came into my room."

"What do you mean?"

"He came into my room."

He tried to rape me.

Adrian leapt back and stood, wordless but for the expression of panic on his face. He asked, barely maintaining calm, "All right, so he came to your room . . . he probably had a valid reason, right?"

"In the middle of the night?" she asked, outraged. "For what?"

"I— He might have been checking in on you. I mean, you've been having nightmares, right? Maybe you were sleepwalking, or yelling in your sleep, or . . . I don't know, something!"

"The walls here are thick, Adrian. Fuck, listen to yourself! You don't even believe what you're saying."

"My fucking dad?" He paced around the sala, holding his head with his hands and squeezing as though he wanted to pry his skull open. "And you're not delirious or anything? I mean, you haven't been sleeping, you're sick, you . . . it wasn't these, these—nightmares?"

"It happened, Adrian. It was real."

Sophie had decided to spare him the details, but then found herself talking about the creaking door, how it sounded like the balbal. She told him how his father's hand menacingly grazed the kulambo before he lifted it. How she got a good look at his face in the moonlight. With each word, Sophie bargained for Adrian's faith.

This is how it happened, in painful, graphic detail. Do you believe me now?

"I tried to resist but I couldn't move. I was . . . frozen . . ." she said, tears flowing down her face. "But see, nothing happened. It was bad and could have been a lot fucking worse, but I managed to scare him off. I got out of bed and threatened to scream. He freaked and ran out of the room."

Another lie, but it was in service of a greater truth. She could never tell him about Alondra; it would all but convince him that everything was made up.

"Nothing happened?" he asked, pleading.

Sophie shook her head. "Nothing happened. This is the worst way to find out, but it's the truth. Your dad is a predator."

Adrian bristled at the word. He had a look on his face that was both distant and distressed. "That's why you've locked yourself up in your room . . . because of Dad? And now you're here . . . to be away from him?"

Sophie nodded at each question. She imagined what he must be thinking, how he must see her. She wept, hiding her face in her hands. He knelt beside her, himself weeping, and took her hands in his.

"I'm so sorry," he said. "This is a lot, and I know I said the wrong things. I'm so sorry you had to endure all that."

"You believe me, right? You have to believe me. I need you to believe me."

"This hurts so much, Soph. But yes. Of course I do."

April 18

Good Friday

SOPHIE HADN'T LEFT THE COUCH SINCE YESTERDAY. She had no strength, as though it had left her body along with every word of revelation. Her blood felt like sludge. Sleep came and went. Adrian dropped by, bringing her some soup of beef shank and bone marrow, but she had no appetite. Her sense of time had also abandoned her. All she knew was that the sala in that small cottage became too bright, too hot, so it must be the next day. When Adrian left her to return to the manor, she burrowed into the folds of the couch drenched in sweat.

Lethargy had overcome her. It was a delirious kind of lethargy, or maybe a lethargic delirium. She'd gotten up once and gone to the bathroom, only to realize that it was nothing but a nascent sort of dream, a subconscious expression of her needs, and so she had to raise herself from the couch, dragging her feet. She looked at herself in the mirror. She had done this very thing, felt herself doing the thing, seen herself doing the thing, and yet it was merely déjà vu. It was not her after all.

Under the moth-eaten blanket, she dreamed she was on the plane again. Another manifestation of her needs? No, this was a memory; she was not leaving, she was yet arriving to this cursed land. Another moment she was in her cobalt blue Dodge, books and clothes in the back and the trunk, the passenger seat vacant save for her acceptance and scholarship letter. Her ticket out. She was in the Bentley, the rain beating against the window. She was entering the wrought-iron gate. She was passing the exit sign from Ruskin. She was in Keystone Methodist wearing a frilly white dress, pink bow in her hair. She was singing a psalm. *The Lord is compassionate and gracious*. She was in the cab of a sixteen-wheeler. Not a memory. She could see nothing, but she heard the damp final breaths of her mother and the others dying with her. She felt herself soaked in blood and afterbirth. She felt her nanay's hand on her, stroking her scalp. *Forgive me.* She felt life leave her, leave them both.

Then, she awoke back in the room.

The guest room. The old general's room. The room with the peephole. The too-permeable room.

She was back at Villa Sepulveda.

"Don't worry about the family," Adrian had told her at the cottage. "Don't worry about me." Sophie could barely lift her head when he came. Her voice was weak, but when he'd asked if she wanted to come back to house, her answer was clear: No. Never.

He'd promised to take care of her and shield her from his dad. She couldn't muster disappointment or annoyance or outrage. She only said no.

He had crossed the lawn, come and gone, bringing her medicine when it was time. He had brought the same questions too. Come back with me? No. Are you sure? No. More food? No. Change of clothes? No. Do you want me to stay? No.

Then there were new questions. Have you seen your phone? No. Has anyone else come? No. Did you tell Remedios what you told me? No. What about Tiago, Dante? No.

You're the only one I told.

She would never get to tell anyone; he never allowed for the possibility.

"She's picked up what Mom has," he explained when he carried her into the villa, drug-addled and barely on her feet. The voices returned to her in snatches. "Make sure she hydrates," his auncle suggested. "There's still soup on the stove," his great-aunt offered. "Let me help you with her," his father said, but Adrian insisted he stay away. "Go find a doctor instead. We need to contain the sickness before it spreads even more."

Now she was back in the room. The room with the peephole. The too-permeable room. He had brought her back there after the Xanax had done its work.

"I'm sorry," he said as he lay her down the bed. He tied her hands with a rough hempen rope. "I love you."

Maybe it was foolish for Sophie to have hoped. As was her way, she never let doubt overpower compassion, yet that only meant that doubt did exist. Part of her knew that this boy had never been as stalwart as he believed himself to be. He was pampered, sheltered. His two decades on earth did not make him any less of a child. What he called experience and what he considered wisdom were culled from films and books and late-night bull sessions in smoky rooms with other boys exactly like him. His so-called principles had never been tested by time, battered by adversity. And when the test did come, he reverted to the only things he truly valued. Loyalty, family. The things that made him who he was. He had no other lodestar. Not even love.

It was midday when her wits fully returned to her. Her body felt weak, but at least she now saw her half-conscious dreams for what they were, and she now saw Adrian for who he was.

He was sitting at the end of her bed, head in his hands. He was crying. He didn't notice her stirring.

She had the good sense to feign sleep. There would be no arguing with him in that state; no appeal would be heard. No help would come, either, not from the Sepulvedas. Maybe from Remedios, but the family would never allow it, not if Adrian had already told them what Sophie knew. She shut her eyes and eased her already shallow breath. When Adrian finally finished crying, he wiped his face dry and left the room. He didn't even look back at her. The sound of the lock was deafening.

Sophie struggled with her restraints, kicked her unbound legs, but it got her nowhere. Adrian had been sailing at the Belvedere Marina since he was eight. He knew his knots. Even without the drug coursing through her body, she wouldn't be able to undo them.

She cried, but barely any tears dampened her cheeks. She had run out. A plea rose in her, the stirring of a prayer. Despite her upbringing, she'd never been a believer. Yet in this moment she gained a desperate sort of faith. Her heart cried out to the heavens.

Then she realized what day it was. Good Friday. God was dead, and so was any hope of salvation.

Adrian didn't check on her for the rest of the day. No food, no water, no bathroom breaks. Sophie was forced to wet herself. Her body squelched on the bed and the pungent smell of urine stung her nose. The sorry display at least elicited enough pity to sway her captor when he finally visited her late that night. He'd left her in the dark, so it took him time to find the source of the smell. Despite his evident disgust, he rushed to her side.

"I couldn't bring myself to come in here," he explained, remorse painted on his face. "I didn't think. I wasn't thinking. I thought you'd just be asleep. I'm so, so sorry, Sophie. I didn't mean for this to happen."

He didn't ask if she needed to go now. He didn't offer to untie her. He let her keep lying in her filth. He only apologized for the indignity of this one oversight, as though that were his only sin.

"Let me go, Adrian."

"I can't. Not until I can be sure that you won't do anything rash."

"What could I do? Where could I go?" she asked evenly. He needed to be convinced of her docility. She gestured at her bound wrists. "This is unnecessary."

"I can't risk you acting crazy." Adrian shook his head as if trying to exorcise his thoughts. "Hurling accusations against my family when everyone is on edge . . . and, and grieving, and dying and—my mom is dying and I can't do anything about it and Dad is at his breaking point. I'm the only one holding it together. Don't you see that?"

"I do. I'm sorry. I shouldn't have told you. But it doesn't have to change anything. I won't tell anyone. We don't even have to talk about it. If we need to, we can deal with it when we leave. Yes. I understand now."

Adrian edged closer to her, his eyes probing. His voice wavered as he said, "Tell me again. What you told me. I need to hear you say it again."

"What? Which part?"

"You know which."

"You said you believed me."

"I've had some time to think, and . . . I don't know what to believe anymore."

Yes, you do, she wanted to say. Her bonds proved it. She wanted to call him out on the lie but instead she said, "Ask Manang Remy. She'll tell you the same thing."

"No, I don't care about that," he spat. "Yes, people fucking died and my family has blood on their hands. The knowledge is crushing, Sophie. I've lived in fear of it for so long. But I can't do anything about it now, except bear the guilt of their crimes."

"They're not your crimes," she answered, maintaining her calm despite knowing his own guilt, his own crimes.

"Maybe. But that doesn't matter to me right now. What matters is you. What you say happened to you. Tell me that part again."

"Adrian, please. You already know. My story won't change. Don't make me repeat it."

Adrian stood over her, arms crossed. "I didn't say anything about changing your story. I just want to hear the truth."

"I told you the truth."

"That's what they all say."

"What can I say that will make you believe me?"

"Say you made a mistake."

"I didn't."

"Soph, I keep on telling you . . . people do things differently here," he said, almost apologetic. "You've seen how Dad's been taking care of everyone. He's trying to be hospitable and . . . I think you misunderstood."

"There's nothing to misunderstand."

"Look—not everything is a violation. You know, with the peepholes and everything, you're just worked up, thinking about agency and consent and . . . and white feminist bullshit."

Sophie was stunned speechless, her contempt overshadowed by confusion. Where had this come from? More terrifying still—had he always been this way?

"Ever since you got here, you've done nothing but complain," Adrian continued, his voice finding steam. "The food, the peepholes, the beetles, the legends about this place—and don't get me started on your nightmares!"

"What the fuck does any of that have to do with anything?"

"Everything—because I thought you were different." His lips thinned into a pained wince. "But you're just like the others."

He loomed over her and checked her restraints. His skin grazed hers for an instant and it gave Sophie a jolt.

"What others, Adrian?"

"You're all the same . . . Dad's a very handsome man, y'know. Everyone says so. And he's kind, attentive. I can see why you'd have the wrong idea. They had the wrong idea too. I just thought you were different. I'm really disappointed."

Sophie's breath caught on her throat as realization dawned on her. His exes. They all broke his heart, he'd told her. They all cheated on him.

"Who else?" she asked, her voice stilted in trepidation.

"Tara. She was a one-off, I thought. Said my house gave her the creeps. At first, it seemed to me she meant Lola or Lolo. Eventually she told me *Dad* gave her the creeps. I mean, what the fuck! He was always so nice to her. He chaperoned us when we hung out, went to movies with us, that sort of thing. And he was so welcoming. He always invited her to dinner, and he always let her sleep over."

"Adrian . . . "

"One day, she just stopped talking to me. Found out she'd started seeing some dumb varsity jock on the swim team. Do you know how much that hurt? She was my first love. And I don't care what you think about middle school romances. It was real to me."

Sophie gasped. "Jesus Christ."

"I know, right? Crazy." Adrian scoffed. "Vanessa was worse. Her family's rich as fuck but she was such a simple, down-to-earth girl. Never put up a front, never tried to be one of the popular girls, even though she easily could have been. That's what I loved about her. She was so sweet and meek. She collected stuffed animals for way longer than any girl should.

Yeah, I know, she seems kind of dumb, but I didn't mind that too much. Until I found out it was all an act." Adrian shot her a scornful look. "Fed me the same kind of bullshit you're feeding me now."

"It's not bullshit, don't you see?"

"She wanted Dad. I saw it in her eyes, way before I caught her in the pool house. She lost her towel, she said. Didn't know Dad was there. Yeah, right. 'Oopsie, I'm such dumb, innocent liddle girl,'" he said with a mocking accent. "Fucking bimbo."

"And Lexie? What about her?" Sophie recalled the anguish on his face when he had told her about her latest ex. The rich blonde who got invited to every function, who was embraced by the Sepulvedas and deemed worthy of Adrian. The one Sophie envied, no matter how hard she tried to deny it.

"Now her . . . I really thought we would go all the way. Marriage, kids, the whole deal. Everyone approved of the match. Lolo said it was about time for me to be thinking about suitable partners. I was fucking seventeen." Adrian laughed wryly. "But that's what happens when you're the heir of an empire. And Lexie was basically American royalty, so."

"Adrian . . . what happened with her?"

"Don't get me wrong—I'm not an idiot. I kept my guard up. I mean, you learn things after getting burned—twice. I kept Lexie from coming over, made sure she had as little contact with Dad as possible. I couldn't risk her doing what the others did. That was hard, though. Her fam always got invited to our parties, and I ran out of excuses for when Mom and Dad asked why they haven't seen her lately and why don't I bring her over for brunch or dinner or whatever. They really liked her. They were super lenient with sleepovers too. So, yeah, eventually I brought her around. I couldn't help myself. Apparently, neither could she."

"What did he do?"

"What did *he* do?" Adrian asked, almost shouting. "She

was the one backing up on Dad in the kitchen. Yeah, leaning over the counter and rubbing up on him like a damn stripper. I saw it with my own two eyes and she still had the nerve to say it's not what I think. That Dad tried to . . . " He cleared his throat. "She was class valedictorian, have I told you that yet? Smart enough to think on her feet and play the victim. Oh, she cried. Made me cry too. I loved her so much—I can't stress that enough. I loved her so much I almost believed her."

Sophie wept. "Why didn't you? After everything you've witnessed, why the fuck didn't you?"

"Because she was lying. Dad said so himself."

It was so simple, so natural, the way he said it. The weight of reality devastated Sophie. There'd been other girlfriends. Younger girlfriends. Adrian had heard this all before. He knew. And despite the others, despite Sophie being one in the long line of his father's prey, Adrian still sat there, comfortable in his willful ignorance, confident in his choice to disbelieve her.

"You were supposed to be different," Adrian said, lifting Sophie's chin with a gentleness that matched his tone. "I told myself, this time, I'll be a lot smarter. I tried to make sure you wouldn't get any ideas, the way the others did. It was for your own good. But you were so . . . persistent. Two years was a good run, but honestly, it was silly of me to think I could keep you away for long. The family would have to meet you at some point, right? And the funeral was the perfect opportunity to ease you in. Lolo's dead, everyone would be distracted, and surely you'd be on your best behavior."

"Me?" she asked with bitter incredulity. "I'm the one who's supposed to behave?"

"I tried to protect what we have for as long as I could," he answered, not taking the bait. "Because it felt right, being with you. Like I said, you're different. You're Filipino, same as me. You were smarter, kinder, more mature. You're not a liar or a slut. You're a dalagang pilipina. The ideal woman. *My* ideal woman."

The thought made Sophie sick. "What, meek and compliant? A paragon of virtue? You know I've never bought into that crap."

Adrian fell silent, reflective. Then he smiled, which only unsettled her more. "I've tried to educate you, teach you what you said you wanted to learn. I was so proud to be on that journey with you, Soph. And I was so proud to finally show you off to my family. I watched you grow into the woman you always wanted to be. The woman I always saw you as.

"I should've known better." His face darkened. "You'll always be a redneck from Nebraska."

Tears ran down Sophie's cheeks. "I'm a fucking human being, Adrian. I'm not some toy you can play with to fulfill your fantasies. Call me what you want, but I know who I am. And now I know who you are. You're just like your dad."

"Shut up!"

"You are. What's worse is that you think you're better than him. You honestly think you're a good guy. Well, guess what? You're the one who tied me down to this bed."

Adrian put a hand over her mouth, a manic look in his eyes. He pressed so hard Sophie felt her teeth cutting against the inside of her lips. "Yeah, that's right. You wanna be gagged too, you bitch? Keep talking. I dare you."

Sophie whimpered in fear. In that moment, she knew there was no more use arguing. She could repeat her entreaties, but Adrian wouldn't be moved. This was a man who had been denied what he believed he was entitled to. At first it seemed she was imprisoned to protect the Sepulvedas, to preserve Adrian's deified notion of who they were. Sophie now knew that it was never about those things at all. Adrian wanted control and he wouldn't stand to be denied it. Nor would he relinquish it, no matter how much she begged.

When she calmed down, Adrian released his hand. He stood, took a deep breath, and grimaced at the yellow-stained sheets. As he retreated to the door, he put a finger to his mouth. “I’ll be back later.”

Sophie sank into the bed, her arms hanging above her like a limp marionette. The rope burned the already raw skin of her wrists. She pulled up her legs, avoiding the stain and its stench. After a while, something else stung her nose. Something rotten.

Barely two days dead, Olympia’s corpse already suffused the air with the vile miasma of death.

April 19

Black Saturday

The sun was already low when Tiago returned. He'd confirmed yet again that the roads hadn't been cleared, and his attempts to reach the municipio and the capitolio were also in vain. "The country is in deep mourning for the Lord," he'd kept telling his amos, and he was right. No one picked up his calls, not even to the direct lines to important people that Eric had told him to call. Yet that was not the news that caused the usually taciturn groundskeeper to look alarmed.

He made his report from the bottom of the grand staircase, much to the Sepulveda siblings' confusion. He believed now, he told them, and he practiced what he previously dismissed as superstition: He refused to bring evil into the house.

"It's better if I keep the gaba away," he shouted from the foyer.

With a grim formality, he then unfurled the bundle tucked under his shirt. "I found this on the way back," he said, laying its contents on the polished tile. A shinbone, one end sharp and jagged. It was dry and chalky white, stripped of any remnant of flesh. Its joint end had been chewed clean, teeth marks scoring its rounded surface. There was no question: This belonged to a human being.

"Is it his?" Divina asked, clutching her chest.

Tiago hung his head. He didn't know for sure, but he had a bad feeling. The bone proved his wife's superstitions, this family's accursed lore. Only took him forty years to come around to believing.

"But how?" she asked.

"I don't know," Tiago replied, "But no animal could have dug up a corpse and done this kind of damage,"

It fell upon Javier to accompany the groundskeeper to the roadside where the rest of Raul's remains might be found. He welcomed the excuse to leave the manor.

"It was definitely an animal," he told Tiago as they closed the gate behind them. "The bite marks look like they could be a wild dog's. And it rained after Papa's funeral," he continued. "Maybe the ground shifted and made it easier for a pack to dig the body out."

The older man was unconvinced, and Javier couldn't convince himself either. He only knew that whatever did this, it was impossible they'd find the rest of his father.

The two climbed the uphill road. On the horizon Javier took in the coconut trees far below them, stretching as far as he could see. He saw, too, the gash in the escarpment and the fallen pile of earth that separated them from the town. The landslide was more massive that he'd imagined, even from a distance.

After a while, Tiago stopped and pointed to the spot where he'd found the bone. They bent low to search for tracks. Bones, torn-up clothing, Raul's rings, maybe. Nothing. They ventured deeper into the brush but also came up empty-handed. When the sun dipped behind the trees, they switched on their torches.

"What do you think it is, if it wasn't an animal?" Javier

asked. The older man responded with a noncommittal grunt. Javier asked more directly: "Do you think it was the balbal?"

Tiago hushed him. It was risky enough that they trampled in these parts at this dark hour, on this dark, unholy day, he whispered. They didn't need to tempt trouble by making pointless noise. He gestured toward the bolos that hung from their waists. There was a reason they had to carry them.

A rustling sound halted their steps. Javier spun around, the light from his torch sweeping the area around him. The blades of grass were completely still. There was no breeze. The crickets' song, which had grown louder the farther away they got from the villa, had all but ceased. Javier looked every which way, alert and on guard.

Another rustle came. The sound grew and soon enough, the two men saw where it came from. The tops of the tall grass parted. Something was coming toward them. A beastly figure, running on all fours. Branches and dead leaves crackled underfoot in a sort of gallop.

Javier ran, Tiago right next to him. They weaved through the trees, the beams of their torches frantic and unhelpful in guiding the way. Through a small clearing Javier saw the edge of the road and sped toward it. The firm asphalt let him run faster and at full tilt. He looked back and saw Tiago catching up, but barely. Some meters behind him, in the middle of the road, Javier caught a glance of their pursuer.

The balbal.

It stood tall, two heads above him, at least, even as it hunched over. Its entire being was covered in black, matted fur. The bright amber of its eyes glowed in the gloom of dusk. Clawed hands raised above its head, the demon unfurled what at first looked like wings, until Javier saw they were taut membranes that connected its limbs. It opened its mouth, its rows of sharp fangs wet and gleaming.

Eeeek eeeek eeeek. Eeeek eeeek eeeek.

The demon dropped and sprinted on all fours, bounding with stubborn ferocity.

Javier picked up his pace, spurred by the screeching cries behind him.

When they reached the gate, he and Tiago hurriedly wrapped the chain around its bars and locked it. The old man held himself upright against Javier, who felt like his legs would give out. At least they were safe, for now. As far as he could tell, the balbal had disappeared farther back on the road. The screeching had softened, as if it had quit giving chase.

The two men went into the manor. Tiago barred the large wooden doors and called for everyone to bar all possible entryways. The family had only just gathered in the oratorio for the six o'clock Angelus. Javier breathlessly reported what he'd seen, shutting the windows as he went. Remedios swiftly joined him, needing little explanation. Dante went into the silong to fetch bolos.

"It's because of her," Remedios said in exasperated panic. She pointed accusingly at Olympia's lifeless body. "She brought it here. We should have buried her right when she fell."

"She hasn't rotted yet," Javier argued, yet was quick to add, "Not that much anyway. But we can't take any risks."

Eric turned to Adrian. "Go and keep your mom safe. The rest of us will stay with Mama."

A scraping sound came from the roof. Claws scratched on the terra-cotta tile. Divina screamed.

"Run!" Javier said, taking hold of his aunt's wrist and dragging her after Adrian. Kai followed, and Remedios too. Margot didn't stir at the commotion as they all barged into the room. The old women huddled in a corner next to the bed. Kai held their great-aunt close, joined in nervous prayer by the caretaker. Javier handed his bolo to his nephew. "Use it if you have to." Adrian barely held himself upright, let alone the blade, but he feigned courage and stood guard by his mother's side.

Javier gestured for everyone to be quiet, pointing up at the ceiling. He slowly backed out of the room. Before he could close the door, Kai shot up from their corner, agitated. They looked around the room in search of something. Then, heedless of the noise, they pushed past Javier and sped out into the hall.

The insistent knock at Sophie's door struck her with both hope and fear. She'd heard screaming, and now someone tried to come for her.

"Sophie, wake up." The voice was muffled through the door. It was low and furtive, yet it had an edge of urgent distress. "Can you hear me?"

Kai. Could this be a trick? What sick game was Adrian trying to play?

"Come on, wake up," they said, louder this time. "You're not safe in there."

They didn't know. They couldn't know. Sophie let herself believe. How much worse could things get for her?

"Kai? I'm here. I . . . I can't open the door," she rasped, her throat burning. "I'm tied to the bed."

"Tied? What are you—?" A pause. "We're running out of time, all right? The balbal is on the roof and we need to hunker down, so open the fucking door."

Heavy footfalls passed right above her. Talons clicked and scratched to and fro. Sophie blanched. It was as Remedios said. *The monster is coming*. Now it was here.

"Adrian's keeping me locked up in here. Please, you gotta find a way in. I don't want to die in here."

The footfalls grew louder and more regular, repetitive. The balbal was jumping on the roof, trying to break through.

Then, a slam fell against the door, then again, one after

another. The wooden frame began to creak from the assault. The knob shuddered. An earsplitting bang threw the door open and Kai fell to the floor. When they got to their feet, Kai froze in stupefied horror.

"What the fuck did he do to you?"

Sophie tried explaining, but she didn't know how far back to start. There were too many causes and effects. All she could say was "He's lost his mind."

The scratching on the roof grew fainter, as if the monster had been scared by the racket. Kai took the opportunity and unbound Sophie.

"You tried to tell me, didn't you?" they asked while undoing the ropes. They kept their voice low, glancing up the ceiling as they went. "The other day, when you asked for help. I'm so sorry . . . "

For someone who was all about energies and vibes and intuition, Kai was hardly intuitive when it counted. Yes, they could have helped, but that conversation felt so long ago now, and so insignificant. "Just get me out of here," Sophie replied.

Once done, Kai got Sophie to her feet and led her out the hall. "This way—we're all in Margot's room. We can barricade ourselves there while—"

"No! Not if he's there!"

"—only until it's gone. Please, you can't be here alone," they pleaded. "And it's not after any of us. It just wants Mama. We'll be safe—" Kai grabbed Sophie's arm and made to run.

"Let me go! I'm not going with you." Sophie pulled away, panicked. "It's not the corpse—that thing is coming after all of you."

Dust and debris fell as the balbal's onslaught continued. The roof tiles cracked and the hammered metal ceiling tiles tremored under the monster's weight. Javier found his brother,

Tiago, and Dante crouched around Olympia's corpse, their weapons pointed at the ceiling. The thudding and scratching and clawing seemed to come from everywhere. Javier unsheathed his bolo and held it with both hands, the closest to a prayer that he'd ever come.

The balbal was real. Here it was, flesh and blood and fangs and talons, as real as the curse he'd denigrated and the ghostly visions he'd tried to ignore. He'd heard and seen the signs and still refused to accept, and now, the curse had sent its monstrous embodiment. Here was the reckoning of the Sepulvedas, coming from above as though the heavens itself beat down on the crumbling villa.

Javier pleaded for mercy. *Papa and Mama are dead. What remains of the family took no part in their crimes. Spare them, O God. Deliver them from judgment.*

Suddenly, the clangor stopped. All the men heard were each other's wet, heavy breaths.

Javier looked to his kuya, then to the groundskeeper, but neither knew what to do next. Dante then said "We should move her. Somewhere not as wide open, with doors we could close. The oratorio is closest."

The others agreed. With haste, the men wrapped the doña's body with the linen on which it had been laid. Javier and Eric took one end, father and son the other. On Dante's signal, they lifted it off the banquet table. The corpse squelched and its stench grew stronger.

Then came an explosion of wood and capiz shells, splinters and slivers flying all over the room, as the balbal crashed in through a window. The men lost their grip and dropped their cargo on the floor, each retreating into corners and behind their weapons.

The creature rose from the floor and stood to its full height, its arms above its head, its flaps outstretched. Its cry pierced the air as it bared its long, sharp fangs dripping with viscous slime. Dried blood coated the matted fur around its jowls, its webbed hands, its yellowing claws.

Eric slowly backed away from the balbal, one hand brandishing a knife and the other showing an open palm, as though trying to calm a lion. Javier saw intelligence behind the monster's eyes, and it seemed to comprehend his kuya's gesture of appeasement. He also saw, however, that this monster would not obey. It swatted the knife out of Eric's hand, slashing him with its claws. Blood spurted out of his arm and sprayed the monster, making it look more fearsome. Javier ran to his brother's side and pulled him back, folding Eric's arm to arrest the bleeding.

The demon turned away from them and lurched toward Olympia's corpse. Tiago took one of the lit candelabras and swept it before him like a trident. He told his son to flee, but Dante pulled on him. "We don't have to die here," he implored his father. The paltry candle flame did nothing to repel the balbal. The stench was too tantalizing. Tiago lunged with his makeshift spear, but the attempt did not land. The demon swatted the candelabra away, then parried with its long limbs.

"No!" Dante dived in front of his father, but it was too late. Tiago had earned two vicious swipes across his gut, his flesh and insides shredded into ribbons. The groundskeeper, stunned and eviscerated, fell where he stood.

Dante swung his bolo at the monster, driving it away from his father. It circled him slowly, and Javier took advantage of the distraction. He rose to his feet, crept behind the balbal, then hacked into its haunch. The monster shrieked. Black ooze spurted from its back; it, too, smelled of rotting flesh. Javier brought his blade down again. The monster retreated and ran around the room in a frenzy, knocking over chairs and jumping on the dinner table, then the buffet, before clinging onto a corner of the ceiling, cowering upside down like a giant bat. Ooze and gobbets of its gray flesh fell onto the floor.

Javier went to his mother's side, his bolo pointed straight at the creature. He yelled toward Dante, "Bring her into the oratorio!"

Once the two started dragging the corpse, the balbal shrieked, the sound more piercing, but it did not move from its place. It watched Javier warily, and without breaking eye contact, he called out for his brother.

"Kuya!"

Eric took a second too long to respond.

As Javier turned, the demon leapt from its corner and pounced, pinning him to the floor. Its massive hands pushed down on Javier's arms, cracking his joints. It loomed over him menacingly, then brought its face inches away from his. Its damp, rancid breath suffocated him. It raised its head then swiftly sank its teeth on his shoulder, skewering skin and flesh. The wound felt like it was on fire.

Javier screamed, flailed, and kicked at the demon's hindquarters, swinging his blade erratically. He heard its jaw click, bear down on bone. He went blind with pain. The balbal pulled back. Blood rushed out of Javier's body and the monster lapped it up as though it savored victory. As though it taunted him.

Then, it lifted its head and searched the room. With the last of his remaining strength, Javier raised his bolo and stabbed the demon in its gut. He dragged the blade down as far as he could reach, screaming in anger.

The balbal responded in kind, opening its maw. The scream that came was unlike anything Javier had ever heard. It wasn't a screech; it was a roar, and it thundered like a battle cry and a summoning and an exultation all at once. Like the horns that obliterated the walls of Jericho, like the trumpets that heralded the end of days. It dulled all other sounds, even that of Javier's flagging heartbeat.

The monster roared and kept roaring, and though his

senses began to depart him, Javier could yet feel a sudden and powerful jolt, one that shook not only his body but everything around him. The sensation left him with one final, horrified thought: Something had called back to the balbal. Something ancient and vast and deep.

The very land itself heeded the monster's cry, and it answered with a swelling, deafening rumble.

The roar was inhuman, and it shook the very floor beneath her feet. Sophie tried to steady herself. It wasn't her weakness or a drug-induced delusion—the tremor was outside her, all around her. A side table wobbled, a vase on a pedestal rocked in its place. A coat rack tipped over and fell to its side. The villa's bones creaked, its high-pitched wails blending with the balbal's own keening.

"Is that a fucking earthquake?" Kai asked.

Sophie turned to head toward the back staircase. It would be the closest way out. She grabbed Kai's wrist, a reversal of sorts. "We gotta get out of here."

"The others—they need help."

Screams came from down the hall. Sophie thought about Adrian and hated herself for it. There was Divina, and Remedios. Margot. They were blameless, collateral damage in the Sepulvedas' curse. Dante, too.

"There's no time," she told Kai.

"I can't leave them behind."

Their certainty felt like a rebuke. Against her better judgment, Sophie found herself following Kai as they headed toward greater peril.

By the time the two of them reached Margot's room, the exodus had begun. Margot was conscious, eyelids fluttering and head lolling, but she couldn't stand on her feet. Remedios and Divina kept her upright, carrying her by her arms. Kai steered all of them toward the kitchen and told them to take the staircase that led out to the veranda.

"Where's everyone else?" Sophie asked. No one bothered to answer her in the rush of the moment.

The quake intensified. The floorboards widened and narrowed and cracked, so did the walls. A grandfather clock crashed, clanging discordantly, its glass shattering.

"Get as far away from here as possible!" Kai yelled, then headed back down the hall.

"Where the hell are you going?" Sophie asked.

"To my brothers—and Adrian."

Sophie gave chase, trying to talk sense into them. The quake showed no signs of abating, and the balbal was on the rampage. She couldn't keep up, still weak from her captivity and running on such unstable ground. There was no use, anyway. She now knew Kai would fight their instincts and dive into certain doom if it meant saving their family. Sophie shared no such impulse. She broke off and ran the opposite way, hoping against hope that Kai would make it out alive.

She turned down the main hall but was soon stopped in her tracks. She only caught a glimpse of it at first. The large black creature was covered in rough fur, a cross between a simian and a wolf. She couldn't believe her eyes. The sight of the balbal both alarmed and fascinated her, enough to distract her from getting to safety.

The demon was bent over a body. Olympia. Chewing with relish, it drove its snout deep into her guts like a starving dog.

Then, an explosion went off somewhere behind Sophie, jolting her back into her senses. The smell of gas reeked, and soon, flames consumed the remains of the ruined kitchen. The balbal rose to its hindquarters. Its gut was scored with a fresh, gaping wound. It struggled to lift its quarry and, after a few tries, ended up pulling it by the legs. Olympia's innards left a bloody trail on her polished floor. Sophie gasped, and the sight of her startled the beast in kind. Seeming to find its strength, it grabbed the disemboweled corpse and carried it off in its arms, bounding down the splintering steps of the manor's grand staircase.

Stamped metal tiles fell from the ceiling, and a section of the roof broke open, sending shards of terra-cotta to rain down on Sophie. A section of the corridor seemed to recede as the floor went askew. The spot she stood on shifted and she lost her footing. She crawled, her arms and knees buckling.

The rumble grew louder as the house seemed to subside, setting the whole place on an incline. Sophie only then noticed how the motion didn't rock her side to side. It pulled down and apart. She felt the pang of nausea that usually came from a sudden freefall.

This was not an earthquake. This was a sinkhole.

She scrambled on all fours, trying to find her way, which seemed to change by the second. A post split apart and fell, almost hitting her. Then, an earsplitting crack stunned her, and she saw the north end of the manor sink into the silong. The oratorio and the conservatory, and most of the bedrooms, now lay in a chasm below her, thirty feet deep or so, amongst the storeroom's contents and the mahogany columns that once held the manor upright. The kitchen, too, had fallen, and its flames engulfed the bottom of the pit, fanned by the breeze that blew in through the hollowed-out house.

Villa Sepulveda had sunk and settled. Everything went still. The cloudless night sky was visible overhead.

Wary of aftershocks, Sophie stayed low and close to the floor, which remained stable for the moment. She crawled through the puddles of blood in the dining room, inching her way toward the back of the house, where she hoped to find a way out.

Harried footsteps came from some distance behind her. Adrian. He looked hurt but still moved with some vigor. He didn't spot her as he ran toward his father, who sat against a slanted wall, half-conscious, legs pinned under a large beam.

Adrian strained to lift the beam, but it didn't budge. He tried pushing it off with his body, but all that did was crush Eric's legs even more. Eric screamed, his breath short and ragged.

Sophie rose to her feet and approached them, her footing steady even as the ripple of an aftershock made its presence felt. Past the smoke that billowed around them, she watched father and son struggle, a chill seizing her body. No—a numbness.

Soon, Adrian caught sight of her. His shock lasted but a second and quickly gave way to panic. "Please," he said, tears streaming down his face. "If you take the other end, we can lift it just enough for him to slide away."

The ground rumbled once more, but like the beam of lumber, cut and smoothed from the trees that grew on this very plantation, Sophie remained immovable. The tremor did nothing to prod her into action.

"He'll die here! Please, Sophie!"

Even mercy didn't move her.

The fire blazed from far below and lit Sophie's surroundings. Another rumble, another plaintive cry from Adrian. She couldn't hear him among the din. She was so rapt by the crater, its metes and bounds, the destruction it held in its maw.

Then, in the distance, past the collapsed roof and rooms and walls and foundations, she saw something. A vision, pointing toward a pile of rubble. A fallen wall and a section of the back staircase formed a clear, if precarious, path to higher ground, away from the pit and its consuming flames.

Her savior had returned.

Sophie took one final look at Adrian and Eric, then turned toward the woman that beckoned her. Without a word, Sophie walked over the ruins and away from the manor, leaving the Sepulvedas to the fate she knew awaited them.

It was time.

The earth roared again, widening its jaws. The crater's sides cascaded into its depths, taking everything along with it: the broad-winged angel on the fountain that greeted the villa's guests, the gravel driveway that stopped the mud from sticking to the Bentleys' wheels. The stone vault of the zaguan, the aforementioned vehicles. The rows of dwarf coconut trees, the landscape meticulously tended by the devoted groundskeeper. The shrubs and the bushes around the caretaker's cottage. The cottage itself. The sprawling lawn, the plot where the mausoleum was to be built, where the family pool used to be.

That other, smaller, more crowded pit and all its unfortunate occupants, their skulls and bones and tattered clothes and rusted blades all commingled beyond recognition.

The desaparecidos, disappeared no more.

AFTER

AT THE LAST, WHEN SHE THOUGHT ALL WAS lost, Remedios still played the part of caretaker. The fires raged from fathoms beneath the pit, which could yet grow larger, and she needed to tend to the girl. She found her sitting near a damaged section of the garden wall, right by the lip of the sinkhole, hugging her knees. She resembled one of the paintings that used to hang in a corner of the conservatory: a nymph gazing forlornly at her reflection on a pond. When Remedios asked her to step away from the edge, the girl didn't stir, enthralled by the flames. She lifted the girl up by her arms and led her to the stone fence, a good distance away from the ruin.

Remedios peered down the hole. It was all gone. Villa Sepulveda. Her cottage. The land had taken everything and everyone. She didn't know the ground could open up like that and swallow them whole. They all tried to flee, dispersed in all directions, but there was no safe harbor. It was only by a perverse miracle that she survived, clambering out from the edge of the earth. The look on her son Dante's face as he realized he couldn't make it, as the land crumbled under him, would forever be burned in her memory.

Her tears fell in earnest as her dog came and lay by her feet. The world was quiet. Not a breeze stirred the trees. The crackle of burning wood was the only sound. Still, she kept her senses sharp. She kept vigil as the girl fell asleep. She waited all night but never saw a sign of the balbal, never heard its shrill cry. It might be down there in the pit, along with her entire world, burning to a crisp. She didn't feel assured by the thought.

A helicopter circled overhead the next morning. It was Easter, Remedios then realized. The day of resurrection.

"What will we tell them?" she asked Sophie.

The girl looked her dead in the eyes. "We tell them everything."

Remedios feared this would be the answer, but Sophie was right. The balbal, the disappeared, it all had to come out. Tiago was gone and Dante was gone. The Sepulvedas were all gone. Wisps of smoke rose from the wreckage. Yes, she would confess to mass murder. For what else was there? The woman with two homes, two families, had nothing left to lose.

She would even confess to fratricide. That, at least, she'd done of her own volition.

For she'd seen how the master of the house was afflicted by nightmares. Like a madman, he warned of monsters, of gaba. Of Alondra's revenge. Remedios felt his torment was deserved after what he orchestrated that night forty years ago. After what he made her do. She herself deserved torment, and she had been waiting for her own accounting.

Yet he was her brother, and from her, he deserved some compassion. She loved him as a sibling despite never being acknowledged or treated as such. It was an unfair, lopsided kind of love, Remedios knew that, and she'd made her peace with it. She was the caretaker's daughter, and then the caretaker herself, and that was simply how things were. Her acceptance didn't erode even in the twilight of their lives. And so when he got worse, his mania increasing as his lucid moments became shorter, rarer, how could her heart not break?

Over and over, he begged Remedios for release. *Don't let her get me. Don't let her get us. She is coming.* His final night was no different, for the most part. His screams had beckoned her from the next bedroom, and as was her duty, she came to his aid. He repeated the same ramblings about Alondra and the balbal, and he asked her again. He couldn't stand to do it himself.

That night, however, she'd heard him say something he hadn't said before.

"Parang awa mo na. Tapusin mo na, Remedios. Sundin mo ang kuya mo."

Please, end my suffering. Your brother demands it.

Kuya.

Older brother. A term of respect for an older boy or man, regardless of blood relation or social status. A title used even by the help to refer affectionately to their amos, especially the younger ones, before they were rightfully the don or the señor. A title Remedios herself had once called Raul.

He said the word differently that night. The weight of the word and all that it carried was unbearable. She heard the desperation in his voice, and it slaked the desperate longing in her heart. Yet she felt bitterness too—from the decades of waiting, decades spent treated as less than, expected to do the family's every bidding, even the ones no person should be forced to accept; and from the voice telling her that she was being manipulated to do yet another inhuman act.

Remedios clung onto that bitterness as hard as she

gripped the edges of the pillow. She cried as she placed it over his face. As her brother went into reflexive spasms of resistance, her fingers trembled, slackening in doubt. This was murder still, wasn't it? Even though the man himself had begged for death, even though his passing could easily be explained as bangungot. Even if no one ever found out. But she would know, and she already knew too much. Remedios steeled herself. She was doing it out of mercy. Out of love. She had been called, and she would be the one to release her brother from his suffering. She deserved that recognition at least.

Alondra never crossed her mind, but Remedios felt now, in hindsight, that when she'd committed that fateful act, her family should have been spared from the curse. It all started with Raul, hadn't it? And she had put him out of his misery. Didn't that purchase protection? Immunity for her and for her husband? For Dante, who had nothing to do with any of this? Her heart cried out. Why did Alondra have to take him? She recalled what Tiago had always told her: *There is no bargaining with God*. But Alondra had been a person. Flesh and blood. Was there no bargaining with her too?

Even as the aid workers whisked her and Sophie into the helicopter, Remedios felt no safety or rescue, not even as they ascended to the clouds. She looked down onto the sinkhole. It was much larger than she'd thought. It took the entire property, stopping short of the plantation's tree lines. She pondered the abyss and felt a foreboding sense of emptiness. She imagined life behind bars. She hoped she would live long enough to return, for she wanted to return, despite it all. After she'd served her time, she would come back to the land she called home. Down there, where that pit was. Where she was born and grew up, where she loved and lost, where she committed grievous and unimaginable crimes. She would die there, amidst the coconut trees, waiting for the day the balbal finally came for her.

"Wounds inflicted when God is dead never heal right," Remedios had explained to Sophie the morning after, when she saw the bruises on her arms and the abrasions on her wrists. The doctor's order seemed to bear it out. She needed to stay, he said. She needed more time to recover. She was still severely dehydrated. She might have a concussion too, or some other invisible injury that needed confirmation. Yet every second in that provincial hospital, where the paint peeled off the walls and the air had no hint of antiseptic, felt like an eternity. She was still too close to the villa. She doubted she could be far enough away. And so Sophie insisted she felt fine. More than fine, actually. The feebleness of her voice eroded her argument.

Over FaceTime she told her parents about the sinkhole and its casualties, but not much else. She didn't tell them about the monster, or the attempt on her, or being kept prisoner. Roy and Frances wanted to come and bring her home, but she told them no. She knew they couldn't afford the trip. She promised she'd head straight back to Nebraska as soon as she was discharged. The lie was enough to deter them.

By the time she got to Manila, the incident was all over the news. One long-form feature traced the villa's history from its noble beginnings to the events of the past Holy Week. The sinkhole and the revelation of the mass grave, the article said, was "a bloody and ignominious end to the Sepulveda curse."

Sophie knew better. *The past is present. History repeats.*

At Ninoy Aquino International Airport, she learned what flying commercial was really like. It had none of the glamor of her prior trip, nor of what she'd imagined. The terminals were ancient, the queues overlong with passengers who crammed their entire lives in their checked luggage. She finally saw the famed balikbayan box—the cardboard crate Filipinos preferred over normal suitcases, to maximize space and minimize freight charges. Her purple Samsonite stood out in the row of boxes lashed with nylon cords, mummified with duct tape.

The plane cabin was claustrophobic. Even with her slight build, she barely had any room to move. Her senses also had no place to rest. People moved about restlessly, finding their seats, fumbling with their backpacks and duffels, blocking the aisles as they chatted in diverse tongues. She only caught a few familiar terms, and the smatterings of Taglish helped little, but she could decipher the sentiment behind the words. Anticipation, eagerness, excitement. They were going to America, the land of milk and honey.

The place meant something different to them, and she envied them for it. She envied the hope in their eyes. She envied the strength it must take to leave one's home and cross treacherous seas to enter even more treacherous lands in pursuit of a better future.

Some rows in front of her, a baby cried.

She'd had such grand notions coming here. She'd hoped to fuse her two halves, led by the hand of someone who thought he knew better, whose love of country and love for her were as false as the stories he told. And now everything felt severed, either-or and irreconcilable: There was good and evil, the real and the unreal, the sacred and the profane. There were two Sophies, the one before and the one after. The one who might never heal right.

She envied their wholeness.

The crew announcement came on. *Estimated flight time: fifteen hours and twenty-one minutes.* She pulled up her window shade. As she did, a flight attendant came by and asked if she would be interested in a seat upgrade. "We have a no-show," she said, glancing at Sophie's bandaged wrists. "And the pods in business class are very comfortable."

"They're worse than they look."

"Did I mention it's free?"

She declined; she was fine with what she had. With little enthusiasm, Sophie asked the woman next to her if she'd rather take it. The woman, underdressed for the cold of the cabin, had been watching the conversation intently and jumped at the chance.

The engine hummed alive and the wheels began to turn, starting Sophie on another journey, one whose end was yet unknown. She planned to come back to Stanford, but only to clear out her dorm. She possessed so little; sans textbooks, she could fit it all in the trunk of her old Dodge. Once the packing was done, she'd hit the I-80 out of the city. She'd go away for a while, to some place where she didn't have to think about coding or neural networks or the trees and branches of recursive systems. She might find herself in another small town, smaller than Ruskin and filled with nicer, kinder folks. People who didn't gossip or pry. Live-and-let-live types. She'd stop there for some time, work at a diner or a grocery store. Then, when that got stale, she'd move on to another small town where no one knew who she was.

Somewhere she could disappear. With her.

Alondra. The mother Sophie never had, and never lost.

She looked different now, sitting next to Sophie. No longer dark and fearsome, she looked more like herself in that faded photograph, but older, as though she'd survived all these years. In a way, she had. She was as beautiful and complex as the land outside their window, this land they both came from, so hard to love, so full of the nameless dead.

Her face was clear to Sophie, as clear as it was the night she walked away from the country house as it burned into ashes at the bottom of a hellmouth. The night she left the Sepulvedas to die. Then, as now, Alondra offered her solace and safety, her kind eyes telling Sophie she'd done the right thing.

The plane rumbled as it took off. Sophie nestled into her seat, quivering as she reached for Alondra's hand. With interlaced fingers, Alondra lifted it to her lips.

I'm here. I'll always be with you. Forever.

ACKNOWLEDGMENTS

MY HEARTFELT THANKS GO TO MY EDITORS: Sarah Guan, who first saw the potential in this story and helped me grow it from a seed of an idea; and Diana Pho, who helped me untangle its more difficult parts and ushered it toward fruition. Thank you, too, to the brilliant team at Erewhon and Kensington for all the care and support in bringing this book to life, especially to the following:

Viengsamai Fetters, Associate Editor
Cassandra Farrin, Publishing Director
Kelsy Thompson, Production Editor
Rayne Stone, Copyeditor
Rin Ryan, Proofreader
[To Be Determined], Cover Artist
Lou Malcangi, Art Director
Shannon Gray-Winter, Senior Marketing Copy/ARC Manager
Martin Cahill, Campaign Manager
Kasie Griffitts, Sales Associate

None of this would be possible without my agent, Eddie Schneider, and the entire JABberwocky team. Thank you for always being a steadfast champion of my work.

This book also would not exist without the folks at the pub and the no-drama crew, who did early reads and who inspire me every day to be a better writer and human being.

I'm forever grateful to my family, the Manibo and Boco clans. Finally, to my husband Sean, to whom this book is dedicated—mahal kita.

Discussion Questions

THESE SUGGESTED QUESTIONS ARE TO SPARK CONversation and enhance your reading of *The Villa, Once Beloved.*

1. As a genre, the Gothic is about the past bearing down on the present. With this in mind, what role do the supernatural entities and phenomena play in the story, aside from providing chills and thrills?

2. Villa Sepulveda's long history is inextricably intertwined with the family who inhabits it. What similarities and differences do you see between the manor and the Sepulveda clan itself?

3. The book has several point-of-view characters as well as captivating secondary characters. Which one is your favorite? Whom do you most relate to and why?

4. One of the ways that the text develops the characters is through showing or describing their fear responses. How does

Sophie generally respond to fearful situations or characters? How does she differ from Javier, Adrian, Remedios, or Kai? How is her fear response similar, and how is it different, from your own?

5. Folklore and religion feature heavily in the book. What roles do local folklore, superstition, and Catholic rituals and traditions, play in the story? How do they affect the characters' view of events? Of themselves and the people around them? How do they impact the decisions they make?

6. At various points in the story, the characters become privy to, and complicit in, some form of cruelty or atrocity done by others. How do the characters react in those situations? How do they justify their choices to themselves? How do they justify it to others? Which of these choices do you think are defensible, if any?

7. The story is told from the point-of-view of a character who immigrated from his homeland (Javier), a character who was not born in and had never been to her homeland until the start of the book (Sophie), and a character who never left the homeland (Remedios). How does this part of their identity affect each of these characters' attitudes toward the country's dictatorial past?

8. The concept of legacy is something the characters grapple with throughout the novel and one of the Sepulveda family's legacies is toxic masculinity. How does it come up in the beliefs and actions of the male characters? How does it relate to the family's complicity to authoritarianism?

9. Although the story is set in the Philippines and features mostly Filipino characters, America is a looming presence in

the story. How does America as a physical place, as a state, as an idea, or as an ideal, affect the characters' lives? How does it affect their views of themselves and their choices?

10. The novel is bookended by plane rides. How are these two journeys different? In what ways did Sophie change from her outbound trip to her return?